"Marilyn Campbell has another winner . . . futuristic romance at its best."
—Johanna Lindsey

"COMPELLING, IRRESISTIBLE, IMAGINATIVE . . . passion of searing intensity."
—*Romantic Times* 4+

"SUPERB, FASCINATING . . . this one is the ultimate in putting your imagination into overdrive."
—*Rendezvous*

"AN INSPIRED, BRILLIANTLY CONCEIVED NOVEL."
—*Paperback Trader*

"MESMERIZING AND ENTHRALLING."
—*Talisman*

STOLEN DREAMS

by

Marilyn Campbell

A TOPAZ BOOK

TOPAZ
Published by the Penguin Group
Penguin Books USA Inc., 375 Hudson Street,
New York, New York 10014, U.S.A.
Penguin Books Ltd, 27 Wrights Lane,
London W8 5TZ, England
Penguin Books Australia Ltd, Ringwood,
Victoria, Australia
Penguin Books Canada Ltd, 10 Alcorn Avenue,
Toronto, Ontario, Canada M4V 3B2
Penguin Books (N.Z.) Ltd, 182–190 Wairau Road,
Auckland 10, New Zealand

Penguin Books Ltd, Registered Offices:
Harmondsworth, Middlesex, England

First published by Topaz, an imprint of Dutton Signet,
a division of Penguin Books USA Inc.

First Printing, June, 1994
10 9 8 7 6 5 4 3 2 1

Printed in the United States of America

PUBLISHER'S NOTE
This is a work of fiction. Names, characters, places, and incidents either are
the product of the author's imagination or are used fictitiously, and any resemblance to actual persons, living or dead, events, or locales is entirely coinciden-
tal.

To my grandmother,
Margaret Bickart,
with a lifetime of love and respect.

A very special thank you to my editor, Hilary Ross,
for believing in me and books that cross genres.
I really couldn't have done this without you,
my friend.

1

Innerworld-Planet Terra (Earth)

Shara slid her tall frame a little lower in the chair and pretended to concentrate on the food in front of her. A practiced dip of her head made her straight, shoulder-length hair fall forward, creating an effective, sable-brown veil to shield her expressive eyes. This was one time her kid brother would not get her support. She was going to stay out of this family discussion if it killed her.

"*Drek*! But that's unfair."

"Mackenzie Locke!" Aster glared at her son, whose sullen face had taken on a tinge of pink when he realized his slip. "I will not have that language in our home. In fact, I don't care for your attitude at all this evening, young man."

Shara watched Mack sneak a look at their father. He should have known better than to expect sympathy from that corner. Aster and Romulus *never* disagreed in front of their two children, at least not out loud. Beneath the table, Shara gently tapped her brother's shin with the toe of her shoe to warn him to give it up. He was spoiling their weekly family dinner . . . again. She wasn't surprised when he continued his argument.

"Shara has her own residence. All I want—"

"Shara," Romulus interrupted, "is a grown woman

with an established career. You aren't even out of school yet."

Mack's rebuttal was cut short by a sound similar to the whisper of distant wind chimes.

Shara gasped as thousands of sparks of white light exploded in the corner of the room where the sound seemed to originate. A second later the sparks consolidated into the shape of a person. As the lights flickered out, Shara discerned that their intruder was a very old, bald-headed man. His lavish attire compounded the shock of his abrupt appearance. The long-sleeved, floor-length caftan he wore was striped with a dozen brilliant colors and gathered at the waist by a wide belt decorated with large, rectangular crystals, which glowed with a light of their own. As Shara collected her wits, the man swayed and collapsed on the floor.

Romulus reached the still figure first, but Shara was right behind him. Quickly kneeling and pressing her finger to the side of the man's neck, she said, "He has a pulse, but it's very weak." She moved her hand so that her fingertips hovered above his temple. Since they both knew her abilities to mind-touch were the strongest of the Locke family, she looked to her father for the required approval.

Before Romulus could decide if the circumstances justified such an invasion of privacy, the man's eyes twitched and slowly opened. Moving his watery gaze over each of the group around him, he settled on Shara. In a strained, halting whisper, he asked, "Where . . . am . . . I?"

"You are in my home," Romulus answered in a terse voice before Shara could speak. "More precisely, you have trespassed into the residence of Romulus and Aster Locke. We are the Co-Governors of the Noronian colony of Innerworld, in the inner core of the planet Terra, known to the Outerworld natives as Earth. Who are you and why are you here?"

The stranger's eyes closed and a smile deepened the lines in his leathery face. "I made it. Thank the Supreme Being." When he reopened his eyes, he spoke to Shara again. "Please . . . if you will . . . help me to rise a bit . . . I could breathe more easily. I have so much to tell. And so very little time."

Shara placed an arm under his shoulders and gently lifted him. He was so thin, she could feel his frail bones beneath the silky caftan. When she saw how much effort it took him to remain upright, she continued to support him as he began to explain.

"My name is Lantana. I have come from . . . the future."

The Locke family's shock was unanimous, and their questions came faster than Lantana could respond.

"Time travel experimentation is prohibited here," stated Romulus.

"Why have you come here, now?" Aster queried.

Lantana paused to take a wheezy breath. Raising a trembling hand to Aster, he continued. "I wanted to meet you before I died."

Aster raised her eyebrows in confusion. "Me?"

Giving her a small smile, he let his hand drop limply onto his lap. "Yes, you, the Mother of the Transition, the woman who did so much to bring the cultures of Norona and Outerworld Earth into the Cooperative Age. Aster Mackenzie Locke, the first Terran woman to join with a Noronian man and bear children of the future." With those words he nodded at Romulus, Shara, and Mack, then returned his gaze to Aster. "What Earth year did I arrive in?"

"Two thousand thirty," Aster answered. "What year are you from?"

Lantana sighed. "Then the Transition has not yet begun. I was trying for a later date. I come from a desperate time for both Innerworld and Outerworld, a tragic result of events that never should have happened. But I escaped . . . to meet you . . . and seek your help."

"Escaped?" Romulus asked. "Are you a criminal?"

A dry laugh turned into a hacking cough as Lantana tried to answer him. "Yes, I suppose I am. You see, in the future, time travel is still against the law." He ran his index finger over the beveled edges of the crystal rectangle on the front of his belt, and it sprung open like a miniature drawbridge. All four heads leaned closer to inspect the workings inside. "This is the culmination of a lifetime of labor: my tempometer. I began designing it to prove time travel was possible. In spite of the law, I always intended to use it myself before I died. I have admired you for so long, Aster. Your petitions to the Ruling Tribunal of Norona are in every child's history book."

Aster's face flushed with shock and pride. "My petitions were recorded? For history?"

"And your speeches, like the one you made to convince the Tribunal that you and Romulus should be joined." Lantana's expression contorted as he seemed to be searching his memory. "By this time, have you not already delivered your petition requesting permission for Innerworld's people to begin making contact with certain Terran leaders of Outerworld?"

"Yes, I have, but that was over a year ago, and they never responded."

"Aah, then it is yet to come. You will hear soon. And do not be discouraged by the Tribunal's caution. When they review your suggestions for a universal trade agreement, they'll come around."

Aster stuttered in confusion. "But I haven't even . . . that is, I was only thinking of—"

Romulus touched her shoulder. "I don't think it's wise to know too much of our own future."

Lantana grabbed Romulus's arm and pulled himself closer. "You're wrong. It's vital that I tell you, and you must help. I don't have the strength or the time left to find someone else. My life will end before this day is through."

Shara automatically renewed her support of him when he slumped backward once more. His show of defiance obviously drained what little energy he had. For a moment he was deathly still; then he drew in a ragged breath and spoke again.

"In my time, there is an evil Terran leader in Outerworld, Khameira Chang Sung. Everyone thought he was just another religious zealot. No one realized until it was too late that he possesses tremendous mental powers. His followers are mindless in their devotion to him. One day he was merely a Chinese farmer. Ten years later he controls all of the Asian continent.

"Because of Khameira's ambition, there was a third great war on Outerworld. Powerful weapons were used which ravaged the surface and decimated the population. Khameira still lives, but he rules a dead planet from a protective underground shelter. It will be thousands of years before the atmosphere will be cleared of all poisons. And in the meantime our people are trapped." Exhausted, Lantana closed his eyes.

Shara gave him a slight shake to rouse him again and demanded, "What do you mean, trapped?"

Romulus added his own question. "Why wasn't he stopped? Surely the Tribunal would have approved of interfering with Terran culture in the face of such a threat."

Lantana's body trembled as he attempted to summon enough strength to continue. "There wasn't time. You see, Khameira's powers blinded the Noronian emissaries in place on Outerworld as effectively as he had hidden the truth from the Terrans. By the time Norona was notified, the tunnels to Innerworld were already destroyed, sealing us inside the planet. Even after the atmosphere stabilizes, there are so many live bombs buried in the surface, it will be impossible for Norona to safely rescue us for centuries."

Shara observed her parents communicating mentally and guessed by the expression on Aster's face what was being discussed. As a Terran, Aster was skeptical of strangers and was obviously questioning the veracity of what they were being told. But Romulus would be reminding her that Noronians lived by a code of honesty. Lantana's words should be accepted as truth.

"When will all this take place?" Romulus asked, his brows narrowing in concern.

Lantana tried to respond, but was gripped by another hacking cough for several seconds. When he caught his breath, he was so agitated that his words ran together. "You mustn't know the date. All could be lost. You would leave warnings that might be forgotten. Or worse, the people will wait for proof before acting, and it will be too late. No, you must do as I say to save Innerworld. Khameira must never be born. Unfortunately, he was an orphan, so the logical solution of preventing his mother from conceiving him is not viable."

Shara shook her head, thinking she must have misunderstood. "How would we be able to prevent his birth if we don't know who his mother is and we don't warn future generations?"

Lantana shifted against her arm to face her directly. "*You* can do it, Shara. Your work makes it possible . . . without violence."

"My work? I'm a genetic researcher, not a diplomat."

"Yes, yes, I know. You are also well known in my time for your discovery of the memory molecule within the DNA structure.

Shara was almost afraid to ask, but curiosity won out. "You mean my theory is correct? It *is* possible to trace an individual's direct ancestry, back to the beginning, through the deoxyribonucleic acid?"

Lantana nodded. "That, and more. I was not certain precisely what time I would arrive here, so I brought a copy of the monograph you wrote—or rather, will write—regarding your findings." He pulled a sheaf of papers out of a large pocket in his caftan. "I was not certain if my information chip would be easily compatible with the readout units of your time, so I printed this out for you. In this, you should find whatever you need to move up the completion of your research."

He reached back into the pocket and handed her an envelope. "A lock of Khameira's hair is inside. By analyzing it, you will find the genetic identification of his ancestors. Khameira claimed to have Noronian blood. His mental powers seemed to confirm that supposition." Another coughing spasm prevented him from continuing for several minutes.

Finally he held Shara's gaze with his and spoke in a raspy whisper that sent a chill down her spine. "Go back. Back to the beginning on Norona. Find the rebel who was Khameira's ancestor." His bony fingers grasped her hand and squeezed. "You *must* prevent that one from being exiled to Terra. Then all will be well." His fingers released their hold as his head fell back on Shara's arm.

After a moment Shara searched for a pulse, but found none. Quickly she touched his temple, then shook her head. "Nothing." As she lowered Lantana to the floor, Romulus left the room.

When he returned, he said, "A team is on their way from Medical. They'll revive him so we can question him further."

Shara tried to participate in her family's speculations, but she was too torn by her own conflicting emotions. Sadness for an old man who died in her arms, fear of the future he described, and elation that her theory would be proven correct were all secondary to an overriding sense of anticipation. A trip back in time would be an unprecedented event. She could be fundamental in saving the planet, justify her entire career, *and* learn the truth about her own ancestry, all in one glorious adventure.

While they awaited the medical team, Romulus removed the tempometer belt from Lantana and locked it in the hidden security drawer of his desk. A short time later the team arrived, but swiftly determined that there was no life spark remaining in Lantana's body to be revived. His time had come to an end, and the soul had immediately departed the body.

"So," Romulus said as his family took seats in the living area, "our options have just been narrowed. Without being able to question our visitor from the future in greater depth, there is no way of guessing the exact time period he spoke about. A warning to all future generations might be sufficient. Then again—"

"Then again," Aster broke in, completing her mate's sentence, "depending on how far in the future this takes place, the warning could be forgotten or misconstrued, just as he prophesied."

Mack had his own ideas on the matter. "If we knew the date, we could use the old guy's time device to send someone forward to snatch Khameira before he gains control. Since we can't do that, maybe we could get to one of his ancestors in our time. What about that theory of yours, Shara? Can you really figure out who the tyrant's ancestors are by that lock of hair?"

"I think so. I'll have to read my own research paper to see how I finally figure it out, but basically, I believe that the memory molecule contains the pattern of every direct ancestor of an individual. Each person has his own identifying pattern that gets added to those inherited. Analysis of a hair sample should result in a complete list of ancestral patterns. The method involves testing other people and looking for a matchup. In other words, somewhere in Outerworld right now is a direct ancestor of Khameira. Prevent that person from breeding, and Khameira would never be born."

Aster shook her head doubtfully. "I don't see how you could accomplish that. There are billions of people out there. Besides the physical impracticality of testing that many people in your lifetime, it would be impossible to force everyone's cooperation."

"That leaves only Lantana's suggestion," Shara declared. "He obviously thought out all the same possibilities that we did. I must go back to Norona, to the time before the rebels were exiled to Terra. There were only a few hundred people sent to live on the surface. All I'd have to do is test each person in that group, find the one with a pattern that matches one of Khameira's, and stop that person from going."

Before Shara completed her last sentence, Romulus was up and pacing. "Hold it right there. You've jumped right over three important facts. One, Lantana did not explain how to use his device. Two, even if he had or you could figure it out yourself, time travel is prohibited. And three, you are hardly qualified for a mission that would obviously entail considerable risk."

"On the contrary, Father, it is my theory that will be on trial and my equipment that will be used. No one is better qualified than I. As far as any risk involved, I am no less qualified than mother was when she helped prevent this planet from being destroyed by an asteroid and rescued you after you were abducted by that demented Terran, Gordon Underwood."

Romulus clearly was not happy with the comparison. Despite what he had said to Mackenzie earlier, he still thought of Shara as his little girl, even though she was approaching her thirtieth year. "Remember, your mother was not alone. She had a highly skilled tracker accompanying her." Romulus preferred not to think about what might have hap-

pened to him or Aster had it not been for the special
mental talents of his empathic friend, Falcon.

"So I'll engage a guardian to protect me. Perhaps
Falcon would like a change of scenery. It must be
about time for him to take a break from Outerworld's stress factors again."

· "You know he rarely leaves his Terran family these
days." Giving her suggestion only a moment's consideration, Romulus returned to the original problem.
"At any rate, a guardian wouldn't help if you don't
have authorization to make the trip. I'll compose a
communication to the Ruling Tribunal tonight, relaying Lantana's warnings. Too bad we didn't have a recorder on while he was speaking, but perhaps
together we might be able to reconstruct his exact
words. I'll add a request for permission for someone
to make the trip, *if* the tempometer can be figured
out. Either way, we have to leave the final decision
up to them."

Shara frowned, but said nothing. At least he
hadn't refused her outright. It seemed obvious to her
that every avenue, even one against the law, should
be investigated to prevent the disaster Lantana
warned them of. But no one could predict how the
Tribunal would respond. As she helped her family
recall Lantana's description of the future, she leafed
through the pages of the research monograph he had
brought her.

It took only a quick scan to confirm that this was
indeed her work and that completion of the genetic
tracking program she had been struggling with was
now in her hands. While they awaited the Tribunal's
decision, she would go ahead with her research.
When approval for the time travel came through,
she wanted to be ready to go.

It was inconceivable to her that the Tribunal would refuse permission when the future of both Norona and Earth depended on it. It was also beyond her imagination that they could turn down her request to go when she was so close to proving her theories about the memory molecule firsthand. No one needed to know that her research had a personal as well as scientific basis.

She was only a child when she had set her goal, and it was one of her classmates who had pushed her toward it. The little boy had called her a Terran and made an awful face when he said it. Shara had asked her teacher what the word meant, but the definition—a human born on the surface of the planet and whose ancestors were also Outerworld natives—did not seem to apply to her. Nor did she understand why being a Terran, even if she was one, would cause the boy to sneer at her.

When, a few days later, that same boy had made up a cruel song about Shara being a "mixed-breed" and encouraged the other children to join in the fun, Shara asked her parents to explain. That day she learned the truth. Her father was pure Noronian, but her mother was a Terran, an inferior species of humanoids. In order for Shara to understand, her parents had explained how they had met.

When the Noronians first established their mining colony in the center of the Earth, they had considered the fact that the native Terrans being humanoid like themselves was an advantage, since a group of Noronians were to be left on the surface. They could easily integrate with the primitive inhabitants. It was never intended for any Terrans to be brought into Innerworld, however.

Tunnels were bored through Earth's twelve magnetic fields for the Noronian ships to travel in and out. Unfortunately, as Earth's population grew, accidents began to occur. Because of the magnetism, a Terran vessel occasionally moved into a tunnel doorway undetected just as the doorway was being opened, and the people on board were transported into Innerworld. The Noronians considered these Terrans dangerous and inferior, but they could not risk revealing their presence in the Earth by sending them back.

Aster Mackenzie arrived in Innerworld because of one of those accidents, but fate had surely had a hand in it.

At the time Aster arrived, there was a strong taboo against Noronian Innerworlders fraternizing with the transplanted Terrans. Nevertheless, Romulus, who had just been nominated for the Governorship of the colony, was irresistibly drawn to Aster and she to him. When they were both stricken by the Noronian mating fever, Romulus knew they were destined to be together. But merely being together was not enough to satisfy the fiery craving of the fever. Although there was no record of it ever happening before between a Noronian and a Terran, Aster and Romulus's souls were crying out to each other. The only cure was joining, which eternally bonded two people mentally and spiritually, and a joining between their races was forbidden by law.

After risking their lives to prevent Earth's collision with an asteroid, Romulus and Aster petitioned the Ruling Tribunal of Norona for special permission to join. Aster's bravery and loyalty during the crisis carried considerable weight, but it was the proclamation by the Tribunal that Aster was distantly related to one of the original Noronian colonists that tipped the scales.

Aster became Romulus's mate through the sacred joining ceremony, and they were appointed Co-Governors of Innerworld—a post they had held ever since.

The Tribunal's proclamation satisfied most of the people, but there were die-hard bigots who refused to accept it as truth and others who accepted it, but assumed the drop of Noronian blood Aster inherited had to have been from an inferior Noronian to begin with. In their minds, a Terran could never be their equal, and they passed that prejudice down to their children.

As the first child born from a mixed joining, Shara was considered a precious symbol of the future by some and an unholy freak by others. Her parents' joining had been expected to mark a change in the way Noronian Innerworlders viewed Terran Innerworlders, but prejudice occasionally still bubbled beneath a facade of civility. Only a handful of other mixed joinings had been publicly recorded since, and just two of those had borne children. Because of their parentage, Shara and Mackenzie's status as "mixed-breeds" was common knowledge throughout the colony.

That fateful day, over twenty years ago, Shara had determined to find a way to prove Aster's Noronian ancestry and thereby remove the clouds surrounding her own heritage. Her choice of a career in genetics had been based on the desire for that proof, her excessive ambition driven by that goal. Now, unexpectedly, the means had been handed to her, and nothing was going to stop her from taking advantage of the opportunity.

With part of her mind listening to her family and part still wandering in the past, she almost overlooked the last few pages in her hand. The word *tempometer* caught her eye and she took a second look. The final pages did not detail her research, but Lantana's. He had included his experimental findings, schematics for the device, a set of operating instructions, and a final, handwritten note which read:

My life is ending. There is no more time to perfect my tempometer. I must try it as is and hope that I come close to the time period I seek. Although I believe I have figured out how to make a time-hop from one century to another, I have not uncovered the secret of making a time-hop shorter than a hundred years.

Shara was about to show everyone the pages, but something held her back. It occurred to her that her father was only going through the motions of requesting permission to time-travel because he didn't really believe she could figure out how to use the device. For a while, she decided, she would keep this information to herself.

A month later there was still no word from the Tribunal, but Shara had made considerable progress on all her projects. Her genetic tracking program for her micropputer was nearing completion. After secretly borrowing the tempometer for analysis, she began studying Lantana's notes and gained a fair knowledge of how to operate the device.

With much less enthusiasm, she had done some research into the time period she was intending to go back to. She had always excelled at science and math. History, on the other hand, was a subject that left her in the dust. But she realized the necessity of understanding the era in order to return to it even for a short time.

She knew the basics as well as any other Innerworlder. A little over ten thousand years ago, a fuel shortage threatened to cripple the entire planet of Norona. Expeditions were sent throughout the universe in search of a new source of volterrin, the rare material upon which the technology of Norona was structured. After centuries of futile exploration, volterrin was discovered in abundance in the inner core of the planet Terra.

Now, so many centuries later, Norona was still dependent upon Innerworld to provide its volterrin. The disaster Lantana had spoken of would cause all trade to be cut off, creating another crisis situation on Norona. Shara was certain that fact alone would convince the Tribunal to approve her journey into the past.

Although most of the population of Norona had rejoiced when the volterrin source was first discovered, there was a small group of dissidents who attempted to sabotage the efforts to import the mineral. These rebels wanted Norona to be forced to return to simpler times and to give up modern technology completely. The rebellion was short-lived and a suitable punishment decided upon. A primitive species of humanoids inhabited Terra's surface at that time. Since the rebels wanted to live in a simpler time, they were exiled to live among those less civilized humans.

Shara knew she would have to learn a lot more about those rebels in order to obtain cell samples from each. The easiest sample to collect discreetly would be a strand of hair, but it still required her to come in close contact with them. Wishing she had paid more attention when she was in school, she promised herself to set aside a few days to study whatever material could be found on the rebels.

Though she heard the door to her lab open and close, Shara needed to complete a calculation before she greeted her visitor. She knew someone was speaking, but she blocked out the voice and kept her gaze locked on the monitor before her so as not to lose her train of thought. The pressure of a strong hand on her shoulder accomplished what the voice had not.

"Ahem!"

Annoyed at the interruption, Shara slanted a glance at the fingers spread over her shoulder. The closely pared, unpolished nails and the smattering of fine blond hair on the large hand identified her visitor as a man. Her gaze continued up a bare forearm to an aqua jersey loosely covering a pair of muscular shoulders. Intending to deliver a glare that would have most men pleading for forgiveness, she swiveled her chair toward him and raised her eyes.

Her intended glare lost its hostility as she caught sight of his attractive, almost boyish features. His crown of blond curls, sky-blue eyes, and long eyelashes would have seemed more fitting on a Terran angel. But the warm body standing much too close to hers was definitely not that of a spirit. A plain gold earcuff on his left lobe was the only adornment that was not given him by nature. He epitomized the type of man she avoided at all costs. Her irritation increased as she realized that instead of pleading, he appeared to be patiently waiting for an apology from her.

Lifting his wrist with her thumb and forefinger, she removed his hand, then brushed the spot on her shirt where his hand had been. "Now that you've succeeded in interrupting me, what is it you want?"

His features lost some of their angelic quality as he glowered at her. "You mean you didn't hear any of what I said when I came in?"

Shara gave an exaggerated sigh. "Of course not. I was in the middle of a calculation. Everyone knows better than to try to talk to me until I look up from my work."

"I'm afraid your personal work habits are not as widely known as you'd like to think. If you don't wish to be disturbed, you should put a sign on your door. That's what I do, and it is most effective."

Shara got off her stool to face the exasperating man on a more equal level and was disturbed at having to look up to meet his eyes. At a height that topped 180 centimeters with her bootheels, she didn't have to do that very often. "I don't particularly care what method you find effective. You've interrupted me and I would like to get back to work. So you may either repeat yourself or leave." As she had done a moment ago, he now took a turn scanning her from head to toe. He stared at her eyes for so long that Shara blushed—something she couldn't remember doing for years. "Well?"

"Very interesting," he said, continuing to stare. "I had been told Shara Locke was a forerunner in her field, although a bit impatient and not the friendliest person one might meet. Obviously that was a fair description. On the other hand, I had expected a much more . . . *mature* woman. Tell me, do you have any control over the way your eyes change, or is it all involuntary?"

Shara opened her mouth to respond, but wasn't certain what she wanted to say. It sounded as though he had just complimented and insulted her at the same time. And she certainly didn't intend to volunteer the truth about her eyes. She didn't know who he was, but she was positive she shouldn't give him any ammunition that might later be used against her. Like her father, Shara's hazel eyes changed colors depending on her moods, which made it virtually impossible to hide her feelings from anyone who knew her. She always thought of it as fate's way of counterbalancing her special mental gifts.

Deciding it was better not to answer him at all, she turned back to the calculation displayed on her monitor. "Please excuse me. I really am very busy."

"Getting ready for your trip back in time?"

She gasped as she spun around again. "How do you know about that?"

He smiled, a wide, self-assured grin that showed off perfect white teeth and a deep dimple in his cheek. "Surely you didn't think you could keep something like that a secret. The rumors are flying throughout the academic community."

When he didn't receive the response he expected, he stopped smiling. "Perhaps it would be best if I simply began again." He held out his hand to her and waited until she accepted it for a brief, impersonal shake. "I am Gabriel Drumayne, Professor of History and Chief Procurer of Antiquities for Norona. Although I do have an office and residence in Innerworld, I spend very little time here, so I realize you may not recognize me. But you must be familiar with my name."

Shara did not hesitate to stick a pin in his arrogant little balloon. "I am very sorry to disillusion you,

Professor, but your fame is not as widespread as you imagine it to be. I've never heard of you."

His smirk told her he found that hard to believe. "Nevertheless, you are hoping to receive permission to travel back in time. You will undoubtedly need an expert on Noronian and Terran history to accompany you on such a landmark venture. As I am the most qualified historian available, I will be going with you."

2

Shara swallowed the retorts that popped into her head, *Says who* and *Don't bet your airship on it* being two of the less profane comments his egotistical declaration prompted. Smothering a laugh at her own contrariness, she opted for a less aggressive line. "I believe I might have something to say about that." With a dismissive air, she returned to her work.

Again his hand closed over her shoulder, this time turning her back toward him. "You aren't just unfriendly, you're rude. I can't believe the Governor's daughter hasn't been taught better manners."

She bristled at his reference to her father. "And you . . ." she glared at his hand until he released her, "are a brute. If you manhandle me once more, I will call security."

His mouth dropped open in shock. "Manhandle? You are not only rude, you're unbalanced. Perhaps *I* shall have something to say about who goes on this trip."

Shara paused, not certain whether he really might have a say in the matter, and attempted to regroup. "I apologize if I've been . . . rude, but I dislike being interrupted when I'm in the middle of a difficult calculation. I will be glad to discuss the trip with you at another time, when I'm not so busy."

Gabriel studied her for a second, then apparently decided it was the best he could do. "Fine. How about first thing tomorrow morning . . . before you get involved in another difficult calculation?"

Even though she heard the sarcasm dripping from his words, Shara nodded in agreement. "Meet me for breakfast in the dining room downstairs at oh-eight-hundred."

Gabriel nodded in return, aware that she had made a point of giving him an order rather than a suggestion. As he left the lab and headed out of the building, he shook off the uneasy feeling he had had from the moment he heard about the venture. Before he approached Shara, he had asked several people about her. Regarding her work, she received the highest praise—brilliant, devoted, obsessive. Descriptions of her personality were less flattering— humorless, cool, antisocial.

Naturally, with warnings like that, he had been prepared for the worst upon meeting her. And maybe that had caused him to be on the offensive . . . but a *brute*? He had never committed a violent act on a woman in his life. Unless one counted the Kesian female who had decided he would make an excellent main course for her dinner.

All in all, he had to admit he'd handled the situation badly, but he would have the chance to correct his error tomorrow. Rumors abounded about the purpose of the trip, but the consensus was that she was the one behind it. Being the Governor's daughter practically ensured her having her own way in the matter . . . *if* she got the approval of the Tribunal.

A trip back in time could be the apex of his career. And, for that opportunity of a lifetime, it appeared to be vital that he gain Shara's approval. It had been a long time since he had tried to court a woman's favor.

The problem was, although Shara looked like a woman—and a beautiful, well-formed one at that—she hadn't reacted to him the way most women did, with soft smiles and inviting glances. He knew what those women wanted from him and, when he chose, he gave it to them. Having spent most of his life on the fringes of civilization, he hadn't the slightest idea what else might influence a woman like Shara.

Perhaps his assistant, Ferrine, could give him some advice.

Shara switched off her monitor and set her work aside for the day. Gabriel Drumayne, professor, procurer, and general nuisance, had broken her train of thought, and she couldn't seem to get it back on track. He had been right about her being rude, not that she would ever admit it to him.

She never liked being interrupted, but it was much more than that. One look at his handsome face and the smile that said he knew just how good he looked, and her self-defense mechanism had kicked in. From previous experience, she should be immune to attractive, self-confident men. But since she wasn't, rudeness usually sent them on their way and protected her from her own weakness.

They say a woman never forgets her first love, but Shara wished she could. Like the professor, her first love had had fair coloring and broad shoulders, and she had fallen so fast she never wondered whether he felt the same. She gave him her love and her virginity, two things her Terran mother had convinced her should not be given lightly.

Shara had always understood that her mother's sense of morality was not the norm in Innerworld. The average Noronian accepted coupling as a pleasurable physical experience that did not require any emotional entanglement. At the Indulgence Center, a sexual encounter was just one of a long list of entertainments available. Yet Shara had felt more comfortable adopting her mother's more reserved attitude toward intimacy.

She had mistakenly believed her first young man had wanted more from her than a biological release, but even that would not have been as bad as what he had really wanted. After they made love, he let her know how disappointed he was with her. He had thought sex with a mixed-breed would be a unique experience; yet not only was she not unique, she wasn't even skilled.

It had taken Shara a long time after that to let any man get close to her. The fear that they were interested in her only as a freak of nature was always with her, and she thought she had become adept at interpreting men's ulterior motives. But one day another man slipped under her guard. Although this one had dark hair and eyes, he was still extraordinarily handsome. Her instincts insisted he was interested in her as a woman, not a breed, and she fell again, a lot slower, but the landing was familiar.

Her second experience at love proved that her instincts were never to be trusted again. True, this one didn't care that she was of mixed blood, but his attraction to her still had to do with her parentage. He was politically ambitious, and once Romulus helped him get a position he desired, his devotion to Shara dwindled rapidly.

It was bad enough that Gabriel Drumayne had interrupted her and was so gorgeous he made her insides flutter, but when he made a reference to her father, he committed his third and most serious offense. Shara had always made sure that her accomplishments were her own rather than due to her father's influence, and she was extremely sensitive about it.

Recalling why she automatically reacted to the professor the way she did relieved her of any guilt for her poor manners, but it didn't remove the problem. She had agreed to talk to him tomorrow morning. Considering his position, he probably carried as much influence as she did to recommend who went on the trip. And considering the way she felt about history, a historian would be a logical choice for the companion she promised to take along.

Perhaps there was some quirk in his personality that would justify her refusing to accept him. Maybe he was really a brute after all. She realized he had had a distinct advantage over her at their first meeting because he had gotten information about her beforehand. In order to take away that advantage, she would have to find out a little about him. Ten minutes and several telecommunications later, she located a friend who could introduce her to the professor's clerical assistant, Ferrine.

"Thanks for meeting me on such short notice, Ferrine," Shara said, smiling across the table at the tiny female with the bright orange hair.

Ferrine twitched her freckled nose and smiled back. "I've been wanting to try this new dinery, but my mate's been away and I didn't feel like coming alone. You didn't have to bribe me with a meal, though."

Shara's smile faded. "It wasn't—"

"Oh, don't worry. I'm joking. Your friend Kiku told me you wanted to get some background on my chief, and I figure that's only fair, since he was checking on you first. Don't get me wrong. I'm loyal to Gabriel, but there are times when I have to do what I think will be best for him. You know he spends most of his time journeying, don't you?"

"Actually, I don't know much more than his name and title." And that he's annoying and egotistical, she added to herself.

"Well, let's see. In spite of the title, he spends very little time lecturing and only a fraction of his time procuring antiquities. His primary function—and his life's passion—is researching primitive civilization. He's compiled a number of monographs on the subject. From time to time on his journeys, he comes across a valuable artifact and acquires it for Norona. Because of the remote places some of these research journeys take him, he's often without human company for months at a time. But it doesn't seem to bother him. Even when he's here, if he's involved in a project, he's liable to forget there are people around. Sometimes I have to remind him to eat and sleep."

"So he's a loner and dedicated to his career." Shara couldn't find fault with that.

Ferrine nodded. "He's not shy or introverted; he just doesn't go out of his way to encourage relationships. Of course, the way he looks, he's never had to encourage *female* relationships anyway. Women tend to overlook his lack of interest and readjust their schedules to suit him. As far as I can tell, the only thing he gets excited about is his work. Personally, I can't imagine making love to a man whose mind is off in another time or place, but I guess there's no accounting for taste." She noted the slight flush on Shara's cheekbones and added, "You really confused him today."

Shara's eyebrows lifted a notch. "I beg your pardon?"

"I don't know what happened when he went to see you, but he came back and asked me what I thought he should do to make himself more acceptable to you. Knowing Gabriel, I assumed he meant in a working sense, not personally."

"Uh, yes, he intends to work with me on a project," Shara said, trying not to care that he might not be as sure of himself as he had appeared.

"And again, knowing Gabriel, he probably forgot certain amenities like saying hello or excuse me, or introducing himself."

"Well . . ."

"Believe me, I know," Ferrine said with a laugh. "But I'm used to him. Truly, he's not inconsiderate. It's just that his mind is sometimes miles ahead of his mouth. When he's not distracted by a project, he's quite pleasant and actually fun to be around. He really seemed anxious to get along with you."

Shara gave a noncommittal shrug, realizing she had been hoping for some negative information and wound up talking to the professor's one-woman support team instead.

"Listen," Ferrine said, leaning closer and lowering her voice. "He wouldn't want me to tell you this, but it's not as much of a secret as he likes to believe,

and it might help you to give him a little more lee-
way, as far as his behavior is concerned."

Shara tilted her head expectantly. A secret about
the professor could be just what she needed.

"He was born in Parson's Colony."

That simple sentence told Shara more than
enough to fill her with panic. She thanked Ferrine
for her time and returned to her lab, but her mind
was occupied with thoughts of the experiment that
had taken place at Parson's.

Although it was not widely publicized, as a geneticist she had studied the few details recorded. Six
couples with exceptionally developed mental abilities had formed a group family in which no one
spoke aloud. All communication was by thought and
all minds were always open to the others, the theory
being that together they would form a dynamic mental union.

Most Noronians were trained to communicate
mentally by pressing two fingers to another's temple
and concentrating. Despite having a Terran mother,
Shara had been born with a few exceptional mental
abilities. Though she couldn't discern another's
thoughts without making physical contact, she could
send specific thoughts or simple instructions, usually without the receiver being aware of it.

She had several other extraordinary skills besides
that, but only her immediate family knew about
them. The curious attention she drew by being a
mixed-breed was bad enough; she didn't want her
special skills being talked about as well.

However, those abilities could be useless against
someone from Parson's. The professor could have
the power to manipulate her to do whatever he
wanted. Although she had no problem blocking an

average intrusion, such as her brother had occasionally attempted, she had no way of knowing if her mind was strong enough to hold off a more talented trespasser. She would just have to keep her guard up around the professor at all times.

Her reasons for making sure he did not accompany her had now doubled. But she thought it would be best to let him think she was being cooperative while staying a step ahead of him.

The next morning she arrived in the dining room precisely at 0800 prepared to pretend she was open-minded. By 0900 she headed to her lab, more annoyed with the self-centered boor than before. He had not shown up, nor canceled their appointment.

Her morning took another downward turn when she received notice that a highly skilled research assistant had chosen to work in another department rather than accept her more generous offer. This had happened before during the years she ran the genetics research lab in Innerworld, but only once did the prospective employee let it be known that Shara's questionable breeding had affected his decision. After that, she always wondered about the true reasons when she lost a qualified employee or when a choice assignment was passed on to a geneticist on Norona.

Three hours later, Gabriel finally appeared in the lab. This time he stood quietly beside her until she looked up at him.

The explicitly graphic directions she had intended to deliver if she ever saw him again slipped away. It was impossible to curse at an angel. The only thing missing was his halo. She decided to let him have the first word, because she fully intended to have the last.

Rather than speak, he handed her a brown leather

pouch. Shara glanced suspiciously at the small bag, then back at him.

"It's for you," he said, loosening the drawstring at the top of the pouch.

Turning the bag upside down, Shara shook the contents onto her worktable. A gray, crescent-shaped stone about two inches long fell out with a thud. "You're giving me a rock?"

Gabriel frowned and shook his head at her. "That's not a rock. That's the foreclaw of an Umerian trenchrat." When she still looked skeptical, he explained. "In ancient times on Norona, if one person offended another, it was customary for the one to offer the other a gift that held sentimental meaning for the giver."

"Let me get this straight. This . . . thing . . . has sentimental value to you?"

"Very much so! It saved my life. I was on the planet Umer when I accidentally met the gaze of one of the amazons there. It isn't that I didn't know better, mind you, but she caught me by surprise. Before I could blink, she had me half entranced. Let me tell you, if that trenchrat hadn't attacked me right then, I might never have escaped. I killed the beast, but this claw broke off in my back. I've had it for years."

Shara wondered if he could be making up the story. The thing still looked like a rock to her. But Ferrine *had* said his journeys took him to distant places on a regular basis, so his tale could be true. And she had heard of the hypnotic powers of certain Umerian females. Just as she had heard that some men went there hoping to be forced into their exotic brand of captivity.

"I could how you the scar," Gabriel said seriously. "I never had it repaired."

She tensed at the thought of his removing his shirt for her to inspect his back. "No. That's not necessary. I was just thinking about your story. I've never been anywhere but Innerworld and Norona."

"Then you are probably in need of this adventure you're planning. Oh, I almost forgot. I apologize for missing our appointment this morning. I'm afraid I started translating an ancient Terran scroll last night and failed to note the time until a half hour ago."

"You mean you haven't been to sleep yet?" Shara asked, remembering what Ferrine had said about his forgetfulness. More than likely, it was Ferrine's suggestion that he apologize.

"No. I'll catch up with it later. I always do. Since I missed our breakfast appointment, would it be possible to have our discussion over lunch?" Rather than attempting to sway her with the boyish grin and dimple ploy, his expression remained sincere.

She preferred not to have the discussion at all, but she reminded herself that it would behoove her to play along. "That would be satisfactory." After putting the claw and pouch into her desk drawer, she gave her computer instructions to run a program while she was gone.

Neither spoke until they had ordered a meal; then Gabriel got right to the point. "As I understand it, you have a time-travel device in your possession and substantiating evidence to justify its use. Do you have a good case?"

"Excellent." Shara had already decided to fill him in on the situation. It would not be that difficult for him to find out on his own anyway, and she wanted him to believe she was accepting him.

Meanwhile, she stayed alert for any attempt on his part to touch her mind.

He paid close attention as she told of Lantana's insistence that she go back in time to prevent one rebel from being sent to Earth. By the time their meal arrived, he knew as much as she did about the reason for the trip.

"And what about the device? It won't matter what you intend to do if you can't operate it."

Her study of the tempometer was still a secret, but she didn't dare lie. "I think I'll be able to manage. Once approval comes through, of course."

"Of course." Gabriel couldn't prove she was withholding something, but the irises of her eyes had changed color twice since they sat down. They started out a soft brown-green hazel, but turned bright emerald green as she talked about Lantana's appearance and her plan to go back in time. Then, just as suddenly, when he asked about the time device, they darkened to a dull shade of olive.

Not for the first time, Gabriel thanked the heavens that he had not inherited the emotionally reactive irises common to so many Noronians. Of course, without that trait, the Code of Honesty would be difficult to enforce. But he had never seen a pair of eyes in which the changes were as drastic as Shara's.

He decided it was time to terminate the preliminaries and state his objective. "I understand why you want to make the trip, and it makes sense that you should be the geneticist to go. But, as I told you yesterday, I believe a historian should participate in the venture and that I should be that historian."

"I've given that some thought, Professor, and—"

"Gabriel. The title is an honor, but not necessary."

Not necessary for him perhaps, Shara thought,

but she preferred to keep familiarities to a minimum. "As I was saying, I have come to the conclusion that a historian would be a logical addition to the team. Since history is out of my area of expertise, I would leave it to the Tribunal to select the individual best qualified."

His eyes narrowed at her implication that it would not necessarily be him. "And I'm telling you, there is no one more qualified than I. The moment I heard the rumor, my mind was made up that I would be part of this. The research would be invaluable to my text. But now, after hearing exactly what you plan to do, I realize there is more at stake here than my work."

With his elbows on the table and his hands clenched in fists, he leaned closer and spoke in a deceptively soft voice. "I will do everything in my power to make sure I'm right beside you all the way, Shara Locke. You think you're going to go back in time, alter an event that occurred ten thousand years ago, and everything will be just wonderful when you return. Well, I don't believe that's possible. In fact, I don't believe it should be permitted. I won't stop you from going, because I want to make the trip myself, and you seem to have my ticket. But I'll be *drekked* before I let you do anything that might affect history as we know it!"

Shara was so stunned by his pronouncement, it took a moment for her anger to flare. "Since you were so thoughtful as to give me fair warning, *Professor,* I'll give you one right back. I'm going to do everything in *my* power to make sure you do not get to accompany me. But if you still manage it, you had better stay out of my way. I will do whatever needs to be done to save this planet. And if that means altering history, so be it."

Shara stood up to walk away from the table, but before she took three steps, Gabriel blocked her path. When she tried to go around him, he grasped her upper arms and held her in place. She tipped her head back to give him the full effect of her yellow-flecked glare and met a fury that matched her own.

"Some people might be intimidated by your tough act, Shara. You *are* a big girl." He moved closer and stared down his nose at her. "But I'm bigger." Stepping back again, he released her. "Let me give you another warning. Know your enemy before you threaten him."

"I'm sorry, Shara," Romulus said, his hazel eyes revealing that he truly did sympathize. "There's nothing more we can do. The Ruling Tribunal has made its decision. They believe it's too dangerous to tamper with time."

When Romulus had asked her to come to his office, Shara's heart had started to pound with excitement. She had been so sure the news would be good. She appreciated his difficult position: As Governor, he had to abide by the Tribunal's edicts; as her father, he always wanted to give her everything she wanted. But this was one time he had no idea how badly she wanted something, nor the real reason why. "Didn't they believe what Lantana told us?" she asked.

"According to the transmission I just received, they apparently believe all of what he related will happen, because they have decided to prepare warnings for future generations."

"But I thought we made it clear that a warning would be too precarious." Shara's frustration forced her to rise from her chair and pace the large room.

"I'm sorry," Romulus repeated with a shake of his head. "Our hands are tied."

Maybe *your* hands are tied, Shara thought, but mine are still free. She turned away from him, knowing that if he saw her eyes, he would know she was scheming. Trying to appear resigned to the decision, she promised to be at his house for dinner in two nights, as usual, and left the office.

Later that evening, when Shara was certain her parents and their staff had gone home, she returned to the Governor's office. Having worked there during her academy years, she was familiar with the storage system and where to find the week's entry code. Within minutes she had an emergency travel visa good for a round trip between Innerworld and Norona. She couldn't be certain how many times she might need to make that trip, so she took a few more. Copying her father's signature and applying his seal took special care, however, and a man's voice in the outer office let her know she had taken a few minutes too long.

"Is someone in here?" the voice called out.

Security, Shara deduced, knowing they would have been alerted to activity in the Governor's office. She had expected to be in and out before they would investigate.

"Yes," she returned. "I'm in the storage room." Her mind clicked through her options. If her father learned of her late-night excursion, he might guess her purpose. She couldn't let that happen. As the security man entered the back room, she remained seated at the desk, as if it were perfectly natural for her to be there. Relief eased her shoulders when she recognized the black-uniformed man. "Good evening, Tomas. I didn't mean to pull you away from your office. I guess I should have told you I'd be here tonight."

Tomas lowered the small stunner in his hand. "Good evening to you also, Shara. Has your father got you working nights in his office these days?"

She laughed, but braced herself inwardly for what she had to do. But she had no choice. "Not really. I was on my way to his house, and he asked me to pick up these visas for him." Tomas walked toward her, frowning slightly as his gaze fell on the visas in front of her, and Shara panicked. If he recognized the signatures and seals, she would be caught in a lie—a small crime compared to the one she was about to commit.

She had been taught never to misuse the gifts the Supreme Being had granted her, but as the security man leaned over the desk to get a closer look, she acted in self-defense. Her mind entered his and planted a suggestion.

You must return to your office, and you will not remember seeing me. You investigated the Governor's offices and no one was there. Everything was in order. Go now.

Tomas stood erect and left the room. Shara took a deep calming breath, but when she picked up the electronic writer, she couldn't stop her hands from shaking. She had just broken one of the most serious Noronian laws—invasion of mental privacy.

She assured herself that when her mission was over she would be forgiven for everything: the lie, the illegal mind-touch, stealing the travel visas, and forging her father's name, all leading to defiance of the Tribunal's decision not to use the tempometer.

Listing her crimes in such a way gave her an anxious moment. They were adding up terribly fast, and she hadn't even left Innerworld. She repeated the litany that had brought her to this point: *The reward is worth the risk.* With a lot more haste, she completed her chore and returned to her residence.

In order to go back to the time of the rebellion, she first had to get to Norona without being discovered. There were two days before her father expected to see her, and she wanted to be well on her way by then. An express mail ship was scheduled to leave in the morning, but even that speedy transport took a week. In an attempt to put off suspicions as long as possible, she programmed her telecommunicator to send a message to her parents' home right before she was supposed to arrive for their weekly family dinner, saying she was tied up on a project. A second message two days after that would tell them she had decided to take a brief holiday and would contact them when she returned.

Romulus had not been aware that the tempometer had been removed from the desk in his residence, and Shara hoped he wouldn't go looking for it now. All she needed was a little luck. With the tempometer's help, she might even be able to get back without her parents realizing she had been gone.

Although she tried to sleep for several hours, it was a futile effort. Finally she arose and got dressed to leave. Using the clothing she planned to take along, she carefully concealed the tempometer and the notes Lantana had given her, and packed it all in a small bag.

Though she knew she wouldn't feel anything there, she touched the spot behind her ear where the universal translator chip had been inserted last week. Since she rarely left Innerworld, she had never had a use for it before. With the chip in place, she would be able to understand and communicate in any known language or dialect being spoken wherever or whenever she visited.

Ready to depart hours before the appointed time, she headed for her lab to pick up the microputer and make sure she had left adequate instructions for her research team.

As departure time neared, Shara's excitement mounted. Suddenly the door to her lab opened, and the unexpected sound caused her to spring off her stool.

"Going somewhere, Shara?"

For several wild heartbeats, she could only gape, speechless from the shock of being discovered by the worst person possible. How could the professor have known what she was planning? She hadn't made advance reservations or even spoken to anyone. There were only the preprogrammed messages for her parents. But there he stood, like an angelic centurion, with his feet spread and arms crossed. Her resentment toward the odious man increased another degree.

She tried to mentally order him away, but discovered that she was locked out of his mind for some reason. She tensed, expecting him to be furious with her attempted invasion, but he didn't seem to notice that she had done anything. Carefully avoiding an untruth, especially with the evidence of a travel bag at her feet, she hedged. "I don't believe my itinerary is your concern." He marched across the room and cupped her chin in his hand before she had a chance to object. As she jerked her head away from his touch, a slow smile appeared on his face.

Gabriel had seen what he was looking for, but decided not to let her in on his realization quite yet. At the moment her eye color was a drab olive green, and he knew she was hiding something this time. He mentally catalogued that information for further analysis.

Shara backed away from him, discomfited by the way his brief touch had warmed her skin. "What do you want, Professor?"

"Tch, tch, tch. Still angry, I see. Too bad. This journey will be difficult enough without you scowling at me the entire time."

Shara straightened her spine and gave him the scowl he was expecting. A week had passed since their last encounter, and when he hadn't made another appearance, she had hoped he had gone off on another one of his research treks. "And what journey might that be?"

"You're not a good enough actress to pull off the simpleton routine, Shara. I know the Tribunal turned down your request to travel back in time. I also know you're planning to ignore their decision." Her small but audible intake of breath confirmed his assumption.

"How do you know that?" she whispered.

He gave her his most charming smile. "Because, fellow scholar, that is precisely what I intend to do as well." He paused for that dart to sink in, then continued. "I could stop you right now. All I'd have to do is let the Co-Governors know you have the tempometer." Her look of dismay told him he had guessed correctly. She *did* have it in her possession.

"They would never permit their offspring to become a criminal. But in that scenario, I wouldn't get to go, either. I gave this a lot of thought, and I believe I came up with the same conclusion that you did: The reward is worth the risk. Give it up, Shara. You have no choice but to accept me as your partner for the duration."

She was briefly taken aback at hearing her litany come from his mouth, until she recalled their last argument. Since she couldn't get through to his subconscious mind, she tried for a bluff. "Go ahead. Call my parents. They know what I'm doing."

He noted the olive color of her eyes had grayed a bit more, and bet she was lying, despite the fact that it was prohibited by the Code of Honesty. Striding past her to the communicator on her desk, he wondered what laws were left for her to disregard. He touched a button and said, "Connect me with Governor Romulus."

Shara's finger touched the same button a heartbeat later and disconnected the communication. "All right. You can come. But I have one question. Do you still intend to prevent me from altering history?"

"Absolutely," he stated emphatically.

"Then I'd say *partner* is the wrong term, because I still intend to carry out my mission, even if I have to do it over your unconscious body."

Gabriel raised one eyebrow at her. "I'm accustomed to going long periods without sleep. And when I do sleep, it's very lightly. Or are you still harboring notions of overpowering me with physical violence?"

She cocked her head, thinking physical violence should not be ruled out. "If you're not with me, I don't need to do anything."

Gabriel closed his eyes and pinched the bridge of his nose. He had never known such an argumentative, unreasonable female. "Regardless of your delusions, here's the situation: You can accept my presence in spite of our difference of opinion, or return the tempometer and give up any hope of proving your theories firsthand. Well? What will it be?"

3

"Do I at least get to specify terms?" Shara used her most caustic tone of voice, but his smirk let her know he was finding her more entertaining than threatening. Physical violence was sounding better all the time.

Gabriel shrugged. "It doesn't have to be war between us. You admitted to me that you thought a historian would be helpful. With me you have a historian and a seasoned journeyor. Your lack of experience in primitive cultures could put you in serious danger. Though you're not really in a position to request favors, I'll show you how easy I am to work with. I will agree to one contingency, as long as it has nothing to do with altering history."

Shara frowned, caught as she was between logic and emotion. His points were valid, but she refused to admit she needed his expertise. With a sigh of unwilling surrender, she chose her single request. "My one condition—and it's imperative you agree—is this: Stop putting your hands on me."

"What?"

"I thought I spoke very clearly. Four times now you have put your hands on me in an aggressive manner. I don't like it."

Gabriel searched for an appropriate response. It

wasn't the first time a female had commented on the effect his touch had had on her, but it was the first time one was repulsed by it. Shara had even counted the number of contacts. He, on the other hand, could only remember thinking how warm her flesh had felt against his fingers, as opposed to her chilly disposition. "I assure you, those offenses were unintentional, but I do apologize. I will try to curb my tactile impulses in the future. So when do we leave?"

She resented being forced into a corner, but there didn't seem to be any acceptable alternatives. As soon as Shara told him the time and gave him a travel visa, Gabriel left to pack his necessities for the trip.

Shara's fantasy wish that the professor would change his mind dissolved when she saw him at the foot of the boarding ramp to the sleek mailship. He had changed into a loose-fitting, dark-brown jumper with short sleeves and long pants, similar to the forest-green one she was wearing, but with two notable differences. Where hers had a high collar that reached her chin, his neckline was opened to his diaphragm, allowing her to see that the hair on his chest was the same shade of pale gold as—

She put a halt to that line of thinking. The other difference was that his jumper had dozens of various-sized pockets, most of which seemed to have something inside them. Floating beside him was a large satchel, at least three times the size of her bag. A guide strap wrapped around his wrist kept it from drifting away. Apparently he had attached an antigravity device to save himself the trouble of carrying it.

"Professor," she said stiffly in acknowledgment.

He nodded. "If it makes you more comfortable to keep my title between us, go right ahead. But I will answer much more readily to Gabriel, the name I'm accustomed to. Keep that in mind if you ever need my attention quickly. Shall we board?"

Shara didn't bother to answer, walking past him up the gangway and into the ship. She would have preferred to have their cabins a kilometer apart, but one didn't have much choice on a mailship. The ship was built for speed rather than comfort, and passengers had to stay in whatever crew's quarters were available, which in this case were the last two sleepers at the end of a passageway.

Gabriel waited for her to enter the first room before moving on to his own. One look at the cubicle he would be inhabiting for the next week dampened his spirits. The single bunk against the wall looked just a bit too short and too narrow for him to use it comfortably. The floor space between the bunk and the lavatory with its minimal shower cell was barely wide enough to roll out his sleeping pouch, but it would have to do.

Normally the lack of comfortable facilities would never have given him the slightest problem, but after dealing with the female anomaly next door, the room's limitations bore the brunt of his dissatisfaction. It irritated him that she should give the appearance of being an enticing woman while she acted more like a spoiled child. He surmised that her selfishness and misconception that she could always have her own way could have been brought about by her being the Governor's daughter.

Her disagreeableness was almost enough to make him forget how his body responded each time he caught sight of her. Almost. But it was exceedingly difficult to ignore how his heart rate increased or his temperature rose a notch. Impossible to forget that his lower regions were being stirred at completely inappropriate times. In the past, his sex drive had always been controlled by conscious decision, not an involuntary reaction like this.

He recalled what she had said about his touching her and again wondered why she should find him so unappealing. Had she responded as other women had, he and Shara could have had a pleasant week ahead of them. As she requested, however, he would keep his distance from her.

Avoiding her entirely was out of the question, though. They had plans to make and for their mutual safety he wanted to make sure she knew what to expect when they went back in time. He decided it would not be necessary to make any move toward peace between them yet. They would both have to go to the common dining room to eat. Eventually she was bound to accept the fact that they were a team.

By the third day, Gabriel realized he had underestimated her stubbornness. Unaccustomed as he was to being ignored, he hadn't considered that Shara would remain in her sleeper except for the odd times she chose to dine. And when he happened to see her in the dining room, she simply offered her icy, "Professor," and looked away.

He usually avoided company himself and was perfectly content to be alone in his own room, but he and Shara really needed to communicate. Suddenly a possibility occurred to him that he hadn't thought of before. Perhaps she was avoiding him because she intended to leave him behind once they reached Norona. With her eyes as expressive as they were, she might be afraid he would guess what she was up to if he spent enough time with her. Certain that he had guessed her plan, he only had to thwart it. But his intuition told him he would fare much better if she were the first one to break the silence.

Retrieving a small mercury-filled sphere from his satchel, he determined to get her out of her room and into his . . . for purposes of communication.

Bonk!

Shara bolted off her bunk and stared at the wall she had been using as a back support while she was reading.

Bonk!

The second thud sounded close to the same spot.

Bonk!

The thuds continued to come, spaced about five seconds apart, as if someone were playing screwball in the next sleeper. And she knew who that someone had to be. She put up with it for several minutes, vowing not to let him get to her. Ignoring him for the past three days had been one of the most difficult tasks she had ever assigned herself. Every time she saw him, she could sense him wanting to talk to her, and her terrible weakness had her wanting to let him. Added to that, the boredom of staying in her cramped quarters was definitely playing havoc with her nerves. Perhaps, she thought, scolding the professor would be just what she needed to break up the tedium.

Before she could give it a second thought, she was knocking on his door.

"Shara!" Gabriel greeted her with a smile that lit up his angel eyes. "What a nice surprise. I was just thinking how much better double screwball is than solitaire. Care to join me?" He stepped back and waved his arm to invite her inside.

She remained in the passageway, reminding herself she had not come over to play a game with him, especially not inside that tiny room. "No. I, uh, only wanted to check on you. I heard the thumps on my wall and thought—"

"Oh, *drek*, I am sorry. I guess the rooms aren't soundproof. If you don't care to come in, would you like to get some fresh air with me? The biodrome on board is small compared to one you'd find on a regular passenger ship, but it's still a change of scenery."

Shara's boredom won a brief skirmish with her caution. "Yes, that sounds fine."

"One moment, then." He tossed the screwball onto the bunk and picked up a small white bag. On their way below deck, Gabriel was careful not to touch her, in spite of an irrational, overwhelming urge to do just that.

As soon as they entered the biodrome, Shara inhaled the humid air and smiled.

Gabriel nodded at her appreciation. "Did you know that only forty years ago, tropical rain forests like this one had almost been obliterated on Outerworld Earth? It's incredible what progress they made out there once they finally realized what danger they were in."

Shara took another breath of oxygen-rich air provided by the carefully cultivated plants and trees. Sounds of a rushing waterfall and native jungle creatures had been realistically simulated to enhance visitors' sensual pleasure. "Yes, as a matter of fact, Professor, I do know a bit of the environmental history of Outerworld."

"Oh, of course. For a moment I forgot who your mother is. Aster Mackenzie's contributions to the planet will be legendary."

She laughed. "At least that's what Lantana told us, but my mother found it hard to believe. She's really a very modest person."

"Would you care for a Caress?" Gabriel offered, holding open the bag he had brought from his room.

Shara peeked inside to make sure she understood precisely what he was offering. Recognizing the red shimmer-wrapped hearts, she dipped her hand in and brought out one of the dark chocoberry treats. "Thank you. Where did you find these?"

"I always bring a supply with me. They're my only bad habit."

She didn't buy that for a minute. Gabriel unwrapped a sweet as if it were a rare treasure, then placed it in his mouth. His expression left no doubt about his extreme enjoyment as he savored the chocoberry slowly melting in the heat of his mouth. Shara felt as if she were a voyeur and he were performing a very private act. Dragging her gaze away from him, she ate the piece she had chosen for herself. It was good, but not *that* good.

"I'm glad you decided to end the silent treatment," Gabriel said when he finished his chocoberry. "We do need to go over your plans."

Shara started to correct him about why she had shown up at his door, but realized her desire to have a confrontation with him had melted along with the chocoberry. For a few minutes, at least, she wanted to continue the peaceful mood he was attempting to establish. Discussing her specific plans was a sure way of destroying that mood, particularly since she had no intention of including him in them. Yet she was aware that any information she could glean from him could be helpful. She decided to see if she could get him talking instead of the other way around.

"From what I've read about the time of the rebellion, the insurgents were scattered over the planet, but at the end, the leaders all gathered in First Province to rise against the Ruling Tribunal. Obviously, I'm hoping to hit that time period."

"Hoping?" Gabriel asked, carefully watching Shara's eyes for clues.

"Yes, hoping. Lantana had not perfected the tempometer. I can program it for the year I want, but, according to his notes, I may end up as much as a century off. I'm counting on the theory that there are eddies and flows in time, and certain events—those with historical significance—have a stronger pull than other times."

"If you're right, there shouldn't be a problem. Nothing in that time period was as significant as the rebellion and colonization of Innerworld Earth."

They came to a small pond and sat down on two smooth boulders. Shara tested the temperature of the water with her fingers and smiled when a group of tiny fish rushed to the surface. "Sorry, guys, all we have is sweets." After a moment, she returned her attention to Gabriel. "I've been reading about that era, but I'd appreciate anything you could tell me that might help prepare me."

Ferrine had told Shara that Gabriel spent very little time lecturing, but it was immediately apparent that he enjoyed it. With no further encouragement on Shara's part, he shared his knowledge and love for the past. Rather than the sort of dry dissertation she remembered from some of the professors of history she had had in the academy, Gabriel made the past come alive for her.

He described the fears of the Noronian leaders as the shortage of energy began to threaten their way of life and the renewed hopes for a glowing future after the discovery of volterrin in Terra's core. Likewise, he gave her an insight into the motivations of the rebels. The fuel crisis had given them a golden opportunity to spread their views and gather followers, despite the fact that they had previously been considered fanatics.

"The leaders of the movement called themselves Friends and preached a return to the old ways, before technology removed the challenge of survival from their lives. In their minds, this also meant a return to the time when there was no Ruling Tribunal or central planetary government. They wanted to give the people more freedom by putting the power back into the individual provinces. Naturally those leaders were ready to take control of the new local governments to ensure harmony.

"By the time the crisis ended, the Friends had gone from dreaming of change to believing they could force their wishes on the population. Despite the fact that peace and love were supposed to be the basis of their movement, legal protests gave way to attacks on government-owned property. A large portion of the administrative center of First Province was destroyed before the rebels were brought under control."

Shara found herself so fascinated with his tales that the afternoon sped by. On the way back to their rooms, she didn't hesitate to accept his suggestion that they dine together. Several of the crew members joined them shortly after they arrived in the dining area and the evening turned out to be surprisingly enjoyable.

The next two days followed a similar pattern. All Shara had to do was ask a few questions and Gabriel was pleased to educate her. When he had covered every aspect of the rebellion and ancient Noronian history, she urged him to tell her about his journeys.

The day before they were due to arrive on Norona, Gabriel was determined to bring their discussion back to the present. They were once again in the biodrome, walking along the winding path and sharing his stash of Caresses. "I think we should make some contingency plans, in case we get separated," he began.

While he outlined a procedure that he thought would be workable, Shara's mind wandered. Although she had come to appreciate his company and his vast knowledge, she hadn't lost sight of the fact that they had opposing goals. As far as she was concerned, it was still in her best interest to make the time-hop without him. For the past several days, she had successfully sidetracked him. Surely she could manage it a little longer. The moment he concluded his idea for regrouping, she asked, "Tell me about yourself. You know everything there is to know about me, and all I know about you is your work."

Gabriel narrowed his brows in confusion. He could not comprehend the connection between their plans and his background. Thus far, none of their discussions had veered into personal areas. Under the circumstances, there didn't seem to be a need for an exchange of trivial information. On the other hand, Ferrine had assured him that shared confidences could put Shara into a more cooperative mood. "What do you want to know?"

She figured some basic questions could get him started talking about himself, and then, as he had with other subjects, he'd carry on from there. "Where were you born? Do you have siblings? What do your parents do?"

He was automatically suspicious about what prompted this line of questioning. He had stopped revealing any information about his origins long ago, after he realized how uncomfortable it made most people. And yet, what greater confidence could he share? "Parson's Colony, one older sister, diplomatic councilors."

Shara hadn't expected him to be so forthright.

He noted her surprised expression and nodded. "My parents were two of the original twelve."

"That must have been an incredible experience," she said with sincere fascination. Though the possibility of him having superior mental powers frightened her, she also had the desire to know more about it, from both a professional and personal standpoint. "If I remember correctly, for a short time Parson's Colony was considered one of the greatest brain trusts in the galaxy, then it abruptly dissolved. Several reasons were officially cited—personality and control conflicts and something about a problem with the offspring." She scrutinized his head of soft golden curls, past his beautiful blue eyes, and down over his well-developed form, and said the opposite of what she was really thinking. "You seem fairly normal to me, Professor."

He shrugged his shoulders. "*Normal* is a very relative term. Our parents thought open mental communication was perfectly normal, even healthy. As children we never had to be warned of dangers because our parents' eyes were on us whether they were with us or not. If I was about to trip over something, that item would vanish or I would be caught by invisible hands in midair and gently set on my feet.

"We never had to go to academy because all of their joint knowledge was automatically imparted to us. They had expected the offspring to have even greater mental powers than the parents, but only a few did. My sister, Janna, was one of them. Others inherited abilities equal to their parents. Some acquired none at all."

Shara asked the question that had been on her mind since Ferrine first mentioned his birthplace. "And what abilities did you inherit?"

Gabriel gave her a sly smile. If he truly wanted to gain the upper hand with her, he could let her wonder indefinitely—worrying that he could hear her every thought whether she directed it at him or not, fearing that he could send thoughts or suggestions without ever touching her, and she'd never be the wiser. Reminding himself that he wanted to gain her cooperation, he revealed the truth.

"Some of the skills developed within Parson's Colony were so powerful that outsiders began to fear that the colonists might misuse their abilities. The group finally broke up due to the pressure of those frightened outsiders. Your reaction to where I was raised was one of intellectual curiosity, but I assure you it is much more common for someone to become immediately distrustful of what I might be capable of doing to them.

"Just so you know you have nothing to fear from me, I'm going to tell you something I usually keep secret. I didn't inherit any of my parents' extraordinary talents. Unlike most Noronians, I can't even direct specific thoughts to you if I touch your temple. Unfortunately, I also lack the ability to block out other people's thoughts. I'm what they call an *open receiver*."

"Are you telling me that you hear what I'm thinking all the time?" Shara's stomach knotted at the possibility, and his laughter did little to calm her.

"No, your privacy is intact." She didn't need to know that once he figured out the color key to her moods, her eyes would tell him all he needed to know without hearing her thoughts. "You mentioned that the offspring had problems. Imagine what it would be like to have twenty-three other people in your head at all times. That's how many open minds there were after each couple had two children.

"There were other open receivers like myself, who could never block anyone or sort out the individual voices. As children, we never knew a moment of quiet, let alone privacy. Before the group disbanded, they invented a jammer for the less fortunate minds." He pointed to the plain gold cuff on his left earlobe. "With this on, my reception is effectively jammed, and I'm protected against any unscrupulous person trying to invade my mind without my knowledge or permission."

The last he added as a warning, in case she should get the idea that she could manipulate him. Already having broken at least two laws that he knew of, she could be capable of more.

Though she still didn't trust him and would rather not have to deal with him professionally, Shara felt deep sympathy for him and those other children. It was impossible for her to imagine growing up without ever having time to herself, the chance to dream private dreams, or to keep special secrets that only one or two dear friends shared. No wonder Gabriel spent most of his adult life alone and journeying to civilizations where they had no telepathic abilities. He was making up for lost years.

"Any other questions?" he asked without looking at her.

She had plenty, but if the answer to a simple question about his birthplace could cause her to want to reach out to him, she was afraid of what might happen to her good sense if she learned anything else. "Not at the moment."

As they strolled along, she contemplated his account of his childhood. She wasn't sure he was being completely truthful about his lack of skills. After all, it would be to his advantage to keep her in the dark about that. At least she now knew why she hadn't been able to get through to him back in her lab.

If he *was* being honest about his background, however, she realized, he'd be even more distrustful of her if he discovered the extent of the extrasensory abilities she possessed. She wondered whether it was her or Gabriel who really had the upper hand.

"All right," he said after a moment. "It's your turn. I already know your parents are the Co-Governors, you were born in Innerworld, and you haven't ventured far from the cocoon."

"There's nothing wrong with that," she said in a tone that let him know she was ready to defend her way of life.

"I didn't say there was, but you must admit you've

had a fairly charmed existence so far." He realized he was baiting her, but he couldn't seem to help himself.

She stopped dead in her tracks, with her hands fisted on her hips. "Charmed? Do you think you're the only child in the universe who had a difficult time growing up? You don't understand anything about my life. Yes, my parents are important people and wonderful to me. I love them very much, but—as with you—because of what my parents wanted out of life, I have had to live with the consequences."

Gabriel stepped closer, wanting to confirm the color her eyes took on in anger, even though he didn't understand the cause. The hazel was now sparked with yellow. He pushed a little harder. "I'm sure being the center of attention all the time would make life simply unbearable."

Rather than rage at him, her voice quieted as she turned away. "There is a vast difference between being the center of loving attention and the focus of hatred."

His hand raised and stroked her hair before he remembered his promise not to touch. When she didn't pull away, he did it again. "I shared a confidence with you, Shara. I can't read your thoughts, but I can tell I've said something to offend you again. Why would you think you were the focus of hatred?" His fingers slipped through the dark, silky strands at the nape of her neck, and the way her head tilted suggested she liked what he was doing. "Why?" he repeated.

She turned to meet his gaze, but his fingers remained tangled in her hair, gently kneading the back of her neck. If it hadn't felt so good, she would have stopped him. "I assumed you knew all important data about me, Professor. My mother is a Terran."

His hand stilled. "And?"

Studying his face, she decided he was not being obtuse on purpose. "And that makes me a mixed-breed, an oddity . . . a *freak*."

He was well aware of the prejudice she referred to, but had not connected it with her. How could anyone call this exquisite creature a freak? "It also makes you rare, like a black orchid-rose." With the slightest tug on her hair, her head tipped back, and his free hand came up to caress her cheek. He watched, totally fascinated, as her eye color softened to the shade of rich, dark chocoberry. And, oh, how he did love the taste of chocoberry.

Shara held her breath, knowing he was going to kiss her, knowing she shouldn't allow it, yet knowing she didn't have the willpower to resist something she suddenly wanted so badly. As his lips brushed hers, a tingling sensation caused her to gasp. She inhaled his Caress-tinged breath, her eyes closed, and her arms snaked their way around his neck.

His tongue teased hers until she shivered with the pleasure he was giving all her senses at one time. Taste, touch, and smell blended together in his kiss. The sound of need coming from deep in his chest spurred her passion in return. In her mind she pictured his gorgeous face and the muscular body that her fingers were suddenly free to explore.

He deepened the kiss, and she felt his hands easing down her back, bringing her closer. The pressure of his splayed fingers on her bottom held her firmly against him and she gave in to the temptation to rise on tiptoes to better fit their bodies together. Her hands roamed impatiently over his back, relaying her own wish for more.

Tearing his mouth away from hers, he whispered in a voice hoarse with rampant desire, "Someone could come in here at any time. We should go back."

She swayed in his arms as the sweet fog cleared from her mind. *Holy stars!* What had she done? Her body continued to throb with the need for immediate satisfaction, but her mind was jangling alarms. The moment he released her to retrieve the bag of sweets he had dropped, Shara hurried back the way they had come.

Gabriel smiled as he fell in behind her and quickened his own pace. After their rough start, he was reassured to see her in as much of a hurry to seek privacy as he was. He must not be as unappealing to her as she had led him to believe.

His reassurance was abruptly shattered as she entered her sleeper and the door slid closed before he could follow her inside.

"Shara?" When she didn't respond, his tone changed to a demand. "*Shara!* Open this door." It whooshed open again, but she stood blocking the doorway, as if she could keep him from entering if he really wished to do so. The sensuous chocoberry color of her eyes was marred by streaks of angry yellow. "What's going on?"

She lifted her chin defiantly. "Maybe you should tell me. One minute we were talking, and the next, you . . . you had your hands on me again."

"I *what*? I distinctly remember you being involved back there. If you want proof, I probably still have impressions of your nails in my back. You were just as prepared to couple as I was."

She spun away from him, hugging herself against his words. "Couple? I hardly know you. Why would I want to couple with you?"

Stepping inside the sleeper, he waited for the door to close before replying. "Know me? What does knowing me have to do with coupling? I've coupled with females who don't even know my name."

"Employees of the Indulgence Center are paid well to overlook their customers' shortcomings. My gifts carry a price also, but it's nothing so simple as signing over a number of credits. When I share pleasure with a man, it will be because there's a mutual caring, a meeting of the minds as well as the bodies. A *relationship*. You and I have nothing in common. You must have done something to my mind to make me forget that so easily. I should have expected as much from someone raised in Parson's Colony."

He yanked her around to face him, fury tightening his throat. "And I should have known better than to trust a Terran. How dare you twist my confidence into a weapon against me? I told you I have no power. Nothing! I can't even keep you from crawling inside my brain without an artificial device. I'm untalented, but still a Noronian, which means I do *not* lie, and that's more than I can say for you." He let go of her arm, moved to the door, and slammed his palm against the control panel.

Before exiting, he turned to her once more. "You're right about one thing. We certainly don't have anything in common. *I* am completely rational. Don't fret about giving away any of your precious gifts. I wouldn't want to chance freezing to death."

A moment after the door closed behind Gabriel, Shara slumped down onto her bunk. She couldn't

believe what she had just done. It had been wrong
to strike out at him when it was herself she was furious with. All she wanted was to avoid repeating old
mistakes. Professor Gabriel Drumayne was another
man interested in her only for what she could do for
him.

She had previously come to the conclusion that if
she didn't couple with a man, she wouldn't get emotionally involved, and thus, he couldn't cause her
pain. The ache in her chest was proof that she was
wrong about that, too.

What had come over her? She should never have
let herself get carried away like that. She certainly
knew better, and he would have no way of knowing
that she didn't share his uninhibited attitude toward
coupling. It hadn't been fair to him, but she couldn't
help feeling as she did. The sharing of one's body
should have a meaning deeper than a simple biological function resulting in a release of stress and a
few minutes of pleasure.

So why was her body still demanding that she go
after the man who offered a meaningless release?
Because, no matter how hard she tried to deny or
bury it, she was cursed with a passionate nature and
a weakness for incredibly handsome, self-sufficient
men . . . like Professor Gabriel Drumayne.

It didn't matter. After the scathing insults they
had just hurled at each other, even a meaningless release would be out of the question. Gabriel thought
she was cold. From now until the end of the flight,
she would be a block of ice.

All that remained was to get off the ship and
time-hop before he realized she was gone.

* * *

Gabriel knew he had destroyed any possibility of peaceful coexistence with Shara the moment he called her a Terran. Ferrine's advice about gaining Shara's cooperation had certainly backfired with a vengeance. He still felt Shara's slur against him like a poison dart in his throat. He prided himself on his ability to remain calm in the most dangerous circumstances and cool-headed in the most hostile situations. He couldn't remember ever losing his temper over something as trivial as coupling.

How could they have gone from kissing to name-calling? He remembered having thought she was childish. Obviously he wasn't much more mature.

But their bodies hadn't been acting childishly in the biodrome. There was no question in his mind that they both would have thoroughly enjoyed themselves had he not paused to suggest they seek privacy. Not only was he bewildered by his overly passionate reactions to her, he was utterly confused by her reasons for rejecting him. She spoke as if she required some sort of emotional bond before she could enjoy coupling with a man. He knew that was the norm in some cultures, but . . .

The answer came to him instantly. Her mother's culture was one of those. Apparently Aster had passed on her personal values to Shara. He had always been a firm believer in each person having the right to practice his or her own lifestyle, as long as it didn't overlap his.

Since he was not looking for a long-term relationship with a female, he would be certain not to initiate any further physical contact with Shara. Such a relationship carried responsibilities that would interfere with his studies regardless of who the female was, but an attachment with an irrational creature like Shara would undoubtedly tie his brain in knots.

It wasn't as if he had to have a female. There were plenty of times in the past when he remained celibate for months on end without giving it much thought. His hunger for knowledge had always been the strongest driving force in his life.

This would simply have to be another one of those periods of celibacy, in spite of the fact that he couldn't remember ever feeling the need to make physical contact with a woman the way he did with Shara. Though he had promised to curb his tactile impulses, he hadn't even known he had any. Until he met Shara, he had never experienced such strong urges to put his hands on another person.

Though the incident was entirely her fault, he supposed it would be up to him to ease the tension between them before they set off on their journey.

As docking time neared, he knew he could no longer put off making the apologies that he assumed she required before they could go back to communicating with one another. When she didn't answer her door, he followed a hunch and pressed the control panel. The door opened to his touch, verifying she had already vacated the sleeper and canceled the inhabited code.

Within seconds, he retrieved his satchel and headed for the deboarding area. Several crew members were there, preparing for the all-clear to open the gates, but none of them had seen Shara. Deciding this was the best place to waylay her, he waited. And waited.

The mailship docked, the gates opened, and most of the crew disembarked, but Shara had not yet appeared. Suddenly that problem became critical when he caught sight of four black-uniformed men striding toward the gangway. He didn't need any special talents to know they were coming for Shara and the tempometer.

4

Inside one of the emptied cargo holds, Shara considered making the time-hop from within the ship rather than risk running into Gabriel. The problem with that was that she was at least twenty kilometers from where she wanted to arrive—near the administrative buildings in First Province—and she had no idea if any transportation would have been available from this point back then. Besides that, she'd always had a slight difficulty with her sense of direction.

When she guessed that sufficient time had passed for Gabriel to have left the ship in search of her, she headed toward the deboarding area. Her dismay was obvious as she saw the one she wished to avoid striding toward her, pulling his floating satchel behind him.

"It's nice to see you, too," Gabriel said sarcastically. "But, believe me, *I* am the least of your problems." He grasped her by the elbow and pushed her back the way she had come. When she balked, he told her, "There's a security team right behind me. Guess who they're looking for?"

"*Drek!* I'm going to have to hop from here, then."

"You mean *we're* going to have to hop from here," he corrected her. "But only if you make it fast." He glanced behind him, then gave her another nudge forward.

Shara quickly led him down two passageways and back to the hold.

"Is this where you were hiding for the last hour?" he asked as she secured the door.

Ignoring him, she pulled the tempometer belt out of her bag and snapped it around her waist. She had already preset the program so that all she had to do was implement it. From Lantana's notes, she understood that anything she was holding would time-hop with her, so she tightly clutched her bag in her left hand and worked the tempometer with her right.

Gabriel watched her finger trace the beveled edge of one of the large crystals on her belt. He was about to question why she was wasting time when the front of the glowing stone flopped open and he realized he was looking at the tempometer. As Shara took a step away from him, he instinctively pulled her into his arms and grasped the handle of his satchel.

A firm knock against the sleeper door alerted Shara that the security team had probably found her. She couldn't send them a suggestion and concentrate on escape at the same time. She had no choice but to time-hop immediately and take the professor with her.

"Let's go!" Gabriel ordered.

Shara moved the tiny switch beneath her finger from left to right three times, then held her breath.

The knocking increased to pounding as someone called out, "Security! Open the door!"

Panic gripped Shara as seconds passed and nothing happened. Suddenly she felt as though they'd been hit by a wall of energy that hurled them across the room. But they were no longer *in* the room. In fact, they didn't seem to be anywhere at all.

She clung to Gabriel as they and their baggage seemed suspended in a black void. As abruptly as they had arrived there, they were slammed by another force that sent them spinning through a tunnel of illuminated, swirling colors. A deafening, high-pitched squeal sent needles of pain into her mind as they tumbled over and over within the eerie kaleidoscope.

Just when Shara was certain they were either going to die or be driven insane from the noise, their bodies slowed to a gentle float and the squeal quieted to the tinkling of wind chimes. She remembered how that sound had accompanied Lantana's appearance and hoped it meant they were coming to the end of the time-hop. A moment later, she felt solid ground beneath her boots.

A blast of frigid wind greeted them. Wherever . . . or *when*ever they were, it was ice cold, and there was no sign of inhabitance. Snow covered the hilly ground and icicles hung from barren trees. It made no sense. Even if they had arrived in the winter season, winters in the First Province were mild and rarely yielded more than a few snow flurries on the coldest days. Only seconds had passed, yet Shara could already feel her toes going numb.

With chattering teeth, she looked up at Gabriel. "What do you th-th-think?"

"I think we're going to freeze to death if we just stand here. Maybe you'd better take us back and re-check your programming."

She hadn't realized how much his body had been protecting hers until he released her and moved away. Her hands trembled as she tried to reverse what she had done. "It's not responding, and I'm af-f-fraid I'm g-g-going to t-t-touch the wrong thing the way I'm sh-sh-shivering."

Gabriel shook his head with a sigh. "All right. Give me a minute." As he lowered his satchel to the ground and opened it, he asked, "Do you have any idea where we are?"

She rubbed her arms and stepped in place to keep her blood circulating. "According to Lantana's n-n-notes, we sh-sh-should be exactly where we were, only in a d-d-different time p-p-period." She watched him remove several squares of silver material and two short metal poles from his bag. With a flick of his wrist, the two poles telescoped out to a little over a meter in length. Within a matter of minutes, he had constructed a small tent with an inflated mattress for a base. Before her eyes, the silver turned white and was effectively camouflaged against the snow.

Gabriel was digging something else out of his satchel when a loud roar echoed around them. With the howling wind blowing gusts of snow in her face, it took Shara a moment to locate the source of the beastly sound. Less than a hundred meters away, atop a high rise, a bulky creature tipped back its head and roared again. Another roar, then another answered the first as several more dark shapes lined the horizon.

They were unlike anything Shara had ever seen, with their squat bodies and long horns curving upward out of the sides of their heads. Shaggy brown hair concealed the legs and face entirely.

"*Wartbulls?* Don't move a muscle!" Gabriel ordered Shara as he slowly straightened and faced the animals. "They may only be—" He didn't bother to complete his sentence as the pack of animals charged down the hill. "Get behind me!"

She dashed to his back as fast as her frozen feet allowed. Staring at the animals, she flung a mental order at them to stop, then sent an image of them turning around, but neither method had any effect on the primitive creatures.

Gabriel was braced with legs apart and both hands clasped around the grip of a paralyzer rod. Choosing the animal in the forefront, he pointed the weapon and fired. The red beam hit the beast between the horns. It stumbled, momentarily confusing the others in its pack as they slid to a halt around their leader. A few seconds later, however, the leader recommenced its roaring charge.

Gabriel had no choice. He increased the setting and fired again before the animals could close in on them. One creature after another collapsed in a hairy heap as they were hit by the lethal blue light. In seconds the snow was littered with carcasses.

Shara's violent trembling was now caused as much by fear as the cold. She had never felt so utterly helpless in her life. "Th-they would have k-k-killed us," she muttered.

Gabriel didn't waste time responding. He shoved his satchel and her bag into the tent, then transferred the antigravity device to the outside. "Get in and sit still while I move us away from here. Who knows what sort of creature will come to prey on our welcoming committee?"

Shara hurried to do as he said and instantly felt some relief once she was out of the icy wind. She was surprised to discover that the material was transparent from this side. The entire tent abruptly rose, tipping her sideward, but she tried to remain as still as possible after that.

For several minutes, Gabriel guided the floating shelter until he reached a spot where the wind was partially blocked by high snowdrifts. Shara wondered how he was managing to tolerate the cold so much better than she, but when he lowered the tent and crawled in, she realized he was merely more stoical. His lips and fingers had turned blue and his hair and clothing were covered with frost.

His entire body was shaking as he began rooting through his satchel again. "He-he-heater," he whispered, placing a crystal ball in the center of the tent. Instantly it emitted a soft golden glow. Seeing him place his hands close to the orb, Shara did the same and sighed as a mild warmth seeped into her stiff fingers. She barely began to thaw when he took several small metal boxes out of his satchel and crawled toward the tent opening.

Grasping his arm, she asked, "What are you doing now?"

"Have to . . . s-s-set b-b-barriers to k-k-keep animals away." As he spoke, two of the boxes fell from his trembling hands.

Shara picked them up and held out her hand for the other two. "Give them to me and tell me how to do it." When he hesitated, she added, "It's very clear that I need your help, Professor. You will be of little value to me if you're frozen to death."

He gave her the two boxes and pointed out the activator button. "Just p-p-push them . . . under the s-s-snow . . . at the f-f-four corners of the tent. And hurry."

She rolled her eyes at him. "No kidding!" Opening the tent flap as little as possible, she went back out into the cold. The snow was packed so hard she had to use the boxes to dig out holes to set them in the way Gabriel had instructed. By the time the fourth barrier projector was activated, she was again shivering from head to toe.

Crawling back inside, she noted that Gabriel was now huddled in his sleeping pouch, but he was still quaking something awful, and she wasn't doing any better. Because she'd had to open the tent flap and let in the freezing wind, the space heater had yet to make a substantial difference.

Shara tugged on the edge of the pouch he had tucked under his chin. "Let me g-g-get in th-th-there with you." When he merely arched an eyebrow at her and kept his grasp on the pouch, she explained, "Hypoth-th-thermia. B-b-body heat helps."

"Only if . . . you t-t-take off those . . . c-c-clothes."

Shara blinked at him, then realized her body suit was covered with melting frost, and his damp clothing had been discarded on the floor next to him. Another violent shiver racked his body, and she set aside her natural modesty in light of practicality. Reminding herself that most of the people she knew would think nothing of being seen in the nude, she stripped to the skin as quickly as her shaking hands permitted. Nevertheless, she kept her eyes averted and hoped he did the same.

"Sh-Sh-Shara—"

"Don't s-s-say a word," she warned as she slipped into the pouch with him. "You s-s-saved my life. I owe you." The pouch, made for one large man, expanded enough to accommodate her once he straightened himself out. She had thought her body was as cold as a human could get until she stretched out on top of his length with her cheek on his shoulder.

He was one giant icicle. Though her extremities had almost no feeling in them, she pressed her feet to his and rubbed her hands up and down his upper arms. Her efforts finally paid off after what seemed like an eternity. The numbness left her body and his shivering lessened to an occasional spasm.

As his skin took on a more normal warmth, he moved his hands from where they had been sandwiched between their chests and massaged her back, returning the favor of getting her blood circulating.

At least that's what she thought he was doing. But what began as a vigorous rubdown changed to a light skimming over the flesh from her neck to her thighs. Another shiver passed through her, but this one had nothing to do with the cold.

"Professor, I—"

"Don't you think you could call me Gabriel, under the circumstances?" His hand cupped her bottom as he said it.

She kept her head against his shoulder to keep him from seeing her flushed cheeks. "I suppose so . . . Gabriel. Are you warm enough now?"

"I still can't feel my toes. Can you?" He sucked in his breath as her hips and thighs shifted to enable her toes to search out his.

"No wonder you can't feel them. They're like ice. But the rest of you feels . . . normal again, so—"

He stopped her from squirming upward to get out of the pouch. "You don't want to do that yet," he said, keeping his arms wrapped snugly around her. "You may feel comfortable in here, but the heater hasn't raised the overall temperature by more than a few degrees so far. Give it a little more time."

Shara inched back down to her previous position, but she was no longer as concerned about freezing to death as she was about incinerating. His muscular body felt *too* good beneath hers and his fingers were awakening all the nerve endings in her skin. Suddenly she felt a movement between her thighs and realized her nerves weren't the only things standing at attention.

Since there was nowhere for her to run at the moment, she opted for conversation. "I've never seen anything killed before. Did it bother you to do that?"

His lips brushed across her forehead. "When I first started journeying, I tried to abide by the nonviolent doctrines I'd been raised with. But I soon learned that civilized ethics don't always have a place in primitive cultures. Sometimes survival has to take priority."

"It never occurred to me to bring a weapon. If I had been alone, I'd be dead now."

He pressed a light kiss on her temple. "You can't know that for sure. You might have found some way to frighten them away."

She grimaced. "Then I just would have frozen to death slowly, instead of being devoured instantly."

"There's also the possibility that the security team would have stopped you from hopping at all."

Even though he had to realize she was no longer chilled, his hands continued to stroke her. Since it would be ludicrous to order him to remove his hands from her while she was lying naked on top of him, she continued to pretend that she didn't notice how sensual his touch was . . . or that he was aroused.

She rose on one elbow to meet his eyes for what she knew had to be said. "At any rate, I'm aware that I owe you an apology. Two, actually."

"Oh?" By lifting her upper body, she partially revealed the full breasts he had only gotten a brief glimpse of earlier, and then he was too cold to care. He knew it was rather primitive of him, but he really *appreciated* a woman with a well-developed figure. He forced his gaze back to her face and worked to keep it there.

When he had lowered his eyes, Shara wondered if he might be nodding off, but when he looked at her again, she was immediately aware that sleep was the last thing on his mind. "Um, yes, an apology. I, uh, was wrong to try to leave without you. I am very obviously not prepared for this journey. Thank you for preventing me from making a terrible mistake. And thank you for helping me to avoid the security team." His hands eased slowly up and down her ribs as she gave her little speech, and on each upward stroke, his thumbs skimmed the sides of her breasts.

He watched the irises of her eyes change to chocolate brown and fought the smile that threatened to give away his thoughts. "And the second apology?"

She swallowed hard, finding it more difficult by the second to ignore how he was making her feel. "I was very rude yesterday and said things I didn't mean."

"Which things?" he murmured as he rolled the two of them onto their sides.

"It's nice of you to act as though you've forgotten my insults, but I haven't. You trusted me with sensitive information about yourself, and I behaved abominably. You had a right to be furious and insult me in return." She wasn't quite sure how he managed it so smoothly in such a confined space, but their positions were now almost reversed. She was lying on her back and his body partially covered hers as he smiled down at her.

"I don't think two wrongs make a right," he said, his gaze drifting lower. Her breasts were even more beautiful than he'd guessed and her eye color had confirmed the fact that the contracted nipples weren't entirely caused by the cold. "I owe you an apology also." He had thought seeing would be enough, but the need to touch every part of her was overruling all else. His fingers trickled over her stomach and crept upward. "My throwing your heritage back at you was completely unreasonable. My only excuse is that I was confused."

"I'm sorry about that," Shara said, trying not to think about her racing pulse. "But I'm afraid you confused me as well. I don't usually . . . forget myself so easily."

His hand had finally reached the swell of her breast and, with great effort, he stopped himself from proceeding further. "I can't say that I understand your attitude, though. I know you were enjoying our kisses as much as I was." He watched her gaze move to his mouth while her tongue sneaked out to moisten her lips. "In fact, I think you're wondering the same thing I am right now: Was it really that good?" Her sharp intake of breath was her verification of his guess.

"I don't want to *take* any of your gifts, Shara. I want to give you some."

The only response she could manage was to furrow her brow.

"The first gift I'd like to give you is satisfaction . . . of your curiosity."

She knew this was a mistake. She should get out of the pouch, stop his velvety touches, which were clouding her mind while seducing her body, and, above all, avoid kissing him.

Her lips parted to deny him, and he lowered his head.

How could an act so simple as two mouths making contact tip the world off its axis? His tongue teased hers, and she had the answer. This was no simple act. The tender caress he started to give her instantly turned demanding and all she could do was respond to that demand with her own shocking need.

He gave up the fight to keep his hand from capturing her breast. When she covered that hand with hers and encouraged him to squeeze harder, his erection stretched to its limit against her hip.

Gabriel had never known such uncontrollable desire, but now was not the time to analyze it. His body demanded that he seek immediate relief and he moved over her. Yet, in spite of the fact that she spread her thighs to cradle him and her hands urged him to complete the union, the recollection of what she had accused him of before gave him the willpower to hold back.

"I think our mutual curiosity is satisfied," he murmured against her mouth. Sliding his aching shaft up and down over her nerve center, he kissed her again, then said, "I would like to give you another gift, but you'll have to tell me you want it. The pleasure is yours for the taking, Shara. Will you accept it?"

There was no doubt in her mind. If she didn't take it in the next few seconds, she would go up in flames. "Yes. *Please*." He entered her so quickly, she gasped, but her body had been well prepared and welcomed his with a shudder of relief.

Her body had previously welcomed two other men, but now she realized they had merely taken from her without giving anything in return. Gabriel's body was doing things to hers that she hadn't known were possible. There was a harmony to their movements, and every stroke, every touch, made her more aware of how much *she* could take from *him* . . . if she just reached out for it. If she could only quiet the whispers of uncertainty in her mind.

His intention had been to please her first, then satisfy himself at a leisurely pace. That was the way it had been in every encounter he had previously had. But this wasn't like anything in his previous experience. Being inside her increased his passion tenfold. He couldn't seem to control his body's powerful thrusts. Raging need hammered at him until he could only drive forward.

Harder.

Faster.

He heard her pleading with him, but couldn't sort out the words. He needed more and nothing would stop him from having it all. The level of pleasure at which he normally peaked had passed and still his body strained higher. When the shattering release finally came, he felt as though he had gone through another time-hop. He was breathless and dizzy. His head throbbed and his body felt battered.

And he wondered how long it would be before he could do it again.

His selfish thought replayed in his head and awoke his conscience. What had come over him? It was almost as if he'd completely lost his sanity for a few minutes.

Shara gave him a nudge. "Please. You're very heavy."

As soon as he shifted them onto their sides, she shimmied upward and out of the pouch. He watched her pull a long-sleeved bodysuit out of her bag and slip it on. What had happened to him was so unusual, he didn't know quite what to say.

Had he pleased her at all? She wasn't acting like a sated woman. Had he left her unsatisfied, then? Perhaps he had even hurt her in his energetic pursuit of his own elusive release. He instantly rejected that possibility. He had been with females who were too small for him, and it had been noticeably uncomfortable for both of them. Shara had effortlessly taken in every centimeter he had to give and enveloped him as if nature had created their body parts from one mold.

Why the *drek* had she been in such a hurry to get away from him? How could he have been so strongly affected and she remain so aloof?

Perhaps her Terran genes *did* make her different. He had always heard that Terrans were excessively emotional, sometimes volatile people, and he had assumed their sexual passion would be heightened as well, but that didn't seem to be true in Shara's case. He told himself to let it go. Her lack of response was her problem, not his. And yet his ego refused to accept the fact that she hadn't enjoyed their coupling in the least.

He couldn't see her eye color the way her lashes were lowered, and she was obviously not planning to offer him any insight, since she sat down and began reading some papers she'd pulled out of her bag. His fingers touched the jammer on his ear. For the first time in years, he was tempted to remove it to hear her thoughts rather than any words she might choose to say if he asked for them. He knew that invasion of privacy was unnecessary, however, when all he had to do was make her look at him to learn the truth.

Sitting up in the sleeping pouch, he considered the best way to approach the problem and decided to follow her lead by getting dressed.

Shara concentrated on steadying her hands and her breathing as she stared at the papers in front of her. Too bewildered to rationalize what had just happened, she tried to block it out with cold, logical work—something she had had a lot of practice doing over the years.

She forced herself to break the tense silence. "If I had any idea what year we arrived, I might be able to figure out what I did wrong."

"I think I can help with that," Gabriel said, sitting down in front of her. "Assuming we didn't change locations, the last time this section of Norona was this cold and covered in snow and ice was during the Frozen Era. Besides that, those animals I killed were wartbulls, a vicious species of carnivores that became extinct about one million years ago."

"A *million*? I was trying for ten thousand." She picked up the tempometer belt, opened the crystal, and peered at the workings as if it might tell her the answer. "And why couldn't I reverse the time-hop?" she asked herself aloud.

"The cold?" Gabriel suggested.

"I suppose that's a possibility. Lantana made no mention of external temperatures having an effect, but he also never performed any actual tests on the device."

Gabriel's eyes widened. "You mean it was all theory before today?"

Shara frowned. "Not entirely. He *did* make it back to us."

"Great," he said with a smirk. Since it was too late to change his mind about accompanying her, there wasn't much to be gained by sarcasm. "So how can I help?"

"I've spent the last few weeks studying these notes and schematics, but you're welcome to go over them. Maybe, between the two of us, we'll get it right on the next hop."

He nodded and took several sheets of paper from her. After scanning the pages quickly to get an idea of the information covered, he went back to the beginning and started reading, but his mind and his gaze kept wandering to Shara. Although he believed he was doing a fine job of hiding it, his body was still vibrating with the aftereffects of the most incredible climax he'd ever experienced. She, on the other hand, seemed totally engrossed in comparing the inside of the tempometer to one of the Lantana's drawings. Was she truly unaffected by what they had shared, or was she also hiding her feelings?

Again he was tempted to remove his earcuff, but he was now close enough to analyze her eye color, so he felt obliged to try that method of reading her first.

"Shara?" She glanced up at him. Her eyes were hazel, but more brown than green. As her *natural* hazel color was more green, he wondered if some traces of desire might still be lingering. "Do I owe you another apology?"

She returned her gaze to the tempometer. "Of course not."

"I can't explain what happened. I really meant to please you."

"I'd rather you forget about it."

Gabriel took the tempometer out of her hands and set it aside. "I can't forget about it. Did I hurt you?"

She cocked her head at him. "Not at all."

"Were you left unsatisfied? I'm not normally so inconsiderate—"

"*What is this?* A test?" Shara shed her cool façade. "I'm trying to be casual, the way I might have reacted if I hadn't been raised by a Terran mother. But I can't sit here and dissect our coupling as if I do that sort of thing with strange men all the time. I don't! I have been with exactly two men, both of whom I thought I had an emotional bond with. And *neither* of whom ever caused me to behave the way I just did with you. I don't understand what happens when you touch me, but I don't seem to have much control over my . . . my . . . *biological urges* once you do. And that does *not* please me in the slightest!"

The thought crossed her mind that he possessed a power he had denied having, but this time she held her tongue. "Now, I accept this incident as being partially my fault, but in the future I'd appreciate it if you did not take advantage of my weakness."

Gabriel tried to sort out everything she'd just confessed and correlate it with her eye color. If she had been lying, the color would have been drab olive rather than hazel. Thus, he deduced she was being honest, but the truth embarrassed her. She reached for the tempometer, and he moved it behind him. "You didn't answer my question."

Looking down at a drawing, she murmured, "Which question?"

He leaned closer and touched her chin with his forefinger. "Look at me." She frowned, but raised her lashes. "Were you left unsatisfied?" He watched with fascination as her eye color altered to a rich, warm brown.

"Why is it so important?" she asked in a breathy voice.

"I don't know," he admitted. "I'm just trying to understand what happened to me. I offered you a gift of pleasure, and it was very ungentlemanly of me not to be certain you received it. Shara, you're not the only one in this tent having trouble controlling your behavior. You say my touch disturbs you, yet I can't seem to keep my hands off you. I have coupled with enough females that I can't claim inexperience, as you have. And yet I don't remember ever losing myself so completely in the act that I didn't know if I satisfied my partner."

She turned her head away. There was no way she could admit that, even unsatisfied, he had given her the most moving physical experience she'd ever had.

He stroked her flushed cheek and urged her to face him again. "I could do better . . . whenever you wish." He closed the slight gap between their mouths.

"No!" Shara exclaimed, scooting backward. "You're doing it to me again. What happened between us isn't some mystery that you have to work to understand. It's called lust—a strong chemical attraction—and that is *not* something I want in my life. Giving in to it is against everything I believe in. We are not going to do any more kissing, and that's my last word on the subject. Now, if you don't want to help, at least don't hinder me. I want to get out of this time while that heater still has energy in it."

He didn't agree to her declaration, but he accepted the subject change for the moment. "It's solar. Unless there's an extended eclipse, we'll stay comfortable enough. Also, the ice and snow should provide us with plenty of water.

"Food could be a problem, however. I only brought enough compressed meals to last a week for two people. I have a protective suit for poisonous atmospheres, but it wasn't meant to protect against cold this extreme. Nor do I have anything else that would allow me to remain outside long enough to hunt for fresh game. The wartbulls have probably been devoured by other animals, so we can forget that. Unfortunately, one of the reasons they and other creatures faced extinction at this time was an extreme shortage of food."

Once again Shara was relieved that he had forced his company on her. She hadn't thought to bring food, had nothing in her bag that offered protection from the raw elements they had encountered, and even if she had brought a weapon, she wasn't sure she could kill anything, even if it meant her survival. Dealing with adverse situations was apparently part of his normal routine. For his experience, she was grateful enough to forgive him for almost everything else.

To herself, she admitted that concern for their well-being was not the primary reason she wanted out of that time. She was anxious to escape to a time where she could keep a safe distance from him—a time with lots of open, *warm* space and plenty of people.

The scientist in her attempted to analyze what had happened. Though she had previously felt attraction, even strong desire, mindless lust was completely unfamiliar to her. She hadn't known it could strip her good sense and turn her into a wanton without her conscious approval. In a way, though, she wished he *had* satisfied her more fully. Then perhaps she wouldn't be even now fighting the urge to move closer to him.

She should not have been aroused at all. There had been no gentle foreplay or coaxing of her desire. There were no words of admiration, let alone devotion. Now that she gave it more thought, there had been few words of any kind . . . with the exception of his straightforward offer and her unhesitating acceptance.

She should have been able to warm his body without being overwhelmed with desire. She should have been able to resist satisfying the need to feel him inside her.

He'd been aggressive, somewhat rough, and so hurried that she should have been disgusted. There were a lot of *shoulds* and none of them had mattered at the time.

At least he had admitted to a certain bewilderment also. She hoped he would accept her decision not to explore the attraction between them any further. As soon as she had the thought, she felt a twinge of regret. Her scientific curiosity wanted to examine it until she understood how it worked. She knew instinctively, though, that she lacked the ability to impersonally study the feelings without involving her heart.

The sharing of one's body should have more meaning than a biological release, and coupling without an emotional bond went against her personal morals. *There.* She felt better after repeating her beliefs to herself. She would remind herself of those beliefs whenever the weakness came over her. If that didn't work, she would recall the fact that he was only with her because of her tempometer, and not due to any sincere personal interest, which put him in the same category as her other two lovers. She was simply the available body to him.

If that was still not enough, there was the most important reason of all not to give in to the weakness. He intended to stop her from completing her mission. Her one foray with him into the halls of lust let her know she could be controlled by her own passion, and she didn't put it past him to use any method available to achieve his goals over hers.

If he tried to kiss her again, she would force herself to refuse and hope he was convinced that seduction was a waste of time with her.

The future of Innerworld depended on her remembering that Gabriel Drumayne was her enemy.

5

The contents of Gabriel's satchel continued to amaze Shara as the day wore on. The compressed meals he referred to looked like thin crackers and could be consumed in that form if necessary. However, the addition of melted snow and a few seconds in his collapsible cooker turned the crackers into tasty vegetable omelets. He also had a choice of several powders to mix with more melted snow to make soups and drinks. He explained that he had the equipment to create a limited supply of water, but that it wasn't necessary to waste what he'd brought under the circumstances. And, of course, they had his seemingly endless supply of Caresses.

She found using his portable sanitary unit embarrassing, but more practical than baring her bottom outdoors to relieve herself. At least he had been considerate enough to bundle himself in his sleeping pouch and go outside for the minute it took her to use the unit. She assumed he took care of his own needs while he was out there. Nature definitely gave men a few advantages when it came to survival.

By the time the sun slipped below the horizon, they had reviewed and analyzed Lantana's notes and checked and rechecked what Shara had done, yet they hadn't been able to discern her error.

Underlying it all had been a current of crackling tension that had both of them jumping at the sound of the other's voice and being overly cautious about their movements.

Frustrated, tired, and cramped, Shara sighed aloud. "There must be something missing from his notes."

"Considering his advanced age, that could be a possibility. I'd suggest we start looking for what is *not* written here, like the effect of external temperatures. Why don't we have our evening ration of food and get some sleep? Maybe we've been at it too long to see clearly."

She nodded and set aside the tempometer belt and notes, but she couldn't set aside her fears as easily. In theory, it had all seemed so simple. In reality, she might never get back to her own time, let alone fix something that happened before. If they didn't figure out what went wrong, they could soon be facing slow death by starvation. To get her mind off the gloomier possibilities, she asked him to tell her about another one of his adventures.

He gave it some thought as he prepared their meal, then said, "You might find my very first journey interesting. I was young, mind you, and lacked practical experience, but I thought I could handle anything. Rather than visit a culture that had been written up in detail, I wanted to uncover something totally new, right away.

"I chose a settlement on a small planet in the Telvar system, where the inhabitants were a humanoid species on the lower end of the evolutionary scale. What interested me most was that they supposedly lacked the power of speech, as well as any telepathic ability. You remember what I told you about my childhood, so you can imagine how enticing a completely silent culture would be to me. I was determined to find out how they communicated.

"I had heard tales of journeyors allowing primitive tribes to believe they were gods, and I had sworn I would never do something so unethical. I was prepared to put these people at ease and show them I was not much different from them as soon as I arrived.

"When my ship landed, however, I never even made it outside before they attacked. A small army of the local residents surrounded the ship and tried to beat it to death with sticks. The brief information I had found regarding their evolutionary level seemed accurate. They were short, with almost no necks, or foreheads, and had arms long enough to rest on all fours. The men and women were both covered with hair, but their faces and general forms were decidedly humanoid.

"For the next two days, they continued to bang on the outside of the ship. Replacements came to relieve the original attackers, then the replacements were relieved in turn. I felt like I was sitting inside a metal drum. Even after I plugged my ears, the vibration from the noise was driving me insane. I refused to give up on my first journey, but I wasn't about to leave the ship and be instantly killed, either. I kept thinking they'd get tired and back off long enough for me to show them I had come in peace, but it didn't look like they were going to give me that chance."

Shara took a plate of food from his hand, but her attention was on him. "What did you do?"

He shrugged and made a slight face. "I took off

my jammer to find out just how dangerous they were. At first, because I didn't pick up any mental voices, I thought something had happened to my ability. Then an image flashed in my mind and I realized they thought in picture form. They all had a similar picture in mind.

"Apparently they thought the ship was a sort of giant nut that had fallen from a tall tree, and they were trying to crack it open to get to the food inside."

Shara smiled along with him. "So they meant you no harm after all."

"Not unless they were cannibals . . . which they weren't." He took a bite of his dinner and washed it down with a fruit drink. "Once I'd given in to using my mental disability to solve the first problem, I threw out most of my other resolutions as well. Using the ship's defense system, I dazzled them with a fireworks display, while I broadcast a lively symphony recording out to them.

"They may not have thought I was a god, since that concept was too complex for them, but they were sufficiently awed to give me the break I needed to leave the ship unharmed. I performed a few tricks, like making fire come out of a box, and they accepted my presence in their village. That was the first time I realized that I hadn't learned everything I needed to know in Parson's Colony. Sometimes unethical methods are the only ones that work."

"I understand what you mean. I've been telling myself everything I've done recently will be worth it in the end."

"The only problem with that line of thinking is you don't find out if you made the right decisions until it's too late."

Shara grimaced. "Do you think that's what happened when the Noronian rebels first infiltrated Outerworld Earth? They did what they thought they had to do, but it turned out to be the wrong choices."

"I believe so," he replied, nodding thoughtfully. "History reports that the rebels abused the natives' trust and became power hungry. I'm hoping to confirm or refute that information firsthand."

As soon as the discussion veered into the explosive topic of their individual goals, Shara drew him back to his story. "Did you ever figure out how those people in the Telvar system communicated?"

"That and everything else about them. From what I could tell, they had no enemies other than nature, so they had no reason to fear me or hide anything. I wrote my first published monograph on their culture. The reason they didn't speak was that their vocal chords were only in the early stages of development. A few of them could manage a grunt, but they rarely used it. Their language was pictures."

"Like hieroglyphics?"

"Not precisely. They didn't use symbols or stick figures. They actually created realistic drawings. Almost every one of them was gifted with tremendous artistic ability. Any available surface was used to express themselves—rocks, trees, cave walls—or they just scratched their pictures into the dirt with pointed sticks. Of course, getting an idea across sometimes took hours, but time had very little relevance to them."

Shara could not imagine ever being that patient. "Tell me, did you enjoy the silence as much as you expected to?"

Gabriel laughed. "For the most part. Though I'll

admit, after a few months I occasionally felt the need to converse with my ship's computer."

"A few *months*? I'm not the most sociable person, but I doubt I'd last that long without any sort of dialogue."

Gabriel collapsed the cooker and stowed it away. "I find that brief interludes of sociability are more than adequate."

"Yet you seemed to enjoy teaching me about old Norona and telling me about your journeys."

He rubbed his chin. "I suppose I do. It must be because you're a good listener." Again it struck him that his normal behavior had been altered in her presence.

Gabriel was well into his third tale when the glow from the heater orb abruptly dimmed. Shara stared at it fearfully and asked, "What's happening to it?"

Glancing up at the darkened sky, he could see the first stars had begun to appear. "It's conserving the energy it stored all day. A small amount of energy can be absorbed from the reflected light off the stars and moon, but not enough to maintain all night the warm temperature it's been emitting so far. Don't worry, though. The sleeping pouch will keep us quite comfortable."

Shara's gaze darted from the orb, to the pouch rolled up in the corner, to Gabriel. He didn't look like he had any ulterior motives in mind, but those angel eyes of his were impossible to read. "I don't believe we should share your pouch again. I'll put on some extra clothing and—"

"Don't be foolish. You may not freeze to death outside of the pouch, but you would be too cold to get a decent night's sleep. We're both rational adults. If you don't wish to repeat what happened before, we won't." Gabriel couldn't understand why she would *not* want to repeat something so pleasurable when it had not left his mind all day, but he would abide by her decision regardless of how unreasonable it was.

Shara held to her belief that she would be fine without his body heat, while he summarized his last story, unrolled the pouch, removed his clothing, and climbed inside. But as the temperature inside the tent gradually grew chillier, she admitted that she was indeed being foolish. Hugging her knees to her chest, she waited until she was certain he'd dozed off.

As she attempted to discreetly make an opening for herself, he said, "You'll be much more comfortable without your clothing."

Then she remembered his comment about being a light sleeper. "No, I won't."

"Stubborn woman. You're cold," he complained, but made room for her anyway.

She tried to find a position where the least amount of their bodies would be touching.

"Give it up, Shara," he finally said in a tone that showed he was losing patience with her. With little effort, he shifted them both onto their sides with her in front of him. His arm, wrapped snugly around her waist, held her against him. "Now go to sleep. We'll get up at first light and start again."

She took a shaky breath and ordered herself to relax.

This was practical, not intimate. But if it wasn't intimate, why was she so aware of how solid he felt against her back, or precisely how large his hand was where it covered her ribs? Or how she could feel his body changing because of her nearness?

He was an opponent, not a lover.

Her heart should *not* have been racing. The pulse between her legs should *not* have been awakened. In spite of her mental insistence that she would not succumb to her weakness, her body had acknowledged his touch and began readying itself for him.

"Are you frightened?" he whispered in her ear.

His warm breath sent a shiver down her spine. "Yes, a little."

"I can feel your heart pounding," he murmured. His hand slid up and pressed between her breasts as if to slow the heavy beating. "Is it the situation . . . or is it me?"

She opened her mouth to answer, but his palm brushed over one tightened nipple, then the other. Her soft moan encouraged him to cup that breast while his thumb continued to tease its peak through the thin layer of cloth. She felt him getting harder and bigger as he moved against her bottom, and she sighed with the frustration of wanting and not wanting.

His warm lips planted a trail of teasing kisses along her jaw, luring her mouth closer and closer to his, as his hand crept down her stomach in search of an even more sensitive area. Her mind was rapidly losing the battle of willpower against her body, and she knew if she could not withstand his advances this time, it would be easier for her body to win the next time, and the next, until her mind had no say in the matter at all. Until *he* and his delicious mouth controlled her every thought and deed . . . as long as he needed her.

And when his need of her was ended, he'd be gone, and she'd have nothing and no one. Again.

"*No!*" she said, pushing his hand away and sitting up to face him. "I said I don't wish to couple with you, and I mean it. I intend to find the Noronian rebels and stop one of them from getting to Earth and none of your sly tricks is going to stop me."

Gabriel raised his brows in surprise. "Tricks?" He sat up beside her. "What are you raving about now?"

"I am not raving," she said, purposely lowering her voice to prove her point. "I am simply warning you that I know what you're trying to do. Perhaps someone more naive would have fallen for your little seduction act, but—"

"Stop it!" Grasping her shoulders, he gave her a light shake. "What you're accusing me of is not only untrue but insulting. You're a beautiful woman, and I'm physically drawn to you. Period. Your self-appointed mission was the last thing on my mind a moment ago. If anything, *you're* the one who could end up influencing *my* judgment with your sexuality."

Shara shook her head and looked away. "I don't need any false flattery. I'm fully aware of just how resistible I am to men."

He started to argue with her, but held back. There was no sense in convincing her that she might have some power that she didn't know about, especially since he hadn't yet figured it out for himself. He stopped her from leaving the pouch. "Wait. I'm not going to pretend I understand you when I don't, but I won't try to *seduce* you again. Lie back down, Shara. I've never forced myself on a female before. I'm not going to start with you."

With a frown, she inched her way back into the pouch. This time, however, their backs were turned to each other. Sheer exhaustion overcame Shara's nervous condition, and she eventually fell asleep.

A very vivid dream awakened her just as dawn was

breaking. Her name was being called, but she couldn't tell where the voice was coming from. A frantic search through a house of doors, then a snowy forest, led her to the foot of an erupting volcano. The ground was shaking violently and fiery lava threatened to burn her alive, yet she couldn't make herself run away. Whoever was calling her was inside the volcano and she had no choice but to go to the caller.

The flowing lava parted and made a path for her to climb the mountain. As she reached the top, the shape of a man formed amid an explosion of volcanic ash. The burning figure held out his arms to her and called for her to join him. She turned to flee back down the mountain, but the lava had closed the path. She was trapped on the rim of the volcano, surrounded by fire. The only escape was to awaken from the nightmare.

As she lay there, breathing heavily and trying to sort out the dream from reality, she realized she was truly suffering from excessive heat, and the ground did seem to be quaking beneath her. The next second she found the cause.

Gabriel was still turned with his back to her, but he was trembling and scratching at the skin on his arms and chest. His breathing was raspy and labored. Tentatively she touched his shoulder and was stunned by the intense heat radiating from him. "Professor?" He didn't answer. "Gabriel, are you ill?" He kept his back to her.

She raised herself up on an elbow and saw that his eyes were squinted shut in an expression of severe pain. She gently placed her hand on his cheek and his forehead. "You're burning up! You must have picked up some virus during the time-hop. Come out of here," she ordered, tugging on his arm. "We've got to cool you down."

She found it easier to get out and drag the pouch off of him than to get him to move. The first thing she noticed was that his penis was so engorged it was purplish and jerking involuntarily. Dragging her gaze upward, she saw several long, angry welts where he must have scraped himself. She knelt beside him and forced one of his eyelids open. The cornea was blood-red.

With an inhuman growl, he suddenly pulled her down beside him and smothered her mouth with his. She squirmed and pushed, but her efforts were futile against his incredible strength. He used every part of his body to hold her in place for his unexpected assault. She was completely enveloped by him and his overwhelming heat. The moment he freed her mouth, she cried, "*Please,* don't—"

Again he uttered the animalistic snarl and, in a deep gravelly voice that seemed detached from his body, said, "*I . . . must.*" With one savage yank, he tore the top of her suit down the middle.

She could only assume that the high fever had twisted his mind and caused him to act out some horrid hallucination, but giving him a reasonable excuse did not lessen her panic. It was quite clear that she couldn't stop him or defend herself. She could, however, try to prevent any serious injury. Though she didn't help him remove the remains of her bodysuit, she stopped fighting him.

In a matter of seconds, he rammed himself into her, roared a sound that was more pain than pleasure, then collapsed on top of her.

Shara was repulsed, furious, and terrified that his seizure wasn't yet over. She felt bruised and debilitated. But beneath it all she was also shamed, for, despite the violent intrusion, her body had opened and welcomed him, and wanted to hold him inside for much longer than it had taken him to gain his release.

"Get off me!" she demanded with a shove that had no effect on his dead weight. He seemed to be unconscious, and she could barely breathe. Using her whole body, she gave him a heave that sent him rolling onto his back. His shaft was still erect and swollen, but not quite as enormously as before. Shara touched his neck and found a rapid yet slowing pulse.

The amazing thing was that his damp skin felt cool. She had never heard of such an extreme fever coming and going so quickly. His breathing appeared to be almost back to normal also. She raised one of his eyelids and noted the redness had gone away. The only symptoms left of whatever ailed him were the scratches on his upper body.

She yelled at him, talked to him, nudged and shook him. When he still didn't awaken after several minutes, she began to worry anew. Could the strange fever have left him in a coma? However would she manage without him in this frozen wasteland? In desperation, she decided to try to reach his unconscious mind directly.

As her fingers touched his temple, she remembered that his jammer would prevent her from reading or sending him her thoughts. She grasped the gold earcuff and gave it a tug, but it held tight. Before she could figure out how to remove it, Gabriel's hand clamped over her wrist.

"What are you doing?" he asked in a normal, yet accusing voice that inferred he knew the answer.

Shara stuttered a moment before she could defend herself. "I thought you were in a coma. I was trying to help."

His disbelief was evident. "I told you I'm a light sleeper. All you have to do is speak to awaken me."

"*Speak?* I did everything but drag you out into the snow. Up until a few minutes ago, you were terribly ill—burning up with a fever. Your eyes were all red, and you . . . you . . ." She was so angry, she couldn't find the words.

"I *what?*" he asked, obviously not at all convinced by her explanation.

"You *raped* me!"

"Hah! Now you've gone too far. I would never commit such a barbaric act. Why not just admit why you were trying to remove my jammer and forget trying to fabricate an excuse? Did you think you could plant a suggestion in my mind to go along with your scheme to change history?"

She couldn't believe he had no recollection of any of what had just happened, let alone accuse *her* of taking advantage of him. "I'm *not* making this up. You were feverish and having trouble breathing, and . . . and scratching yourself. Look at your arms."

He glanced down where she pointed, then at his erection. "I can't explain how I got the marks, but I certainly don't appear to have had a release in the last few minutes."

"That's nothing compared to what you looked like before! How do you think you got out of the pouch? And who do you think ripped my clothes off?" She grabbed the torn bodysuit and shook it in front of him, but there was still a hint of doubt in his eyes. "And this," she said, discarding the last of her modesty and bringing his fingers to the inside of her thighs to discover the ultimate proof. "Do you see another man in this tent who could have left this behind when he was done using me?"

For several seconds he was dumbfounded. His gaze darted from one piece of evidence to another, but he saw only clues, not answers. His last words to her before they went to sleep haunted him: *I've never forced myself on a female before. I'm not going to start with you.* Shaking his head in confusion, he muttered, "I really don't remember."

Shara stared into his eyes for several heartbeats, then replied quietly. "I believe you. I thought it might have been some sort of virus picked up during the time-hop, but I don't seem to be affected, and I've never seen a virus leave the body so swiftly. You have a lot more practical experience than I have. Perhaps it would help if you saw how you behaved. If you will allow me to touch your mind, I'll show you my memory of exactly what happened."

He hesitated, always fearful of allowing anyone access to his mind, but if he had committed the offense the evidence implied, he needed to try every avenue to learn what caused him to behave so insanely and to prevent it from happening again. "All right. It's worth a try. Just so you understand, I will receive everything in your mind, unless you consciously block it from me. It's entirely up to you to control what you want to send. I'm incapable of separating new information from past memory. And please don't speak aloud while my jammer is off; it causes such echoes I can barely comprehend anything. Ready?" His hand lifted to his earcuff.

"Yes. I mean, no. Please get dressed first." Though he was no longer in a fully aroused state, his nude body was still a formidable distraction.

He complied, but could not resist one lingering look at the gifts nature had given her, before she concealed them. His preference would have been to forget about clothing completely for the remainder of the time they were alone there. He had always found the various usages of clothing in different cultures of great interest, possibly because he had grown up in a group that had no need for it.

Then again, considering Shara's negative attitude toward coupling with him, it was probably best to put the only available barrier between them. Although he could never remember having any difficulty controlling his body's physical reaction to a female, dressed or undressed, subduing his arousal had become a full-time effort around Shara.

And he didn't like it one bit.

As soon as they were both dressed, they sat down across from each other and he removed the jammer. Pressing two fingers against his temple, it was instantly apparent to her how vulnerable he was. She could have easily wandered through his thoughts at will until she knew every detail of his life. The unlimited power he had handed her made up for his earlier distrust a hundred times over. She let him know she appreciated his faith in her and promised to be careful not to abuse it if at all possible.

Shara re-created the scene for him, from her point of view, from the time she awakened until she reached for his earcuff.

"*Drek!*" he whispered as he replaced the jammer and she backed away from him. "I thought I was dreaming . . . only you came to me . . . you were willing."

Shara straightened her spine and looked at him warily. "Tell me about the dream."

He frowned. "I didn't even realize I'd had one until just then. It's not clear. There are only flashes. I was hot, too hot, and somehow I knew you could cool me. I called you, you came, and the fire went out. That's it. An apology is hardly adequate under the circumstances, but—"

"I had a dream also," she interrupted, and he stilled. As she described the images she had had, he began nodding his agreement.

"Yes, that was it," he exclaimed. "Fire and lava, explosions of volcanic ash. Until you described it, I forgot why I was so hot. The fever might have caused me to have such a dream, or the heat I was radiating might have triggered it for you, but as long as I was wearing the jammer, we shouldn't have shared the same dream. And I definitely should not have been so deeply unconscious that I would act it out without being at all cognizant of it afterward."

"It wasn't exactly the same dream. I wasn't aware that it was you calling me."

"All right. Any other variables to consider?"

As long as they were analyzing it as if it were a scientific experiment, she could separate this man from the one who had raped her. "I wasn't having any physical difficulties, nor was I unaware of what was going on." She frowned and shook her head in dismay. "Something's very wrong here."

"Did the dream arouse you?" When she lowered her lashes, he prodded. "From what you showed me, I didn't have any problem entering your body. Were you prepared for me?" He had picked up a brief sensation of pleasure from her before she blocked it. "Shara, this is important."

She crossed her arms in front of her and met his gaze. She resented having to admit that her body had betrayed her again. "Yes. My body seemed to be well prepared. But that doesn't mean I find that sort of act exciting."

"I wasn't implying that you did—only that your body was responding in a manner opposite your conscious will, similar to what happened to me, but on a much less aggressive level."

Shara maintained her defensive pose. She had touched his mind and knew he hadn't purposely raped her, but she had also discovered that he didn't have the mental power to force a physical response from her. "So can we draw any conclusions as to what happened?"

"I've only once seen a man show the same symptoms and behavior that I exhibited, and the cause couldn't possibly apply to me. Thus, your theory that I contracted a strange virus is probably the best one we have. I feel fine now. More than likely it was an isolated incident."

Shara wanted to believe that. The only problem was that it didn't explain her responsiveness. Why was she drawn to him against her will? Why did his nearness constantly cause her to behave in such abnormal ways? Since she met him, she'd been angrier, more frustrated, and more passionate than she'd felt in many years.

It was all unfamiliar, and terribly uncomfortable.

By the end of the day, they had completely dismantled and rebuilt the tempometer, analyzed and reanalyzed every alternative, then chilled it outside to determine if external temperature had any effect on the device, then did it all again. Their original hypothesis was proven when they saw that several of the tiny chips changed color and contracted slightly when exposed to the icy weather.

Now that they were as certain as they could be that the tempometer would work again as long as it was kept above freezing, they only had one problem to concentrate on—the destination time.

"We may not be able to figure it out before we have to use it," Gabriel said during their evening meal.

"We're not running out of food yet, are we? I thought you said we had a week—more, with the reduced rations you've been serving."

He shook his head. "It's not the food. It's the time period that concerns me. We've been working so hard on the tempometer, we both forgot about something you said to me before we got here. If you're right about the eddies and flows in time, why were we pulled to this particular moment of the Frozen Era?"

Her spoonful of chowder stopped an inch from her open mouth, and she lowered the utensil back to her bowl. "The cataclysm."

With a slow nod, he confirmed her guess. "It's the only event of any importance in this time period. The asteroid could be on its collision course right this minute and we'd have no way of knowing it."

Shara's mind soared through the facts she knew. The Frozen Era came to an abrupt end when a sizable asteroid hit Norona, knocking it onto an orbit closer to its sun. The impact caused a series of earthquakes, floods, and tidal waves that temporarily wiped out every living thing on the planet's surface. Thousands of years passed before nature calmed and the life cycle resumed. The period after the cataclysm was the only time of Norona's history that would have been less hospitable to humans than the Frozen Era.

Before they went to sleep, Shara set the tempometer next to her in case they needed to leave in a hurry during the night. It was programmed to return them to the time they had left . . . she hoped. This time, exhaustion was not sufficient to allow her to sleep soundly. Too many problems were playing screwball in her head.

Thus, shortly before dawn, when she felt the temperature within the sleeping pouch begin to rise, she immediately tensed. Needing to confirm what she feared was happening, she turned to Gabriel and placed her palm on his back.

He was burning up!

6

"**R**omulus!"

Aster's shout sounded in his mind a second before Rom heard her call him aloud, and by then he was already on his way to their living room.

"Did you do this?" she asked, her voice a nervous pitch higher than usual. She was pointing at a chair with brown-and-beige-striped upholstery next to the fireplace.

Rom frowned. Her confusion was interfering with his ability to read her thoughts. "Did I do what?"

"Exchange the chairs," she replied with some annoyance.

He took another look at the chair, then realized what she was referring to. Now he was as confused as she. "Wasn't that the material that was my first choice when we picked out that chair?"

"Yes. But I convinced you that the floral print would brighten up the room. Remember?"

Rom gave her a wink. "In fact, I have a very pleasant memory of precisely how you convinced me, too." He cut off his affectionate thought when he realized she was growing more agitated. "Wait a minute. You think I exchanged the chairs?"

Aster threw her hands up, knowing he had done no such thing, but grasping for a satisfactory explanation. "Last night when we went to bed, the floral chair was here. Now the striped one is in its place. Even if I went so far as to suppose Mack was playing a trick on us, he didn't know that the striped upholstery was your preference. But how else could it have gotten in here during the night and the floral chair taken away?"

Before Rom could formulate a guess, their son opened the front door, slammed it behind him, and stood there glowering with his hands fisted on his hips.

"You're not going to believe this!" he exclaimed.

"What's the matter?" Aster asked, momentarily setting aside her questions about the chair.

"Why aren't you in class?" Rom added.

Mack marched across the room shaking his head and flopped his long body into the striped chair. "Somebody's pulling a twist on me, but I can't figure out who or why. I got to class this morning and the professor said I wasn't on his roster. He admitted that I was there yesterday and the day before that, but today my name's not on the list, so I must not be in the class."

Frustration had him out of the chair again. "Then I went to the admin clerk to straighten it out, and guess what?" He paused and made sure he had both parents' full attention. "I'm not in their records at all. According to the computer, I never registered for school this year. Do you believe that? After how hard I tried to talk you out of making me attend academy this year, and how I killed myself to earn a passing mark in calculus last term, nothing I've done shows up in the files!"

"That's ridiculous," Rom said, striding over to the

telecommunicator. "I'll get this straightened out right now."

While Rom contacted the academy, Aster questioned Mack about the chair. When he seriously asked "You mean that's not the same one that was here yesterday?" she knew he wasn't the culprit responsible for the strange switch.

"No one can explain it," Rom told Mack after ending his call. "All traces of your attending classes this year have been erased. They're investigating the matter, but in the meantime, you can go back and reregister right now."

"Oh, lucky me," Mack muttered sarcastically.

As soon as he had gone, Aster and Rom shared the same thought. Something wasn't right. Both of them had the feeling that neither incident was simply someone pulling a twist.

They were already worried sick over Shara taking off with the tempometer. It seemed unlikely that she would get past the security officers on Norona, but a confirming report that she had been stopped could not reach Innerworld's communication center for at least another whole day.

The moment they had realized what she had done, Rom had sent a message to Norona, vaguely explaining that due to a family emergency, Shara needed to be detained immediately upon her arrival there and put on the first return flight. He and Aster firmly believed that Shara's unusual defiance would end the moment she knew her deception was uncovered. But that didn't really prevent either of them from worrying.

By the end of the day, they knew Shara wasn't the only thing they had to worry about.

A number of people they talked to had weird stories about something in their lives that had inexplicably been altered. Each involved a choice that had previously been made, but had now been reversed. Like Aster's chair fabric and Mack's attending the academy, one man swore he'd decided to park his vehicle in his garage last night, but in the morning it was in his driveway. A woman spoke of how the kalani bushes that had been in front of her residence for months had somehow been replaced by roses, which was what she had almost planted to begin with.

Rom called in several trackers who had the ability to "see" events that occurred within the past twenty-four hours. None picked up a single image of something changing in any way, despite the clear memories of those affected.

Rom and Aster called a meeting with the Chiefs of Security and Scientific Research that evening. They, too, had heard some peculiar tales during the day. Nothing suggested any imminent danger, but neither could the incidents be ignored, no matter how insignificant.

The only immediate actions decided on, however, were to search the universal history data banks for similar circumstances, while a team of scientists would be set to work theorizing how such changes might have logically happened without the interference of some alien culture in possession of magical powers.

Whatever had caused the alterations, the Innerworlders were determined that they would stop it before anything more serious was affected.

7

Shara crawled out of the pouch and huddled in a corner of the tent. If Gabriel was about to have another attack, he was going to suffer this one on his own.

The starlight, combined with the dim glow from the heater orb, illuminated the tent enough for her to see how the fever progressed. She sympathized with him as muscle spasms racked his body, and he began clawing at his neck and chest as if biting insects were eating him alive.

His groan of pain was so excruciating, she had to stop herself from going to him. There was really nothing she could do to help, and she had no intention of becoming part of any hallucination he might be having this time.

Shara.

She heard it clearly, the voice from her dream, but it didn't seem to have come from Gabriel.

Shara.

Panic trapped the air in her lungs. Her name hadn't been said aloud; it was *thought* to her. But Gabriel had no such ability, nor was she touching his temple to read him. And yet she was intuitively certain it was Gabriel calling her.

She wiped at the annoying film of perspiration on

her upper lip. It seemed incredible that his body temperature could be so high that it heated the entire tent, but that seemed to be the case.

Gabriel thrashed from side to side, kicking at the confining pouch and moaning in pain and frustration. She *could* do something to help a little, she realized. Careful to keep out of his reach, she freed him from the pouch and opened the tent flap a fraction of an inch to let in a draft of icy air.

The cold was such a relief from the suffocating heat, she knelt in front of the opening and let the biting wind curl around her. Still, it was not enough to cool her. Urgently tugging at her clothing, she stripped to the skin and opened the tent flap a bit more.

Come to me, Shara.

She whirled around, expecting to see Gabriel right behind her, but he was where he had been, curled into a fetal position and twitching uncontrollably.

Help me!

The desperation in the words almost rent her in half. The cold air was so soothing, yet she felt compelled to obey his call.

Something crawled up her arm and she brushed at it, but she could see nothing there. She scratched at the skin where she had brushed to ease the itch left behind. An insect must have invaded their shelter! A few seconds later, a similar itch irritated her neck, then her other arm. She suddenly felt as though her nerve endings had moved to the outside of her flesh.

I need you.

The words stroked her body as if they had substance. Despite the cold at her back, fingers of fire caressed her breasts and danced between her naked thighs, creating a burning need that even the freezing wind could not cool.

You need me.

Her perspiring body trembled from the effort it took to remain where she was rather than give in to her weakness.

Suddenly awareness flashed through her discomfort. She was suffering from all the same symptoms as Gabriel. The virus had affected her after all. She wasn't hearing his thoughts; she was *hallucinating!* Without her realizing it, the mysterious fever had taken control of her mind as well as her body. While logic remained, she closed the flap, no matter how good the cold felt at the moment.

A pounding drum had taken up residence between her thighs, demanding immediate appeasement. The fever seemed to begin and end at the core of her womanhood. Her fingers confirmed the excessive dampness she knew would be there, but it was not her own touch that her body craved.

She cried aloud from the pain of a need so great she would surely die if it went unsatisfied, yet she continued to fight against it.

Until her mind could fight no more and retreated into darkness.

"Shara? Are you asleep?"

She heard his voice and knew it was him and not the fever talking, but held her response in order to analyze the situation.

She was lying on top of him, naked, and she could feel him deep inside her. How could she not remember how she had gotten there? With her next breath, she realized her body's temperature had returned to normal, as had his, and she could feel the chill in the air from when she had opened the flap. The fever that had driven her to the brink of sanity was gone. The overpowering desire that had held her in thrall was now only a mild humming through her body.

What sort of virus would carry so many radical symptoms, and yet be completely neutralized by sexual gratification? Before she could give that question further consideration, Gabriel's shaft throbbed within her and her own muscles clenched around him in automatic response.

"Shara, as good as this is to wake up to, I have the distinct impression I've missed something again."

With an embarrassed groan, she separated their bodies and eased to his side. The light tone of his voice contrasted with the humiliation she felt at finding herself in such an intimate situation and not knowing how it had come about. Only the concern in his eyes gave her the courage to speak.

"You had another . . . seizure a while ago. However, it now appears I have contracted the same virus. The symptoms seem to be identical. High fever, tremors, oversensitive skin, possibly brought on by agitated nerves—everything, exactly like that night. Unlike you, though, I was wide awake, at least for a while. I heard a voice call me, like in my dream, only this time I knew it was you. I heard you in my mind. Or I thought I did. It must have been a hallucination brought on by the fever. I blacked out. I swear to the Supreme Being, I have no idea how I came to you, or . . . or . . ."

Gabriel stroked her cheek. "Considering the position we were in when I awoke, I will assume I did not force myself on you this time."

She couldn't meet his eyes, but she shook her

head. "No, I . . . I believe it was I who took you. I'm afraid I don't remember."

Gabriel couldn't resist a small joke. "Doesn't say much for either one of us, does it?"

Shara made a face at him and sat up. With a quick scan of the tent, she located their discarded jumpers and tossed his onto his lap. "I don't see any humor in this situation."

"No, I don't suppose you would." As they both dressed, he suddenly became angry. Very angry. And he wasn't going to put up with her bad humor or unreasonableness another minute! "You know something? You're right. There's nothing funny about this situation at all. But it's not my fault, and I'm sick and tired of you treating me like it is!"

Shara turned on him in shock. "I never said this was your fault!"

"Hah!" Her denial fueled his frustration. "Every time I get near you, you flinch away; every look you give me is suspicious. *Drek,* woman! You touched my mind. You *know* I don't have the power to manipulate you."

"Then who is doing it?" she shouted back at him. "What's happening to me?"

"I certainly don't know, but losing your temper isn't the way to figure it out!"

Breathing heavily, they both glared at each other for several seconds as if deciding whether to escalate their fight to physical blows.

Belatedly, the perverse humor in this situation struck Shara and she quelled the urge to laugh. "I never lose my temper," she stated as seriously as possible.

He noted her attempt to smother a smile and felt his anger slip away as quickly as it had come upon him. "Neither do I. Shall we find someone else to blame for our loss of reason as well as our bodily control?"

Now she felt foolish. She hated these quicksilver mood changes she had been going through, but without understanding the cause, she didn't know how to control them. "I'm open to suggestions."

He was relieved to hear that, though he wondered just how open she'd remain. "I told you I had only seen these symptoms one time before. Until you were stricken, I was certain it couldn't be the same problem, but now I think we may have to consider the possibility."

When he hesitated, Shara assumed the worst. "Is it . . . incurable?"

"Not normally. Before I explain, please understand, I'm only guessing. I could be completely wrong."

Growing more impatient by the second, Shara insisted, "Just tell me and get it over with."

"The man I referred to was a Noronian also. The joining ceremony with his chosen mate-to-be was scheduled to take place in a short time. She had to make a brief business trip and was delayed in returning. By the third day of her absence, his mating fever became so intense, he descended into a deep coma."

Like every Noronian, Shara had been taught that she had someone destined to be her mate. When Noronians' mating time arrived, usually about halfway through their lives, and the two people found each other, they would be stricken with the mating fever. Normally the couple realized they were meant for each other right away and joined so that the fever had little or no chance to be bothersome. The formal joining was physical, mental, and spiritual, as their minds became one in two bodies and their souls joined for all eternity.

Gabriel was waiting for Shara to draw her own conclusions, but she needed more input. "What were his symptoms?" she asked, hoping his answer would differ from what she expected him to say.

"High fever, itching, red corneas, violent body tremors, and finally the coma. During all of it, his body remained in an aroused condition. He would become violent if anyone tried to touch him. His mate-to-be returned, coupled with him, and he had a miraculous recovery."

"It can't be the same," she stated firmly, shaking her head.

He shrugged. "You're the scientist. Consider the facts. We're both Noronian; your Terran ancestry is recessive. I'm a male. You're a female. The symptoms we are both suffering are most definitely those of the mating fever, and we are relieved by coupling . . . whether we remember doing it or not. Even the first time seemed somewhat mind-stealing, especially when you had so vehemently denied any desire to couple with me before."

"No. *No!* It can't be. There is no way we could be destined for each other. We weren't instantly drawn together by a strong physical attraction. When my father first saw my mother, even though she was an Outerworlder and forbidden to him, he knew. Nothing could keep him from being with her. And my mother had had dreams of him long before she arrived in Innerworld. She recognized him as the man from her dreams the moment she saw him. You and I don't even like each other half the time. It's impossible."

"I agree. It's absolutely impossible. I shouldn't reach my mating age for another thirty or forty years, and you're even younger than I am."

Shara frowned. "When my parents joined, they were almost the same ages we are now, as were my father's parents. I'm afraid age is not a valid negative in my case. There is a possibility that my time could have come, but instead of being with my intended mate—"

"Wrong. It doesn't work that way and you know it. Only one's true soulmate should be able to put out the fire for someone in the throes of the mating fever."

"But only one's true soulmate should be able to trigger it to begin with. Do you honestly believe I am yours?" His automatic expression of dismay added a bit more acid to her caustic speech. "Of course you don't. No more than I believe you could be mine. *When* I find my mate, I'll know it's him the moment our eyes meet. When he puts his hand on mine, I'll feel tingles of electricity run up my arm. We'll have everything in common, and he'll love me, unconditionally, for myself. Not because I'm a mixed-breed, or who my father is, or what I can do for him!"

Though he couldn't quite understand his reaction to her little speech, he felt that he had been insulted. "Your conception of finding a mate sounds very romantic and if that's the way it's supposed to be, I'm sure it will happen for you. I have a few preconceived notions of my own. *If* I am destined to have a mate, she would have to be an experienced traveler, have a mild disposition, a good sense of humor, and a rational, mature attitude about physical contact—none of which characteristics describes you."

He noticed how she bristled at his words, but he continued before she could start another argument. "Personally, I hope I never find a mate. Not only do I prefer a solitary life, I am adamantly opposed to altering my lifestyle or my career to satisfy another person's comforts or interests. I've spent half my life running away from having people inside my head. The last thing in the universe I want is to join with a female who would become a permanent fixture in my mind."

"Good," Shara said stiffly, telling herself his negative opinion of her character didn't matter in the slightest. "We're in agreement, then. Whatever this is, it cannot be the actual mating fever, but a simulation of it. The only thing I can figure is that something happened during the time-hop that affected our bodies' metabolisms, triggering the same symptoms as we would have experienced during our mating time, and because we were physically touching at that moment, we each became the target of the other's, um . . ."

"Desire?" he finished for her, then tried to respond in the same clinical manner she had used. "Continuing with that assumption, perhaps there's a logical reason why the fever is reaching a peak while one or both of us is unconscious. Neither one of us is willing to accept the fact that we are destined to be mates. Though I have demonstrated a desire to couple with you, you firmly rejected my advances . . . with one notable exception." He paused to see if she would blush for him. She did, and he considerately held back his knowing grin. At least whatever caused the sparks of hostility between them had vanished.

"I would never *consciously* force you to satisfy that

desire. Therefore, let me suggest another possibility that should at least be considered. Although we do not accept this situation as the genuine mating fever, our souls may not share our attitude on the subject. Those entities may have taken it out of our hands by forcing us together without our conscious participation."

Shara held up both hands in protest. "I cannot accept that theory. I do not believe for one moment that a spiritual power has taken over our minds and bodies to force us to ... to ... have sexual relations against our will. For that matter, it could be some alien being that we picked up during the time-hop who's getting a vicarious thrill through us."

Though she was clearly upset and perfectly serious, Gabriel couldn't stop himself from laughing. "At the very least we should be allowed to enjoy ourselves while we're performing!"

"Very funny."

"I'm sorry. This situation seems to have put me in a peculiar mood. However, I do have another, more constructive thought. If this is a simulation of the mating fever and it was caused by the time-hop, another might take it away again."

"I certainly hope so. I don't care to repeat the last two nights indefinitely."

"Nor do I. What do you suggest, madame scientist?"

Shara pinched the bridge of her nose and tried to analytically separate her feelings from the facts of their dilemma. "The only permanent cure to the mating fever is to be joined. That solution is obviously unacceptable. We are also agreed that the fever may disappear during another time-hop. If not, it can surely be dealt with medically once we return to our own time. Therefore, all we need is a temporary cure for the symptoms."

"Which, as we have already discovered firsthand, is coupling. Agreed?"

Shara took a deep breath. "Yes, agreed."

"Since I have made it quite clear that I have no objection to sharing my body with you, it is up to you to set aside whatever personal resentments you're harboring and be reasonable—"

"I am not unreasonable, nor do I resent you . . . precisely. Just because my attitude toward intimacy differs from yours—"

"*Enough.* There is no need for further debate on the matter. I am attempting to look at our problem in a purely scientific manner." Perhaps it was a remnant from the fever, but he was finding it increasingly difficult to maintain a serious expression. "We both need our wits about us to get through whatever lies ahead. And if that means it becomes necessary from time to time to satisfy our . . . biological urges . . . I can only recommend that we do so. As efficiently as possible, of course."

She saw a twinkle in his eye and suspected he was secretly delighted that she was being coerced into agreeing to the one thing she most wanted to avoid. Under the circumstances, however, she had no logical rebuttal.

When she made no reply, he took her hand in his and shook it in a very businesslike manner. "It's agreed, then. I will expect you to tell me when you need me to accommodate you, and I will do the same. *Before* the fever becomes a hindrance or steals our consciousness."

Without looking at him directly, she gave him a

brief nod, despite the fact that she had no idea where she would ever find the nerve to ask him for such a favor if such a need arose again.

Gabriel lifted her chin. "Did you get any sleep?"

"Not unless you count my blackout. You?"

"Enough. If you require a nap, I can—"

"No. Thank you. I keep thinking about the cataclysm. I'm sure that has to be the event that pulled us here; we could even be sitting in the area where the asteroid hit. In which case, we might not have the ten seconds we'd need to escape."

Gabriel rubbed his jaw. "I was thinking the same thing. Do you want to try to return?"

"Give me one more hour . . . and some light. If I can't come up with anything better, we'll reverse the hop we did."

Gabriel fixed them a meal, recovered the barriers from outside, and stowed everything in his satchel except the tent, while Shara went through Lantana's notes and examined the tempometer one last time.

"I don't believe it!" she exclaimed. "It was so simple, I completely overlooked it."

"What?" Gabriel asked, instantly catching her excitement.

"What's the difference between ten thousand and a million?"

He angled his head at her. "Nine hundred ninety thousand?"

"No. Two zeros! Lantana didn't come out and state it anywhere, but there are references I should have picked up on. He worked with a base of a hundred. Instead of one year equals one, one year equals one hundred." She was astounded that she could have missed something so easy. Gabriel's suggestion that spiritual forces were involved in what was happening to them came back to her. Perhaps the same force had prevented her from seeing the obvious until she and Gabriel had come to an agreement of sorts. Again, she firmly rejected that possibility.

"I can have the tent dismantled and packed in sixty seconds. If you hold the heater orb in front of the tempometer, it should stay warm enough until I'm done."

"Right." She secured the belt around her waist and put the notes into her bag. As she turned to go outside, Gabriel grasped her arm.

"Not that I don't trust you," he said in a tone that hinted otherwise, "but my historical knowledge and journeying experience are no longer the only reasons you need to take me with you."

It took her a moment to understand that he was referring to the fever. Ignoring the warmth that flooded her system, she lifted her chin in defiance. "I'm counting on the time-hop to eliminate that particular necessity. But even so, I wouldn't abandon my worst enemy to this place, and I think it's horrid of you to imply that I would."

She turned away from him so that her eyes could not reveal the truth. For a brief moment, she *had* considered leaving him. She had never had such a wicked thought in all her life, and she only felt slightly guilty about it.

Shara had thought he'd been exaggerating about packing up the tent in sixty seconds, but he actually managed it in less than that.

This time they knew what to expect during the hop and without the fear, the journey seemed to go much faster.

Shara felt the warm sunshine even before the tinkling sound of wind chimes drifted away. They were in a fragrant place of fruit-bearing trees and rolling hills covered with tiny multihued flowers.

"Welcome to paradise," Gabriel said, surveying the area. "It's hard to be certain, but I think we're at least in the same location we were before. We definitely managed to pass over the planet's rebirth and, considering the lack of construction in the area, I'd guess we didn't overshoot our target date of 5750, either."

Shara shielded her eyes as she noted the sun's position in the sky to get her bearings. The white ring around the large, fiery sphere suggested they were still on Norona. "From what I researched, the administrative center of First Province was approximately twenty kilometers east of where our ship docked. If we're anytime near when I wanted to arrive, the rebels should be amassing in that area."

Gabriel extracted a triangle-shaped mirror from the left breast pocket of his jumper. "Beauty, record," he said. Then, holding one corner, he raised it above his head and turned in a full circle.

"An audiovisual recorder?" Shara asked with open interest.

"Recorder, computer, confidante," he replied, and tilted the mirror toward her face. "Smile for the camera."

Instead she smirked and reached for the device. "May I?"

He handed it to her. "Ask whatever you wish to learn. It will respond to the voice of whoever is holding it." As she examined the mirror, he decided it might be quite nice to have some recordings of her that he could play back sometime in the future, when he was far away and very alone. "Look at your image as you speak."

Shara thought that seemed a bit odd, but she did as he instructed. "Where are we?"

INSUFFICIENT DATA

"Oh!" The printed words on the mirror's surface surprised her. "It doesn't use a voice?"

"It has one, but I prefer—"

"Silence," she surmised. "Did I understand you correctly? You call it Beauty?"

Gabriel grinned.

Shara thought of a biting retort, but instead she looked at her own reflection and said, "All right, *Beauty,* based on your analysis of the environment, plant life, and atmospheric conditions, could we be in First Province on the planet Norona?"

AFFIRMATIVE

"Obviously, you didn't program it for friendly chatter," she said to Gabriel. "Beauty, what is the date?"

15761.52 NORONIAN

That was the date in their own time.

Gabriel explained, "Its internal clock wouldn't have been affected by our time-hop." He took the recorder back and asked, "Is there a concentrated group of life-forms in the area, evolution level five or above?"

YES

"Locate."

19.8 KM

A flashing arrow appeared below the numbers. Gabriel held the mirror parallel to the ground and slowly turned clockwise. When the arrow stopped flashing, he halted and pointed at a hill in front of him. "That's where we want to head. But we need to change clothes first. The object is to try to be as inconspicuous as possible. Any minor differences can be gotten over by claiming we're travelers from another province. Beauty, show me the style of clothing worn by the average male and female rebels on Norona in the year 5750."

Instantly a holographic image of a man and woman appeared before them. They were both wearing lightweight material draped loosely from the left shoulder to about midthigh and gathered with a braided rope at the waist, and sandals with toe and ankle straps. Gabriel asked Shara, "Did you bring anything that you can make look like that?"

After her lack of preparation for the Frozen Era, she was proud to show him that she had made some provisions. She opened her bag and pulled out a length of thin white fabric bunched together in the middle by a gold brooch. "I did do *some* research."

"Good. Now put it on." The mere fact that the temptation to watch her change was almost overwhelming convinced him to turn his back while he unearthed his own garment and put it on. He attached Beauty to a thin strip of leather and hung it around his neck, then transferred the paralyzer rod from his special jumper to the hidden sheath he'd designed into a fold of his tunic.

Since the tempometer belt might attract too much attention and was too bulky to hide beneath either of their tunics, Shara buried it beneath her clothing in the bag.

Shara thought that the simplicity of the covering seemed appropriate to the goals of the rebels, but she was used to covering more of her body even in the privacy of her own residence. Accustomed as she was to wearing long pants and shirts or full bodysuits and jumpers, she felt uncomfortably exposed. After tying a length of gold braid around her waist, she rearranged the material to shield her sides, but she still felt underdressed.

Gabriel turned around and gave her a look of approval that had more to do with his being a man than a historian. His grin would have made her nervous even if he'd been fully dressed. As it was, she was staring at an awful lot of perfectly developed male flesh and it was impossible not to think about how it felt pressed to hers.

He picked up her bag and strapped it to his floating satchel. "It sounds like we have quite a hike ahead of us. No sense in carrying a burden when you don't have to."

Ignoring the jittery feeling in her stomach, Shara said "Thank you" and they started toward what they hoped was civilization. After a few minutes of silence, she asked, "How do you feel?"

He glanced sideward at her. "Fine. And you?"

"Fine. No noticeable aftereffects." They walked a bit farther before she asked the question that was really on her mind. "How long do you think it will be before we, uh, can tell whether or not the, uh . . . the *problem* was taken care of?"

Gabriel had the devilish urge to make her explain the *problem* just to see her blush again, but since her blushes tended to stir his desire to touch her, he asked for her scientific evaluation instead.

As long as he put it that way, she found it somewhat easier to discuss the subject that was making her so abnormally nervous. She just wished she could stop tripping over her tongue every time she tried to say anything remotely personal. "Based on the timing of the two . . . incidents . . . following the first . . . coupling, it should be safe to assume that if twenty-four hours passes without any, uh, significant metabolic fluctuations, the fever has been neutralized." She felt her cheeks flush in spite of her attempt to pretend she was speaking of someone else's body.

Except for his offer of a Caress, neither of them attempted to maintain a conversation during the subsequent hours while Beauty kept them on course. Even when they had a meal break about four kilometers from their destination, their individual thoughts remained private. A short time after that break, they were standing atop a high ridge looking down on a peaceful valley.

There was only one concentration of life below, and it appeared to be a small but productive farm. Several large wooden buildings were surrounded by rows of crops. Cows, goats, woolies, and horses grazed together in one fenced area, and pigs, chickens, and farbits were in pens near the buildings. A number of people were performing chores outside.

"Record," Gabriel said, touching Beauty. "Note the absence of any mechanical equipment or vehicles."

Shara had simply thought the idyllic scene was pleasing to the eye. Gabriel was working. As they descended the grassy slope, she accepted the fact that it would be to her advantage to follow his lead until she became acclimated.

Several men and women stopped what they were doing when they caught sight of Gabriel and Shara approaching. Gabriel raised his arm in a friendly greeting.

Instead of any return wave of welcome, two arrows cut into the earth, centimeters ahead of their toes.

8

"State your business," a female voice shouted at them.

Shara traced the order to an attractive young woman with curly blond hair, who was perched on a high branch of a tree a short distance away. She was dressed in the traditional rebel garb and aiming a bow and arrow at the two trespassers.

"Hello," Gabriel called back. "We are weary travelers seeking a new way of life. We heard that we might find Friends in this place."

The dozen workers to whom Gabriel had waved formed a circle around him and Shara. They were a fit-looking group of adolescents, several of whom held long-handled tools that could double as lethal weapons. Shara thought Gabriel seemed awfully relaxed under the circumstances.

A tall woman with masculine features stepped forward and scrutinized Gabriel's face and body. She wore a leather helmet over her hair and an owl was perched on a leather pad on her shoulder.

"Artemis," the woman called to the archer in the tree. "Do you know this man?"

"No, but he looks familiar," Artemis replied.

"I would think so, since he could pass for your twin brother." The woman with the owl turned back to Gabriel. "I am Athena, mentor of this commune. Are you of Artemis and Apollo's family?"

Gabriel smiled at the woman. "Not that I'm aware, though I have been told before that I bear a resemblance to that distinguished man, and I'm flattered."

As soon as Shara had heard the names Artemis, Athena, and Apollo, her heart picked up its rate. From her studies she knew they were three of the leaders in the Noronian rebellion. She and Gabriel must have made it to the correct time!

"My name is Gabriel, and this is Shara, my mate-to-be."

Shara's eyes widened. Why would he say such a thing? His next words were even more surprising.

"We have vowed not to be joined until the cause of freedom is won. Have we found the Friends we have heard so much about?"

Athena's expression remained stern. "If you heard so much, then you must know of a sign that would identify you as a true Friend."

Gabriel tapped his left breast with his right fist two times, then extended that hand, palm up, toward her. After she repeated the gesture to him, he lifted Beauty off his chest, turned in a full circle, and said, "To friendship, peace, and love."

Everyone around him reached into the tops of their tunics and brought out triangular-shaped pendants made of a variety of stones and woods. "To friendship, peace, and love," they all returned to Gabriel and Shara, as smiles replaced their threatening scowls and their postures relaxed. Athena introduced each of them and told of their contribution to the commune. Though most of this group tended the crops and small animals, others not present were shepherds, smiths, and hearth tenders.

"Have you traveled far?" one of the younger boys asked.

As Gabriel related the background information he and Shara had previously decided upon, she had to admit once again that having Gabriel along was to her advantage. Despite her studies of the period and his numerous stories, there were still small details, like the hand sign and three-sided pendants, that she hadn't known about. She wondered how many other important pieces of information he had forgotten, or neglected to mention, in all their talks. Could he have left them out intentionally to ensure her continued need of him?

She felt her heart begin to race from the anger that instantly surfaced. He had no right to— She cut off her own thoughts as she realized what a strong reaction she was having to such a small thing. It had been *her* responsibility to be prepared, not his. There was no logical reason for her to be so upset about it. But logic seemed to have abandoned her lately.

Cold fear stabbed at her stomach. Was that overly emotional reaction a sign that the fever was still with her?

The group was most interested in how the newcomers' baggage remained in the air. Gabriel showed them the degrav and modestly told them it was the only antigravity device of its kind because he'd invented it.

"We have forsaken modern technology here, Gabriel," Athena said somewhat testily. "If you wish to be one of us, you will have to make adjustments."

Gabriel immediately lowered his burden to the

ground, removed the degrav, and slipped it into an outside pocket of the satchel.

With an approving nod, Athena said, "Your timing is excellent. The Friendship Summit will take place on schedule at sunrise tomorrow. Representatives of factions from all over the planet have been arriving here throughout the past week. There is more than enough room and food for you to stay with us."

"Wonderful," Gabriel said with a broad smile. "We were hoping we would not be too late to observe the meeting."

"You are welcome to do more than simply observe," Athena assured him. "One of our beliefs is that everyone's opinion is of value, regardless of their birth condition. The Ruling Tribunal's decision to colonize Terra must be overturned before the ships depart."

"When are they to take off?" Shara inquired. The curious expression on Athena's face and the frown on Gabriel's told her she had asked a question that she should have already known the answer to.

"I'm afraid long days of traveling combined with the delay of our joining has my *shalla* a bit confused," Gabriel explained. "The first day of the second season is a date everyone is talking about."

Shara didn't have to stretch her limited acting ability to look embarrassed over her forgetfulness. His calling her his *shalla*, the intimate term for soulmate, and referring again to their joining had her quite flustered.

Athena was apparently convinced. "We will have two sunrises after the Summit to force the Tribunal to see our point of view."

"Force?" Gabriel asked, as if he didn't know what the future held. Athena stared at him with eyes that seemed to be trying to read his mind, but, of course, even if she had the ability, his jammer would prevent it.

After a second, she frowned and said, "The Friends will do whatever they must. Come, let us go to the lodge."

Without the degrav, Gabriel had to drag his satchel along the ground by the guide strap.

"Allow me to assist," an auburn-haired young man named Misha said, and the satchel rose off the ground and hovered in the air.

At the same moment Shara realized Misha was using his mind to lift the satchel, she felt a mental intrusion and instantly blocked it. There was no way to tell who had attempted to read her without opening up to it, however, so she simply determined to keep her guard up against all of them.

Gabriel had told her that, although it was kept secret at the time, a few of the rebels possessed extrasensory powers that they didn't hesitate to use. She had thought it was somewhat contradictory that these people would reject advanced technology while having no qualms about using superior mental abilities, but he had explained that they considered those abilities *natural*, as opposed to man-made.

One of the many objections the Friends had against the Ruling Tribunal was the edict that strictly limited the use of any special mental skills. Some of the Friends believed they were given the gifts to help others. Others believed the powers made them superior and they were given these powers because they were meant to lead rather than follow.

Seconds after the first probe, she felt another. This one was gentler and seemed different enough to make her think it was not from the same person. These people might call themselves Friends and speak of friendship, peace, and love, but Shara wondered why such friendly people needed an armed guard at the edge of their farm and why they were so distrustful that they would try to read her thoughts even after Gabriel had given them the appropriate signals.

What would they have done to her and Gabriel if Gabriel hadn't known the hand sign? For that matter, what would have happened to her if he hadn't been with her to smooth the way? The group had seemed very menacing when they first surrounded her and Gabriel. Were they prepared to kill to protect their privacy? As suspicious as they were, she doubted if they'd believe a story as outlandish as her being a time traveler.

Again, she had a reason to be grateful for Gabriel's presence, but she was still annoyed that he hadn't filled her in completely.

By the time they entered the large building Athena had called the lodge, at least twenty others had joined them, and more introductions were exchanged. The inside of the lodge had no interior walls on the ground floor, but the overhead loft that rimmed the cavernous room was partitioned off into narrow, draped cubicles. Several rows of long wooden tables and benches were at the far end of the room and mats, blankets, and pillows were scattered over the rest of the floor.

"As you can see, we have a rather full house at the moment. I regret that we cannot offer you a separate cell, as they have all been taken, but if you wish less crowded sleeping arrangements, you can always bed down in the meadow, as some of our other visitors have." She motioned for Misha to set the baggage against one wall. "There are over two hundred people staying here tonight and I am asking all to help where they can. If the two of you would not mind, there is a desperate need for more hands in the cookhouse."

Shara and Gabriel quickly agreed and Athena took them out the door at the other end of the building. The heat from several crackling fires wafted over them. Portions of large animals were being cooked on spits and a small army of adults and children were basting meat, stirring the contents of various pots, and preparing greens.

Once Athena left them under the supervision of the hearth tenders, Shara excused herself for a moment. Under the pretense of needing something from her bag, she went back into the lodge. Making sure no one was watching too closely, she activated the special security guard she had attached to the bag before leaving Innerworld. With the guard on, the bag was locked and its weight increased to make it impossible for anyone to open or move it. The contents were far too valuable for her to be as trusting as she normally would be.

The moment she returned to the cookhouse, she was assigned a task. Fortunately for Shara, she was asked to wash a basinful of tubers, something that required no previous experience. Gabriel was put to work turning the spits over the hot fires. It was beginning to look as though they would either be freezing or burning up throughout their journey.

As soon as she thought of burning up, she made a quick mental check of her body's condition, then relaxed when she was positive that she was perspiring from the heat of the fire and not an inner fever.

Now that she was in the time period she wanted, she was going to be too busy to have to deal with a biological impediment. She sincerely hoped the last time-hop had expelled the simulated fever permanently.

Shara's gaze automatically shifted to Gabriel. With his back to her, she didn't hesitate to watch the play of muscles in his arms and back as he rotated the spit. His muscular legs were braced apart to keep his balance and the tunic was insufficient to stop **her** from thinking of the rest of his perfectly sculpted body. On Outerworld Earth he would have been compared to a Greek god, but now she was among the men who were the Greek gods and she considered Gabriel's physique quite superior.

Not that she was going to allow that incredible body, or his handsome face, to affect her judgment. As long as there was no fever forcing her to give in, she would resist the urge to stroke those muscles or thread her fingers through his silky blond curls, or—

She pulled her gaze back to the vegetable in her hand. Looking at Gabriel was *not* the way to control her weakness. With a little effort, she filled her mind with her mission.

Because their arrival occurred precisely when all the rebels were gathering, she was reassured about the theory of eddies and flows in time. Athena had said they had two sunrises after tomorrow before the ships departed for Terra. Surely that would be more than enough time for her to test a hair sample of every rebel in the vicinity for a DNA match with Khameira. All she had to do was wait for everyone in the lodge to go to sleep. Any Friends not in residence that night should be at the Summit in the morning. She would have to be discreet, but she felt confident that she could accomplish her work without arousing suspicions.

To make sure she didn't miss anyone, her micropmuter contained the list of the names of the two hundred twenty rebels who were originally exiled to Terra. In order to check off those names, she had to learn each person's identity. While Athena was introducing those on hand, Shara had memorized names and faces, but she didn't expect it to be that easy with everyone else in the camp. Though improvising was not one of her strengths, she was determined to find a way to test every single participant in the Friendship movement.

If only she could be sure Gabriel would not interfere! As she scrubbed the skins of a bottomless pile of tubers, she concentrated on how to get around his belief that history should not be tampered with. Reasoning with him had failed. She briefly considered offering the use of her body in exchange for his noninterference. However, she didn't believe he wanted to couple with her badly enough to forget his personal goal of preventing her from altering the past . . . to say nothing for the fact that coupling with him could influence her thinking instead.

"*Drek!*" Gabriel shouted, jumping away from the fire and shaking his right arm.

"He's been burned," a woman named Hestia called out. "Get Apollo's case!"

As a little girl dashed into the lodge, Shara dropped the tuber in her hand and rushed to see how badly he was hurt. A bright red splotch on the inside of Gabriel's forearm marked the injured spot, and his clenched jaw let her know it was painful. The moment the girl brought out a small chest, Hestia removed a bottle of liquid from it and poured some over the burn.

"That will do until Apollo arrives to take care of it," she assured him. "Until then, perhaps you should help Shara."

He accepted her suggestion as everyone returned to his or her individual chores.

Shara grimaced at the blistering flesh on his arm. "Did the liquid help at all?"

"It numbed the area," he said, picking up a brush and a tuber. He lowered his voice to a murmur meant only for her ears. "It will be interesting to see if Apollo really was a healer, as legend says, or just a good pharmacologist."

Shara leaned toward him and whispered back, "You didn't burn yourself on purpose just to find out, did you?"

"Do I seem that unbalanced to you?"

She cocked her head at him. "As a matter of fact, you do. What the *drek* possessed you to say we were waiting to be joined?"

He casually looked around to make sure no one was paying attention to their conversation. "It was the first thing that came to mind that made us sound a bit fanatical, like true Friends. Plus we can now use it to explain any sort of aberration, including the possibility that the fever is still with us."

She wasn't at all happy to hear him bring *that* up, but his reasoning did make sense, so she moved on to her next complaint. "Why didn't you tell me about the hand sign and triangle pendants?"

"Frankly, it never occurred to me." He saw a hint of yellow in her eyes. "Are you angry with me, Shara?"

Since such a reaction was uncalled for, given his

explanations, she started to deny it when she noticed how intently he was starting at her. He wasn't guessing; he was analyzing the color of her eyes! Her shoulders slumped with the realization that she could no longer keep her feelings private. "How much have you figured out?"

Though he hadn't meant to reveal his one advantage over her, he saw no choice but to tell the truth. "Your eyes are like emeralds when you're pleased or excited about something, olive-gray when you're lying or evading, yellow-streaked when you're angry, and an absolutely delicious shade of chocolate when you—"

"Hush! I have no control over the changes, and I don't care to wear shields all the time. Normally it's not a problem. Only a few people have spent enough time so close to me that they can read my eye color like that." Now her cheeks were flushed.

"Shara, even without your overly expressive eyes, anyone could probably guess what you were thinking. I told you once, you're not much of an actress. You show your feelings with every part of your body. If it's not your eyes, it's the set of your chin, your posture, the way you move your hands." His gaze slid to her thinly covered breasts. "The way you move your body when I—"

"Please stop saying things like that," she whispered urgently, glancing around for eavesdroppers. "You know how I feel—"

"Oh, yes," he said over the rest of her sentence. "I know *exactly* how you feel. Like velvet and satin that's been warmed by the sun."

"I'm not listening."

"You promised to be accommodating."

She narrowed her eyes at him, then touched the back of her hand to his brow. "You're not feverish."

"You didn't touch the right part of me."

Without thinking of the consequences, she looked down at his lap and her cheeks heated even more. The loose tunic had a small tent formed in it.

He didn't bother to hide his grin. "It's not my fault you look so desirable in that scrap of cloth." He leaned a little closer. "The only reason I got burned was because I kept thinking about what I saw when you bent over to place that stool you're sitting on." Her lips formed an *o*, and he took advantage of her surprise with a quick kiss. "If you don't want me to say things like that, try not to tease."

"I . . . I . . . wouldn't, I didn't . . . not on purpose." His smile told her *he* was the one who was teasing, and she grimaced at him rather than give him the smile she felt inside. She then made an attempt to distract him before she gave away her true reaction to his teasing. "I think you should know, someone— two people, actually—tried to enter my mind while we were being greeted. I blocked them, but I'd say we should assume we're not as accepted as they'd like us to think."

Before he could respond, Hestia came over to take a look at his arm. When she saw how many tubers were left in the basin, she pulled up another stool and helped them out.

The sun had set by the time all the food was prepared. As Shara helped bring it inside, she was pleased to see that the lodge was now filled with people she hadn't met yet. Though they all appeared to be humanoid, and the majority looked younger than her, Shara noted a wide range of differences in their individual features.

There were rather small people with yellow-brown skin, black hair, slanted eyes, and prominent cheekbones. There were fair men and women as tall as Gabriel with wild manes of red and blond hair and bright blue eyes. Others had skin and eyes in shades of ebony. The most unusual were the men and women whose bodies were covered in intricate tattoos rather than clothing.

As the people started making their way toward the food, Hestia grasped Gabriel's elbow. "Come with me. Apollo has arrived with my brothers."

Shara followed close behind as Hestia guided Gabriel across the room to where Athena and Artemis were speaking to a group of men. One of those men stood out, even amid such a diverse crowd. Noticeably older than those around him, he was of giant stature and physique, with a riot of light brown curls that fell below his shoulders and a full beard of similar springy coils. Beyond the physical, however, there was something so regally imposing about his bearing, he could only be one of two men—Zeus or his brother, Poseidon.

Quickly Shara ran through the legendary family history Gabriel had given her. Zeus had another brother, Hades, who was less dramatic in appearance, but had a penchant for fire and destruction. His sisters were Hestia, Demeter, and Hera, whom Zeus made his mate once he was free of the moral restrictions of the Noronian Tribunal.

By this time, he had already fathered a considerable number of children with several of his female followers, in direct opposition to the regulated birth edicts of the Tribunal. The twins Artemis and Apollo were born of one of his women. Athena from another. The way he spread his genes around before and after going to Terra, Zeus was a prime suspect in Shara's search for Khameira's rebel ancestor.

"Good eve, brother," Hestia said cheerfully as she approached the group. "I hope that scowl you are wearing is caused by an empty stomach and not a bad day. We prepared all your favorites in anticipation of either circumstance."

The big man hugged her to his barrel chest and loudly kissed her on the forehead. "The day was frustratingly unproductive. The Tribunal has once again refused to hear our petitions and the councilors are afraid to challenge them. I have no doubt your wonderful cooking will bring me out of my foul mood, though." He set her away from him as abruptly as he had hugged her. "But if you were truly concerned about my disposition, you would have brought my nectar, as you usually do."

Hestia looked to Athena, who answered for her. "That was my doing, sire. I recommended that no wines be served tonight, as we should all have clear heads for the sunrise meeting. Of course, if you wish—"

"No, no," Zeus said firmly. "You made a wise decision, as always." His gaze landed on Shara, and his scowl softened. "Do I dare hope you have come to join our family?"

Hestia spoke before Shara could reply. "Shara, Gabriel, I present Zeus, leader of this commune of Friends. They are newly arrived, brother, but I fear I must disappoint you. They are to be joined soon."

His narrowed eyes cut through Shara's tunic as he scanned her length. "Soon is not already done. Perhaps you will share a cup or two of my special nectar with me tomorrow evening."

Thinking that would be an ideal opportunity to

test him, Shara opened her mouth to accept, but Gabriel's hand clamped over her bare shoulder and squeezed a warning.

With an easy smile, Gabriel said to Zeus, "Perhaps you'd sleep better tonight if you withdrew that offer."

Zeus's laughter echoed through the lodge. "You not only look like my son Apollo, you must have his courage as well."

"Actually," Hestia said, raising her voice to turn everyone's attention to her, "Apollo is the one I brought Gabriel over here to see. He was burned while helping at the hearth."

As Apollo moved to Gabriel's side and Hestia made the formal introduction, Shara could see the resemblance between the two men. After she obtained Apollo's genetic codes, it would be interesting to compare them against Gabriel's. They were both golden specimens of manly beauty, and yet there was something remote about Apollo. Gabriel was so much more . . . touchable. Her fingernails dug into her palms to keep her hands from following the route her mind had taken.

Apollo held Gabriel's forearm as he examined the burn. Gently his fingertips stroked the blistered skin. In a surprisingly soft, melodic voice, he said, "Please close your eyes and picture your arm as it was before the accident." Gabriel did as he was told. "Now hold on to the image of the healthy skin tissue until I tell you to open your eyes." Apollo placed the palms of his hands over the burn and closed his fingers around Gabriel's arm.

Shara wondered what Gabriel was feeling. After an initial muscle twitch when Apollo enveloped the injury, Gabriel visibly relaxed except for a slight wrinkle of concentration on his brow.

Barely a few seconds passed, but it seemed much longer. No one around them spoke or moved until Apollo removed his hands from Gabriel's arm and stepped back with a confident smile.

No evidence of the burn remained!

Delighted, Gabriel flexed his fingers and rotated his forearm. "I had heard reports of your skill, Apollo. I'm honored to have experienced it personally. Thank you."

Apollo nodded. "And now perhaps we should discuss how you appear to be more of a reflection of myself than my twin sister."

"Speak of whatever you wish," Zeus grumbled, "but let us do it with food before us." Holding out his huge hand to Shara, he said more pleasantly, "You will sit by me, lovely lady. Your guardian angel cannot object to that much."

Although he said nothing, Gabriel's expression suggested he objected *very* much. She assumed he had a good reason for not wanting her so near Zeus, but she could think of no polite way to refuse. Thus, she accepted his hand to walk beside him.

Platters of food awaited them at one long table where no one had sat down yet. As soon as Zeus was seated at its head, however, the benches were soon crowded. Shara sat to his left, as he directed, and Hestia sat next to her. Apollo and Gabriel were situated a few feet away on the other side.

Hestia introduced those Shara had not met before, while everyone filled their plates. All the people at the table were followers of Zeus and resided in the commune. Most were related to him in some fashion.

When Hestia finished identifying each person, Shara could not resist commenting, "Your brother has certainly done his part to enlarge your family."

Hestia shrugged. "You must not judge him by the standards of average men. He has great appetites and believes in appeasing them."

Shara noted the mountain of food Zeus had piled in front of him, but she understood Hestia was not referring only to that.

"He is determined that our family will spawn a great dynasty. Unfortunately, he is having to do it almost singlehandedly. None of his sisters have a desire for power, nor have we proven fertile thus far. Our absent brother, Poseidon, keeps to himself most of the time. Though he has sired only a string of mutants with his mate, Amphitrite, he has taken no other women to his bed. And Hades . . ."

Shara followed Hestia's glance down to the other end of the table where Hades sat. He was dark in coloring and personality.

"Hades supports Zeus, but he has his own ideas of how changes should be accomplished, and he has yet to father any children. Of all Zeus's offspring, only a few have added children to his ranks. Apollo prefers to spend his private hours alone or with young boys. Athena and Artemis have taken vows of purity . . . though I do not believe what they do in the privacy of their cells would be considered totally pure by some."

Shara returned Hestia's knowing smile and encouraged her to continue sharing her family's secrets. The woman apparently loved to gossip, and Shara was mentally recording every detail. When Hestia ran out of tidbits about her own family, she went on to talk about the leaders of other factions of

Friends who were temporarily in residence: the barbaric Odin and his mate Frigga; the dark-skinned beauty Isis and her competitive brothers, Osiris and Set; and Scot, the eccentric leader of the tattooed clan.

Listening attentively to Hestia, Shara failed to block a mental probe for several seconds. Though unfamiliar with this type of telepathy, she was now certain that it was as individualized as fingerprints. This was the gentler of the two intrusions she had felt earlier. She looked at all the faces around her, but none gave away anything.

The touch had been so brief and light she didn't think the person would have been able to glean anything before she blocked the probe, but it was impossible to know for sure.

She held her breath, waiting for someone to alert the others that she and Gabriel were not what they claimed to be. Time passed, but no one pointed an accusing finger at her, nor did anyone attempt another probe.

The conversation grew louder and more animated as the platters of food emptied and were cleared away. All had their own ideas about how the Summit should be handled and what direction the majority of the Friends would vote to take. Shara noticed how Gabriel fingered Beauty and moved it from one angle to another as different people spoke. The light in his eyes let her know he was ecstatic about the historical recordings he was making.

Shara was asking Hestia a question when she felt a warm pressure against her leg. She shifted in the small space available without crowding Hestia. When Zeus moved as well, she was certain the contact was not accidental, even though he appeared to be totally involved in conversation with Athena.

Under the circumstances, Shara thought it would be better to ignore him than make a scene. But when his meaty hand slipped under the table and onto her knee, she changed her mind. As his fingers inched their way beneath her tunic and up her naked thigh, she leaned close to Zeus's ear and murmured, "If you wish to continue fathering your dynasty in the future, I'd suggest you remove your hand from my leg."

His hand stilled uncomfortably close to the juncture of her thighs. "You would risk your love's life over a trifling?"

Shara met his gaze with a smile. "No, I wouldn't tell him that you took his warning as a joke. I would handle the matter myself."

He continued to stare at her for several more heartbeats, then let out another roarlike laugh as he brought his hand back to his own lap. "Gods above, I like you, Shara. You could be one of my own."

I just might be, Shara thought. *We'll find out the truth soon enough.* As she turned away from him, she caught sight of Gabriel glaring at her as if she'd committed some terrible offense. Even after she resumed her conversation with Hestia, she felt him staring at her.

Despite his obvious displeasure with her, however, she hadn't expected him to do anything about it in front of so many people. She was wrong.

With a few words to those around him, Gabriel rose and came to stand at Shara's side. "It was a pleasure meeting all of you," he said, grasping Shara's upper arm and practically lifting her upright off the bench. "We are especially grateful for your kind hospitality, Zeus and Hestia, but we traveled a great distance today, so we must ask that you excuse us until dawn."

Shara barely kept her balance as he started to pull her away before she had climbed over the bench.

"Aah, the mating fever strikes again!" Zeus exclaimed, much to everyone's amusement, except Shara's.

She was going to strangle Gabriel the moment they got out of here. By the time he stopped by their bags to fetch his sleeping pouch, she was certain every person in the entire lodge assumed the same thing Zeus had—that they were rushing outside to couple before the fever reached a peak.

Walking rapidly toward the hill from where they had first seen the commune, neither she nor Gabriel said a word until they were a good distance away from the lodge. The exercise did not mellow his irritation with her, however. "Hadn't I told you enough about him? Or had I told you so much that you were tempted to try him yourself?"

"What the *drek* are you talking about?" Shara shot back as she lengthened her stride to keep up with him.

He came to a stop so abruptly, she was several steps past him before she halted as well. "I'm talking about the way you were toying with Zeus. For someone who claims to have no interest in coupling without establishing some sort of bond first, you certainly were anxious enough to share your *gifts* with him!"

Shara's mouth dropped open in shock. "You can't really believe that."

"No?" He threw the sleeping pouch onto the ground. "I told you about that special nectar of his. It was a rare, addictive aphrodisiac that not only kept him potent, but made his women so desperate for relief that they didn't mind sharing him with every other woman who caught his eye. And there you were, ready to accept his invitation to *share a cup or two with him!*"

Shara propped her fists on her hips and glared up at him. "I am not brainless or lacking in recall. I wouldn't have drunk any of it. It would have been a perfect opportunity to test him."

Gabriel narrowed his eyes at her. "Oh? Then perhaps you'd like to explain why you practically had your tongue in his ear after dinner?"

Shara gasped. "I have no idea why you think you have the right to question anything I do or with whom, but you're completely out in space on this one." She took a step closer and poked him in the shoulder. "I'll have you know, that vile man was sliding his hand up between my legs as if it were nothing more personal than a handshake. The only reason I was anywhere near his ear was so that no one else at the table would hear me threaten to castrate him!"

The stiffness went out of Gabriel's stance. "Really?"

"Look at my eyes, if you still doubt me."

The moon illuminated her face sufficiently for him to see the yellow flecks of anger and no hint of olive. He took a deep calming breath. "I'm sorry. I overreacted."

"I'll accept your apology if you'll tell me what I have done to make you think I am completely without common sense."

"I don't think anything of the sort," Gabriel retorted. "I was simply worried about you. Zeus is of a time and culture very different from ours. He was the type of male who considered a smile from a female consent enough to act on his desires. It was not beyond him to use force to gain whatever he wished, including women."

Shara still thought the excuses he was giving for his irrational behavior in the lodge were only part of the truth. "I see. Then I suppose I should thank you for preventing me from getting raped a second time in one week." She turned to walk away from him, but he caught her arm and pulled her back.

"A *second* time?" Gabriel felt the tension vibrating between them and was furious all over again that she could cause him to lose his self-control so easily. "I thought we were past that, but if you wish, we can rehash the entire sequence of events . . . including *my* rape!"

Her eyes widened, and she was about to hurl a more direct insult at him when he pressed his fingertips to her lips.

"No more. Listen to us. Sniping at each other like spoiled children." He traced her mouth, then brushed her cheek with the same fingers.

The soothing touch made her realize how foolish they were being . . . again. "You're right. I'm sorry I overreacted as well. I swear I am not usually so unreasonable."

His hand trailed down her throat and around to the nape of her neck beneath her hair. "Nor am I usually prone to jealousy."

Angling her head, she leaned a bit closer. "Jealousy?"

He nodded and held her gaze with his. As his

one hand continued to stroke her neck, the other moved to her lower back and urged her closer still. "Yes, jealous. A perfectly reasonable response, given the facts of the situation. You rejected my attention, yet you appeared to be welcoming another's. My male ego was bruised. I'll stay aware of it in the future."

She wanted to tell him she understood and appreciated his honesty, but his hands were working some sort of magic on her spine, and the way he was looking at her made her forget the words she would have said. His head lowered ever so slowly, and she willingly tipped hers in anticipation of his kiss. The thin layers of material separating their bodies could not conceal the physical changes occurring as they came together more fully, but this time those changes weren't quite as alarming to her.

Ping

Shara and Gabriel both started at the faint sound that arose from between their chests. Since he knew what had caused it, he recovered more quickly than she did.

"Yes, Beauty," he said, lifting his triangular recorder so that he was looking at its mirrored surface.

"What is it?" Shara asked anxiously. "A warning?"

"Of sorts," he said with a frown, then pressed the back of his recorder against his inner wrist. "Beauty, physiological analysis. Display pulse rate and body temperature."

Shara read the illuminated data as they appeared. His readings were in the high-normal range.

"It must have been you," he said with a crooked grin. "Hold up your hand."

She wasn't sure why he was doing this, but she obeyed. With Beauty held against her wrist, he turned her arm so that she could see herself in the mirror.

Shara's anxiety increased as she noted the new readings.

Her pulse rate was slightly above normal and her temperature was up 1.2 degrees.

9

Crossing her arms defensively, Shara said, "I have admitted that I'm . . . responsive to you. If you'll recall, I once asked you not to take advantage of my weakness by purposely seducing me. I think it's rather unkind of you to request a computerized confirmation of my vulnerability versus your near indifference to me."

His expression was one of stretched patience. "What is unkind is that you believe I would do such a thing. A moment ago you were close enough to me to know very well that I am far from indifferent toward you. I programmed Beauty to warn me of any rise in my body temperature over one degree, because I knew you would deny any evidence that the fever was still with you as long as possible. Given some notice, I thought to make the *cure* more acceptable to you. Beauty alerted me of the temperature rise, but it was you she was reading, not me."

"One degree does not necessarily mean it's the fever. We were walking very fast, then we were arguing, and then . . ." She shook her head. "A slight increase in pulse and temperature is perfectly normal under those circumstances."

"All right," he said calmly. "Let's just sit down here and talk for a while. No touching, and you choose

the subject." He unrolled his sleeping pouch on the
grass and lowered himself onto one end. "If you're
correct, our bodies' readings will both stabilize in a
few minutes."

She sat down facing him and picked an impersonal topic. "Hestia told me a lot of gossip that you
might want to add to your notes."

"That could be helpful," he said in the same pas-
sive tone he'd used before. "Tell me what you
learned."

From his perch in the tree where he had hidden
after following the strangers out of the lodge, Misha
continued to observe them for a while. It had been
a lovers' quarrel just as it had appeared to be.

And yet, in the moment he had touched the female's mind, he sensed something alien about her,
as if she weren't Noronian. Not being able to read
the man at all caused him even greater confusion.
No one knew them, and they gave no sect affiliation.
Athena had automatically assumed they were spies
for the Tribunal, but if that were the case, Misha
would have been officially notified by his superior.

Satisfied that they weren't leaving the commune,
Misha climbed back down the tree and returned to
the lodge. He didn't believe there was any new information to be picked up, but he couldn't stay away
for long without someone questioning his where-
abouts. Among the Friends, trust was in short supply, even within the family. And Zeus's habit of
ruthlessly eradicating suspected enemies was legendary.

What had begun as an exciting assignment had
quickly become tedious. The constant tension was
beginning to unnerve him and the farm chores were

demeaning, but if tomorrow's Summit proceeded as he had warned the Tribunal it would, Misha promised himself he'd be on holiday by sunset.

All the while Shara related what Hestia had told her, she worked hard to shut out any thoughts that might cause her any agitation. But her efforts seemed to have the opposite effect. The more she tried not to think about what the increased readings meant, the more nervous she became. When she lost her train of thought in midsentence, she gave up the struggle. "Show me your readings again."

He held out his arm so she could see what Beauty had to report. His pulse rate and temperature were only a fraction higher than they had been before, but the fact was, they should have been going down, not up. Unless he was ill.

Or his mating fever had been triggered.

"Your turn," Gabriel said, removing Beauty from its chain and handing it to Shara. When she hesitated to request her own readings, he asked, "Would you rather wait until you're mindless, like the last time?"

With a sigh of resignation, she asked Beauty for an update, even though she could feel a burning sensation behind her eyes and her heart was beating as if she'd just run a race. As she had guessed, the increases in her readings were greater than his had been.

"Analysis?" Gabriel asked with one raised eyebrow.

She suspected he kept using scientific words and phrases for the same reason she did—to keep her from thinking of their relationship in emotional terms. But the truth was, her emotions were in a greater state of upheaval than her body. If she could just keep the two separate, it might not be so disturbing.

With that thought in mind, she gave the analysis he'd requested. "Both our pulses and temperatures are rising, though mine are increasing at a faster rate. I suspect it has something to do with our different attitudes toward the problem. It appears that the mating—er, *simulated* mating fever did not disappear with the time-hop. Thus, we have no basis for a supposition that it will go away with the next hop, either."

He gave her a moment to continue, and when she didn't, he said, "You didn't mention the one other very important factor: The timing between attacks was shorter this time. There were about twenty-three hours between the first and second attacks. Nineteen between the second and third. If it follows the fever's standard pattern, the periods of relief will continue to diminish until we are forced to—"

"That's not going to happen! We'll be back in our own time and seeking medical treatment long before we lose all control."

"You sound very sure of that, but the fact is you have no evidence on which to make that statement. There is no record of a couple fighting the mating fever for any length of time without medical assistance. But it is known that eventually coupling will not be sufficient to cool it. If we do not get treatment and we do not join, we may both fall into a coma from which there is no return.

"In this time period we don't have many options, as far as I can tell. There is no known treatment here, and a formal joining ceremony cannot take place without two of the couple's parents to act as witnesses. Add to that the fact that we are in a volatile situation, probably being closely observed, and may not have the freedom to find privacy before the mindlessness forces us to seek relief wherever we are. I think we should consider returning to our time immediately and—"

"*No!* If we go back to be treated, we may never get the opportunity to return. You may be satisfied with the recordings you've made of this period, but I—" She stopped herself from reminding him of her goal. "I'm not ready to go back yet." She was glad she hadn't yet mentioned the additional probe during dinner. That would probably make him more determined to return. "At any rate, how can you even consider returning before tomorrow morning's meeting? Think of the invaluable research for your monograph."

He *had* been thinking of it, but he hadn't wanted to be the one to bring it up. "Then that brings us back to my earlier question. If we don't go back for treatment, we have only one cure available to us here. So what shall it be? Oblivion or conscious pleasure? Personally, I'd like to be aware of what we're sharing, for a change, but I'll leave the choice to you . . . this time."

When Shara had previously agreed to couple with him to control the fever, she had been certain it wouldn't actually be necessary. To wait for oblivion to make the decision for her was too painful and clearly dangerous to her sanity. However, she knew conscious pleasure could be almost as dangerous for her. Once she allowed her sensual nature to surface—and it would if she repeatedly shared her body with him—it would only be a matter of time before her heart became confused and thought she was in love again.

But it was a risk she would have to take. She could not go back to be treated and give up this chance to confirm her heritage when she was so very close to the answer. The only thing she could think to do to protect herself was to withhold her emotional participation from the biological act.

With her lashes lowered, she murmured, "I, too, would prefer consciousness." Keeping her gaze averted, she removed her belt, tunic, and sandals, then laid down on her back on the pouch.

Gabriel grimaced at the picture she presented. She looked as though she were about to be sacrificed. Her body was stiff, her hands balled into fists at her sides, and her eyes were squeezed shut.

And even like that, she was more beautiful than all the stars in the heavens. He felt his fever rise a degree as his body strained to be joined with hers.

Shara opened one eye. "What are you waiting for?" When he simply cocked an eyebrow at her, she thought she understood the problem and sat up. "Oh. I hadn't thought you would require my assistance. You seemed quite . . . capable of performing a few minutes ago. It would probably be most efficient if you would tell me precisely what you'd like me to do to prepare you."

"Efficient?" he asked, bewildered by the stilted words that had no correlation with the fire building in his blood. He removed his own covering and knelt beside her.

She quickly scanned his body and looked away again. "You don't appear to need any help."

"No, I suppose not. But I'd like you to touch me." His hand caressed her breast. "As I want to touch you. The fever isn't near its peak yet."

She gingerly set his hand from her. "Please don't.

If it's not absolutely necessary, I'd rather we skip any ... peripheral contact." She scratched at her arm. "My fever is building, and I'd like to get this over with as soon as possible."

Gabriel's mouth fell open. He could hardly believe what she was saying, but he could see for himself that she was being honest with him. She really didn't want him to give her pleasure, just the physical joining needed to cool the fever. It was so cold and insulting, he was tempted to walk away from her. Let her suffer from the fever's symptoms until she mindlessly attacked him again. The problem with that was, in spite of her insult, the swelling and throbbing of his genitals was becoming more uncomfortable with each of his heartbeats.

"All right, Shara. We can do this *efficiently*. Lie back and open yourself for me. I wouldn't want to *contact* you more than absolutely necessary."

She heard the hostility in his voice and knew she had hurt his manly pride, but he would get over that much easier than she would get over a broken heart. Closing her eyes, she positioned herself for his entry. When he didn't proceed immediately, she worried that her attitude had cooled his desire for her, but then he pushed inside her and began pumping without completely lowering his body onto hers. As she requested, he was touching as little of her as possible.

The act did not take long, and Shara managed to keep her mind elsewhere while her body received what it required. As before, the fever cooled once it was fed. She had gotten exactly what she asked for.

And it was more repulsive than when he had unknowingly raped her.

As soon as he was finished, Gabriel moved away.

For a while he just sat there with his back to her, taking deep, slow breaths. Then he rose and put on his tunic and sandals. "I was told there's a small lake on the other side of the west ridge. I'm going to rinse off. I suddenly feel extremely unclean."

As he started to walk in that direction, Shara had the irrational yet frightening thought that he might not come back. "Gabriel."

"What?" he asked without turning around to her.

"I won't ask you to do that again."

His shoulders relaxed slightly. "Good. Because I would refuse."

She watched him walk away, knowing he was hurt and angry with her, but certain he would return. His mention of the lake and rinsing off had her swiftly dressed and heading for the showers behind the cookhouse. Lanterns had been lit inside the lodge and multiple conversations could be heard through the open windows. It would be a while before everyone was asleep and she could begin her tests.

Feeling somewhat better after the shower, she walked back to the sleeping pouch on the hillside. Gabriel hadn't returned, but he had had much farther to walk and probably needed more time to cool down than she did.

Considering the task she wanted to perform later that night, she decided to take a short nap while she could. She got undressed, crawled into the pouch, and dozed off seconds later.

She awoke as Gabriel slid into the bag beside her, but she pretended to remain asleep. All she had to do now was wait for him to drift off, then go back down to the lodge and obtain her samples. If all went well, she would return before he missed her.

She was wondering how long he would remain angry with her when he tucked her against him with his arm around her waist. Relief that he seemed to have forgiven her caused her to nestle more comfortably in his embrace. But she was careful not to relax too much. She had work to do—work that he didn't approve of.

She waited until his breathing became shallow and the arm around her went slack. Then she began easing her way out of the pouch. She almost made it.

Gabriel's hand closed around her ankle the moment she stood up.

"Going somewhere, Shara?"

"Uh, yes, to relieve myself."

He tightened his grasp. "Lean down and give me a kiss first so I can go back to sleep."

Since that was what she wanted him to do, she knelt down to comply. He exchanged his hold on her ankle for a fistful of her hair.

"Olive," Gabriel said flatly as soon as she was close enough for him to see her eyes. He was still stinging from their mechanical encounter and this didn't improve his disposition. She tried to back away, but only succeeded in having her hair tugged. "You know better than to lie to me, and I've warned you about how lightly I sleep. I also warned you that I wouldn't allow you to do anything that might alter history, and no matter what is happening between us, I won't change my mind about that!"

Shara attempted to reclaim her hair, but his grip was too secure. "And I told you I didn't care if I had to accomplish my mission over your unconscious body. I *have* to do this!"

It occurred to him that he may have underestimated how strongly she felt about her self-assigned mission. "Fine," he said, releasing her hair and sitting up. "Let's debate the issue calmly, like two *reasonable* adults. Convince me that you're right and I'm wrong."

She wondered if there were any way she could win a straightforward debate with him. Though she doubted it, at least she had to try. "I've already told you what Lantana warned us about. The only sure way to prevent that from happening is to stop Khameira's ancestor from going to Earth."

"The Ruling Tribunal of Norona didn't agree with you," Gabriel countered.

"They didn't see him or hear him. If they had . . . if *you* had, you would understand. Lantana was a desperate man. Rather than pass away peacefully, he used the last breath in his frail body to try to save Innerworld from disaster. He spent years working on the only solution he could come up with. If I don't follow through with this, all his efforts, his entire life, were futile."

Gabriel rubbed his chin. "There are some pieces that simply don't fit here. You're not a coward, but you don't strike me as a brave, lone crusader, either. You've never had any desire to leave your home to go adventuring before this, and I'd bet you never opposed your parents in your life. Suddenly you're breaking laws and defying the greatest power in the universe to set off on a journey with practically no experience. It would make more sense to me if you had found someone who shared your opinion to go for you—someone more seasoned and less noticeable when he or she disappeared. Why take such an enormous risk yourself?"

"I had to. It's my equipment and my theories being tested."

"You could have taught someone what was needed."

"No! That wouldn't be the same. You just don't understand how important this is to me."

"Hmmm," Gabriel said, nodding slowly. "I think we're making progress now. You said, 'how important this is to me,' not to us, or to Innerworld, or Earth. Why is this mission important to you *personally*? Is it the prestige you'll earn if your theories are proven?"

She frowned at him and briefly considered lying or refusing to answer at all, but every minute he delayed her was one less minute she had to run tests. "All right. I'll tell you. While I'm searching for Khameira's ancestor, I'm hoping to find my own as well."

"It's really that important to you?" he asked, already guessing her answer.

Her eyes pleaded for his understanding. "I've existed under a cloud of doubt my whole life. This is my opportunity to learn the truth."

"And what if the truth is that you have no Noronian ancestor among the rebels? Wouldn't it be better to leave it unconfirmed?"

She shook her head. "It couldn't be worse than it's been. I want to know, one way or the other." She could see by the concerned expression on his face that she had scored a point in this debate of theirs, and quickly pressed her slight advantage. "What possible harm can my testing the rebels do?"

"I have no objection to the testing you want to do, only to your plan to interfere with events already past. The smallest change now could have horrendous repercussions thousands of years in the future. Like tossing a tiny pebble into a pond, it makes a minuscule splash, but the ripples circling out from it grow larger and larger."

She was about to argue with his theory when she realized it wasn't necessary.

As long as he didn't prevent her from testing the subjects, she didn't need to change his mind about anything else until she found the right rebel. When she did . . . well, she'd worry about dealing with Gabriel and his theories then. "I see what you mean," she told him, careful not to actually lie while he was watching her eyes so closely. "If I promise to be very careful not to cause any ripples, will you at least agree not to interfere with my testing?"

He had the strangest feeling his idea to debate the matter had somehow backfired, but he couldn't put his finger on exactly what felt wrong. His intuition told him to keep a very close eye on her. "I will do better than agree not to interfere. I'll help you. The faster you test everyone, the sooner we can go home. The fever has tied us together for the moment, and although you may not be worried about it escalating, I am."

"I'm as worried as you are; I'm just not going to let it stop me from doing what I need to do. I accept your offer to help. The hardest thing is going to be identifying everyone, but maybe between the two of us we'll remember the names of most of the people we met or were told about."

"Beauty can help with that. Remember, she was taking pictures as we were being introduced."

"Great. There are still several hours left before dawn. If we're lucky, we could be gone before their big meeting begins."

As they donned their tunics, Gabriel said, "I know

I said I'm in a hurry to get back, but since we're here, and it would only be a few more hours . . ."

Shara smiled. "It would be a real shame not to get a recording of such an historic event." In fact, Shara thought, it could work out perfectly. If they identified both people she was looking for, she could easily find her way to the Ruling Tribunal's headquarters, while Gabriel was absorbed in the proceedings of the meeting. Once the triumverate heard her story, they would surely detain the one rebel to prevent a future disaster.

They were ready to go when Shara placed her hand on Gabriel's arm. "Wait, I . . ." His eyes met hers in question. With a sigh, she made herself do the proper thing. "I really am sorry. About . . . before. It was irrational."

Gabriel brought her hand to his lips and kissed the palm. "We're both suffering from irrationality. I don't know how to make this easier for you—"

She touched his lips with her fingertips. "Just accept my apology."

He smiled and enveloped the fingers that had hushed him. "Accepted." He kept her hand in his as they began walking back to the lodge.

Shara used the time to explain how her microputer worked. Once inside, they wouldn't speak for fear of waking someone. Gabriel instructed Beauty to review the recordings and print out the name of each person he directed the mirror toward. Then if that name was on Shara's list of rebels that were exiled, she would run the test.

There was a boy in the tree where they had first seen Artemis, but since his name was not on the list, Shara didn't need a hair sample from him. They waved at the young sentry, told him they'd decided to spend the rest of the night indoors, and continued on. Only a few lanterns remained lit inside the lodge and the silence let them know their timing was good.

As they entered, it was immediately evident from the amount of floor space now vacant that a fair number of adults and children had chosen to sleep outdoors. But there were still enough in residence to put a dent in Shara's list.

She tiptoed around the edge of the room to where their bags had been left to fetch her micruputer and a tiny pair of scissors. Slightly larger than her hand, the micruputer would be difficult to conceal, and it would be impossible to pretend that it was something other than a technologically advanced piece of equipment. Possession of such a device could cause suspicion among the Friends even if she weren't sneaking around in the middle of the night. Soft snores and gentle rustlings had her gaze darting from side to side as she expected to be caught any second.

Gabriel pointed to the individual cells up in the loft, and Shara nodded. It was logical to assume that was where Zeus and his immediate family would be found, and all of them went to Earth. Shara and Gabriel climbed the ladder in one corner and began their search.

Shara bolstered her nerve and peeked into the first draped cell, but it was too dark to see. Gabriel stepped forward and extracted his paralyzer rod from inside the top of his tunic. Shara's eyes widened with confusion until she saw him change the setting, and a beam of soft white light brightened the interior.

When she recognized the single occupant, she

touched the key on her microputer that brought up the list of names and scrolled down to Hestia. Another key checked off the name and prepared the device for input. Holding her breath, she approached the sleeping woman, snipped off a single hair, and hurried out.

Her hands were shaking a bit as she fed the hair into a slot at one end of the microputer. The unit analyzed the cell structure and recorded the memory molecule's combination of genetic codes under Hestia's name. A third key instructed the microputer to compare the codes with those of Khameira's, and a fourth triggered a comparison with Shara's.

She did not tell Gabriel which was which, for if a match to hers came up, he would undoubtedly insist they stop the search, and she had no intention of stopping until she found Khameira's match as well.

When no match occurred for Hestia, Shara went on to the next cell. Beauty was needed to identify the young couple inside, but only the woman required testing.

Shara got braver as they moved along the row of sleepers, though she found herself flustered by some of the situations she witnessed. It was soon clear why *love* was part of their traditional greeting.

It was also obvious that they believed in freedom from any moral strictures. Although the average Innerworlder's attitude toward sexual relations was much freer than what Shara's mother had been raised with on Outerworld, they drew the line of acceptability at incest and using children.

Artemis slept with her head on Athena's bared breast. Apollo shared his cell with a pretty, preadolescent boy named Hyacinthus. Isis and her two brothers were intimately entwined as if they had all fallen asleep in the midst of foreplay. Very few people slept alone and several cells were occupied by more than two.

Shara and Gabriel were three-quarters of the way around the loft when they found Zeus's cell. They had not located a match among any of Zeus's children, but Shara still wanted to test him to be completely certain.

The huge man was sprawled on his back, embracing a woman on each side of him. Shara had been slipping in and out of the cubicles, trying not to look at anything but faces and hair, but she couldn't help but notice Zeus's manhood. Even at rest it was abnormally large. She felt a shiver of fear at the thought of the pain he could cause if he wasn't in a gentle mood.

Distracted, Shara accidentally bumped into someone's foot. One of the women's eyes blinked open and she squinted at the intruders.

10

The beeping of the telecommunicator awoke Rom from an already fitful sleep. Peculiar nightmares kept disturbing him, and he was uncomfortably aware that Aster was having a similar problem. All day they had been bothered by the sensation that they had forgotten something, without having any idea what it could be.

Aster sat up as he accepted the call.

"This is Illana in Communications. I'm sorry to disturb you, Governor Romulus, but you had requested that we contact you as soon as a message was received from Norona."

Aster reached for Rom's hand as he said, "Yes. Go ahead."

"The security squad assigned to locate Shara Locke reports that, although there are witnesses who report she was on board and no one saw her leave the ship after it docked, authorities were unable to locate her after a thorough search. Another passenger, Gabriel Drumayne, Professor of History and Chief Procurer of Antiquities for Norona, is also unaccounted for."

"A history professor?" Rom asked aloud, though he knew he'd heard correctly.

Aster squeezed his hand. "Shara always had problems in her history classes."

Rom ended the call before responding to his mate. "Apparently she's now having problems obeying orders also. *Drek*! If she used the tempometer in direct defiance of the Tribunal's decision, she's actually broken laws."

Aster gaped at him in disbelief. "Are you saying our daughter is now a criminal?"

"I think we'd better start assuming the worst."

"Dear Lord! What could have possessed her to fool around with that device?"

Rom shook his head. "It certainly doesn't sound like her to do this. At least she had the sense to take someone knowledgeable with her, though I would have preferred that she had a guardian more resourceful than most of the academy professors I've known."

Aster rose from the bed and was out of the room before Rom caught up with her. "What are you doing?" he asked as she sat down in front of the computer.

"I'm checking on the professor."

Before she began her query, the telecommunicator beeped again. This time it was Gerald, Chief of Scientific Research. He skipped the usual pleasantries. "Sorry to disturb you, but I didn't think this should wait. We've just had another incident, only this one occurred in front of witnesses. A new cargo ship changed shape."

Rom and Aster glanced at each other, then asked him to explain.

"The ship was in Hangar B, looking normal; then, in the blink of an eye, the structural design changed. Because of the other incidents, we immediately checked with an engineer who had worked on the ship. He verified that the new body was the one discarded when the ship was first designed."

"Excuse me, Chief," Rom said, feeling very confused and almost overwhelmed by the sense of forgetfulness. "What are the other incidents you mentioned?"

"You don't remember either?"

Aster's stomach was getting queasier by the second. "What is it we've forgotten?"

Gerald pinched the bridge of his nose. "The day before yesterday, you were one of several people who reported an alteration." He reminded them about their chair and some of the others. "We have it all recorded, and my team has been working on an explanation, but now it seems that the individuals who noted the changes don't fully remember them. For instance, tell me what pattern is on the new chair by your fireplace."

Aster looked at it and said, "Stripes."

"Was it always striped?"

"Well, of course—" Abruptly she had a mental picture of the exact chair with a floral print, and Rom sent her a thought that it seemed vaguely familiar to him as well. "Now I'm not sure."

The chief sighed. "That's the same thing I've heard several times. Apparently there were a number of things that changed around the same time, but now people's memories seem to be adjusting to the changes as if they had always been that way. However, the records we made after the alterations have remained intact as far as we can tell.

"Based on what has happened so far, we are assuming the ship alteration will not be the only one reported in the next few hours when people start waking up, but some time afterward, they may not remember it being any other way. It's as if history is being changed in very subtle ways and it takes a while longer for the memory to catch up."

Aster's eyes widened at the word *history*, and Rom's fears mirrored hers. If Shara had truly traveled back into the past, she could be doing small things that were affecting present time.

Rom cleared his throat nervously. "There's something you need to know about, Gerald. Call a meeting of your team immediately. Aster and I will meet you in your office."

They disconnected and quickly got dressed to go. Aster wrote a brief note to inform Mack where they were going, and went into his room to set it on his nightstand. The moment she entered the room, the blood rushed from her head as panic stabbed her chest.

The room was decorated entirely differently—the way it had been before Mack was born. None of Mack's favorite pictures were on the walls. None of his belongings were on the furniture, or the floor, or in the closet.

But worse than that, there was no Mack, as if all traces of him had been completely erased!

11

Shara was momentarily frozen with fear as she stared at the woman she had awakened. The last thing in the world she wanted was to be caught in Zeus's private cubicle. Just as Shara was certain the woman was going to alert her lover to their unexpected visitors, the woman's gaze focused on Gabriel, and she smiled her willingness to have him join their group.

As she held out her hand and her mouth opened to speak, Shara threw a mental suggestion at her. Instantly the woman's hand dropped, her eyes closed, and she fell back to sleep.

As quickly as possible, she had Beauty confirm the two women's identities and collected hair from all three of the sleepers. Hurrying out of the cell to run her tests, she noticed the way Gabriel was glaring at her and guessed the reason. However, she couldn't risk defending the misuse of her ability while they might be overheard.

By the time they'd visited every cell in the loft, ninety-two names were checked off the list without a match turning up. They eliminated a dozen more on the ground floor before their luck ran out. Gabriel saw Hestia climbing down the ladder and motioned for Shara to hide the microputer. She barely managed to get it into her bag before Hestia walked up to her.

"Good day," Hestia whispered. "You're up very early."

Palming her miniature scissors, Shara smiled and kept her voice hushed as well. "We thought you might need help in the cookhouse extra early, with the Summit set for dawn."

Hestia beamed her gratitude and waved for them to follow her. On the way out, she nudged several people who must have been assigned to help with breakfast. That started a chain reaction, and before long, everyone was coming awake despite the early hour.

Shara and Gabriel were given the chore of scrambling eggs and cooking them in an enormous frying pan over one of the fires. As he began cracking shells, she hurried back to her bag for a quantity of static paper and a pencil and tucked those items and the scissors inside her tunic. Though she wouldn't be able to refer to the list or run the test, she could still collect samples if she was careful and quick enough.

As soon as she returned to the cookhouse, she told Gabriel she'd be moving around all morning trying to get to people they'd missed, and that he shouldn't be concerned about her. When he did no more than nod and look away, she knew he was still upset with her. "I know you don't approve of what I did, but I didn't think I had any other choice under the circumstances."

Out of the side of his mouth, he murmured, "I could have put her back to sleep with my paralyzer."

"My way was faster and ensured that she wouldn't remember seeing us." He was only partly convinced.

"All right. I panicked. I *never* use that ability . . . well, hardly ever. And you know I can't use it against you as long as you're wearing the jammer. There was no harm done. Why are you so angry about it?"

"Because my sister had the same skill, and she wasn't the least bit discriminating about how she manipulated other people with it. I was one of her favorite targets, since I had no way of sensing what she was up to. Of course, you wouldn't have had to use it at all if you'd been paying attention to what you were doing instead of fantasizing."

His change of attack made no sense to her. "I beg your pardon?"

Rather than answer, he transferred the cooked eggs into a large bowl and carried it into the lodge.

She had another batch started before he came back. "Explain your last comment about my fantasizing," she demanded.

"If you didn't limit your relations with men so drastically, Zeus's overendowment may not have distracted you. I'm sure if you're curious about just how big it could get, he'd be more than willing to give you a private demonstration."

"Gabriel Drumayne! You're being a dolt. I was stunned, not *fantasizing*." She remembered what he'd said earlier about feeling jealous. After what she'd put him through last night, he probably had reason to be a little insecure if he thought she was aroused by a man with greater proportions than his formidable self. However, it was still surprising that his ego could be shaken so easily.

"Listen to me, Professor, and listen well because I am not prone to flattering men very often. You are the most attractive, appealing man in this whole place, including the lovely Apollo. *If* I wanted to couple with someone I did not have an emotional bond with, you would be the one I'd choose, even without the fever. You have absolutely no reason to be jealous."

"Jea—" His scowling expression turned sheepish. "Oh. I apologize. Once again, I'm afraid the fever has me behaving in very unfamiliar ways."

"It's partially my fault," Shara admitted. "I've been acting as if my feelings in this are the only ones that matter. I believe my attitude has made a difficult situation worse." She touched his cheek to make him look at her. "From now on, I'll try not to be part of the problem."

He took her hand in his and kissed her palm the sensual way he had done before. An almost imperceptible shiver let him know Shara liked that more than she would admit. With a teasing grin, he said, "And I'll try to remember that I'm the most attractive man around."

"You're going to make me sorry I said that, aren't you?"

He gave her a wink and took another bowl of scrambled eggs into the lodge.

Gabriel felt as though he were a boat caught in a terrible storm, being helplessly tossed to and fro. The only thing to do was ride it out and pray for salvation. There was some relief in Shara promising to change her attitude and admitting that she found him appealing. He didn't welcome the symptoms of the mating fever any more than she did, but fighting it was not the answer.

He hated what she had forced him to do last night, but it had helped him understand something she had said before. Where she didn't want to share her body without an emotional bond, he had cou-

pled with women after little more than an exchange
of smiles. What he and Shara had done shouldn't
have bothered him in the least.

But it had, because with Shara the physical release wasn't enough. He wanted her to like him. He
wanted her to like touching him. He wanted her total attention.

He wanted more than she was willing to give.

That realization stopped him in his tracks. He had
always backed away from females who wanted more
from him than a pleasurable hour, and he had never
had the desire for more than that from any of them.
He supposed this possessiveness with Shara could
be another side effect of the fever, but it still had to
be dealt with until they received treatment.

"Gabriel!"

He was startled out of his reverie by the realization that Shara was standing in front of him and had
apparently asked him something. "I beg your pardon?"

"Take this," she said pushing a platter of meat into
his hands. "Are you all right? You were standing
there with a strange look on your face."

He nodded. "I'm fine. Just daydreaming a bit. This
is all pretty incredible for a history fanatic."

As he helped carry the rest of the cooked food
inside, he purposely thought about the unique opportunity he'd been given and what priceless information he was gathering. Within moments, however,
his mind drifted back to Shara's admission.

Surely her finding him appealing was a step toward the kind of bond she felt was so important.
The fact that they had helped each other survive
their sojourn in the Frozen Era and were now working together on her personal project should be an-

other big step or two. What else would she need to allow herself to enjoy coupling with him?

She had mentioned wanting to have everything in common with the man who would be her soulmate. From what he could tell so far, they had absolutely nothing in common . . . except the fever. Everything, from their upbringings to their lifestyles to their careers to their mental abilities, was at opposite ends of the spectrum.

Considering just how opposite their mental abilities were made his stomach clench, and he felt as if he were on a storm-tossed boat. Shara possessed the one ability he feared most. If he didn't have his jammer, she could twist him into anything she wanted, dangle him like a marionette from strings she carelessly controlled, and he would never know she was doing it.

That was what Janna had done to him for years, until their parents found out and mentally ostracized her for a week. The same silence Gabriel had hungered for had frightened his sister so much, she abided by every rule from then on.

When he had misbehaved in an attempt to earn the same punishment, they took pity on poor untalented Gabriel and waived the usual ostracism. He couldn't win then, and his luck didn't seem to have improved in all these years.

The first female that he desired to spend more than an hour with also made him want to avoid involvement with her at any cost.

Again he ordered himself to concentrate on his work. *That* was why he was here, not to moon over a woman like some lovesick adolescent. But his research—the one and only passion in his life—had abruptly taken a second position behind his preoccupation with Shara.

He knew it wasn't logical, but he resented her more for that than any of the things she had done to him consciously. If she would at least stop fighting him about coupling, perhaps he could get his mind back on his work.

As they sat down to eat, he decided that Shara seemed to be suffering from a similar contradiction of wanting and not wanting, though their mutual discomfort was little consolation. He remembered her heated response to their first kiss in the biodrome and how she had welcomed his body into hers when they had first landed in the Frozen Era.

With her mind on saving his life, she hadn't refused his touch and by allowing that, her passion flared before she had a chance to analyze it to death. On reflection, giving her a chance to think was what had ended the interlude in the biodrome.

She had asked him not to touch her more than necessary last night. Actually, she had voiced objections to his touching her from the minute they met. That fact presented an interesting supposition.

Perhaps it was her own passionate nature she was fighting, rather than his. Wanting him without that bond would go against her personal moral code. Understanding why she acted as irrationally as she did, however, did not help him figure out a way around that code. There had to be something they had in common that would put her at ease about this peculiar relationship they'd been forced into. However, as long as they disagreed on the subject of altering history, he wasn't sure that it was possible for him to put her at ease.

The first hint of daylight interrupted his further

contemplation of their dilemma. Everyone pitched in to clean up so that the Friends could get on with the morning's business. He chuckled to himself when he noticed how quickly Shara took advantage of the commotion to get a few more samples. Without anyone being the wiser, she stole a hair, stuck it to a piece of static paper, and wrote a name beneath it. If she didn't know someone's name, she simply introduced herself first and then found out.

As more people arrived, he accompanied Shara to the entranceway so that Beauty could record the multitude of introductions. He then stayed by her side, helping with identification, shielding her actions from onlookers, and keeping conversations going while she labeled each sample she acquired.

The crowd inside the lodge swelled to capacity by the time the sun was fully above the horizon. The sect leaders gravitated to one end of the hall while everyone else milled around, exchanging information and opinions. As chairs were being placed in a row atop one long table, Gabriel let Shara know he was leaving her to claim a spot in front for Beauty and himself.

One representative from each sect climbed up on the table and took a seat, with Zeus commandeering the center position. At his sides were Odin, Isis, Scot, Albion, Danu, Pele, and three more men Gabriel hadn't met.

Odin motioned to his son standing below him, and the younger man pounded on the wooden table with a large mallet. The banging continued until everyone quieted and faced forward.

"Thank you, Thor," said Zeus in a booming voice that easily carried to the back of the room. "And thank you all for coming to this Summit. I wish you friendship, peace, and love." He struck his left breast twice and offered his hand in the gesture that stood for their beliefs. Almost in unison, the motto was repeated and the sign returned to him by everyone in the lodge.

"Please extend our greetings and appreciation to all of the loyal Friends who remained behind to tend your communes while you tended to their futures. For those of you who just arrived in our region, I will bring you up to date."

For the next half hour, he detailed the various endeavors made by the representatives on the dais. They had tried every method available to voice their concerns and protest Tribunal actions through the legal system. They met with regional councilors to state their objectives, filed a multitude of petitions, and submitted the proper forms to request a hearing in front of the Ruling Tribunal.

Repeatedly the Tribunal refused to grant them an audience, thereby refusing to recognize the Friends as a legitimate interest group. Two of the councilors had attempted to speak to the Tribunal for the Friends, but they, too, were refused admittance to the private chambers of the powerful triumvirate.

Zeus had remained seated as he outlined their activities in a flat, rather bored voice, and the people in the room grew restive. But when he paused and rose to his full, imposing height, they immediately stilled.

"Yesterday we met with those two councilors who had been sympathetic to our views. Although they say they still believe in the Friends' movement, they are no longer willing to risk their positions for us. They feel our battle is lost."

"*Never!*" shouted a man from the back of the

room. A chorus of voices called out their agreement until the chant of "*Never*" was accompanied by stomping feet and the lodge walls trembled from the emotional uproar.

Order was restored with the help of Thor's hammer.

Zeus raised his voice a bit more and allowed his hostility to filter through. "They say we cannot manage our own lives apart from the Ruling Tribunal and its suffocating laws!" His audience protested, but Zeus's words thundered over them. "They say we cannot use our mental abilities to their fullest extent, that only the Tribunal has that right. They say we cannot have the freedom we've requested so peacefully!"

"*Freedom!*" became the chant of the angry crowd, and Zeus made no attempt to calm them. Gabriel could feel the raw excitement building in those around him. Knowing what was about to happen enhanced his fascination with how it had come about.

Like a symphony conductor, Zeus made a slashing motion to silence everyone, then roared, "The decision is in your hands this morning. Do we settle back and allow the Tribunal to prod us from place to place like the cows in our pastures?"

"*No!*" the Friends yelled back at him.

"Then what say you to your elected representatives seated here before you? What is your desire?"

A hushed murmur passed through the crowd like an electrified wave as the row of men and women on the makeshift dais glanced at one another in anticipation and uncertainty.

"*Revolt!*" a woman cried a few feet away from Gabriel. It was Hera, Zeus's sister, and the look that Zeus gave her spoke of his admiration.

"Revolt! Revolt!" The shout was deafening, as one by one the leaders stood up to endorse the cry.

In an exaggerated gesture, Zeus slowly curled the fingers of his right hand into his palm, thumped his breast twice, then shot the mighty fist upward and held it there.

Each of the other leaders imitated his action. Within seconds, the identifying hand signal of the Friends had changed from a show of friendship, peace, and love to defiance, war, and hatred.

"We have a plan ready to be implemented immediately," Zeus told the crowd. "But its success depends on each of you. If there are any among you who are not prepared to commit their lives to the cause, let them depart now, for there can be no turning back once we begin."

Like those around him, Gabriel turned to see if any cowards dared to make themselves known. None did. But history had it that someone betrayed the Friends from within.

Zeus clapped his hands together once and proceeded. "Excellent. The main thrust of this plan is that, through surprise, aggression, and limited violence, we will lay siege to the First Province Administration Building and the Ruling Tribunal's headquarters. Our opponents will discover what it is like to have *their* freedom withheld. At the same time, we will invade all of the councilors' private residences for the purpose of holding their family members hostage. They will become pawns in the negotiating that will commence once the Tribunal realizes how strong and determined we are.

"We will now go outside to divide up into teams. Captains have been preselected and given specific assignments to carry out."

Those words prompted everyone on the dais and a number of people in the audience to don purple headbands. Gabriel had to admire the smooth choreography of Zeus's show.

"You may remain with your sect or join up with another group. My brother, Hades, needs twelve brave volunteers to assist him in setting up distractions while the rest of us are moving into position for the takeovers. Those willing to take a slight risk should meet him in the barn. Once the teams are set, the captains will give each of you individual instructions."

Zeus paused and scanned the sea of anxious faces, then shouted, "In two hours we will march to victory and freedom!" Again he punched his fist skyward and held it there as the gesture was imitated throughout the room. Excited cheers and whistles echoed off the walls as the outer doors were thrown open and everyone began pushing toward the exits.

Gabriel searched for Shara in the crush of bodies. He had been so enthralled by the proceedings, he hadn't noticed what part of the room she was in. Suddenly he caught sight of her near one exit. Her worried face and frantic hand gestures as she spoke to people passing by alerted Gabriel to trouble. As quickly as possible, he fought his way through the crowd to her.

"Please listen to me," she was saying to no one in particular. "Just slow down and think about what you're doing. Someone could be hurt!"

Gabriel grabbed her arm and jerked her toward him. "What the *drek* do you think you're doing?"

She made an attempt to free herself, but the crowd held her captive as much as Gabriel. "I'm trying to save lives! Zeus got them all so stirred up, they're ready to commit suicide for this cause of theirs."

"That's right," Gabriel murmured sternly next to her ear. "And you can't stop them."

"At least I can try!"

He quickly looked around and was relieved to see that no one seemed to be paying attention to them. With her in tow, he elbowed a path through the crowd to an empty corner.

"You're manhandling me again!" Shara glared at him as he blocked her escape with his body.

"You wouldn't have come with me if I'd asked nicely."

She opened her mouth to contradict him, but she knew he was right. "I was only trying to get someone to listen to reason before they—"

He cut her off by giving her shoulders a slight shake. "It's *you* who has to listen to reason, not them. This is the way it happened then and you weren't here to stop anyone. You can't interfere with what's already done."

"But you told me people were killed, *children* were maimed. We could spare some of them if we just—"

"*No!* We can't take that chance. What if you spare one who should have died and another dies who shouldn't have? *Think*, Shara. Use that analytical mind of yours. By interfering with what actually occurred, you could cause the elimination of someone whose descendant was important to our history. Without that rebel's survival, the descendant would never be born."

She could hardly argue with that theory, since she had returned to this time to prevent Khameira from being born on Earth in the future. "I don't like this one bit."

"Are you ready to go back?"

She straightened her shoulders and shook her head. "No. Not yet. I have to run tests on all the samples I collected this morning and check the names against the list. I'm sure I'm missing some."

"Then at least get the tempometer belt and put it on. Everyone's too busy to notice it. I'd like to be able to make a fast exit if—"

Before Gabriel could complete his sentence, Zeus walked up to them with a curious look on his face. "Is there a problem?"

As Gabriel had feared, Shara had been observed. He shook his head and gave Shara a hug. "Just a case of nerves, I'm afraid."

Zeus nodded as if he understood and patted them each on their shoulders, but his eyes revealed a continued wariness. "Do not worry, friends, your oath to postpone your joining in support of our cause was a worthy one, and you will be well rewarded for your sacrifice very soon now. Since you have no loyalties to a particular sect, I would be delighted to have you march alongside me."

12

Gabriel's instincts told him this was a test. He tried to think of a reason to decline that wouldn't raise Zeus's suspicions about them even further, but Shara spoke before he could come up with one.

"It would be our extreme pleasure," she said with a shaky smile. "I'll just get my bag and we'll be right with you."

Zeus waved a hand at her. "Not necessary. Arrangements have already been made to provide everything we might need. Come. Time is wasting."

As they followed Zeus outside, Gabriel whispered to Shara, "Why did you agree?"

"I had a queer feeling about the way he was looking at us."

"Me, too. According to history, the Tribunal received advance notice of the attack from someone who had been at the Summit. Undoubtedly Zeus would have been on the lookout for an informer. He might think we're spies for the Tribunal, since we're not connected with any known sect. In which case, it would make sense for him to keep us close, or at least make sure someone is watching us at all times. But I certainly would have felt a lot better if we had the tempometer with us."

Shara didn't like leaving her micropputer behind, either, but Zeus hadn't left them any choice. Thank the stars she had decided to stow her supplies and hair samples in her bag or he might have noticed the bulge in her tunic and questioned it. She looked around at the people separating into groups. If there was such a spy, he or she probably would have slipped away during the commotion at the end of Zeus's speech.

Athena called Zeus over to her group to ask a question, and Gabriel and Shara took the opportunity to move out of anyone's hearing range. Still, Gabriel kept his voice lowered as he said, "Shara, I'm very serious now. Please keep in mind what I said about interfering and stick by me. We're marching into one of the most violent situations in Noronian history, and even though we weren't around at this time, our lives can be ended all the same."

"Terrific," she said with a grimace. "Well, I suppose we could look on the bright side. You'll be going back with recordings that will have the academic community standing on its head for priority viewing."

"True, but I'm accustomed to taking risks to get to the facts. You aren't. Perhaps my going would be enough to calm Zeus's suspicions. He might accept an excuse of jangled nerves or cowardice from you, and you could stay here. That way at least one of us would be able to get back to our own time."

"Cowardice! No, thank you. That would probably convince him that I am a spy, and he'd leave one of his henchmen behind to eliminate me. Besides, not knowing whether you were safe would drive me insane."

He lifted her face to his for a quick kiss. "How nice. You do care."

"I don't . . . well, I do, but not . . ." She paused to control her fumbling. "I was thinking about the fever."

Gabriel winked. "Of course you were." He locked his fingers through hers and guided her back to Zeus. When she tried to free her hand, he held it more tightly. "We're supposed to be madly in love with each other, remember? I think it would be a good idea to act as if we really are . . . for Zeus's sake, if nothing else. He might decide to make sure we're two of the casualties today if we're not convincing in our roles."

Suddenly Shara felt as though a needle had been inserted in her brain. She instantly blocked the intrusion, but the unexpected pain caused her to stumble.

Gabriel braced her as she swayed. "What's the matter?"

"Someone just tried to probe me again. And none too gently, I might add." She glanced at the group around Zeus and noted the curious expression on Athena's face. The first time Shara had felt a sharp prick of mental invasion like that, Athena had been present. "I think this time it's Athena. She's probably been planting suspicions in Zeus's head because she can't get a reading from either one of us."

Gabriel pretended to be checking Shara's temperature and peered into her eyes. "Can you make her believe she got through to you and that we're loyal Friends?"

Shara angled her head at him. "Probably, but I thought—"

"Just do it," he ordered tersely.

Shara forced the suggestion into Athena's mind and a second later Athena nodded to Zeus. The relaxed smile he gave them as they approached confirmed Shara's suspicions.

"Athena needs two more soldiers for her team," Zeus said. "She will be taking control of one of the councilors' residences. It is larger than the others and he has a staff of employees there with his mate and children who will need to be guarded. At any rate, you will see more action marching with her. My team will be the last to arrive in the city, since I have to see everyone else off to the right posts first. Good luck to all of you."

He strode off before Shara or Gabriel could protest. She wanted no part of anything in which children might be hurt. Regardless of the warnings Gabriel had given her, she could never stand by and do nothing but watch.

Shouted orders caused everyone to look toward the barn. Four large horses plodded out pulling a long wagonload of wheat tied in bundles. An adolescent boy controlled the reins and next to him on the seat was a younger girl. Hades jogged along beside the wagon until it was in the midst of the teams of people. He then told the boy to halt and pounded on the side of the wagon.

Shara was completely surprised as one side of the layer of wheat lifted like a hinged door. The wheat, adhered to a thin layer of wood, formed the lid for a box beneath it, and a group of men and women were opening it from inside. Everyone cheered as Hades' team propped the lid open and began passing out weapons.

"Don't be concerned," Athena said, noting Shara's expression. "The arms are to give an illusion of force only. There will be no need to resort to actual violence."

Gabriel pulled Shara away as her mouth opened to protest. In a hushed voice, he issued a stern reminder. "Unless you're anxious to turn all this negative energy against us, you'd better start controlling your reactions."

He was right; it was just so difficult knowing what the future held. She reluctantly nodded and turned her attention to the activity around Hades' wagon. Somehow Shara had imagined that with their objection to technology the Friends would have used something rather primitive. The arms being distributed weren't as sophisticated as Gabriel's paralyzer rod, but they were considerably more advanced than bows and arrows.

Gabriel identified the weapons for Shara. Most of them were shooters that used caustic ammunition and could be tucked into the rebels' belts, but there were also larger armaments, such as the pipe guns that ejected balls of fire. To his knowledge, the only people permitted to own weapons of any kind were those employed in the Security Services. Thus, these must have been illegally obtained.

When everyone who wanted a weapon had one, Hades joined the team inside the wagon, the lid was lowered, and the children drove it off toward the city.

As promised, precisely two hours after the Summit ended, Zeus gave the signal for the march to begin. The plan was that by the time the various sects neared their destinations, Hades' group would have a distraction of explosions and fireworks ready to blow. Gabriel told Shara it sounded as though he would be detonating incendiary devices by remote control—another odd concession to technology.

The four-kilometer walk was going much too quickly for Shara's peace of mind. With Athena walking beside them, she and Gabriel refrained from discussing anything more important than the beautiful weather the Friends had been granted for their strike. It took a superhuman effort for her to act as excited as everyone around her when the truth was she was terrified.

The only thing that kept her from taking off in a panic was the way Gabriel held on to her hand the whole time—giving it an occasional squeeze, stroking the back of it with his thumb, or bringing it to his lips for a light kiss. The adoring way he looked at her when their eyes met almost made her wish it wasn't just a role he was playing for Athena's sake.

But he'd made it abundantly clear that she would be the last female he could ever fall in love with. She had mental abilities that he resented, she wasn't a seasoned journeyer, she lacked the mild disposition and good sense of humor he preferred, and she had convinced him she was not interested in coupling with him.

Of course, the last negative quality wasn't true, but he didn't know that. And she'd only lost her normally mild disposition after she met him. The fact remained, however, that even if she could change all of those things to please him, he still didn't want a mate in his life and so he would never willingly accept a soulmate, who would take up residence in his mind.

Gabriel squeezed her hand. "Are you all right?"

She forced a smile. "Yes, why?"

He shrugged. "For some reason I just got the impression you were sad about something. It felt strange, as if I were feeling it for you."

She turned her eyes away from his. "I'm worried about what's coming, that's all." Shara told herself Gabriel had probably not picked up an actual emotion from her. More than likely he was reading her facial expression or eye color. After all, he wasn't empathic or telepathic, and they weren't joined, so he shouldn't be able to sense what she was feeling.

Then again, they shouldn't be suffering the symptoms of the mating fever, either.

The closer they got to the city, the faster the army marched. At the first sight of their goal, one team broke into a run and had to be threatened with injury by Zeus to prevent a stampede.

Zeus ordered everyone to halt when they neared the top of the last hill on their march.

Shara looked out over a city that contrasted drastically with the commune they'd left behind, yet bore little resemblance to the First Province Administration Building of her time. Now it was only a small fraction of its future size. Rather than sparkling crystal prisms, the buildings were constructed of white and gray stone. Vehicles moved along on overhead rails instead of cushions of air.

Though different in physical ways, this city still exuded the aura of great power that Shara had sensed on previous visits in her own time. She wondered how the Friends could believe they were capable of overcoming that power with armaments.

Zeus moved from team to team, issuing final orders and wishes for success. The groups assigned to take over the councilors' residences departed first, since they needed to secure the hostages before the main body of Friends surrounded the Administration

Building. As Athena's team made its way down the slope, Shara looked up at Gabriel, hoping he would read the fear in her eyes and say something to reassure her.

Gabriel pulled Shara to a stop and told Athena, "We'll catch up in a minute." Athena narrowed her eyes at him, but continued on with her team.

"What's the matter?" Shara whispered. "She's already suspicious of us."

"She won't question lovers sharing one last kiss before going into battle."

Shara's breath caught in her throat at the mere mention of a kiss and her gaze held to the lips she knew could make her forget the rest of the universe existed. Without waiting for his lead, she stepped closer and placed her hands on his shoulders. One of his kisses was exactly what she needed.

However, as his arms brought her snugly against him, his mouth moved to her ear. "I'm going on," he murmured, hugging her affectionately. "This is too rare for me to miss. But you could still go back or wait here."

The sharp disappointment she felt at not being kissed was distracting, but she made herself reply to his comment. "Zeus is behind us. He'd just drag me along with him, and if I have to go, I'd feel safer with you."

"I appreciate your confidence. I'll make sure you don't regret it." He moved his head back and tipped up her chin. "I'm going to kiss you now. For the benefit of any observers, try to look as if you're enjoying yourself."

He may not have meant the direction as an insult, but she took it as one and determined to repay him instantly. The moment his mouth pressed to hers, she concentrated on giving him the most intense kiss she knew how to give. As her lips moved over his, her body joined the assault. Shifting her hips into his, she received an immediate response.

She nipped his lower lip and gained access for her tongue to play inside. He met her thrust and parried, and returned her efforts with equal enthusiasm.

It was no longer clear who was the aggressor, nor did it matter in the slightest. All that mattered was that they were together, kissing, holding, touching. As Shara had desired, the rest of the world fell away until there was only Gabriel. Wanting to express her need more clearly, she slid her hand down his side and was about to ease it beneath his short tunic when the sound of laughter nearby jolted her back to reality.

Gabriel ended the kiss but continued to hold her tightly as he struggled to regain control of his body. He was disoriented and gasping for breath, but she was trembling, and somehow he knew the reason without having to ask. "It's all right, sweetling. They aren't laughing at you."

She glanced up at him in surprise, then hid her face in his neck. He had guessed what she was thinking! Her cheeks were flushed with embarrassment and her stomach was twisted in a knot.

For a second she had been a young girl again, and the other children were all laughing at her . . . the tall, clumsy mixed-breed.

And Gabriel had understood.

"Gabriel! Shara! Come along!" The shout was from Athena. She had stopped her team part of the way down the hill to await the stragglers.

Shara began to move away, but Gabriel held her in place.

"Wait," he said softly. "I want you to know something before we go on." He combed his fingers through her hair. "That was real just now. Not the fever. Not an act for anyone else. I wasn't thinking about who your parents are or what either of us is doing here. The only thing on my mind was how much I wanted you."

His sincere words were another kind of caress— warmer, steadier—and she stopped trembling. "It was real to me, also," she admitted. "I won't deny it anymore."

"Good," he said with a smile, and took her hand in his to catch up with their team. "Now let's try to stay in one piece today so we can finish what we started in a more romantic setting."

Shara met his gaze and smiled back. A few days ago she would have considered his remark arrogant. Now she thought it was logical . . . and provocative. Changes were being forced on her, and she was no longer sure they were all bad . . . even if it was only temporary.

As they neared the section of the city where most of the councilors resided, their march took on the appearance of a leisurely stroll, but there was no one to perform for. It was almost midday. There should have been a number of residents moving about, but the only people in view were the Friends, getting into position.

Athena posted a soldier at the side and back door of the home she was responsible for, then led the rest of the team straight to the front entrance. Having no reason to expect treachery, someone inside opened the door. Athena and the others carrying shooters pulled them out as they all charged into the large receiving room of the residence. Shara and Gabriel found themselves swept along in the rush.

Before the Friends had a chance to establish themselves, however, they were surrounded by black-uniformed security officers, all of whom had shooters pointed at the trespassers. Every exit from the room was effectively blocked.

"Hold position!" ordered one officer. "Drop your weapons and surrender peaceably."

Instead of obeying, one of Athena's soldiers raised his shooter, and the officer instantly fired at him. The shock of being trapped had momentarily frozen the group, but seeing their friend fall with a smoking hole in his chest inflamed them to act.

Gabriel shoved Shara to the floor as another weapon was fired and a woman screamed in pain. Protecting Shara's body with his own, he ordered her to feign death, while the room exploded into chaos. More deafening blasts struck moving targets. Objects crashed to the floor as tables were toppled to create shields. Everyone was shouting and no one was listening.

As suddenly as the violence had erupted, it ceased. The smell of smoke and burned flesh permeated the air, and painful moans throughout the room were the only sign that told Shara that others had survived. Gabriel's weight kept her pressed to the floor, but at least it reassured her to feel his heart pounding hard against her back.

Sheer terror prevented her from giving in to the nausea she felt from seeing a man brutally murdered. Once Gabriel pushed her to the floor, she had kept her eyes shut tight. If only she could have shut out the sounds and smells of death as easily.

Gabriel opened his eyes a crack. The officer who

had fired the first shot lay a few centimeters away with a gaping wound in his head. Historical accounts reported that the Friends had been responsible for the violence, but now Gabriel knew that, at least in one location, a panicked officer of the Tribunal had caused the altercation to turn deadly.

Cautiously he raised his head to see if it was safe to move . . . and found himself staring at the end of a shooter.

"Go easy, now," the officer standing over Gabriel said. "Hand over your weapon."

"We're unarmed," Gabriel replied, giving Shara's shoulder a squeeze. "If you'll let us get up, you can see for yourself."

The officer backed away a bit, but kept the shooter aimed at Gabriel's forehead. "Stand up slowly and place your hands on your heads."

As Gabriel helped Shara to her feet, the only other officer left standing joined the first.

Shara tried to send him the suggestion that they were innocent bystanders, but her mind was in such a turmoil, she couldn't concentrate. Quickly the second officer ran his hands over her tunic, then moved to Gabriel.

Shara tensed as the officer's fingers discovered the paralyzer rod.

"What's this?" he asked, extracting the rod from the concealed pocket.

"A light," Gabriel answered.

The officer looked doubtful as he examined it. "I thought the Friends only used firelight."

Gabriel shrugged. "That's why I keep it hidden."

"It looks like a weapon to me." The officer gripped the handle and pointed the rod at Shara.

Her heart banged against her rib cage, but she forced herself to remain still.

"How does it work?" the officer asked, watching Shara's eyes.

"Just squeeze the grip," Gabriel told him casually.

Shara stopped breathing as the officer's fingers slowly tightened. She could dive out of the way of the lethal weapon's beam or she could trust Gabriel to know what he was doing.

Her indecision held her in place as a soft white light shone in her eyes. Only then did she remember that he'd been using it as a light during last night's venture. It took a huge effort not to sigh with relief.

"My son would like this," the officer said, directing the light onto the ceiling.

"It's my invention," Gabriel replied proudly. "That's the only one I have, but I'd be glad to make your son another and have it delivered to you . . . after this situation is resolved." Gabriel gave the officer a meaningful glance.

Nodding, the officer calmly gave his address and slid the rod back into its sheath in Gabriel's tunic. Shara desperately wanted to get out of that room. They were being held at weaponpoint, with their hands on their heads, in the midst of a bloody massacre! She could have screamed at the two men behaving as if this were all an everyday occurrence.

"You'll have to come with me to headquarters now," the officer said, then instructed his colleague to remain in the residence until assistance arrived.

They had just stepped outside when a thunderous explosion quaked the ground beneath their feet. A second later another explosion sounded, followed by another and another. Great clouds of smoke arose from the area of the city where the Administration

Building was located. Emergency sirens began wailing almost instantly.

Suddenly they were knocked to the ground by a blast only meters away. In a flash, one side of the residence burst into flames.

"What's happening?" Shara cried.

"Hades—"

Before Gabriel could say another word, several more firebombs went off in nearby residences. The horrifying sounds of the sirens, shattering glass, and collapsing rooftops were nothing compared to the shrieks of hysteria as residents, security officers, and Friends ran from the blazing buildings.

The officer that had remained inside dragged another uniformed man through the front door, shouting, "I need help! There are more wounded inside." Immediately several volunteers came running.

Without thinking, Shara took a step toward the house, and Gabriel grabbed her arm and yanked her back. "You can't go in there!"

"Let me go! We can help."

Gabriel's grip tightened like a vise. "I told you before, you *cannot* interfere!"

The officer guarding them put a swift end to their argument. Using his shooter to point, he ordered, "Move over there where the others are being gathered."

A dejected group of Friends were being herded upwind of the fires by a troop of armed security officers, while other officers frantically checked the burning residences for any survivors left inside.

Shara could see for herself that her assistance hadn't been necessary. But that wasn't what Gabriel had meant. He had warned her repeatedly that he would not permit her to do anything that would alter history. Now she knew for certain that he would stop her by any means available, including physical restraint.

She rubbed the spot on her upper arm where he had held her so securely. There would probably be a bruise there tomorrow. Her angry glare was lost on Gabriel, as he was occupied with Beauty.

Shara looked around at the destruction he was recording, saw the bodies lying on the walkway, and wondered if she was in some sort of shock. How could she be whining about a bruise when others were dead and dying? She could have been one of them . . . if it hadn't been for Gabriel's quick thinking. How could she resent his presence and be so grateful for it at the same time?

A better question came to her immediately. How were they going to extricate themselves from the rebels before they were sent to Earth? She cursed herself for not keeping the tempometer on her person, regardless of how much curiosity it might have attracted.

The crackling fire rapidly spread as burning sparks leaped on the wind from one residence to the next.

One of the officers assigned to guarding the rebels spoke into a box in his hand, then called out an update to the other officers: The rebels were all captured; most of the city was on fire; casualties were mounting; every available medic and fire control squad had been put to work, but there just wasn't enough help to go around.

Gabriel leaned close to Shara and murmured, "My guess is the spy knew about the plans to take over the residences and Administration Building, but hadn't stayed at the Summit long enough to find out about Hades' so-called distractions or Athena's *illusions* of force."

As if similar thoughts had occurred to a number of the corraled Friends at once, a man's voice broke the numb silence. "Someone betrayed us, that much is certain!"

"Stating the obvious is not going to help us now," a woman replied. "Forget increased freedoms. The Tribunal will have our heads for this."

"But I never agreed to any killing!" another protested.

"Nor the firebombs!"

One after another voiced objections and speculations, near panic evident in every statement. No one dared guess who the Tribunal's spy had been, but it was generally agreed that Hades alone was responsible for the massive destruction.

The loud drone of an engine overhead temporarily distracted the rebels from their fear. A large, oval-shaped balloon moved into the airspace above the fire and hovered there. As a snowy substance began pouring down on the flames, relief swept through both factions of the crowd.

The fire was extinguished a short time later, but nothing was left of the beautiful residences that had previously graced this section of the city. The balloon lowered to the ground and the injured were taken inside first. Once that was accomplished, the captured Friends were ordered to board.

Gabriel reached for Shara's hand as the group moved forward, but she held it away from him. She didn't feel like holding hands with the man who was planning to stand in the way of her goal.

"Give me your hand," he ordered.

"No." She crossed her arms in front of her and tucked her hands under them.

"Fine," he said, putting his arm around her and pinning her to his side. "We could get separated. Be reasonable for a change."

Shara held her retort rather than start an argument in front of so many observers. The whole situation was unreasonable. Why should she be any different?

Using his body as a wedge, Gabriel managed to get the two of them next to a window. As the balloon rose into the air, she noted that he kept his one hand on her waist but his other hand was aiming Beauty at the disaster on the ground.

Whole buildings had been reduced to rubble. Others were standing but blackened with soot and there didn't appear to be a glass window left intact anywhere.

Sections of the overhead rails were twisted and bent. At least one large transport had crashed to the ground. From the abundance of activity, it appeared that rescue operations were under way throughout the city, but it was too late for a great number of people.

A park had been converted into a temporary detention center for the rebels, with security officers posted every few meters around a cordoned-off area. Looking down on the group below, Shara surmised that the Friends' ranks had been reduced by at least a third.

The balloon descended and the rebels on board were escorted into the park with the others.

"I hope you have a plan to get us out of here," Shara murmured to Gabriel.

He arched one eyebrow at her. "Me? This is your adventure. I'm just along for the ride. Remember?"

She made a face at him. "Do you want me to admit I'm in over my head?"

"That would be a good start."

"Fine. I admit it."

"I think you can do better than that."

She angled her head at him, trying to guess what concession he wanted. "And I admit that the only reason I've made it this far is because of you."

His expression softened. "Anything else?"

"And I'm terrified out of my wits. Gabriel, please, do you have a plan or not?"

"Maybe. I need a hug first." When she inched away instead, he said, "If I tell you to do something, I have a good reason. If you balk, it could mean the difference between escape and spending the rest of our lives on ancient Earth."

She swallowed her pride and wrapped her arms around his waist for the hug he requested. The moment he held her close, she knew she had needed this more than he had. "Thank you."

He gave her a squeeze. "If we're going to make it through this, we have to trust each other without question from now on. Agreed?"

"Agreed," she said, but privately added, *except where my goals are concerned.*

"That reminds me, thank you for trusting me about the paralyzer rod back there. For a moment you looked like you were going to fall apart."

"I almost did. I was so frightened, I couldn't concentrate well enough to use my power of suggestion to get us out of there."

"It probably wouldn't have helped. There were too many of them between us and freedom." He gave her one more squeeze, then released her. "Here comes Zeus. He obviously doesn't know when to quit."

The big man was working his way through the crowd. As he neared, Shara could hear him offering condolences while at the same time reassuring the Friends that their fight for freedom wasn't yet over. She thought it was interesting that Hades was nowhere in sight.

"Shara and Gabriel," Zeus said, greeting them each with a pat on the shoulder. "Glad to see you made it in one piece. What of Athena? I heard the situation went badly."

Gabriel answered, "Athena was injured, but alive. Several others weren't so fortunate."

Zeus bowed his head for a moment, then said, "Their lives were not lost in vain. This day will prove to be to our advantage in the end."

"Have you heard what's to be done with us?" Shara asked.

Zeus nodded. "We will each be questioned. Speak the truth, for they will be able to know your thoughts. Take the opportunity to reiterate the peaceful motives of the Friends." After another shoulder pat, he moved on.

Shara turned to Gabriel and murmured. "Did you hear that? They will know our thoughts! They're bound to be suspicious if they can't read us."

"We may have to allow them access, but there's no way to predict how they'll react. We'll simply have to wait and see how things go."

"*That's* your plan?" she asked with a skeptical smirk. "Wait and see?"

He ginned at her and shrugged. "It works for me."

In the following hours, two rebels at a time were

taken into the park shelter where the Security Services had set up temporary headquarters. Shara couldn't help but notice that when some of the Friends returned, they had a very strange look about them, as if they were walking in their sleep.

"What do you think is happening in that building?" she asked Gabriel nervously.

"I don't know, but it doesn't look promising. At this time, the Noronian method of reprogramming disturbed minds was in the early experimental stages. Electricity and personality-altering chemicals were still being tested. It could be that there's more than questioning going on in there."

"Dear heavens! We've got to get out of here before our turn comes."

Ping

13

Gabriel and Shara both froze at the warning sound.

"Not now!" Shara whispered, as panic made her pulse race faster than it already was.

Gabriel touched his pendant and murmured, "Beauty, display body temperature."

Shara stood in front of him so that no one but she could see the numbers appearing on the mirror. "You're barely up half a degree. Why did it go off?"

"I reprogrammed it this morning. I thought we might need more time. Check yourself."

Placing her hand between Beauty and Gabriel's chest, she requested her own reading, then groaned softly. "This can't be happening! I'm having a terrible nightmare, that's all." She closed her eyes and took a deep breath. "I am going to wake up now and I'll be perfectly safe in my own bed." She felt his hand touch her cheek, and she opened her eyes.

"You're hot," he said, his voice slightly scolding. "Why didn't you say something?"

She lowered her lashes. "I was hoping it was the fire."

Shaking his head, he muttered, "You are the most unreasonable female I have ever encountered."

Instantly her mood changed from shy to bristling.

"Go ahead, insult me! That will certainly—" His mouth came down on hers so swiftly, she would have lost her balance if he hadn't been holding her up. As soon as her eyes focused on his, she realized he was silencing, not kissing her. Ashamed that she had let her runaway emotions endanger them, she closed her eyes and leaned into him in a gesture of submission. She hated being so out of control, but it really wasn't his fault.

When he was certain her tantrum had been aborted, he raised his head and loosened his hold. One glance around let him know that no one particularly cared if the lovers were having another little quarrel.

Shara looked up at him apologetically. "I don't feel well, Gabriel. I should have told you."

"And I should have known you wouldn't." Suddenly his face lit up. "This could be a blessing in disguise."

She wondered if the fever was affecting him more than her.

"It might get slightly embarrassing, but I think it'll work."

Her gaze darted back and forth to the people on all sides of them. Images flashed in her mind of she and Gabriel coupling in wild abandon on the grass while everyone casually looked on. *Slightly embarrassing?*

He kissed her nose. "Trust me. I'll have us somewhere private before we lose control."

She tried to give him a trusting smile, but her lower lip didn't cooperate. His finger traced her mouth, then he slipped his hand beneath her hair to stroke her neck. His touch was gentle, but when his fingers trickled down her spine, she stiffened. "Please don't. I don't want to be rude again, but when you touch me like that, well . . . I mean, it's very nice, but my skin is getting more sensitive by the second."

Gabriel placed his mouth against her ear. "That's the point. I'm trying to arouse you." She shivered, either from his words or the heat of his breath, and he nipped her earlobe. "The faster the fever's symptoms are visible, the faster I can set my plan in motion. Let me see your eyes, sweetling." She met his gaze and the rich shade of chocoberry told him all he needed to know. "Don't take those pretty eyes off me now. Try to forget that there's anyone around but us. We're all alone here."

He drew her close so that his thigh wedged between the juncture of hers, and she gasped at the intensity of her body's response to the expertly applied pressure. The thin material of their tunics was as nothing between them. She bit her lip as an imperceptible shift of his leg caused her to involuntarily arch into him.

"That's it," Gabriel whispered, slowly rocking her lower body against his. "Do you know how badly I want to be inside you right now? As deep as you could take me. Sliding in and out. Driving us both out of our minds with pleasure. I'd try to go slowly, to make it last, but you're so hot and tight, it's impossible."

Her response was a whimper of pure sexual frustration.

"Give me your sweet mouth, Shara, like you did this morning. Don't hold back. Take whatever you want."

She pulled his head down to hers and dove into an eating kiss that increased rather than satisfied her desire. She was on fire with raw need clawing at her body and her mind. His tongue in her mouth was not enough. She wanted all of him inside her, or she would surely die.

Gabriel almost forgot where they were and what he was supposed to be doing. Her peaking fever was raising his, despite all his efforts to remain conscious of his actions. With tremendous determination he eased her away from him. The corneas of her eyes were blood red as she tried to recapture his mouth.

He swept her up in his arms and rushed to the security officer he had noted was close to his size. He was also an older man who probably had firsthand experience with the mating fever.

"Please help us," Gabriel said to the man in a raspy voice he barely recognized as his own. "We are in our mating fever. Allow us a few minutes of privacy. My *shalla* is very shy. If I take her here, in front of everyone, she may never forgive me."

The officer touched Shara's cheek and lifted her eyelid, then glanced at Gabriel's blatant arousal. With an understanding nod, he let another officer know he was escorting the two prisoners into the shelter.

Gabriel was barely clinging to consciousness as they entered the building. He could see the officer smiling and speaking to several others, but he could no longer hear the words for the blood roaring in his ears. As the officer led him down a hallway, Gabriel felt as though he were walking in slow motion through a thick fog. His body was burning up and his sex throbbed painfully. Shara was moaning and squirming so much in his arms he could hardly hold on to her.

The officer waved him into a lavatory and closed the door. Muscle spasms had Gabriel's entire body shaking violently as his gaze landed on a single straight-back chair in the corner. With the last vestiges of his control he carried Shara to it.

She was so far gone, she fought his efforts, but with his increased strength he was able to maneuver her so that when he collapsed in the chair, she was straddling his lap. Unable to wait another moment, he lifted her hips and buried himself within her.

Their cries of relief had little to do with pleasure and everything to do with salvation from oblivion. As Gabriel's mind cleared, he knew they had come very close to the edge of life itself. Shara continued to cling to him as desperately as he held on to her. He felt dampness where her cheek rested against his head, and as she took a ragged breath, he realized she was crying.

A fist closed around his heart and squeezed. "I'm sorry," he whispered, discovering his throat was tight with an unfamiliar emotion. "I didn't mean to risk your life."

"I know." She raised her head and wiped at her eyes. "Forgive me. I never cry, but it's been one *drek* of a day."

The enormity of the understatement struck them both at the same time. Shara's mouth quivered; Gabriel grinned, and suddenly they both burst out laughing.

"It really isn't funny," she said, muffling her giggles behind her hand.

He shook his head, struggling to keep his own laughter from erupting again, when she surprised him by clenching her vaginal muscles around him. Though her body was no longer burning and her mind had cleared, one look at her eyes confirmed that her fever had not been completely cooled by their frenzied coupling. He didn't expect her to try to appease her need, however, without the fever being at its peak.

His own fire reignited with a vengeance when she slowly raised and lowered her hips. Yet he still hesitated to believe she was actually taking the initiative when it wasn't absolutely necessary. Again she eased her tight, moist sheath up and down his length, then whispered, "More, please."

Tossing aside the last vestiges of her resistance to the inevitable, she covered his parted lips with hers and stole his breath into her mouth. While his one hand captured and caressed her breast, the other kneaded her bottom, urging her to pick up the pace of her stimulating ride. Without relinquishing his mouth for a moment, with her fingers she explored the muscled expanse of his shoulders and back, then combed through his hair, allowing herself to do all the things she'd been fantasizing about.

But now that she had given in to the temptation, she found herself needing more, as quickly as possible. Though she would have liked to make the exquisite shimmering inside her last, she was suddenly too greedy to wait. The moment she felt the first ripples of release approaching, she rushed them both into the deep, and held him firmly until the last wave of sensation washed over them.

Her sigh of extreme satisfaction was her admission to him that she had finally accepted the pleasure he offered along with the relief.

As they both tightened the reins on their overwrought emotions, he withdrew from her body, but kept her on his lap. Brushing a strand of hair away from her face, he murmured, "You certainly are beautiful when you smile."

She bent her head shyly. She knew she shouldn't let his compliment go to her head, but for just a moment she needed to believe he actually cared about her.

"Now comes the fun part of the plan."

His words jolted her back to reality. "Oh, great," she said with light sarcasm. "I was hoping there was more to come."

He gave her a boost up, then rose himself. "We need to give your mind a little exercise. I'm sure the officer that brought us here is still outside the door. Can you suggest he come in without notifying anyone else, then put him to sleep?"

She ran a self-test and nodded. "Yes, I'm fine now."

"Good. Once he's unconscious, I'm going to borrow his clothes, but you'll need a uniform also. How strong is your power?" When she hesitated, he prodded. "I need to know what else you can do to help us get out of here."

She recalled his telling her that sometimes survival takes priority over ethics. And yet, if he resented her mental abilities before, it would undoubtedly be worse once he knew them all. Weighing freedom against his opinion of her, she decided to reveal the truth. "When I concentrate very hard, without any distractions, I can move objects with my mind, and sometimes I can picture things that are beyond my eyesight."

She could sense him trying not to react to her declaration, but his jaw clenched with tension and his hands fisted at his sides for a split second before he successfully hid his feelings.

"Is there another officer down the hall that you could bring back here?"

She closed her eyes and mentally traveled down the corridor. "Yes. But I can only work on one at a time."

"It's still more than I can do," Gabriel muttered under his breath. "Start with the one outside."

Shara wondered if resentment wasn't the only thing he felt toward people with extrasensory abilities, but there was no time to analyze it now. A short time later, they had both donned security uniforms over their tunics, and the two officers were sleeping peacefully with no memories of how they lost their clothing. Unfortunately, the officers' shoes were both too small for either Shara or Gabriel, and they had to keep their sandals on.

"Is there a way out of this building besides how we came in?" Gabriel asked, while he repositioned his paralyzer rod so that he could get to it if necessary.

She pictured the rest of the shelter's layout. "No. There are rebels being questioned in the rooms along the corridor, but those doors are closed. There's only one officer left out front. I can suggest he take a nap while we leave."

"Fine. Once we're outside, stay calm; don't look anyone in the eye. No one should question two officers amid all the confusion. We're going to walk off and keep walking until we get back to the commune. Ready?"

She nodded, made one final check of their exit route, and put the officer on duty to sleep.

They had only taken a few steps down the hall, though, when one of the doors opened and an auburn-haired man dressed in a rebel-style tunic stepped out and blocked their path.

"Greetings, *Friends*," he said arching an eyebrow

at them. "I heard there was a couple suffering from the mating fever and had a feeling it was the two of you." He looked at the uniforms they were wearing. "You seem to have changed sides since I last saw you." When he noted their sandals, he added, "More or less."

Shara quickly sent him a suggestion, but he blocked it before she finished her thought.

"Uh-uh," he said, wagging a finger at her. "You did not let me in. I do not let you in. Shall we talk instead?" He motioned them into the room behind him and gave a signal to the officer inside to leave. The only furnishings were a square table with four chairs around it.

Shara remembered his name was Misha and he had been the one who had levitated Gabriel's satchel when they'd first arrived. He had also been seated at Zeus's table at dinner. From his comment, she surmised that he must have been responsible for at least one of the probes she had sensed. But why would a security officer obey his order to leave?

"Are you the spy?" she asked bluntly.

He gave her an easy smile. "I prefer to think of myself as a man with divided interests. Zeus is my father. The Tribunal is my employer. No matter what happened today, I was coming out ahead. I have succeeded in walking a double path thus far by knowing everything about everybody. So you can imagine how the two of you concerned me. And now I find you dressed as security officers."

"What do you want from us?" Gabriel asked, assuming that he would have reported them already if that had been his intention.

"I would like my curiosity satisfied. Who are you? Where are you from? What is your true purpose in being here? And then we can move on to the more interesting questions. Why did my probe strike a blank wall in you, and what was the strangeness I picked up in her mind?"

"That was you who touched me at dinner?" Shara asked.

He smiled. "Just for a moment, before you stopped me. You are quite gifted—perhaps my equal—which is another reason you interest me. Not many possess my talents."

Gabriel enveloped Shara's hand in his and gave it a squeeze to stop her from answering. She returned the pressure to signify her agreement to let him do the talking.

"I can promise you an interesting explanation while satisfying your curiosity," Gabriel said as if dangling a sweet in front of a child. "But what can we expect in return for our cooperation?"

Misha angled his head in a thoughtful manner. "If you do not tell me, I could turn you over to security again, or I could hand you to Zeus and convince him you are the spies. You may have heard, he is not known for his compassionate nature. In case you were thinking of repeating what I told you about myself, your testimony would hold no weight against mine with either faction."

He walked around the back of the table and took a chair. "Please sit down. There is no reason for hostility between us. I was being honest about my curiosity. If you satisfy me that you are no threat to any concern of mine, I may even help you get out of here."

Shara glanced at Gabriel. She had no intention of doing anything, even sitting down, unless he told her to do it. At his nod, they joined Misha at the table, but he retained her hand. She supposed it was the best method for him to give her signals, but it also went a long way toward calming her.

Gabriel leaned forward and kept his voice low in a conspiratorial manner. "We're historians from the distant future doing research. We didn't mean to get caught up in the actual rebellion."

"Aah," Misha said, smiling. "Yes, that *is* an interesting explanation. But a difficult one to prove."

"Perhaps not. I can show you the recordings I've been making with a device that doesn't exist in this time." He turned Beauty toward a blank wall. "Beauty, project the speech made by Zeus shortly after dawn this morning."

Misha shot up from his chair as a hologram of his father appeared and Zeus's booming voice filled the room. Cautiously he walked up to the projection and passed his hand through it. "*Amazing!*"

"Beauty, discontinue transmission." Zeus vanished.

Misha returned to his seat with excitement in his eyes. "Tell me of the future. What will happen to the Friends? Will Norona colonize Terra as planned?"

Gabriel shook his head. "We are under strict orders not to interfere with any culture we encounter. Revealing future events could be disastrous. But I can assure you that everyone involved at this time will prosper because of the decisions made."

Shara was tempted to tell Misha of her true purpose, but her instincts warned her that contradicting Gabriel at this point could be dangerous to them both.

Misha was obviously disappointed with such a vague answer, but he seemed to accept it as reasonable. "Was the antigravity device also a product from your time?"

Gabriel nodded. "Yes. My skills don't encompass invention."

Misha looked introspective for a moment, then asked, "Are you both Noronians?"

Shara waited for Gabriel to reply.

"Yes, though Shara has inherited some genes from another humanoid species."

"I see. And what of the mating fever? Was it real or an act?"

He held Shara's hand tightly as he spoke. "Real. It struck after we began our journey and has escalated much faster than expected. We are quite desperate to get back to our own time so that we can have the formal joining ceremony with our parents."

Misha chuckled. "Some things do not change with time, I suppose. You have explained Shara's difference, but what of your mind?"

Gabriel shrugged. "I have no idea. Shara can't read me, either. We're especially looking forward to being joined so that we can finally know the joy of sharing one another's thoughts."

Shara wondered how he managed to say that without choking on the words, but his voice was so sincere, she almost believed it herself.

Misha got up and paced the room. "One more question. How did you get those uniforms?"

Gabriel answered that question honestly and Shara added, "All three of them will awaken in a few hours with no recollection of us whatsoever."

"Very interesting," Misha said as he continued pacing. "I don't know of anyone with the power of suggestion, although I've always suspected one of my cousins of being able to do such a thing."

"Really?" Shara asked, her intuition alerting her to

a possible hint of her heritage. "Which cousin might that be?"

"Cyclops—Poseidon's one-eyed son."

Shara hoped that her intuition was wrong. She didn't want to learn that she had a Noronian ancestor if he turned out to be a mutant monster. "I don't believe we met him."

"No. None of Poseidon's followers were at the Summit. They have a commune on the other side of First Province. Zeus and Poseidon have never been able to share anything . . . least of all center stage. All of Poseidon's protests have been submitted separately from his brother's."

Shara caught a warning look from Gabriel and ignored it. "Misha, I wonder if you could help us with something. We were trying to compile a list of all the people involved in the Friendship movement. I believe we got everyone who was staying at Zeus's commune or who attended the meeting. Could you name those who are loyal to Poseidon? You just have to speak and Beauty will record you."

Misha smiled toward the mirrored pendant on Gabriel's chest, clearly flattered to be part of history, and rattled off a list of about forty names.

"Thank you," Gabriel said as soon as Misha paused. "That will be enough. I hope we have convinced you we are no threat and only want to leave this time as quickly as possible."

"I am convinced," Misha replied. "But I am not sure how I could help you."

"We need to get back to Zeus's lodge. Any suggestions?"

"That is easy. As long as you are in those uniforms, you can take one of the scooters in the rear of the building. One word of warning, though. Make sure you are gone by morning. Security does not have the manpower to spare at the moment, but by tomorrow, they will be sending teams out to search Zeus's property for more weapons. If you get picked up again, I will assume you have not told me the whole truth, and I will deny knowing you."

"Don't worry," Gabriel said, ushering Shara toward the door. "We'll be long gone by then."

The scooters were where Misha had said they'd be, and Gabriel quickly examined one. A narrow metal box about a half meter wide and a meter long formed the base very close to the ground. Beneath it was a single runner of four wheels and a pipe extending from the back that suggested it had a propulsion system. Gabriel adjusted the height of the steering column and crossbar affixed to the other end and located the ignition button on the right-hand grip.

Stepping onto the standing board, he told Shara, "Get on and mold yourself to my back as if we were one body. Try to move only as I move and don't let go of me. The last thing we need is to attract attention by having an accident before we even get out of the city."

Shara stepped on behind him, wrapped her arms around his waist . . . and prayed that he was a fast learner.

They had a jerky start and wobbled a bit for a few meters, but Gabriel soon had them pulling away from the shelter. The position of the setting sun advised him which direction to travel, but he had to avoid going by the park, lest anyone should see them too closely, and then he was forced to take a number of detours to bypass the massive wreckage throughout the city.

Another tension-filled hour crept by before they finally reached the outskirts. The moment they were out in the open, Gabriel pushed the ignition button in as far as it would go, and the scooter increased speed to the point at which its wheels barely skimmed the grass. In seconds they were at the top of the hill where the Friends had first looked down on their targets.

Gabriel stopped the scooter and took the time to record the scene as it now appeared. He knew that the city would soon be rebuilt, but it was a depressing sight nonetheless.

He paused again when they reached the rise above the commune, but for another reason. "I don't think anyone stayed behind, but these uniforms make us the enemy here. We might not be given the chance to explain." He directed Beauty to scan the area for evolved life-forms.

As it did so, Shara ran a mental check of her own. She had suppressed her abilities for so long, she hadn't realized she could get such satisfaction from using them.

Assured that no one was about, they discarded the uniforms, and Gabriel drove them down to the lodge. Taking her hand, he hurried Shara inside. "Put the belt on, and let's get out of here."

Away from imminent danger, Shara's mind had reorganized the order of her priorities again. "We can't leave yet."

He turned toward her with a stunned look on his face. "I beg your pardon?"

She scrambled for an excuse he might accept. "Misha said no one would be coming here until tomorrow. I'm filthy, I'm starving, and I'm exhausted. What if we time-hop into another crisis? You may be able to go days without sleep, but I can't. Gabriel, *please*, I can't go on like this."

He didn't like the idea of sticking around another microsecond, but her point was well taken. "All right. We can shower and have a meal here, but then we head back to where we hopped in to get some sleep. It won't take long with the scooter."

She rose on tiptoe and kissed his cheek. "Thank you."

His hands moved to bring her closer, but she spun away too quickly.

"Clean clothes!" she said exuberantly. "I must have clean clothes."

"I'd suggest we wear the tunics until we're ready to leave—just in case we run into one of the neighbors unexpectedly."

She grimaced. "All right. I'll wash it while I shower."

Not certain he could keep his hands off her if they showered together, he suggested she go first while he found something for them to eat.

She reentered the lodge a short time later, feeling much better for having scrubbed from head to toe. Her tunic was still wet, but at least it was clean.

Gabriel's stomach did a somersault as he watched her walk toward him. The way the damp cloth clung to her curves was more alluring than if she had been nude. He cursed his body's instant response, knowing the urge had to go unsatisfied until her fever began to rise again. For a moment he considered telling her *his* fever was mounting to gain her cooperation, but as soon as she touched his cool flesh, she'd know he was lying. Without a word, he headed for the shower.

By the time he returned to her, he had his

thoughts and his body back under control. They filled up on cold meat, bread, and fruit juice, and Shara wrapped up some extra food to take along before they put everything away.

He noticed that she didn't seem to feel any more talkative than he did, and he was curious about what sort of thoughts were occupying her mind.

As they prepared to go, he received a shock. His degrav was missing! He had another stowed inside his satchel, but it bothered him to know that someone had purposefully taken it and that an object from the future would be left in the past.

It took some improvising, but he managed to secure their bags to the steering column of the scooter using his spare degrav and a length of rope.

His nerves would have begun to calm as soon as they started away from the commune, if it hadn't been for his heightened awareness of Shara's voluptuous curves pressing into his back. Within seconds he was back to being unbearably aroused. Quickly he calculated how long he might have to wait for relief. The periods between the fever's peaks were now twenty-three, nineteen, and seventeen hours. Even if this stretch were reduced by several hours, he still had a long, *long* time to restrain himself.

Unless she could be convinced to see the logic of not waiting for the fever to strike again before taking the cure. Surely she would understand the rationale of preventative treatment. He realized that he was once again preoccupied with thoughts of Shara, but it no longer stirred resentment. He told himself he wasn't losing sight of his priorities; he was simply accepting what he had no control over—a reasonable attitude that he desperately wished Shara could adopt as well.

He hoped this torture would be ended in a few more hours. They would be back in their own time, receive medical treatment for their condition, and he could get on with his work ... and his solitary life.

Rather than giving him a sense of relief, that knowledge clenched a fist around his heart again and he wondered if he was developing another disturbing side effect to the fever.

Night came as they rode, but a clear, full moon lit their path. As he stopped the scooter and dismounted, he felt the strength ebb from his body. Shara had been right to suggest they get some rest before attempting the return time-hop. He was exhausted. After removing their bags from the scooter, he pulled out the sleeping pouch. The sooner they took a nap, the sooner they could be on their way.

All things considered, Shara felt pretty good. She had survived a terrifying chain of events, and though her mission was not yet accomplished, it could be soon. *If* one of the many hair samples she'd collected that morning was a match to Khameira's. And *if* she could sneak away from Gabriel long enough to arrange a brief meeting with the Ruling Tribunal.

Gabriel was already tired, and she knew one sure way to wear him down even further. It no longer seemed immoral to consider sharing her body with him. He was certainly not a stranger anymore, and they *had* established a bond of sorts. She was acutely aware of the personal danger of freely coupling with him, but she reminded herself that sometimes the reward is worth the risk.

As fatigued as she was, somehow she would force herself to stay awake a few more hours and accomplish her primary goal.

She inhaled the fragrance of night-blooming flowers and scanned the star-filled sky. It was a warm, beautiful night, and she was with a handsome, desirable man who wanted her badly enough for her to take advantage of him.

The situation could be a lot worse.

14

As Gabriel spread the pouch on the ground, he felt the wind lift the skirt of his tunic . . . only there was no wind. He smoothed the material back down over his buttocks and bent over to straighten the pouch. Again the tunic blew up and bared him from the waist down.

Shara's giggle gave her mischief away. He whirled around to find that she was standing too far away to have lifted the material by hand. He started to question her when she touched a finger to her lips. He didn't understand until he felt a tug on the braided rope around his waist. Looking down he saw it untie itself, then slither down his stomach and between his legs. He held very still as it coiled around one thigh and snaked its way down to the ground, tickling his genitals in the most extraordinary way. Next, his paralyzer rod left its sheath and traveled to the ground on its own.

Normally he would have been angry that she was using her mind to toy with him, but what she was doing was far too erotic to be infuriating. Smiling seductively, she eyed the front hem of his draped tunic, and it began to gather together. Ever so slowly, it slipped between his thighs, teased its way up his back, over his bare shoulder, then floated through the air to land at her.

Ping

Gabriel removed Beauty and tossed it on the ground. He didn't need some stupid device to tell him his temperature was rising. Shara slipped out of her sandals, so he did the same, but otherwise he held still for fear any movement on his part would cause her to change her mind about toying with him.

Stepping toward him, she said, "I think it's time for me to demonstrate that I am the reasonable person I have claimed to be. Whatever this is between us, I'm done fighting it."

As he stood there, naked and more than ready, yet waiting for her direction, a heady power rushed through her. Surely Zeus's nectar would be no match for the exhilaration she was feeling. Letting the power flood her body and fuel her purpose, she handed Gabriel the end of her rope belt. He untied it; then, imitating what she had done to him, he dragged the material of her tunic over her body as if he were in no hurry to reveal what she was finally willingly offering, with no coercion whatsoever.

When he tossed the barrier aside, she stepped into his arms. "Let's find out what we've been missing," she whispered, and rising on tiptoes, she pressed her lips to his.

With the first taste of his mouth, she forgot her ulterior motive for this seduction, forgot why she had been fighting him for so long. Later, when it was absolutely necessary, she would remember her sensible reasons for not wanting to fully share herself with this man. But for now, and as long as they had no choice in the matter, she would enjoy every kiss, every touch, every exciting moment he could give her.

She couldn't tell if it was her fever reigniting or his talented hands roaming over her, but her flesh had begun to tingle, and she felt the stirring of her sexual pulse. Her hands held his hips in place as she deepened the kiss and moved against him to relay her wish to please him, for a change. He had been ready when she removed his tunic but she wanted him more than ready.

Slipping her fingers through his golden chest hair, she teased his nipples until they puckered for her. Then she continued dragging her nails slightly down his abdomen while she lowered herself to her knees before him.

Gabriel groaned aloud as she took him into her mouth and continued to use her nails to tease the rest of his sensitive flesh. It took an incredible amount of strength to remain standing as she pulled him closer to the edge of his control. With every ounce of willpower he possessed, he brought her back up to her feet to face him.

Rather than entwining their bodies more intimately, however, he stepped back from her and took a deep breath. Shara reached for that part of him that was straining to return to her, but he took both her hands in his before she could touch him.

His tongue caressed each of her wrists; then he dipped his head forward to give her a light kiss on her mouth. Still holding her hands, he said, "You wanted to find out what we've been missing. So do I. There's no need for another frantic coupling as long as the fever is controllable."

He brought her hand to his cheek, then touched hers. "We're both a little warm, but nowhere near

delirium. Nothing in life is supposed to be as pleasurable as foreplay and coupling during one's mating
fever. Consider this a rare opportunity to experiment
with something you may have had to wait decades
for. Close your eyes, Shara, and don't think about
anything except what you're feeling. Let's see just
how long we can make the pleasure last."

Shara's attempts to drive him to distraction had
taken its toll on her. She almost demanded that he
satisfy her immediately, but his words had now
aroused her curiosity as much as her body. She obe-
diently closed her eyes.

"Hold your arms out to your sides," he instructed,
positioning them as he wanted. "Palms up and head
tipped back as if you're a goddess beckoning to the
moon to increase your power over me. Spread your
feet a little farther apart . . . to keep your balance."

From the teasing tone of his voice, she guessed
her balance was not quite what he had on his mind.
The pose left every part of her body exposed to him.
It might have been somewhat embarrassing, but
with her eyes closed and her temperature creeping
higher, she had little problem ignoring her usual
modesty.

"Can you guess what I'm doing?" he asked from
behind her. She turned her head toward his voice.
"How about now?" he said at her side. "Or now?" He
was back in front of her. "I'm tempting myself by
looking without touching. Don't you feel my eyes on
you, devouring you, committing every sexy, feminine
part of you to memory?"

Her breasts tightened in response.

"I was once asked to describe what I considered
the perfect female body. My answer then was long
and lush, with full breasts and hips ample enough to

offer comfort to a body as large as mine. I might have added hair like black silk, soft, full lips made for kissing, and eyes that would tell me exactly what she's feeling when I touch her. My answer now would be only one word." His breath was hot against her ear as he whispered that word.

"*Shara.*"

He stepped to her side and was gratified to see her head automatically turn to follow his movement. "You are the beautiful Goddess of the Moon, and I am here to worship at your temple."

A shiver slipped down her spine and into her core. He had claimed to be tempting himself, but his words were playing havoc with her patience. She closed her thighs to try to relieve the throbbing.

"Don't do that," he said, noting the movement. "You wouldn't want to lose your *balance* when there's so much more to come. All I've done so far is look. Now I'm going to touch. Is there any place in particular you'd like me to start?"

The smile she heard in his voice prompted her to shake her head rather than reply. Whatever he had in mind was probably better than any suggestion she might make.

"No preference? Then I think I'll start here." His fingertips tickled the palm of her left hand, then slipped in and out of her fingers.

As lightly as a butterfly's caress he grazed his way up one side of her arm and down the other. The mild tingling she had been feeling grew more intense wherever he touched, and when his fingers trickled over her shoulders to her other arm, smoldering trails of sparks were left behind. His hands sensitized every centimeter of the back of her body, from shoulders to heels. And when she was about to scream at him to be done with it, he came around to her front and began working his way back up from her toes.

She told herself she could wait, that she should appreciate the steady building of her need, that the release would be that much better when it finally happened. But when his fingers moved from her thighs to her stomach, avoiding the neediest part of her, she couldn't hold back the disappointed sigh. "Gabriel, please, I'm dying."

His hands eased up her sides and cupped her breasts. "No, you're not. You're hot, but you're in no danger." She gasped as he scraped his palms over her nipples. "Let me assure you, my Moon Goddess, I'm hot, too. But I'm not ready to finish it yet, because I've been waiting to do this for too long."

She felt him lift and knead her breasts and then his firm, wet mouth closed over one peak. Slow, controlled actions were discarded as he covered one breast, then the other, with eating kisses that became more demanding by the second.

"*Please!*" she cried, clutching his shoulders. He raised his head to take her mouth while he urged her down to lie on the pouch.

She parted her legs, anticipating his immediate entrance, but he stretched out beside her instead. When she tried to turn toward him, he pressed her back again and broke the kiss to say, "Just a bit longer. There is something I wish to learn while I'm still able."

She was beyond understanding. His mouth was hard and hungry when it returned to hers. His fingers were no longer gentle as they raked over her stomach and into the curls between her legs. With a desperate moan, she arched into his hand. As he used her own dampness to stroke her, she grasped his shaft and moved her hand to the steady rhythm he set.

His tortured groan let her know his need was no less than hers, and yet he seemed intent on giving her a release without coupling. She didn't care how it came, only that it should. But wanting it to happen didn't make it so. Simultaneously, their movements became more hurried as they strived to help each other escape the rampaging fever.

Breathing heavily, Gabriel abruptly stopped his efforts and raised himself over her. "It has to be this," he said in a strained voice, and plunged into her body.

Her cry this time was of relief and pleasure combined, but it was only momentary, for now that his fire had joined with hers, the blaze of passion burned even hotter. She wrapped her legs around him and lifted her hips with each of his powerful thrusts so that he was embedded as deeply as possible. Though the need to climax was overwhelming, she didn't want the delicious torment to stop.

Higher and higher into the heavens she rode the spiraling sensations, until there was no heaven, no ground, no bodies. Only pleasure and the raging inferno demanding its tribute.

As it had been in her dream the other night, she was suddenly at the base of an erupting volcano and scaled her way up to its mouth. A tongue of fire shot up from the bubbling cauldron of lava and shaped itself into a man.

Shara! he called, and held out his arms.

In a panic she looked behind her for an escape route, but the path through the flowing lava was no longer there. The only escape from the volcano was through its fiery heart. Leaping off the rim into the man's arms, she spoke his name in return. *Gabriel!*

He caught her as the eruption rocked through them and held her securely against him in the rippling aftermath. It was like nothing she had ever imagined, and it was no less incredible than she had known sharing herself with Gabriel would be.

Shara knew everything had returned to normal when she recognized the feel of the sleeping pouch beneath her and the weight of the man above and within her. She opened her eyes and gave him a shy smile. "An experiment, huh? Did we learn anything?"

He gave her a dimpled grin and rolled them both onto their sides without separating their bodies. "I think so. First of all, we've confirmed that only coupling will cool the fever. No substitutions. Second, either passion can trigger the fever, or the period of relief just took a drastic drop. It's only been about four hours since the last peak."

She didn't want to think about that, so she revealed a different concern. "I saw the volcano again. Only this time I knew it was you."

"Yes," he said, picking up her bewilderment. "I saw it also, and I heard you say my name, but it was more like a hallucination than a dream. So now it's certain: We're not only sharing the fever, there's a mental connection of some kind, in spite of my jammer, and without being formally joined."

Shara had a strong feeling that the vision had a deeper meaning than the obvious, but it made her uncomfortable to think about that also, so she pushed it to the back of her mind.

She felt him flex within her body and her muscles hugged him in return. Having decided to momentarily shelve her personal codes of propriety, she could admit that she liked feeling him inside her. Bending her knee, she drew one leg up to his hip to bring him even deeper.

"There is one more thing we learned," he said in a husky voice. "They were right."

Shara wrinkled her forehead. "They who?" He laughed and a spear of pleasure darted through her.

"Whoever they are who said, 'Nothing in life is as pleasurable as coupling during the mating fever.'" Instead of agreeing with him, she lowered her lashes, and he experienced a very strange feeling in the pit of his stomach. "Shara? What's wrong?"

She shook her head, but kept her eyes averted.

"Please look at me." As she complied, he noticed her eyes were still the delicious shade of chocolate he liked so much and his hunger for her returned full force. But there was something he hungered for even more—assurance that she had enjoyed the foreplay and coupling as greatly as he. "Am I mistaken? Was that not the most incredible physical experience you've ever had?"

She heard the insecurity in his voice and had to tell the truth. "I could count the number of *experiences* I've had on one hand, and none of them could be described as incredible. I didn't know it could be like that for me. It was really quite . . . wonderful."

His reward for her honesty was a kiss so sweet, it almost made her forget that he was the enemy.

As the kiss became less gentle, however, she realized that he wasn't withdrawing from her body or growing tired. And if he didn't sleep, she couldn't do what she needed to do. "Gabriel?"

"Hmmm?" he asked, but his grin hinted that he knew her question.

"As I said, I don't have much experience with . . . intimacy, so I hope you don't mind my asking this. Each time we've coupled there's been evidence that you had a release, even if you don't clearly remember it. But you're still, um . . ."

He shifted his hips forward and she inhaled sharply. "Aroused?"

She nodded. "Is that normal for you?"

"*Drek* no," he said with a laugh, "and thank the stars for that. If it was, I may have had the bothersome appendage removed years ago." When he saw the shock on her face, he laughed again. "I'm joking. But it does get rather uncomfortable going around all day in this condition."

Shara swallowed nervously. "All day?"

"And night. The swelling subsides somewhat, but not completely." He wondered what she'd say if he told her this *condition* of his began weeks before the first time-hop—when he first saw her in her lab.

Though Shara couldn't know precisely how he felt, she could certainly empathize. Each time they'd coupled before this, she had been left wanting. Even now she was far from totally sated. She mulled over the problem and came up with a logical solution that could also help her get on with the task she'd planned. "I think we need to run another experiment."

"Oh?" His hand skimmed down her back and massaged her bottom.

She closed her eyes to hold on to the tiny tremors of pleasure he was giving her. "I . . . *oh my* . . . we should endeavor to find a way to bring us . . . *you* some relief." He partially withdrew and slowly entered her again. "Um . . . we know that once is not enough to . . . relax you. Perhaps a . . . a repetition is . . ." His movements eloquently finished the sentence for her.

The experiment was mutually exhausting, but they worked at it until they had their conclusion: Three couplings were required to bring complete relief . . . and put Gabriel to sleep.

Unable to let go of the lovely feeling of contentment too quickly, Shara lay snuggled in his embrace for some time, yet she couldn't allow herself to sleep. She had work to do.

After a while she whispered his name, and when he didn't stir, she eased away from him, then paused to make sure he didn't awaken before she left him completely. Once she was free, she wasted no time getting to work.

Gabriel reached out in his sleep to bring Shara close again and her absence awakened him. With a feeling of dread, he opened his eyes and searched the immediate area. He felt some relief when he saw her a few feet away sitting cross-legged on her tunic, working her microputer. It was not as bad as if she'd left him, but it wasn't good, either.

Beauty was on her knee, and there was a small pile of static papers on each side of her. As he watched, she picked one up from the smaller pile on her left side, peeled a hair off, inserted it in the microputer, pressed keys, then put the paper and hair on her right side.

He could think of two reasons for her not being asleep. One, she wasn't tired or satisfied enough. He knew without a single doubt that wasn't the case. Thus, the second, more troublesome reason remained. She had stayed awake on purpose—and put him to sleep on purpose—in order to work without his knowledge.

Why would she resort to being devious? He had no objection to her testing the hair samples, and besides, the tests could have waited until she returned to their own time.

There was only one answer. In spite of all his warnings, she was still planning to stop Khameira's ancestor from going to Earth.

It seemed to him that after everything that had happened to them, she would have been frightened enough to realize that she lacked the experience to do anything on her own. But going off alone was apparently what she was planning to do. Just in case he was wrong, though, he decided to wait until she made a move to leave before pouncing on her.

He could hardly believe how foolish and stubborn she could be! What if she had taken off and the fever struck again? How could she place more importance on her search than on her own life?

That question stopped him cold. How many times had he risked his life to obtain one more piece of information? How many times had he been frightened out of his wits and still pushed on toward a goal he'd set for himself? Too many times to count.

Perhaps they were both stubborn fools.

Or was it that they simply had very strong convictions and the courage to test them and persist despite enormous obstacles? Not long ago he had thought they had nothing in common, but there seemed to be some similarities after all.

Thinking of her secondary goal on this venture, he recalled the conversation they'd had about their childhood and realized that a common element existed there as well. She was hoping to learn something that would erase the painful memories of her past. He could have told her that nothing—no discovery, no acclaim, no amount of running away—could change the past. One just had to get on with one's life and let go of the memories. But he knew that was a conclusion she would have to reach on her own.

He watched Shara test her last sample, then slowly set aside the miccomputer. Even before her shoulders slumped and she covered her face with her hands, he guessed that she had not found a match for Khameira. But as she raised her head and looked to the stars, her expression of utter desolation told him she also had not found a match for herself.

He wanted to be furious with her for thinking she could deceive him. He had been ready to lash out at her for using her body to disable him. Instead he lifted a hand to her and gently said, "Come here, sweetling."

Her dismay turned to surprise, then acceptance as she realized she had been expecting him to awaken before she could take off. The relief she felt had her wondering if she'd actually been counting on his interference all along. Since he didn't appear to be angry, she assumed he hadn't guessed her plans.

"I couldn't sleep," she said as she went to his side and lay back in his embrace. "So I thought I'd try to find my ancestor among the samples. It wasn't there."

He waited for her to continue, to admit her deceit and beg his forgiveness, but when he saw the dull shade of her eyes, his initial anger returned. In a flash, he pushed her away from him. "You're a lying witch. You were looking for Khameira's ancestor and then you were going to leave me here while you went to talk to the Tribunal. Weren't you?"

She did her best to look indignant. "I do not intend to argue with you about this again." She moved to get up, but he shoved her back down again. "Let me go!"

As she squirmed to escape him, he grabbed her wrists and pinned them down over her head while he secured the rest of her body with his. Looming over her, he was determined to force his will on her. "Any fool could figure out what you were planning. I was laying here, convincing myself not to be angry with you. But I have every right to be angry.

"I've explained in an intelligent manner the risks of altering history. You know you lack the experience to handle a trip back to the city on your own, and you know how dangerous it is for us to be separated with the fever peaks getting closer all the time. I was even trying to be understanding about the fact that you used my desire for you against me. But I will *not* put up with your lying to me."

She opened her mouth to defend herself, but no words came. She was guilty as charged, on every count. And it had all been for nothing. She wasn't ready to give up, but she did owe him an apology. "I'm sorry."

He frowned down at her. He was ready for an argument and she wasn't giving him one. "Now what are you up to?"

She shook her head. "Nothing. I was wrong to think I could go back into the city without you. I was wrong to consider leaving you while the fever is still with us." She hesitated, to make sure he could read the honesty in her eyes. "But I'm not sorry I seduced you. I only regret waiting so long."

With those words, he was back on the storm-tossed boat again. His mind was still poised for combat, but his body was shaping itself for a more enjoyable form of action. Rather than follow through with either, he released her hands and shifted to her side. "What am I going to do with you?"

The obvious answer could wait a few minutes. An idea was forming. "Take me to Poseidon's commune?" she responded.

"Absolutely not. Besides the fact that they sound even less friendly than Zeus's people, their place will probably be overrun with security in the morning. It's time to go home, Shara. Give it up."

"I can't," she said, as if it were a perfectly reasonable explanation. "I'm too close to an answer. I've eliminated one hundred eighty-three of the two hundred twenty names on the exile list. Thirty-one of the names left are among those Misha gave us as followers of Poseidon."

He could admire the way her mind worked, but he had no intention of giving in. "And what of the other six?"

"The odds are with Poseidon's group."

"The odds were with Zeus's group, too. But the odds don't matter. We're not staying. You heard Misha. If he sees us again, he'll assume we fabricated our story, and I don't trust him not to hand us up to better himself."

"We could leave this time and hop back in again, only head for Poseidon's commune instead."

"That might have been a possibility if the tempometer could be accurately programmed. But as it is, we could hop back in after we'd already arrived the first time. Then there might be two sets of us to escape. It could create a paradox that would disturb the natural flow of time. We don't know enough about this to be sure. Besides, we barely survived this round. We might not be so lucky if we tried again."

"But we'd know exactly what was coming."

He shook his head. "That's the problem. Knowing what was about to happen, we might do something differently and thus change the outcome. Forget it."

She twisted her mouth from side to side. There had to be a way. . . . "I've got it! We could go to where Poseidon and his followers settled on Earth."

"I think you need sleep. You're not making sense anymore."

"Think of it, Gabriel. *Atlantis!* The lost continent about which so many Earth legends were written. There are even fewer details about what happened there after the exiles arrived than there were about the rebellion on Norona." She could see temptation changing his features. "Imagine the marvelous contribution you could make to the historical files."

"There's no way we could get on board one of the ships leaving in two days. Not only would we risk getting caught, but the trip took about seventy years. The passengers were put in a state of suspended animation for the journey and not all of them survived the process."

She noted he hadn't given her a flat refusal. "It would take a little doing, but it's not impossible. First, we would go forward in time from here to take a modern ship from Norona to Innerworld. Then we could transmigrate to Outerworld, take a boat into the Atlantic Ocean to the former location of Atlantis, then time-hop backward again."

He was back to looking skeptical, so she waved temptation a little harder. "You would be able to learn the truth of what happened there firsthand. A monograph on Atlantis's downfall would be sought after by everyone, not just relegated to the files of academic libraries for other historians to use for research." He gave her such an annoyed look, she worried that she had gone too far. "I didn't mean that like it sounded."

"Yes, you did. And it's true. You told me yourself when we first met, you'd never heard of me."

"That's right, partly because I had very little interest in history. But Gabriel, your stories made history come alive for me. You could do that for so many others if they only took the time to find out how fascinating you make it. A text on Atlantis would attract people of all ages; then, once they discovered your way of relating history, they'd begin asking for more of your work."

He captured her chin and turned her face so that the moonlight shone on it. "You really believe that?" he asked, in spite of the fact that her eye color told him she was being sincere.

She took his hand and kissed the knuckles. "Yes. And I'm a very intelligent person . . . when a certain man isn't throwing me off balance."

He turned her hand to return the kiss. "And I suppose if I refuse to go along with this scheme, you've got another one to spring on me."

"I'm not giving up this opportunity to verify my heritage, Gabriel, and even though we disagree about my mission, I know I'm safer when I'm with you. I'd like you to come with me, but if your answer is definitely no, then we can go forward, get treated for the fever, and I'll take my chances on getting away again on my own."

There seemed to be little possibility that she would get that chance, and yet he knew if there was a way, she would find it. Knowing of her intention to alter history, he would have no choice but to follow her . . . again. Logic had brought him right back to where this had all started.

"What about the fever?" he asked, running a finger down her arm.

She absently stroked his chest. "I was hoping to leave that detail up to you. You have such a gift for planning."

He ignored her sarcasm. "I suppose I'll think of something after we hop forward." His hand skimmed down her back and rested on her hip. "Why don't you get some sleep first?"

She eased her body closer to his. "Does that mean you'll come with me?"

"Don't pretend that you gave me any choice," he replied, trying to look stern, but fighting a grin as she brought her leg over his. "You really should take a nap."

"I will," she said with a secretive smile. "But I'd rest a lot better if we reduced the possibility of the fever striking again in the next few hours." Her nails scraped down his abdomen and found him terribly in need of treatment.

He was more than happy to administer the cure anytime she asked, but he let her take as long as she wanted to prepare him for the ultimate service.

Shara felt that there was something very different about this coupling. If she didn't know better, she would have described it as loving. There was no one they needed to fool with a show of false affection. There was no fever driving them. She wasn't doing this because she had an ulterior motive or because she was grateful to him for saving her life.

She was making love to him because it made her

feel so good to give him pleasure ... and because she cared in spite of her wish not to.

Gabriel sensed that something had changed. Her touch, her kiss, her body absorbing his, all felt different somehow. This wasn't a simple coupling between a man and a woman. What they were doing was much more personal, and the way it made him feel was better than any discovery he'd ever made. For the first time he could remember, he wanted to share more of himself than just his body.

He did his best to show her what he was feeling, but it didn't seem to be enough. He wanted to give her something more than a release, something that would let her know he considered her very special. As his body made love to hers, he removed the jammer from his ear and brought her fingers to his temple. *I wanted to let you know how you make me feel.*

Shara was startled by the suddenness of hearing his thoughts, but quickly relaxed and allowed him to hear hers as well. Knowing how much he resented anyone in his mind made his gift all the more precious. *What a beautiful thing to do. Thank you.*

As their passion rose, she maintained her touch so that they were sharing every unbelievable feeling. Her pleasure doubled his and fed back to her.

Suddenly, as they neared a release, they were struck by a sensation similar to a surge of electricity. The eerie power held them captive as the ground beneath them trembled and a golden glow surrounded their joined bodies. The urge to complete the physical act they'd begun superseded any fear of what was happening.

The energy continued to flow through them, growing stronger each second until, with a final heart-stopping jolt, they simultaneously reached an explosive climax.

The glow faded away and stole their consciousness with it.

The sound of birds greeting the dawn brought Shara to partial wakefulness. *What happened?* she thought to herself as she stretched the stiffness out of her back.

Drekked if I know.

Instantly they were wide awake. Sitting up, they moved apart and eyed each other with suspicion.

You said you couldn't send your thoughts, she said accusingly.

I can't. But you can, he mentally replied with a similar edge, then remembered he had removed his jammer some hours ago.

But I'm reading you without touching you. I'm not able to do that.

As he located the jammer and attached it to his earlobe, his brows drew together in disbelief. How could she deny the ability even as she used it?

She heard his doubtful thought as clearly as if he were speaking aloud. *I am not lying!*

With a horrified expression, he touched his jammer, then backed a little farther away. *I heard that! How did you get past the jammer?*

I don't know. I'm not doing anything on purpose. I'm not even trying to direct my thoughts to you. It's . . . it's like you're inside my head!

That's exactly what it is. I remember the feeling all too well!

I don't understand. How can this be? She felt a tightening in her chest and knew instinctively it wasn't her own sensation, but his being transmitted to her.

That's right. I'm tense, and I can tell that you're frightened. He then used his voice, mainly to confirm that he still could. "I don't want to believe it, but there's only one thing that could have caused this." He felt her bracing herself for his pronouncement.

"We've been joined."

15

Romulus felt Aster's tears begin to flow again and had to block her before he fell apart in front of the roomful of department chiefs. He excused himself from the meeting as quickly as possible and headed home.

In spite of everything he'd tried, he hadn't been able to convince his mate to leave their residence since the hour they'd learned both their children were missing. He'd gone about their business, while she'd sat in the striped chair by the fireplace, hour after hour, waiting for Shara or Mack to reappear.

Of course, there actually was a chance that Shara would pop back in at any time. But Mack was a different story. All evidence that he had ever existed had vanished. Only human memories remained and Aster and Romulus had no idea when that would start to fade as well.

Rom had helped Shara redecorate Mack's room exactly the way it had been before. They had an artist draw a rendering of their son with the words MACKENZIE LOCKE EXISTED under it and hung it on his bedroom door. Together they had written out a lengthy explanation and biography that they read and reread to hold on to their memories as long as possible.

He was too distraught himself to come up with any other ideas of how to help Aster deal with the double loss. Neither said it aloud, but guilt was playing a major part in their distress. They had waited ten years before having a second child, and it had been a difficult decision.

In the past two days, a long list of changes had been reported in Innerworld, and Outerworld news was filled with similar stories. In most cases, it was confirmed that a choice had once been made that had now been reversed.

The fact that people's memories were starting to alter to fit the changes was not the only complication added to the original problem. The changes themselves were increasing in severity. Not only had a number of people vanished in both Inner and Outerworld, an entire building under construction in the southwestern United States disappeared in the blink of an eye. Two workers who had been on scaffolds fell to their deaths and a dozen others were injured when the floors they were standing on were no longer there.

A scientific research team agreed on the theory that certain moments in history had somehow been altered, and since it began after Shara disappeared, there was probably a connection. But so far no one had a viable theory as to how to deal with the situation.

By the time Rom reached his residence, Aster had pulled herself together enough to greet him with a halfhearted kiss. They held each other for a long time before she spoke.

"For a moment this morning I had forgotten," she murmured in a shaky vice. "I saw the picture of

Mack and his name on the bedroom door, and for just a second I didn't know who it was."

"Did you reread the bio?"

She nodded. "But I'm not sure if it brought the memory back or created a new one. I found myself questioning some of the things we'd written."

Rom guided her over to the sofa to sit. "The research team is fairly sure that as soon as Shara returns, they'll be able to find out what she's done and go back and correct it."

"And everything would return to normal?" Aster asked in a flat tone.

"That's the theory. Without the ability to re-create the tempometer to go looking for her, we have no choice but to wait for her to come back to this time."

Suddenly the sound of tinkling wind chimes filled the room. They both bolted up from the sofa and stared expectantly at the glittering lights transforming into a body.

"*Shara?*" Aster cried hopefully, remembering that this was how Lantana first appeared before them.

It was a female . . . but not Shara. A heavyset woman of middle years with dark magenta hair smoothed the gathers in her brightly colored caftan. She was wearing a crystal belt exactly like the one Lantana had worn. "My, my. That was certainly interesting," she declared to herself, then smiled at Rom and Aster. "Hello. I hope this is the home of Romulus Locke and Aster Mackenzie."

"Yes, it is," Rom assured her, and introduced himself and Aster.

"Thank the stars! My name is Cattar. I have come from two hundred fifty years in the future in search of an elderly man."

"Lantana?" Rom ventured.

Cattar frowned. "Don't tell me he's already been here!"

"Here and gone over a month ago. He passed on almost immediately after he arrived, but he managed to leave a catastrophe behind. I sincerely hope you're here to straighten it out."

"Actually, I was hoping to be here before him or at least at the same time so that I could force him to fix the mess he caused. Without his knowledge, I'm not sure how much help I'm going to be."

Aster's flash of hope died and she leaned into Rom for support.

Cattar reached out and touched her hand. "I don't mean I'm completely useless, mind you. I am a scientific engineer and I believe I have a grasp of the situation. Perhaps if we all sat down and shared information, we could succeed without the old fanatic's help."

"Fanatic?" Rom repeated as he and Aster sat back down on the sofa and Cattar squeezed her bulky form into the striped chair.

Waving a hand, she said, "He was a very old man whose mind had fogged. But his reasons for doing what he did are not important right now. We must focus all our concentration on what is happening to our world, both in your time and mine. I will need the tempometer he used to come here and any data he brought with him."

Rom and Aster glanced at each other nervously. "We don't have it," Rom said, then told Cattar everything that had happened since Lantana's fateful arrival.

Cattar rubbed at the worry lines across her forehead. "This is much worse than I thought. And yet it provides one of the pieces I was missing for this puzzle. Let's see if I can explain. Lantana had worked on his device in secret, so when he first disappeared, no one suspected he had gone to another time period. All of a sudden, small changes occurred, just as you described happening here. As the type of alterations became more drastic, we suspected time was being tampered with.

"Someone recalled Lantana's preoccupation with time travel, added his fanatical views on certain subjects and his disappearance shortly before the changes began, and came up with a shocking possibility. Upon searching his residence and extracting all the data in his computer, the design for his tempometer was discovered, along with personal journal entries outlining his plans to use it and why.

"We were able to construct the device from his notes." She pointed to her belt. "Unfortunately, it had one flaw that he knew of and one that he didn't. His notes indicated that he hadn't perfected the destination time mechanism. You see, he couldn't figure out how to hit a precise date, but only the right century. I thought I had fixed it. I was trying to get here just before he arrived, but the fact that I'm over a month late shows I still didn't perfect the mechanism."

Aster was stunned. "Are you saying that Shara may have landed in a time a hundred years off from where she thought she was going?"

Cattar shrugged. "*Up* to a hundred years. She could also have missed it by a decade or hit it directly. His theory was that eddies and flows in time had the power to pull a traveler into certain historically important periods. At any rate, that was the flaw he was aware of and that I obviously have yet to correct. The other flaw is the one causing all the havoc, however, and that one will be impossible to fix until your daughter returns with the original device."

Rom and Aster both leaned forward anxiously as Cattar shifted her big body in the chair to find a more comfortable position. Rom prodded her along. "We've made the assumption that Shara has done something in the past that has caused the changes."

"Not necessarily," Cattar replied. "If that was the case, no one would have a memory of anything being changed. The previous event or situation would never have been at all, because history would have actually followed another pattern. No, this is entirely different. It took us a while, but eventually we figured it out.

"When Lantana first used his tempometer, the flaw caused a small disruption or tear in the time-space continuum. Each time the device is activated, it increases the size of the tear. Thus, history is being distorted rather than totally changed. We decided to take the risk of my using the second device in hopes that this trip could ultimately solve the problem, even if it caused a further disruption in the meantime."

Aster massaged her temples as she worked to understand what Cattar was relating. "So every time Shara uses the tempometer, she's causing the situation to worsen. Do you think that suggests that she has used it more than once?"

"Considering the first flaw, she might have had to use it several times to get to where she wanted to go. Then, of course, she'd have the same problem getting back here."

"Is there any way you could figure out where—or

rather *when*—she is and go after her?" Aster asked hopefully.

Cattar shook her head. "I'm sorry. If there's a way to track the movements of a time traveler, we didn't figure it out. Besides, due to the risk of using the device at all, I'm under orders not to activate it again unless I can come up with a solution."

Rom raked his fingers through his hair. "What are we to do, then?"

Cattar's expression revealed her empathy for what they were going through. "We pray your daughter returns soon, and while we're waiting for her, I'll continue to work on correcting the flaws."

Rom couldn't see any other alternatives. "Needless to say, our scientists and facilities are at your disposal."

Cattar thanked him and decided the handsome couple were already suffering too much to hear the rest. Anyway, there was really nothing to be gained by telling them about Lantana's twisted motives. Nor was there any sense in letting them know that there was a strong possibility that, rather than simply changing, their world would soon begin to deteriorate, as it already was in her time.

16

"Joined? That's impossible!" Shara exclaimed. "We didn't perform the sacred joining ceremony. We didn't say the words, or consume the special food or drink. Neither of our parents were present, and most important, neither of us was willing!"

Gabriel's hands pressed to his ears and his eyes squinted shut. *Please don't talk so loud. It's like being in an echo chamber.* He felt her tense agreement, then dared her to come up with a better explanation than he had. *What else could it be? Consider the evidence. The mating fever. The decreasing relief periods between peaks. The surge of power, the glow, the ground tremors, and now we're effortlessly in each other's minds in spite of my jammer. What else could that add up to?* He read her defensive response and lashed back. *Don't you dare blame me for this! I removed the jammer and brought your fingers to my temple because I wanted to give you something special.*

Oh, it was special, all right!

I didn't hear you objecting at the time! he shot back. *How many times have I suggested we go back and get treated before it was too late? But no, you talked me out of it every single time.*

How was I to know that the fever could reach its

natural conclusion without our willing participation? I thought we were coupling to keep the fever from killing us. Instead, we've ended up in a fate worse than death!

They sat there fuming, each one's anger and frustration fueling the other's, placing blame yet knowing that neither had intentionally caused the strange phenomenon. Whatever quirk of fate and time had triggered their mating fevers had also orchestrated its climactic ending.

They were joined, physically, emotionally, and mentally. Based on the evidence Gabriel had listed, it could be assumed that the joining was spiritual as well, which meant it was irreversible throughout eternity.

They had been cheated, their freedom of choice stolen, their futures altered in a way neither could imagine adjusting to.

Gabriel's rage was so painful, Shara threw up a protective mental wall between them. Surprisingly, it worked. After the first few seconds, she was able to keep their minds separated with minimal concentration.

"You're gone," Gabriel noted warily.

"Not really." She slowly lowered the partition and raised it again. "I have no idea how well I can hold it, but I'll do my best." Though she could no longer hear his thoughts, his taut expression told her enough. "I know I haven't always been honest with you, and you have good reason not to trust me. But I swear I did nothing to cause this."

He knew that, but it didn't eliminate his urge to blame someone. He massaged the back of his neck and forced himself to calm down. "It's rather ironic, isn't it?"

"What?" Shara asked, wondering how he could comment on irony in such a seemingly hopeless situation.

He couldn't meet her eyes as he spoke. "For days, you've been trusting me with your life. Now I have to trust you with my mind. I suppose there's some justice in that, but you'll have to excuse me if it takes a while to get used to the idea."

She bowed her head. She knew he was thinking that this might have been avoided if she hadn't been so stubborn about remaining in the past. But she also knew that he was a man who eventually accepted what couldn't be changed and found a way to work around the problem. Though he wouldn't throw it up to her forever, he would resent her for the rest of his life, and she could never let down the wall without feeling that resentment.

"There is one positive note," Gabriel said, standing up. "The question of how we were going to cope with the fever during the next leg of this journey has just been answered."

Shara watched him pull a jumper out of his satchel. "You mean you're still willing to go on with me?" She wasn't sure she felt like continuing herself.

As he dressed and put Beauty and his paralyzer into his jumper, he said, "Roll up the pouch, will you? Of course we're going on. But don't get the idea you've changed my thinking about Khameira's ancestor. I stand by my opinion that history shouldn't be altered. It's just that while our minds were together, I felt how important it was for you to verify your heritage. We're going to do that before we return."

He paused and narrowed his eyes at her. "Then again, my jammer no longer keeps you out of my mind, does it? You could probably convince me that I changed my mind on my own."

Shara couldn't believe he thought so little of her. "I won't take advantage of you, Gabriel. I promise." She could see he wasn't reassured and an idea came to her. "A moment ago you were able to tell immediately that I was dividing our thoughts."

"Yes?"

"Once my parents were joined, my father's mental abilities were passed on to her. If we're truly joined, anytime I let the wall down, you'll feel it. You might even acquire some of my skills. If you want them, I mean."

"I don't really know what I want right now," he said, his voice still tightly controlled. "You'd better get dressed and take out the food you brought from the lodge."

"I'm not hungry," she replied in a flat voice as she handed him the pouch. At the moment she didn't care if she ever ate again, or got dressed, or anything else.

"Yes, you are. I felt it. We'll have a quick snack to replace the calories lost, then you'll program the tempometer. The sun's up and we promised to be out of here by now."

Within an hour they had made the time-hop into the future and were standing in the vicinity of where they had been a few days before, but instead of being inside a ship, they were in the busy transportation hangar. Not far from where they'd appeared was a silver ship that resembled a flying pterodactyl. It was an older model than the one on which they had traveled to Norona. A number of people seemed to be waiting for the doors to open, which, luckily, along with the general noise, kept them from noticing Shara and Gabriel's appearance.

The doors opened and people started descending the ramp to waiting friends and family.

"Dear heavens!" Shara exclaimed, grabbing Gabriel's arm. "Look who that is!"

Standing in the doorway were Shara's parents, Romulus and Aster. Before panic set in, though, Shara realized they looked different . . . *younger* . . . several decades younger.

Aster looked terribly nervous. Romulus said something to her, and she gave him a hesitant smile. As they came down the ramp, Romulus waved at someone below. Shara couldn't resist taking a few steps closer as a woman exclaimed "Rom!" and walked into his open arms.

"You're staring," Gabriel whispered to Shara.

"But that's my parents and grandparents. Don't worry, they won't recognize me. I wasn't even born yet. Listen."

Romulus kissed his mother's cheek and hugged his father. The two men looked so much alike, it was uncanny. Rom stepped back and put an arm around Aster's waist in a clearly possessive manner. "Mother, Father, this is Aster Mackenzie. Aster, Yulan and Marcus."

"They're meeting for the first time," Shara explained. "That means it's about forty years ago, and tomorrow they'll be presenting their case to the Ruling Tribunal. The next day they'll be granted special permission to join, in spite of the law forbidding a mixed joining. I programmed the tempometer for a later date, but I can see how we would get pulled into this time. It was a landmark decision." Noticing the way her parents looked at each other, she couldn't help but add, "It was also very romantic."

Shara knew her parents loved each other, but she'd never given it much thought. Seeing them like this, prepared to defy the most powerful force in the universe to be together, made her own heart swell with emotion. They announced their love with every look, every touch. They were meant to be joined for all time.

Not like her and Gabriel. She had never heard of an accidental joining, but then she didn't know of anyone ever making a successful time-hop, either. As she watched her parents and grandparents walk away, her heart was weighted with despair.

She would never know the joy of finding her true soulmate as her mother had. There would be no romantic courtship or day-long preparation for the formal joining ceremony. She would never know the beautiful oneness of sharing her life with a man who loved her above all else.

Gabriel didn't need to be in Shara's head to see what she was feeling. Sadness emanated from every pore in her body. She had told him days ago of her romantic dreams of finding her true soulmate. She had expected it to happen the same way it had for her mother. Instead, she got him.

Not that he wasn't a good man; he imagined she could have wound up with someone worse than him. It wasn't that she was a poor choice for a mate, either. She had many wonderful traits. He just didn't want a mate at all. And she knew it. Her first reaction to finding themselves joined was numb shock. She'd put up the wall before she got over it. His reaction had been more spontaneous. He was furious.

Now he realized how cheated she must be feeling as well, and his misdirected anger had undoubtedly made it worse.

But what could either of them do? Pray for a miracle? Hope that everything returned to normal when they finally got back into their own time? Risk a paradox by trying to go back and warning themselves not to go?

Make the best of the situation. That was the reasonable path, but it wasn't much to look forward to for the rest of their lives.

Arranging passage to Innerworld was relatively easy. The same mail carrier Romulus and Aster had arrived on was departing again in three hours. Shara had counted on the Noronian code of honesty working in her favor. Since the average person never expected to be deceived by another Noronian, the travel attendant didn't examine their visas too closely. They booked the only available cabin in Gabriel's name so that hers wouldn't come up in any records to raise questions. She didn't want to take the chance of someone noting the fact that Shara *Locke* was leaving on the same ship Romulus *Locke* had come in on.

Rather than taking one week as it did for their flight to Norona, their return would take twice as long, since the stardrive's efficiency wasn't improved until twenty-some years in the future. Neither of them said it aloud, but they were both wondering how they were going to get through the next two weeks in such close quarters with relatively few distractions.

Gabriel figured he could spend the time organizing the notes and recordings he'd made thus far.

Shara intended to use the time to figure out how to program the tempometer for more accuracy.

They were reasonable people. They would manage somehow.

As it turned out, the ship offered a number of distractions, including an exercise room with sauna and whirlpool, a gaming lounge, a movie theater, and a library. The cabin to which they were assigned belonged to a ship's officer who was remaining on Norona. It was furnished with a large bed, a roomy sanitation cell, and a full-service supply station and recycling center from which they could order a wide range of food and clothing. At least they would be *physically* comfortable.

They managed to stay occupied separately throughout the first day and took their meals in the dining room with the crew and a few other passengers on board. Regardless of how much they wished to put it off, however, the time came for them to retire to their cabin . . . together.

From across the lounge, Gabriel watched Shara try to stifle a yawn for the third time in a matter of minutes. Throughout dinner, he noticed how she made an effort to socialize with the other four men and women at their table. She smiled and laughed when appropriate, but he could see she was worn out. He kept telling himself she was a grown woman who didn't need him to remind her when it was time to go to bed.

When he was invited to play a card game with some of the crew, he accepted, but his gaze kept wandering over to where she continued to chat with the group from dinner. Gradually, one after another said good night, leaving her with a young steward who was too handsome for his own good. That one didn't seem to notice how her eyelids were drooping or how many times she'd yawned; in fact, his gaze seemed to be glued to her breasts throughout their conversation.

The moment the card game was over, Gabriel excused himself and went to her side. Putting his arm around her, he smiled at the steward. "I hope you'll forgive me for stealing my lovely *mate* away, but it's been a very long day for us."

"Of course," the man said, smiling back, then nodding to Shara. "We can visit again tomorrow night."

"Don't count on it," Gabriel said under his breath as he led Shara out of the lounge.

"What's wrong?" she asked.

Instead of answering, he had a question for her. "Why didn't you tell him I was your mate?"

Shara was confused by his annoyed tone. "We aren't exactly celebrating the fact. Besides, how do you know I didn't tell him?"

Gabriel snorted. "The man was looking at you like I look at a bag of Caresses. He obviously had no idea you were already taken."

"*Already what?*" They reached their cabin, and he motioned for her to enter ahead of him. She gave him a moment to retract his remark, and when he didn't, she turned on him with her hands fisted on her hips. "You can't have it both ways, Gabriel. You can't wish me out of your life and also be jealous of every man I talk to."

He opened his mouth to protest and she cut him off. "Never mind. I don't even want to discuss it right now. We're both extremely tired and our emotions are still in an uproar. I just want to take a shower and go to sleep." She ordered towels and a conservative nightgown from the supply station and stepped into the sanitation cell.

When she came out wearing the long, loose sack, she ignored the face he made at it and got right into bed. Settling close to the wall with her back to him, she was determined to be asleep before he finished his shower. She felt good about one thing: The fever had left her system, and her cool, rational self was back in control.

Gabriel had assumed that once the fever was gone, his normal behavior would return. But jealousy had never been part of his normal behavior. And why had it bothered him to see Shara dressed in that awful nightgown? She had a right to wear whatever she felt comfortable in. It was just that he had hoped . . .

His body responded to his hope as if it had a chance to be satisfied. That was strange. Excessive lust had never been part of his normal behavior, either. Perhaps some of the fever's symptoms were going to take a while to dissipate.

As he was drying off, he felt Shara's mental partition weaken. She had been right. He'd recognized it instantly. What was she up to? He remained in the cell and waited to see, fairly assured now that she could do nothing without his being aware of it. At first he only had a glimpse into her mind, but the dividing wall continued to crumble, and he soon had a completely unobstructed view. His childhood experience was sufficient to let him know her mind was at rest.

He walked over to the bed and confirmed that she was sound asleep. Apparently she was unable to maintain the partition while sleeping. That realization made him wonder how much energy it had taken for her to hold it in place all day as she had. It hardly seemed fair that she should bear the entire burden, but he lacked the ability to assist her in any way.

Unless she was also right about one mate being able to adopt the skills of the other. He tried to construct a wall, but nothing happened. Perhaps he should ask her more about it tomorrow. If he couldn't learn the blocking skill to give her an occasional mental break, at least he could adjust to having her in his head for a few brief periods during the day. It might not be so bad, if he was prepared for it.

In fact, if the interval when their minds had been open to each other while they coupled was typical, he knew he could tolerate that, as long as he was still able to have his privacy most of the time.

He got into bed beside her and stretched out. After being doubled up in a pouch made for one and sleeping on the ground, he should have enjoyed the luxury of the large, comfortable mattress and fluffy pillow. Instead he found himself looking for an excuse to wrap his body around Shara's as he had been doing in nights past. It made little sense, but he seemed to sleep more deeply when she was in his arms. Considering how much he valued his solitude, that sort of thinking wasn't normal for him, either.

Just to prove he could, he rolled onto his stomach and turned his face away from her. Then he ordered himself to go to sleep quickly, before she started dreaming.

He remembered the dreams too well. And the nightmares. They belonged to all the others. As a little boy they were so frightening and confusing, he woke up crying hysterically every night. As he matured and understood where the barrage of weird images and nonrelated scenes came from, he stopped crying and learned to get by on a few hours of sleep a night, before everyone else's minds went to rest mode and dream mechanisms kicked in.

Although he managed to fight the urge to entwine his body with Shara's, he had no control over the fact that their minds were sharing the same space. There was something different, *unfamiliar*, about the way it felt, though.

He remembered what it was like—hearing disjointed thoughts, one on top of the other, and seeing images that he couldn't sort out or understand. He had always felt as if he'd been invaded by an alien army. To practice his concentration, he'd been instructed to sing songs, recite poems, do math calculations, anything to override everyone else's thoughts, but they were always there in the background.

He tried to identify what was different now. First of all, he wasn't receiving a multitude of jumbled thoughts and memories. There were only his and Shara's, and he could tell which was which. That much told him his jammer was still functioning as far as everyone else on board was concerned.

The second major difference he noted was that he was able to focus on an individual memory of hers and examine it as if it were his own. It wasn't at all like what he had known as a child. *This* was nonaggressive, almost peaceful . . . at least while she was asleep and he had some control over it.

Asleep, she posed no threat to his privacy or his sanity, but she was completely exposed to him. He didn't mean to take advantage of the situation, but he also didn't know how to block her out. Suddenly finding himself on the other side of the proverbial fence, he couldn't resist a little experimentation.

He wondered what her opinion of the steward was, and effortlessly his curiosity was satisfied. She had thought the younger man was pleasant enough as a conversationalist, though too egotistical for her liking, and she was annoyed at the way he openly assessed her feminine attributes. She planned to avoid spending more time with him.

With a pleased smile, Gabriel shifted his body toward her and almost said something before he recalled that she was asleep. What he had just done wasn't polite, but he couldn't stop himself from trying it again. *What did she think of him?*

Gabriel wrinkled his forehead as he felt her confusion. As he already knew, she had gone to sleep a bit angry with him over the steward, and she was wary of him because of his intention to prevent her from doing anything about Khameira.

He also picked up her contradictory attitude about his appearance. She admired him physically and wanted to keep her distance from him because of it. A bit more probing explained that better. She had been honest about only having two close relationships with men in the past. Now he knew how badly she'd been hurt by them and why she'd avoided coupling ever since, especially with attractive, confident men.

Gabriel scoffed at himself, thinking how he'd assumed his dimpled grin and self-assured attitude would affect her as it had other women he'd dealt with. He'd used the wrong approach with her at every turn.

But she *did* like some things about him. She respected his intelligence and expertise, and trusted him to protect her and treat her fairly. Though she didn't want to enjoy coupling with him, she did . . . immensely.

That knowledge pumped Gabriel's confidence back up again. In spite of everything, she had begun to care for him, a little.

The positive feeling vanished the next second as he realized just how deeply he'd hurt her by his hostile reaction to their joining. She had used the expression *a fate worse than death* because she knew that was how he'd thought of it in the first few moments of awareness.

Feeling guilty, he searched for her thoughts about their accidental joining and found nothing. Whatever she felt about it was buried too deeply for him to read, which he guessed meant that she wasn't willing to think about it at all yet.

He didn't really believe being mated with her was worse than death; he simply wouldn't have chosen it if he'd been given the opportunity. But it was only right for him to remember that she wouldn't have chosen it, either. By separating their minds while they were awake, she was doing what she could to make it easy on him. What could he do to make up for her stolen dreams of finding the perfect mate?

Since she didn't know the answer, he couldn't find it in her mind. He fell asleep with the question pending.

When he awoke, he still had no answer, but he did have Shara's warm body curved against his. The fact that they were in the middle of the bed indicated they had each sought out the other in their sleep. The ridiculous nightgown was tangled around both their legs and did absolutely nothing to cool his desire for her.

Realizing his hand was on her breast, he moved it to her waist. He wasn't going to give her an excuse to accuse him of taking advantage of her in her sleep, although he knew that was what his mental probing had been. He was also determined not to be the one to initiate further intimacy between them. Understanding better why she felt the way she did about coupling, he would be careful not to pressure her into doing anything that made her uncomfortable. He wanted her to admit that she desired him. He *needed* her to accept him without the fever hanging over their heads. He couldn't help but wonder how long she'd remain stubborn about it.

He sensed a change and realized she was beginning to rouse. He worried that she hadn't had sufficient rest until a glance at the clock on the wall told him she'd been asleep over twelve hours and he about ten. He'd never slept that long in his entire life!

Feeling her awaken was like watching a flower bloom. *Good morning,* he thought to her as gently as possible, then felt a thrill at being able to send a thought at all after so many years of inability. She stretched and snuggled closer, and the contentment she was feeling made him feel secure as well. He also knew the moment she realized she was not alone in her bed in Innerworld and that it hadn't all been a bad dream.

She sat up with a start and reconstructed the wall between them. "I'm sorry. I didn't let down the wall on purpose, I swear."

"I know. It's all right." But it wasn't at all right. Having her separate from him so abruptly was extremely disturbing to the peace he'd been enjoying. Knowing that she'd expected him to be angry with

her for invading his privacy when she obviously had
no control over it made him feel like a heartless vil-
lain.

"It probably only happened because I was so tired.
I'm sure I'll learn how to hold the partition subcon-
sciously with a little practice." She started to scoot
off the bed, but he stopped her.

"Shara, I'm not upset. We both had a good night's
sleep and I awoke only a few minutes before you.
The truth is, it was very selfish of me to expect you
to hold the partition constantly. I want you to let it
down from time to time when you need a rest. Just
warn me, and I'll be fine."

Her shoulders relaxed with the removal of part of
her burden. It *would* be easier if she could take an
occasional break, especially if she needed to concentrate on something more difficult than eating dinner
and listening to inane flirtations. "Thank you. That
would help." He didn't stop her from getting up
when she moved again. She ordered a clean jumper
from the supply station and carried it into the sanitation cell to dress. "I'll only be a moment," she
assured Gabriel without looking at him.

Waking up to discover the mental wall deterio-
rated wasn't nearly as unnerving as finding herself
cuddled up next to him. She reminded herself that
this was the only available cabin and it would be unreasonable for them not to share the bed. However,
perhaps tonight she would build a partition of something more solid, like blankets and pillows, to keep
her body from gravitating toward his.

They may be joined, but she still had her moral
conscience to answer to. Because of the fever, she
had set aside her conviction that it wasn't right to
share her body without an emotional attachment,

but the fever was gone now, and with the exception of being mated to a man who resented her very existence, things were pretty much back to normal.

As soon as she opened the cell door, she smelled breakfast, but her gaze latched onto Gabriel. He was setting the small dining table for the both of them, which was nice, but she wished he had gotten dressed first. His total lack of modesty might not have bothered her if her mind didn't automatically travel to carnal thoughts every time he showed a little flesh. "You can use the cell now," she said, hoping he didn't notice her flushed cheeks. "This looks good. Thank you."

"You're most welcome," he said with a mock bow. "Order whatever else you'd like, then go ahead and start. I'll be right back." He ordered a fresh jumper for himself, then disappeared into the cell for a few minutes. When he came out and sat down with her, he launched directly into what had been on his mind since she first mentioned it.

"Yesterday you made me an offer that I'd like to take you up on." He could tell by her expression that she needed reminding. "You said if you let the wall down, I might be able to acquire some of your mental skills. If the offer still stands, I'd like to try. I attempted to block you this morning and failed. If I could learn to do that, at least you wouldn't have sole responsibility for keeping our thoughts separate."

"That's a rather drastic change of attitude," she bluntly pointed out.

"I'm trying to be reasonable."

"Oh, yes, we must endeavor to be reasonable, mustn't we?" She studied his face for a moment while she took a bite of omelet. "You understand, I can't promise that your privacy will remain intact. You may not have any secrets left once we start experimenting with this."

He nodded. "I understand, but I don't believe I have any secrets from you anyway."

She wondered if that could possibly be true. If she agreed to this, she'd know soon enough. She would also have to face his resentment of her. She supposed there wasn't much sense in putting it off, though. "Fine. Let's work on it after breakfast."

The speed at which he finished eating and cleared the table revealed how anxious he was to begin, and her curiosity about his real reason for wanting to do this increased.

"I'm going to lower the partition now. Try to relax. If you feel nervous, so will I. Remember, this is strange to me, also."

Gabriel tensed as he sensed her mind melding with his, but it only took him a moment to get used to it. As before, he immediately noticed how different this was to what he had known before.

"Gabriel Drumayne! How dare you crawl around in my head without my knowledge?"

His hands instantly covered his ears to shut out the echo.

Sorry. I forgot. Now, explain.

He gave her a sheepish grin. He should have realized she'd know what he'd done as soon as she read his thoughts. *I couldn't block you out. I told you that.*

You can't tell partial truths when our minds are joined. You purposely looked for answers. Why?

I couldn't seem to help myself. It was a little bit like walking into a room and seeing a whole bowl full of

Caresses. He could feel her annoyance and knew if the situation had been reversed, he would have been furious. *I know it was wrong, but maybe if you can see how it was when I was a child, you'll understand why it was so irresistible.*

Shara felt him making an effort to relax and waited a moment before sorting through his old memories. She was suddenly assailed by a mélange of sights and sounds that all overlapped one another. It was a wonder he remained sane in the midst of such chaos. Then she felt it, the one secret she didn't know about him—the real reason he invaded her privacy and was anxious to experiment with her skills.

Gabriel had never gotten over the tremendous inadequacy he had felt as an average child among so many extremely gifted people.

Perhaps that also explained some of the jealousy he'd exhibited around her. He wasn't nearly as confident as he pretended to be.

I understand. She let him see that she often felt the same way.

You see? Gabriel thought to her in return. *We have several things in common after all.*

Several?

We had difficult childhoods, are devoted to our careers, will take risks to get what we want, and there's that little problem we both have with obstinance.

She made a face at him. *Let's get started. You showed me what it was like when you were a child. Take the jammer off so I can hear what happens now.*

He took a slow breath and did as she asked.

It was incredible! They were hearing thoughts from people all over the ship. *Gabriel. Focus on me and feel what I'm doing.* Slowly, and a little at a time, she blocked out all the outside voices, then let go again. *Now you try it.*

At first he couldn't do it at all. After she walked him through it several times, he still couldn't eliminate the thoughts, but he could at least quiet them to where they weren't so overwhelming.

Shara could feel him tiring and it was wearing on her, but now that she understood why this was important to him, she wanted to give him a treat for making progress, like any good teacher would.

He arched an eyebrow at her. *What kind of treat?*

She clucked her tongue at him as she felt his sex swell in anticipation. *I was thinking of something you hadn't done before! Stay with me, now.* She closed her eyes and mentally left their cabin.

Gabriel balked for a second, but then he understood that she was giving him a demonstration of her ability to see things that were not in her vision. After a quick tour of the ship, she showed him how she could use her mind to move several items around inside their cabin. He enjoyed that a lot, but it made him remember how she had removed his tunic the other night. When he felt how uncomfortable the memory made her, he apologized, but they both knew he wasn't really sorry. Her only response was to reconstruct the partition.

"That's enough for now. Later on, when we're around someone else, I'll let you feel the power of suggestion. We can work on blocking a little more each day. Who knows, by the time this trip ends, you may be able to do it on your own." *And then you could go on with your life the way you'd planned it, as if you'd never been forced to join with me.*

For the next three days, they worked on their separate projects, practiced Gabriel's mental skills, and made an effort to tire themselves sufficiently to be able to sleep in the same bed without touching. Shara figured out how to hold the partition throughout the night and how to hold back parts of both their minds while they practiced, but the constant effort prevented her from ever relaxing completely.

Every morning they awoke in each other's arms and said nothing about it. Every time Shara lowered the wall, she felt Gabriel's restrained desire for her, but he never acted on it.

By the fifth day, Shara was so tense waiting for him to do something more than merely *think* about sex, she probed his mind during a practice session.

What was that? he asked as soon as she tried to do it without his knowledge.

She felt her cheeks flush. It would have been easy to throw the wall back up and keep him out of her mind until she regained control over her thoughts, but that was the coward's way out. *Congratulations. A few days ago you wouldn't have noticed a probe that subtle.*

He narrowed his eyes at her. *That wasn't just a test. What did you want to know?* He felt her struggling to control which thoughts she would allow him to read. She was mentally stuttering, and knowing Shara, he guessed intimacy was probably involved.

She gave up on subtlety and admitted her bewilderment. *I don't understand. I feel your desire constantly. Even when the wall is up, sometimes you look at me and I know you're thinking about coupling.*

Yes, I do seem to be somewhat preoccupied with wanting to be inside you.

His words triggered an involuntary sexual response deep within her. *Then why—*

Why don't I act on it? I am not an undisciplined animal, and there's no fever driving me to satisfy my need without your enthusiastic participation. As long as you prefer our relationship to be platonic, that's what it will be. He waited for her to point out the error in his thinking, hoped she would correct him about what she wanted out of this peculiar relationship, but all he felt coming from her was confusion; then the wall was reconstructed.

No! he ordered, and tried every tool she had taught him to focus his mental energy on tearing down the wall again, but she was too strong for him. "You can't hide from this forever, Shara. You're the one who brought it up, so you can't pretend you're not thinking about it. You've buried your feelings so deeply, *you* don't even know what you want. But I'll tell you this: As long as you can't decide if you want me or not, I'm not going to seduce you into coupling with me. The choice will be completely yours, with no coercion on my part except to let you know how I feel."

She turned away from him, but he spun her around again and held her upper arms. "Let me tell you what your probing would have learned. I want you so much, I ache. I want to hold you, kiss you, touch you. Anywhere. Anytime. And I want you to touch me the same way. We're mated, Shara, whether we wished for it or not. That means neither one of us will ever find pleasure with anyone else, even if we go our separate ways. Is that really what you want? A lifetime of never again feeling what we shared the other night?"

If physical force would have dragged the answer

out of her, he might have resorted to it, but he could tell she simply wasn't ready to answer that question. Releasing her, he turned and walked out the cabin door.

17

Shara took the tempometer out of her bag and set it on the table. She was fairly sure she had found a way to fine-tune the destination date, but until they tested it, she couldn't know for sure. In the meantime, it wouldn't hurt to examine it and go over Lantana's notes one more time.

It didn't matter what Gabriel said. She'd managed a long time without a physical relationship with a man before him and she'd manage after him. Despite her intention not to think about anything but the tempometer, his words kept replaying in her mind. Suddenly she realized why she couldn't let it go.

He'd said "if," not "*when* we go our separate ways." She had assumed there was no possibility of them having a future together. Had her assumption been wrong?

His comment days ago about them having things in common came back to her. She had told him only once that she and her ideal mate would have everything in common, but obviously he'd remembered that and given it some thought. That in itself suggested that he might be considering a long-term relationship. Though she and Gabriel might not have *everything* in common, they did have some common ground to build on . . . if they chose to.

She considered how hard he was working to adopt her skills. Again she had assumed it was so that he could leave her, knowing that he could keep her out of his head permanently. Afraid of what she would find, she had avoided examining his feelings about her too closely. However, she had noticed that the resentment toward her personally had disappeared. Was it possible that he was working so hard, not to leave her, but to adjust to having her around?

That possibility allowed her to bring her own feelings out from where she'd buried them. There was a lot about Gabriel she liked, but did she want to spend the rest of her life with him? With her career in a laboratory and his in the field, she couldn't imagine how they could share their lives even if they were madly in love.

Like her parents were. Romulus would have given up his career for Aster, and she had risked her life for him.

If Gabriel loved her . . .

There wasn't much sense in fantasizing over what she could not have. What she needed to do now was make the best of what she did have.

She had a mate who was trying very hard to adjust to a situation he'd always despised. She had a mate who was intelligent, considerate, entertaining, usually reasonable . . . The list was longer than she'd realized. He made a fine companion, when they weren't arguing. Physically, he was a perfect specimen of manhood. She would never tire of looking at him.

She had a mate who desired her and wanted to please. Now that she permitted herself to think about their joining, she supposed Gabriel was close to being an ideal mate . . . except that he didn't love her and would have preferred not to be mated at all.

Even that might not have been so difficult to accept, if she hadn't already lost her heart to him.

Later that day when he asked if they were going to practice some more, she put him off. Until she had all her thoughts in order, she didn't want him to know what a quandary she was in.

Finally, in the lounge after dinner, while she watched Gabriel playing a game of cards, the only reasonable answer came to her. She couldn't stop herself from loving him, and she couldn't make him fall in love with her, but that didn't mean they couldn't work out a comfortable arrangement. After deliberating all day, she came to the conclusion that such an arrangement might be preferable to never seeing him again. He seemed to be open to the possibility of their maintaining a relationship beyond the end of this journey, so it was now up to her to show him that staying together could be more pleasant than living alone.

If he could discard his resentment and accustom himself to their joined minds, she could certainly forget her girlish dreams of undying love so that they could share their bodies.

Gabriel? She was pleased to note he barely flinched at the unexpected intrusion. He *was* getting used to her being in his head. He looked up from the cards in his hand. *I'm tired. I'm going back to our cabin.*

He started to nod and say good night, when he sensed something lying beneath her words. Before he could question her, however, she raised the partition and left the lounge. He continued playing the game, but that *something* kept tickling at his brain. She hadn't wanted him to know about it, of that much he was certain.

He experienced a moment of panic when he thought she might be abandoning him, then realized how ridiculous that was. They were traveling through space; there was nowhere she could go. So what was she up to?

Excusing himself from the game, he went to find out what she was doing before it was too late. By the time he entered the cabin, he was prepared for a confrontation . . . about *something*.

"Gabriel?" Shara called from the sanitation cell. "I didn't expect you so soon."

Good, he thought, she had not had time to do whatever nefarious deed she'd planned this time. He thought he was ready for her when she came out of the cell. But the sight of her readied him for a very different something than what he'd expected.

An enticing white gown showed off more of her luscious form than it concealed. Two strips of peek-a-boo lace crisscrossed over her breasts and the floor-length skirt was sheer enough to allow him to see a hint of the dark triangle between her legs.

The way he was looking at her made her heart race. She smiled shyly and said, "If I had chosen to be joined, I would have worn a gown like this for my mate. I didn't get to experience the formal joining ceremony, but if you are willing to accommodate me, I would very much like to have the celebration night that would have followed it."

Gabriel had to fight his body's urge to lunge across the room and fulfill her request before she changed her mind, but he wanted one favor in return. "If this had been a normal joining, there would be no barriers between us. Will you lower the partition and leave it down for the night?"

"If you wish."

"I do."

She lowered her lashes so that he would not see the deception in her eyes. Though she would have preferred to open her mind to his completely as he was asking, she knew there were two things he mustn't know. Well hidden behind her thoughts of pleasure was the fact that she still intended to change history if at all possible. And behind that was the true depth of her feelings for him. She could bear anything but his knowing that.

As their minds met, he felt her desire and was assured that she was coming to him with no ulterior motives or conditions except to give and take pleasure. Gabriel didn't even realize he'd been holding his breath until he exhaled with a surge of relief.

His gaze holding hers, he removed his clothing, but requested that she leave the gown on . . . for now. He took a step forward and raised his hands up in front of him with fingers spread and palms facing her. As she went to him and matched her hands to his, their eyes closed and they saw themselves on three separate planes. Their spiritual selves were already blended into one existence. Their minds had melded into one. Only their physical bodies needed to intertwine to complete the joining.

Simultaneously their fingers moved, grazing down each other's arms, and up over the shoulders to their faces. They traced each feature, then eased their hands down and around each other's waist. With deliberate slowness, their bodies and mouths flowed together.

It felt as though they were being immersed in a

sensual pool of liquid warmth. Each time they had coupled before, the fever had demanded urgent completion. This was much more arousing, with their bodies awakening a little at a time, absorbing each other's feelings and hearing each other's thoughts.

His lips on hers were gentle, yet incredibly seductive, and her tongue lured his into a leisurely exploration of her mouth. They didn't move any other parts of their bodies while the kiss went on and on, promising greater pleasure ahead, but they were reluctant to leave this stage behind.

And when they did, their actions remained unhurried, for with each touch they learned more of how to please and be pleased. He slipped the straps of her gown over her shoulders and lowered the lace only a bit at a time, so that her unveiling became a separate act of pleasure for them both.

His mouth on her breast was adoring rather than hungry; her hands stroking his hard muscles were admiring rather than pleading. They moved to the bed and devoted themselves to finding every sensitive area the other possessed until their passion could no longer be held at bay.

Shara was vibrating with the need to have him inside her and yet she didn't want the beautiful waves of pleasurable sensations to come to an end.

Don't fret, sweetling. It isn't ending; it's only beginning.

And with that thought both thrilling and consoling her, he joined their bodies, and together they climbed to the top of the volcano and leaped into its fiery heart . . . together.

* * *

The next morning, Gabriel awoke determined to give Shara a part of what had been stolen from her.

He began courting her. Though confined to the ship, he made a point of keeping her entertained. When he wasn't holding her hand, he was stroking her arm or her hair. He complimented her, teased her, and whispered enticing suggestions in her ear when she least expected it. His supply of Caresses had run out, but Shara's sweetness was better than the finest chocoberry.

Shara found herself responding to his attention with suggestions of her own, and a great deal of time over the next week was spent in the big bed in their cabin. If she didn't know better, she would have thought they were just like any other newly joined couple.

Since he was unable to block any of his thoughts from her, she knew his compliments were as sincere as his desire, and she knew he truly enjoyed everything they were doing together. She also knew he had yet to think of her in terms of love, though he did care for her. Given enough time, she hoped he could learn to love her . . . just a little.

If he loved her enough to want to share his life with her, they would find a way to deal with their different careers.

However, there was still one major problem that could prevent that love from ever developing. They had momentarily set aside any discussion of their opposing goals, but she was aware that he hadn't changed his mind about her tampering with history. Because she was blocking her intentions to defy him, he seemed to be under the impression that she had conceded to his opinion. She decided to allow him that impression for the time being.

Each time she allowed herself to think about it, she became more frustrated. If he loved her, perhaps he would understand the importance of her mission and not attempt to stop her. If he loved her well enough, perhaps she would do anything to keep his love, including giving up that mission.

If only he loved her. . . .

During one of their practice sessions, she sensed him worrying about how their joining would affect his future. Not wanting to face his exact plans quite yet, she blocked his personal thoughts from that moment on.

The morning they were to arrive in Innerworld, Shara awoke to find Gabriel propped up on his elbow beside her with a distinct sparkle in his eyes. *You're looking very pleased with yourself,* she thought to him with a satisfied smile of her own.

"You can speak aloud."

That was hardly the greeting she had expected from him, but it made her realize that she hadn't reconstructed the partition and yet she wasn't hearing his thoughts.

"Go ahead," he encouraged her. "Say something."

"Good morning."

His wide grin was contagious. "I can hardly believe it," he said, bouncing up off the bed and crossing the cabin. "Say something else."

She sat up, her curiosity increasing by the second. "I'll say more when you explain what this is about."

"Look." He held out his hand and showed her the jammer. "I woke up this morning and realized it had come off during the night. When I couldn't find it right away, I tried blocking out the voices, the way you've been showing me." He came back and pulled her up off the bed. "Don't you see? I finally did it!

Once I got used to that, I tried separating our minds, and I did that, too!" Giving her a great hug, he lifted her off the ground and swung her around. "Isn't this great?"

When he set her down again, she tried to give him the happy response he wanted. It was just that she hadn't expected his liberation from her to happen so soon or so abruptly. She thought she had more time.

"Shara? What's the matter?" She lowered her lashes so that he couldn't see her eyes, so he simply let go of the mental block.

Immediately she raised a partition, but his ability had strengthened so much that she had to strain to hold it against his efforts to tear it down. Finally she let him win, but asked, "Would you rape my mind against my will?"

As he realized what he had just done, shame washed over him, and he mentally backed way. "Forgive me. I wasn't thinking."

Understanding how new and tempting this was for him, Shara stroked his cheek as she carefully closed off her thoughts. "The power can control you if you're not careful. Do unto others, Gabriel, and they might give you back more than you can handle."

"Something I said caused you distress, sweetling. I only wanted to know what it was."

"It was nothing. A selfish thought, that's all. I'm embarrassed that it even occurred to me."

Gabriel rubbed his chin. "Now you've got me more curious about what it was. Shall I guess?"

"Why don't we see if you've acquired any of my other skills instead?" She slipped out of his arms and went to the supply station to order something to wear.

"I already tried. I still can't do anything else on my own, but none of those powers are as important as the blocking. I know this is a small thing to you, but . . ."

Shara's pulse pounded in her ears, drowning out whatever he was saying, but his excited pacing said enough. This was it. He didn't need her any longer. As soon as they got back, he'd be leaving on a long journey . . . alone. He would probably take her hand, give it a kiss and say something like *It's been an interesting experience, but there's really no reason to spend the rest of our lives together. Let's keep in touch, though.* And then he'd be gone.

She welcomed him back to bed when he was done pacing and wanted to share his joy with her in a more physical manner. He was too caught up in his own happiness to think there was anything unusual in the way she clung to him, but while he was celebrating his accomplishment, she was saying good-bye.

Once everyone disembarked and went their separate ways, Shara and Gabriel found an empty alcove off a remote corridor of the transportation hangar to prepare for their transmigration to Outerworld.

As she searched through her bag, she said, "I wasn't sure I would need this, but I'm glad I brought it along just in case." She pulled out an ornate gold ring with a large fire opal in its center and put it on her finger.

Gabriel recognized the special Innerworld ring immediately. Only a handful of people possessed them, since they were the key to so much power. Its obvious use was as a means of identification, but it was also a direct connection to Innerworld's central computer and an extension for the transmigrator unit. "Are they issuing those to genetic scientists nowadays?" he asked with a doubtful expression.

She clucked her tongue at him. "I only *borrowed* it from my father's office. With luck I'll have it back before he knows it's gone. I'll need some help with the coordinates."

Gabriel extracted Beauty from a pocket of his jumper. "Beauty, give me a map of the Western Hemisphere of Outerworld Earth showing the former location of the continent of Atlantis in relationship to its neighbors' borders today." A grid appeared on the mirror and the land masses were outlined.

He showed Shara the map and said, "Atlantis covered an area west of Europe and Africa from approximately twenty-two to forty-five degrees longitude and twenty to fifty-five degrees latitude. Beauty, highlight the royal city and the nearest seaport on the coast of Europe."

One dot appeared on the easternmost extension of Atlantis, and another identified Lisbon, Portugal.

Gabriel arched an eyebrow at Shara. "I hate to criticize your plan, but that's a distance of about a thousand kilometers over some very rough seas. Even if we located a boat large enough to safely make such a long trip, we wouldn't know how to pilot it ourselves. The more critical problem would come when we needed to time-hop from the past back to the present. Without being able to pinpoint the arrival time, we couldn't count on the boat being where we left it."

"I've been working on that aspect and I think I've

improved it, but I see the problem." With a thoughtful frown, she studied the map for a moment. "If we time-hop backward from here, then we wouldn't be able to get to a location on Outerworld, since transmigration hadn't been invented yet. And if we migrate out to where Atlantis was, we'd wind up in the ocean. A boat was the only solution I could come up with."

Gabriel put Beauty away. "I think I have another one. Keep an eye out for anyone passing by while I build us a raft."

Shara knew better than to question one of Gabriel's plans, no matter how impossible it sounded. Her gaze alternated back and forth between the corridor and Gabriel. From his satchel he removed the square of silver that had formed the base of his tent, spread it out on the floor, and inflated it.

"The underside is sturdy enough to hold us and our bags on top of water," Gabriel assured her. "And if we don't arrive on solid ground when we time-hop, I can improvise a sail to direct us toward land. The only serious difficulty we might have is, if the ocean is extremely choppy, we could be tossed overboard. I'd suggest you put the tempometer on, program it now, and have it set to go the minute we hit Outerworld."

Shara did as he suggested, then asked Beauty for the exact coordinates of a spot on Atlantis's coast near the royal city. By pressing a series of the raised gold nodes on the sides of the ring, she tapped into the main transmigrator unit and programmed it to send them to their destination. "I'm set," she said, and they both sat down on the raft.

It took a little maneuvering, but with Shara sitting between Gabriel's legs, they managed to maintain contact with each other while he kept one hand on their luggage and another on the raft, so that nothing would be left behind.

"Sweetling, promise you'll stay by me so we can hop out again if the situation is too risky."

"Yes, Gabriel."

Her tone was almost too sweet to be believable. "And another thing: I haven't said it, but I am glad you've come around to my way of thinking about not altering history." He suddenly felt as if she were mentally squirming. "Shara? You *do* agree with me now, don't you?"

Rather than say a word, she turned the opal stone halfway around to the right and they were on their way.

The migration took about two minutes, but it wasn't nearly as jarring as a time-hop. They were simply suspended in a black void until they rematerialized on the Altantic Ocean.

A bolt of lightning streaked across the gray sky followed closely by a crash of thunder. Blowing rain pelted their faces as the raft was carried high in the air by a mighty wave and dropped again with a bone-jarring splash.

"Get us out of here. *Now!*" Gabriel yelled in Shara's ear.

But just as her fingers moved on the tempometer switch, her bag came loose and slipped over the edge of the raft. In a panic, she made a dive for it.

18

Security Chief Varius burst into the Governor's office. "Tunnel number seven just collapsed!"

Rom's stomach clenched violently, but he forced himself to ask, "Casualties?"

"None have been reported so far," the chief replied, making a monumental effort to control his panic. "Two hours from now it would have been a different story. A ship was scheduled to depart for Norona using that lane."

Rom rubbed his eyes. He hadn't slept in days. Couldn't. He mentally contacted Aster before giving Chief Varius his instructions.

We can't put it off any longer. We have to act immediately, Aster thought to him.

In the past two weeks, the changes had taken another giant, disastrous turn. Cattar had reluctantly revealed that she had known how much worse it would get, but had hoped they could have prevented it.

This was the second tunnel to disintegrate; the first had resulted in the death of seven hundred Innerworlders. In Outerworld, most of Europe was now a wasteland because the nuclear accident at Chernobyl in 1986 had been altered.

Transmissions from Norona indicated they were

also experiencing a series of strange phenomena, but the changes didn't seem to be heading for deterioration of the planet.

The only positive note was that Cattar and the Innerworld scientists were certain they were getting close to a solution to both flaws, but they still needed the original device in hand to conclude their analysis.

Cattar deduced that Shara had made another time-hop that ripped the tear in the time-space continuum much wider, but wherever she had traveled to, it wasn't home. And if she didn't get here soon, there might be no home for her to arrive in.

All things considered, Rom knew what had to be done. He met Chief Varius's worried gaze and said, "Notify Emissary R-17 that it's time to make contact with the Secretary General of Outerworld's United Nations. They have to be told what's going on, even if there's very little they'll be able to do about it."

Varius nodded and waited for the Governor to issue the order he knew had to be given.

Taking a deep, steadying breath, Rom spoke the dreaded words. "Commence evacuation procedures."

19

Gabriel grasped Shara's ankle a second before she disappeared under the water. But his hand was slick with rain and he felt her slipping away despite his tremendous effort to pull her back. His other hand was gripping the edge of the raft. If he let that go to get a better hold on her, they could both go down. *Shara!*

Help me! She sent him an urgent image of what he needed to do to save them. Suddenly the raft shot straight up in the air and Gabriel thought surely the end had come. Instead of flipping over, however, the raft hovered there, as if being held up by a powerful geyser of water. But it was their combined mental power, not a physical force, keeping them levitated.

With the raft fairly stabilized, he was able to drag Shara back on board. She lay over his lap, choking and sputtering and drenched from head to toe, but her fingers remained clenched around the handle of her precious bag.

He wanted to comfort her and scream at her at the same time, but both would have to wait until they got clear of the storm. "The wind is blowing us off course. We've got to go." He shifted her back into their former position, and as a bolt of lightning electrified the air around them, they surged into the next leg of their journey.

At the end of the time-hop, it was immediately apparent that Gabriel had been correct about the wind blowing them off course. The late afternoon sun was shining in a clear blue sky, the sea beneath them was flat as a sheet of green glass, but land was nowhere in sight.

Holding the mirrored triangle in front of him and Shara, he instructed Beauty to give them their present coordinates. It wasn't quite as bad as it appeared. "Indicate distance and direction to nearest body of land with dense population of life-forms, evolution level four and above." Their destination was 2.2 kilometers northwest. "How are you at rowing?" he asked Shara.

She twisted her head back to look at him. "I thought you said you could make a sail."

"A sail needs wind. We went from one extreme to the other. I have a personal-sized retropower rocket that I could hook up to the rear of the raft, but it can only be used once and I'd rather save it for a real emergency."

"Then save it and our strength. Take us in with your mind. You can do it now."

"Not without your help."

Shara shook her head. "All I did a minute ago was give you a push start, then concentrate on not drowning. You held the raft up by yourself."

Gabriel didn't know what to say. He'd been too terrified to think about who was doing what. In case it was only a fluke, he focused his mind on elevating the raft. When it rose off the water, he was so surprised, he let it drop again. *Did I really do that by myself?*

Resting her head back against his chest, Shara smiled at the wondrous delight in his mental voice, but it made her realize that she hadn't reconstructed the partition. As she raised it, he stopped her.

"Please don't. We can each block our own thoughts now, and I'd rather keep the channel open between us." He felt her question. "I have a strange feeling that we may need it. Anyway, it's not as terrible as I remembered. I don't mind you being in here with me as much as I thought I would."

Shara smiled again, letting him know his concession was appreciated.

He tightened his arms around her for a moment, then urged her around to face him. "Now that we've got that out of the way, perhaps you'd like to tell me what possessed you to attempt suicide back there?"

His abrupt mood change was jarring, but she knew she deserved his anger this time. "I'm so sorry. I panicked. I saw all my work about to disappear and I didn't think of the consequences."

Crossing his arms in front of him, he kept his expression stern and his thoughts closed to her. "In the future, you will consider the consequences first, *then* act. Both our lives could have been lost because you were worried about losing material possessions!"

"I said I'm sorry. What do you want me to do? *Penance?*"

He closed his hands over her shoulders. "What I want is a promise that you'll never, *ever* do anything so foolhardy again." He pulled her close and embraced her tightly. "In all my journeys, I have never felt fear so great."

Shara held her response, hoping to hear some word of love following the scare of losing her, how his life wouldn't be complete without her, but his analysis was much more clinical.

"It must have been due to our joining. If you feel an extremely strong emotion, such as fear, I suppose I can't help but feel it also."

She sighed quietly and eased out of his arms. "Yes, I'm sure that's what it was. We should change clothes before we reach land."

Gabriel thought she looked awfully dejected. Perhaps he'd been too hard on her, but such an enormous breach of safety required serious handling. He reached over and brushed her hair off her cheek. "I didn't mean to be so harsh. I've become so accustomed to your being around, I forget how limited your journeying experience actually is. You'll get better in time, I'm sure."

Yes, she thought to herself as she dug the rebel garb out of her bag. Better at journeying. Better at hiding her weakness. Better at accepting the fact that she would never have the loving relationship she had always dreamed of—the kind her mother had promised she would find someday, just as her parents had.

In a short time they were once again dressed as Friends, Beauty hung from Gabriel's neck, and Shara had returned the tempometer belt and special Innerworld ring to her bag. Under Gabriel's newly acquired power, they were headed toward land. It had been agreed that if anyone recognized them from Norona, they would explain that they'd traveled to Terra on Zeus's ship, which had set down in Athens, but then decided to explore more of the planet.

With Beauty's help, Gabriel guided them to a stretch of beach with heavy vegetation a small distance from the royal city of Atlantis, where they might be able to make camp. As he lowered the raft onto the sand, he had the feeling they were being watched.

Yes, I feel it, too. When her eyes could see no one about, she used her mental vision. Not far away, crouched amid a thicket of broad-leaved bushes, were a man and woman.

They appear to be more frightened than dangerous, Gabriel surmised. *You talk to them.*

"Hello?" Shara called in a purposely lilting voice. "Please come out. We mean you no harm."

Very cautiously, the couple stood up, came out of the bushes, then fell to their knees with their foreheads pressed to the ground. Considerably shorter and stockier than Gabriel and Shara, they both had brown skin and straight black hair clipped below the ears. The only covering they wore was a short piece of rough brown material wrapped around their hips and knotted at the waist.

Gabriel stopped Shara from telling them they didn't need to bow. *They must have seen us float in on the raft and think we're gods. Remember, these were a very primitive, superstitious people. Don't disillusion them just yet. We need information and they might be more helpful if they're a bit awestruck.*

Whatever it takes, right?

Within reason. "You may rise and tell us your names," he said in an imperious tone.

They stood, but kept their heads bowed. "I am Jarad, and this is my spouse, Ester. You wear the dress of the Friends," the man said, sneaking a look at the strangers.

Shara was instantly relieved to note that her translator chip was programmed with these people's language, whatever it was.

"Yes," Gabriel replied. "That's right. We're Friends, and we're looking for the others like us."

"They're all gone," Ester said with a sad shake of her head, then looked to Gabriel with a hopeful expression. "They promised someone would return to help us. Are you the ones?"

Gabriel quickly improvised. "We were told there would be a man and woman at this location who could guide us and answer our questions. Who made this promise you spoke of, and when?"

"The promise was made by the second visitors," Jarad told him, "and has been passed on secretly through two generations. We had begun to lose any hope of salvation, but then Noe started hearing God's voice, and now we have seen you arrive like birds from the sky, exactly as it was predicted."

Shara thought she knew what Jarad was speaking of, but she wanted to be sure. "What has God told Noe?"

Ester and Jarad glanced at each other with worry in their eyes.

"I will know if you lie," Shara said, gambling a bit.

Jarad raised his head and met her gaze. "God told Noe that the end was coming soon, and the land and all the evildoers on it would be swallowed up by the sea. Noe was ordered to build a huge ark and gather on it a male and female of each animal and tell other good men to do the same. But most vessels have been discovered before they were finished and taken by King Jupiter's soldiers for use in the war against Athens. Noe and his family stay hidden high on the mountain, so their ark has not yet been found."

Gabriel, something doesn't fit here.

He raised his hand to stop Jarad from saying

more. "We have been traveling a very long time and some information is unknown to us. It would be helpful if you could relate to us what has happened here since Poseidon arrived."

Ester nervously tugged on Jarad's wrapper and he gave her a nod. "We do not mind telling the story, but we have work to do. If we don't get back with the potion soon, someone will come looking for us."

From the frightened look on Ester's face, Shara assumed a terrible punishment would be meted out if they failed to complete their task in time. "Is there something we can do to help? Then you could tell us what we wish to know while we all work."

Shara!

How bad can it be?

"You see, Ester," Jarad said. "The stories were true. The Friends *were* good and kind to the people."

Shara ignored Gabriel's mental groan as they followed Jarad and Ester onto a narrow overgrown path through the bushes. A few seconds later, the bushes ended and they were standing at the edge of a large field completely covered by red, white, purple, and pink flowers. A closer look revealed that they were poppies, planted in rows with just enough space for a person to walk between.

The use of narcotics for any purpose was outlawed on Norona a millennium ago, but as a scientist, Shara had studied it. *Opium cultivation?* Shara asked to confirm her analysis.

Exactly. Still want to help?

Whatever it takes, remember?

Ester bent over and tilted a blossom to point out the capsule where the seed develops. "It takes two days to collect the base for the potion from a flower." With her fingernail she scraped the capsule and a milky juice seeped out. "Some practice is required to apply exactly the right amount of pressure. Tomorrow at this time the juice will be solid and can be collected." She stepped over two rows and picked a tiny chunk of dried juice off a seed capsule to show them. "I scratched this row yesterday."

Jarad handed Gabriel a bucket and kept one for himself. "I welcome the help. We have been ordered to provide double the amount we usually collect for the next two suns."

Following Jarad's lead, Gabriel squatted down on his haunches to collect the tiny bits of raw opium, but in seconds his legs and back were complaining, so he switched to crawling in the dirt on his bare knees. He would make Shara pay for this later, that much was certain.

Stop whining and get him talking. After squashing about a dozen capsules, she got the hang of scratching them exactly right to draw milk. She simply didn't allow herself to think about what she was doing.

"Why has the order been increased?" Gabriel asked as they started moving along the row, working first one side, then the other.

Jarad looked at Gabriel as if he had asked a foolish question. "You are unaware, as you said. I will explain. Every twelve moons the princes of Atlantis's lesser provinces meet with King Jupiter in Poseidon's temple in the royal city for seven suns. They and their courts require the potion to keep their great minds in an elevated state throughout the gathering. Today marked the fifth sun, but on the seventh night they will need the most potion."

"Why is that?" Shara asked.

Ester's fingers pinched a capsule so hard the blossom snapped off. "Because a large quantity is required for the final ceremony, particularly to calm the bulls. There are ten that will be sacrificed to Poseidon." She took a shaky breath. "And so will an infant and a maiden."

"What?" Shara exclaimed. *Gabriel, can this be true?*

If we've arrived when I think we have, I'm afraid animal and virgin sacrifices aren't the only atrocities we're going to hear about.

Jared turned to Gabriel with a pleading expression. "The king's servant discovered that our only child, Rebekah, began her menses two moons ago, and he chose her to be the honored maiden. But it is no honor to us. Please tell us that you will be able to save her."

Gabriel opened his mouth, but Shara was faster. "We'll help however we can."

Shara! We're only here to observe.

She gave him an innocent look. *They'll help us with our observations, and we'll help them in return. It's only fair.*

You can't change history!

What I can't do is stand by while a young girl is murdered. They glared at each other for a moment, then Shara looked back at Jarad and smiled sweetly. "Why don't you tell us what you know about Poseidon and his followers from the beginning? Then we'll figure out what we can do for Rebekah."

Jarad shuffled a little farther down the row and began the story that had been passed on to him by his father and his father before that, along with the awareness of what was right and wrong, good and evil.

"God descended from the sky, just as you did, but he brought the Friends with him."

"Excuse me," Shara interrupted. "When you say *God*, are you referring to Poseidon?"

Jarad frowned at her. "Of course. Noe speaks as if it is another, but everyone knows Poseidon is the most powerful of the gods."

Shara decided it was best not to get into a theological discussion at this point. "How long ago did Poseidon arrive?"

"That was eight of my family's generations ago."

How many years would that be? Shara asked Gabriel rather than have Jarad again wonder about her lack of knowledge.

Based on these people's average life span, it could be somewhere between three hundred fifty and four hundred years. And before you ask, yes, that means the continent could blow at any time. Now let the man tell his story before I'm too crippled to walk upright again.

"At first the people were afraid of the visitors that called themselves Friends, but they were very wise and showed the people how to improve their lives. Their great powers were used to help, not hurt.

"The Friends taught the people to build shelters using the trees on the mountains and dig ditches to carry the water to land that was too dry for crops to grow. They built vessels that carried Friends and people over the water to other lands, where they traded things that were plentiful here for things that they did not have. Life was good and peaceful, and some of the Friends took spouses from among the people."

"I heard Poseidon sired children with such a

woman," Gabriel prompted when Jarad paused to move farther down the row.

"Yes. Two, actually. It is said he was very lonely when he first arrived, for his spouse had not survived the journey from the Otherworld. He was brought out of his sadness by Cleito, a girl child of a couple who dwelled on the mountain to the north of the royal city. When she came of age, he took her to his shelter. She bore him five pairs of male twins before she passed on. He chose another spouse after Cleito, who was said to be a witch for the God of Darkness. She gave Poseidon several more children, but made his life so miserable that he chose to leave this land for his kingdom beneath the sea.

"Before he left, however, he divided the land up into ten provinces and gave each twin one to rule. To his firstborn, Atlas, he gave the most valuable portion, which bordered the sea facing the neighbors with whom they traded goods. Poseidon appointed Atlas king of all the land, which he then named Atlantis. Atlas's twin, Gadir, received the property surrounding the royal province so that he might protect his brother's interests, and his back, for God knew that not all of his children had warm hearts."

He stopped his tale to take his and Gabriel's buckets over to a large woven basket and empty them. When he returned, he needed no prodding to continue.

"By the third generation of my family, all the first visitors had gone to join God in his undersea paradise, and Atlas and his brothers began to make changes. The people were put to work building a great temple in honor of Poseidon and Cleito. New laws were set that forced the people to spend a longer time laboring in the fields and quarries and prohibited them from traveling when and where they wished. Punishments were delivered to any who disobeyed.

"Fearing the growing power of the neighboring lands, especially Libya and Athens, Atlas required a certain number of men from each province to train as soldiers in his army to protect the island.

"He also eliminated the law against brothers taking sisters as spouses, since he lusted after his own sister, Hesperis. They had many daughters, but only one son, and he was killed in a storm. So when Atlas went to join his father under the sea, his youngest half brother, Saturn, became king. Saturn was the son of the witch, born the year that Poseidon departed, and it was believed that she taught him her evil spells and removed his heart so that there was no bit of goodness in him."

Jarad noticed Ester checking the position of the sun as it began its descent toward the horizon. "Do not worry, woman. Thanks to these Friends, we will have the basket full and the potion delivered to the palace before the stars begin to shine."

Gabriel desperately needed to stretch his cramped muscles. "Tell me, Jarad, is there a place we could hide our . . . vessel while we're here?"

"If you put everything in the bushes, they should be safe enough."

Gabriel promised to be right back and headed toward the beach to secure all of their belongings. Shara decided he needed help and hurried after him. "Is Beauty getting all of that?" she asked once they were out of earshot.

"Yes, but so far it correlates with most of the information already recorded. What I didn't know is that there was a second set of visitors. As near as I can figure, Norona must have sent an inspection team to Terra to follow up on the development. They would have made note of the problems they saw arising and gone back to the Ruling Tribunal to report. Several hundred years would have passed before anyone could have returned to take action."

"Then it's possible that there's a messenger of death, so to speak, here on Atlantis right now, preparing to carry out Norona's decision to destroy the continent."

Gabriel shrugged. "That could explain Noe hearing *God* warn him to save his family, others like him, and the animals. But I've always thought there was another possibility, and that's the one thing stopping me from insisting we get out of here while we have the chance."

Shara concealed her smile as she noted that he didn't hesitate to use his mind to lift the raft and their bags in the air. He brought it all down in the center of a clump of bushes. "Don't keep me in suspense. What's the theory you're hoping to prove?"

He started to correct her phrasing, then realized she had worded it the way he had in his own mind. "I've always thought the wholesale destruction of an entire continent and a great number of innocents in order to punish the degenerated descendants of the Noronian rebels was too radical on the part of a ruling body as reasonable as the Tribunal.

"Instead, consider this. What if a righteous person was sent here by the Tribunal to issue warnings or place restrictions on the rebels' dealings with the natives? What if that person found a situation so depraved and out of control that he believed the instructions he'd been given were inadequate to stop the cruelty? Knowing how long it would take to go to

Norona for the support of a security force and return, he may have taken matters into his own hands."

"Then why would history state that it was the Tribunal's decision?"

"Perhaps it worked so well to increase their omnipotent image, they chose to take credit for it, then publicly regretted that such extreme measures had been taken."

"The interesting part will come if your theory is correct and you try to release information that could puncture a hole in the Tribunal's power base."

Gabriel winked at her. "Let's take one step at a time." He kneaded the muscles in his lower back. "*Drek,* but I'm going to be sore tomorrow."

Putting her arm around his waist and pushing him back onto the path, she said, "I'll give you a good massage before you go to sleep tonight."

He gave her a quick kiss for the offer. "By the way," he said as they made their way through the thicket, "did you happen to notice that your fine-tuning of the tempometer's destination program had the opposite effect that it was supposed to?"

She pinched his side. "What I did should have worked. But we were practically hit by a bolt of lightning at the same time that we hopped, remember? The electrical charge undoubtedly threw off the balance. You'll see. Next hop, we're going to hit the date we want right on the dot."

"I certainly hope so, since the next hop is going to be home." He waited for her agreement, but she kept silent. "Well? Isn't it?"

She smiled up at him as they arrived at the poppy field. "Of course, Gabriel. Whatever you say."

Why do I detect some insincerity in that statement?

I have no idea.

And speaking of insincerity, you never answered me before the hop—

"Oh, my, Ester. Look how far you got without me. I'm afraid I'm not much help."

"Nonsense," the woman said. "You're doing very well for your first day."

Gabriel's reaction to the idea that there might be a second day for them at this task distracted him from concern over Shara's insincerity. She determined to make sure that he wouldn't spend any more time doing something that would sour his disposition before he discovered her deceit. Besides, they could only learn so much in a field full of narcotic-producing flowers. Somewhere nearby meetings were going on with the descendants of the original Noronian exiles. She needed to get hair samples from every one of them, particularly if Gabriel truly intended to go home on the next hop. "Jarad, please continue your story. Saturn had just become king of Atlantis."

As they continued to creep their way along the rows of flowers, gradually filling the collection basket, Jarad brought them up to date.

Saturn expanded the laws set down by his half brother, further limiting the freedoms of the natives, while also requiring them to give pleasure or receive pain at the whim of the nobility. Like Atlas, he espoused his sister, Rhea, not because of lust or love, but to keep her from running off with a native man. It was said that he forced himself on her when and where he pleased to constantly remind her of obedience, then kept her chained in his room when he wanted her out of his sight.

The numbers of men and boys required to become soldiers multiplied again and again as Saturn altered the purpose of the army from one of protection to one of waging war on their neighbors. His attitude had been, why trade for goods that could be taken by force just as easily?

He demanded that Poseidon's Temple be enlarged and gilded with metals that shone and sparkled, even when no light was on them. Simultaneously, he ordered that another enormous monument be constructed in his own honor. Before it was finished, however, he disappeared and his son, Jupiter, became king. Though some said Rhea killed her brother in his sleep, most suspected that Jupiter murdered his father to gain the power before it was due him. No body was ever found, however, and no one dared accuse the new king.

Jupiter's reign began when Ester and Jarad were children. None of the people believed their fate could worsen, but it did. Jupiter was even more twisted than his father. As if Rhea had not withstood enough, her son continued to keep her a captive, which endorsed the theory that she had killed Saturn; Jupiter appeared to be just punishing his mother for her wickedness. Though he did not use her publicly, she was required to sleep in his bed each night, even when he ordered other women to come to pleasure him. He was also known to keep a number of female animals in his court for variety whenever he grew bored with his human slaves.

Under his rule, perversions were added to the royal ceremonies as well. He claimed that God had demanded human torture and sacrifices. A ceremonial meal often included cooked body organs of his enemies so that he and his princes might ingest the victims' strengths.

The war to conquer all the neighbors to the east escalated, and though he now controlled Libya, rumors were spreading that Athens was not so easily defeated. At each new moon another vessel carrying Atlantean soldiers left for the lands beyond the great rocks and none had returned in a long time. Most of the men remaining on Atlantis were descendants of God or slaves captured in raids on other lands. Those poor souls were forced to work on the monument Saturn had begun and Jupiter now claimed as his own. They were beaten, abused, and often worked to death, because it was assumed that Athenian replacements would be coming on the vessels returning in victory anytime now.

Only the poppy-field workers were free of mistreatment. Each field was maintained by the family that had been its caretaker before Poseidon arrived. The families survived by keeping the secret of how the potion was prepared and convincing the rulers that sorcery was involved.

"We have passed our middle age," Ester explained. "And Rebekah is the last of our family line. If she passes on without having the chance to find a spouse and bear children to inherit our field, it will be given to a child of another caretaker family. Then we will be lowered into the fire pit like all the old ones who are no longer useful."

"It is time to return to the shelter," Jarad said, rising and making one last trip to the collection basket with the buckets.

Gabriel helped Jarad lift the load of raw opium and Shara and Ester each carried a bucket away from the field.

"Where is Rebekah now?" Shara asked as they walked.

The mere mention of her daughter's name brought tears to Ester's eyes. "She was taken to stay in the temple so that her purity could be protected until the final ceremony. We have been told she is being kept in the female slaves' quarters, but we have not been permitted to see her since the meetings began."

"How well guarded are the quarters?"

Forget it, Shara, Gabriel silently warned.

"Extremely well," Jarad said. "The women are used for too many purposes to be allowed any freedoms."

Shara had an idea brewing. "Do any of them serve the nobility's meals?"

"Yes, there are those assigned to the cookfires and meal service."

Shara cut off Gabriel's automatic objection before he could transmit it. *I have to get inside the temple and, since they're at war with the entire civilized world, visitors might be suspected of being enemies. Better that I pose as a household slave.*

"What about male slaves?" Gabriel asked Jarad.

"There are a few in the temple, but most healthy males are put to work on the monument."

Gabriel was torn between wanting to see and record everything he could no matter what the risk and wanting to keep Shara out of harm's way. When they reached a small wooden shelter with a thatched roof, he helped Jarad dump the contents of the basket onto a large stone slab and spread the tiny chunks out for further drying under the next day's sun.

"We will share some food and drink with you," Jarad said. "Then we must make our delivery to the temple, but you are welcome to rest here."

"That's very kind of you," Shara said as they all

went inside the shelter. While Ester rekindled the fire under the cookpot, Shara communicated with Gabriel. *Do you agree with me or not?* She felt his concern for her safety. *We'll keep the channel between us open at all times.*

What if you're in danger, and I'm too far away to help?

I have my powers to protect me. I know you're dying to get a look at Poseidon's Temple and Jupiter's monument. I'll be fine. And I promise to keep our stay here as brief as possible.

Gabriel reluctantly agreed and asked Jarad if he could help them get into the temple. "We need to observe more before we can be of any assistance to anyone."

Without hesitation, Jarad nodded. "We are well known and are familiar with the design of the temple. But I believe the easiest plan would be to take you both inside to the cookery, where we must deliver the potion. There are other slaves as fair-skinned as you, but you will need to be clothed as they are."

Shara glanced at Ester's nearly nude body and inwardly cringed.

Ester walked over to a chest in the corner and took out some folded copper-colored garments. "We have been ordered to serve in the temple on occasion. These robes must be worn by all servants so that they will blend in with the walls of the temple."

Shara breathed a sigh of relief as she noted that the robes were full length, with long sleeves and hoods. They would be somewhat short on her and Gabriel, but it was much better than the wrapper Ester was wearing. Immediately she saw another advantage to the robe. It was large and loose enough for her to wear the tempometer belt and conceal her microputer and supplies beneath it instead of leaving them behind in her bag. While a large pot of lamb and vegetable stew was reheated over the fire, she excused herself to fetch her equipment.

Gabriel felt somewhat better knowing she would have the tempometer on her so that they could make an instant escape if it became necessary.

Suddenly the tin cups on the table rattled. Jarad put his hands over them to stop them from tipping over, while Ester guarded a row of vibrating clay crocks on a shelf above the fire. A thunderous rumble sounded in the distance and grew louder as it seemed to be rolling toward them.

Gabriel felt the floor beneath his feet begin to quiver, and lurched out of his chair. *Shara! We're out of time! Run for the raft and program the tempometer. I'll be right there.*

20

"Jarad! Ester! You've got to get away from here now," Gabriel exclaimed, throwing open the door. The entire shelter trembled as if a giant had reached down and given it a mighty shake, then everything was calm again.

The couple was completely bewildered by Gabriel's actions. In a polite tone, Ester said, "We find it best to stay in one place until the shaking passes."

Only a minor earthquake, Gabriel thought with relief.

Or the local volcano trying to clear its throat.

Are you all right?

Just a bit shaken.

He felt her laughing at her own joke and smiled in spite of the seriousness of the situation. "Jarad, how often is that happening?"

"A few times a day. That one was mild. Sometimes it is so violent the ground cracks wide open. Noe says it is God's warning that the end is near."

"Have you made preparations to leave . . . in case the warnings are true?"

Jarad glanced at Ester. "We have a small vessel hidden. But if Rebekah is lost to us, we have no reason to flee."

Gabriel suddenly realized he had automatically

tried to warn them when he thought disaster was about to strike. *Drek!* He didn't want to feel anything for these people. Whatever happened was done ten thousand years ago. The girl and her family either survived or they didn't. It was wrong to interfere, even if it felt immoral to ignore their need for help. It was definitely unethical to lead them to believe he and Shara might be their salvation.

Interesting dilemma, isn't it? Shara reentered the shelter with the tempometer belt around her waist and a soft black bag tied to the side of the belt. Ester and Jarad looked at her curiously, but they didn't ask about the items and she didn't offer any explanations.

During their meal, Gabriel asked Jarad for another favor. "Please contact Noe and tell him that if he hears from God again, to let Him know that two others are here from, uh . . . the Otherworld. Describe us and where we can be found, then have Noe ask God to contact us. It's vital that we have a talk with Him."

Professor! You're not planning to interfere, are you?

Of course not, but I can't think of any faster way to get to the truth of what happened here than a personal interview with the one who may have been responsible.

A loud trumpetlike noise outside the shelter caught everyone's attention.

"Aah," said Jarad. "He's right on time to take us to the temple."

"He?" Shara inquired as he and Ester both rose from the table and swiftly cleared the dishes away.

"Yes. Elo has been visiting us since he was a calf. Jarad trained him to come to the shelter each day at sunset." Ester took a crock off the shelf and peeked inside it. With a shake of her head, she emptied a quantity of light brown powder from another crock into the first, then put a lid on it. "That should do it. Put the robes on before we go, in case we are stopped on the way to the temple."

Shara was more than pleased with the garment. With the hood up and her head and shoulders bent, she could be mistaken for a man. The last thing she wanted to do was attract attention to herself as a female slave in Jupiter's court.

At least we agree on one thing.

Her self-confidence faltered the moment she stepped out the door and saw Elo. Shara had never in her life seen a creature so enormous. She knew it was an elephant only because she had seen its image in a children's book on Terran animals that her mother had given her when she was learning her alphabet. It had two dangerous-looking ivory tusks that were longer than Gabriel was tall, and gigantic ear flaps that it fanned in warning upon seeing the strangers.

Shara froze in place as the elephant gracefully extended its long trunk up to her face, made a noise that could have been a sniff or a snort, then pushed the hood off her head. The animal gave a mournful squeal, then withdrew its trunk and rocked its great head back and forth.

"He thought perhaps you were Rebekah in disguise," Ester explained. "Elo misses her, too. Elo, this is Shara and Gabriel. They would like to ride with us today, if that is all right with you."

The beast took another whiff of Shara, inspected Gabriel, then folded its two front legs beneath its body. Though less intimidating like that, it was still frightfully large. Shara was wondering how one actually got on an elephant to ride, even with its permission, when it bowed its head with the underside of its trunk on the ground and its nostrils curved upward. Jarad sat down on the trunk as if it were a swing.

"Up," Jarad commanded, and Elo raised his trunk high in the air, tipping back his head at the same time. Jarad stood up on the forehead, walked to the hindquarters, and straddled the hump with his knees bent.

Gabriel went next and looked just as relaxed about the matter as Jarad had.

"Go on, Shara. I should sit in front," Ester said.

Shara thought the animal seemed friendly enough, but it was *so* big. "We really shouldn't put Elo out like this. I can walk."

Don't be a coward.

I am not a coward! I'm cautious.

Then get your cautious behind up here.

"Elo does not mind, and it is much too far to walk," Ester told her.

Shara stroked Elo's trunk and murmured, "I've never been very good at physical things, so don't be insulted if I fall off." Elo's big eye blinked at her as if he understood, and Shara sat down as the men had. Seconds later she was wondering why she was so worried about something that was such fun.

As the elephant lumbered its way north along the coast at a faster pace than one would expect from such a huge creature, Gabriel recorded the beauty of the land. There were steep mountains not far away that were partially covered with deep green forests. The barren peaks had a lavender cast in the twilight. Throughout a good deal of the trip, they were in a meadow with thick grass where herds of animals grazed, unconcerned by the humans passing by.

He was able to identify many of the species that had been in Zeus's commune on Norona, so he assumed a number of the animals must have survived the arduous trip. But he also saw zebras and unicorns, and a few others he didn't recognize.

Shara spotted the royal city a kilometer away because of the golden glow, and the closer they got, the brighter it shone. The entire city was enclosed by a high wall covered with what appeared to be polished brass. The entrance to the city was through a gate of golden bars that was wide enough for a herd of elephants to march through at once. On each side of the gate was a guard tower carved from red-veined black marble.

Ester waved at a guard and the gates were quickly opened for them. Elo carried them onto a bridge as wide as the gateway and paved in the same black stone. As they crossed over a vast waterway, a sailboat passed beneath them.

"When we were children," Ester said, "this harbor was filled with vessels of all sizes. We used to sit on the outer wall and watch them coming and going and pretend that we were directing them."

On the opposite side of the harbor was another wall like the first except that its gate was narrower in size. Again the guard in the tower immediately granted them entrance upon seeing Ester. A paved road led them through a beautifully manicured garden that gradually inclined until they reached another wall and gate. These were coated in a silvery metal and were somewhat less imposing in grandeur and size.

As they proceeded onto another bridge that took them over a waterway half the width of the first,

Shara asked Ester, "Can you go to other parts of Atlantis by way of these waters?"

"No, only out to the great sea. There are three canals that surround the citadel mound, each a little higher than the one before. When we reach the temple, you will be able to look down and see the five-tiered circles of land and water."

They crossed another stretch of upward-sloping land and another bridge before they reached the gate to the citadel. This wall had a different glow than the others—golden, but darker, with the reflective quality of polished copper.

That must be orichalcum, Gabriel told her. *It's referred to in the history texts, but nothing matching its description was ever found elsewhere on this planet or any other, so no one could be certain of the existence of such a metal.*

It's beautiful. This whole place is absolutely breathtaking. I can't wait to see the temple itself. She felt Gabriel's anticipation stirring her own and truly understood how he could get so enthralled by history.

As soon as they were through the last gate, Shara got her first glimpse of the entire temple, since it sat atop a high mound. Around it was a city of glittering buildings, mansions made of a variety of shades of marble, gardens, elaborate fountains, and statues.

But nothing was as awesome as the temple of Poseidon. A copper-plated archway three times Elo's height preceded a spacious courtyard. That open area was surrounded by a gleaming golden wall, atop which was a row of golden statues of men and women dressed in the style of the Noronian Friends. In the center of the wall were double doors, also coated in gold, and a much larger golden figure of a man stood above those.

Beyond the wall were hundreds of white marble steps leading up to the temple itself. Shara guessed the building covered an area of at least two hectares, and the smaller second story brought the building's overall height to over two hundred meters. The structure and its multitude of columns were entirely coated in shining silver except for the pinnacles and trim, which were gold. It was garish beyond belief and yet the sheer splendor had to be appreciated for the incredible workmanship that must have gone into an endeavor of such magnitude.

Elo stopped in front of the double doors and knelt down for his riders to dismount.

"Wait, Elo," Ester told the elephant. "We will return very soon."

Gabriel and Shara both had to fight the urge to race up the long flight of steps to see the interior, but as it turned out, they didn't go up at all. Ester led them around the side to a doorway at ground level.

A stocky man holding a spear taller than he was stood guard in front of the door. He was clean-shaven and his brown hair was cut bluntly above his ears. The only clothing he wore were a white girdle and sandals. As Ester and Jarad approached, he acknowledged them with a nod but tilted his spear forward to stop them from proceeding.

"Do you bring the potion?"

Ester removed the lid from the crock she was hugging close to her body and let the guard look inside. He licked his thin lips in anticipation of a taste.

"You were almost late. I was going to have to report you soon."

Jarad kept his head bowed as he replied in an apologetic tone, "We have been ordered to bring more each day. It takes time to prepare so much."

The guard's attention turned to the two servants standing behind Ester and Jarad. "Why are they with you?"

Keep your head down, Gabriel warned Shara.

"They were loaned to us to work in the field today so that we could supply the princes more adequately," Jarad answered.

"Oh?"

The guard studied each of them as if he knew Jarad had lied, but Shara felt no mental probe.

"How is it that slaves were permitted to observe your work? Are they scheduled for execution this eve so that the secret will die with them?"

Gabriel gave Jarad and Ester a second to give an acceptable explanation. When it was obvious that lying didn't come quickly to them, and with the possibility of a swift execution at hand, he gave the only excuse that came to mind. "Because we know the magic from our homeland."

"Step forward, both of you," the guard ordered, and Jarad and Ester moved aside. The man pushed back Shara's hood. "You are a woman," he said with surprise. "Raise your eyes."

Change your eye color for him, Gabriel suggested.

Shara met the guard's gaze and thought of how he and his people would sentence young Rebekah to a brutal death without hesitation. She felt the anger build and knew it would be obvious in her eyes.

The guard saw the yellow sparks appear in her pupils and jerked back from her. "You are a witch!" He used the tip of his spear to push Gabriel's hood off. "Look at me." Gabriel complied, and the guard stared into his eyes. Unable to perform any magic, Gabriel said, "Her power is much stronger than mine."

"I see." Relaxing a bit, the guard reached up and combed his fingers through Gabriel's blond curls. "You have very pretty hair for one smiled upon by the dark side." His hand skimmed down Gabriel's neck and measured the size of his shoulder and upper arm with a gentle kneading motion.

Shara felt Gabriel's revulsion at the man's touch and realized the guard was stroking him rather than testing his strength. Gabriel stood immobile as the guard's palm scraped over his chest and began an exploratory path downward.

"Why don't you go on, Jarad," the guard said in a softened voice. "I wish to question this slave further."

Ester held out the crock. "Wouldn't you like to sample the potion?"

The guard took his hand and his gaze off Gabriel long enough to wet the tip of his index finger and dip it into the powder. He brought a few grains up and placed them under his tongue, then waved Ester away. "Hurry on, now, before they miss you inside." Gabriel started to leave as well, but the guard's meaty fingers closed over his arm. "Not you."

Shara turned back and hurled a suggestion at him. *The slave is diseased. Touching him is disgusting to you.*

The guard immediately withdrew his hand with an expression of horror. "Be off! All of you."

The moment the door opened, Shara's ears were assaulted by earsplitting clanging, and a wave of heat hit her face. One glance around the cavernous room lit only by firelight told her this was where all the splendorous metalwork was done. Working over fires and pounding on anvils were a great number of naked, sweating men, whose expressions revealed the hopelessness of their situation. Not one of them looked up as Shara passed.

As Ester guided her small party out of that room and down a corridor, she reminded Gabriel and Shara to cover their heads again and hunch down.

"Why are those men working under such terrible conditions instead of outside or at least in an open shelter?" Shara asked.

"The nobility prefers not to mar the beauty of the city with the sight or noise of labor. In the cooler months, the heat from all the fires on this level is directed into the chambers above, but at this time, the vents are closed off."

They passed another large area where women were weaving and stitching copper-colored serving robes and lush garments in a rainbow of bold colors, and farther along pottery was being made. Finally they arrived at the cookery and Shara's first thought was that there were more workers here preparing food than she had seen in all the other areas combined. Surely she and Gabriel could blend in without notice. Now, if only they could get to the nobles themselves.

The heat from the cookfires was a little less sweltering than the first area they had entered, but wearing the robes made up the difference.

Ester took Shara and Gabriel to the overseer. With a friendly smile, she greeted a woman with darker skin than her own. "Good eve, Leah. We were detained by the soldier at the door again. I hope we are not too late."

"They have not sounded the flute yet. The fruit cider has been heated and is ready for you to complete its preparation."

"Good. That soldier asked us to bring these two slaves here to work for you. They are very strong and are to be assigned to service in the chambers above."

"Of course," Leah said with a knowing smirk. "That man will do anything to avoid the heat inside, including sending others to do his errands. Fine. You go about your preparations and I'll show them their duties." With a wave at Shara and Gabriel, Leah said "Follow me" and led them through the maze of workers and tables to a stone staircase.

"The first service will be the cider. You will carry the tureens up these stairs. Be careful not to trip on the hem of your robe. The punishment for a broken serving piece is a broken bone of comparable size. You spill the cider, your blood will be spilled in an equal amount. It is that simple. You do not speak or look into the eyes of the nobility, regardless of their rank, nor do you touch any part of their bodies or garments. Other cookery slaves will do the serving at this meal. Observe their actions and the signals of the nobles so that you can serve at the next. After the first portion of cider has been served, you will bring any empty tureens back down and carry up the next course."

Nice job you landed for us, Gabriel thought to Shara when they were left alone to stand in readiness at the foot of the stairs.

Would you rather go back to the poppy field?

I'd rather get a quick look at the inside of the temple and head home.

Don't pout. It ruins the effect of your pretty hair.

He made a face at her for reminding him of what he'd almost been subjected to. *I suppose I have to thank you for rescuing me.*

Why didn't you try sending a suggestion yourself?

Quite honestly, it never occurred to me. I'm not sure I've mastered it anyway.

Try one now. Something innocuous.

He stared at Leah and suggested that her nose itched. When Leah failed to react, Shara sent the same thought and the overseer promptly rubbed the tip of her nose.

Gabriel frowned. *I don't know what I did wrong.*

Neither do I. Maybe it takes more practice.

Before he had a chance to make another attempt, the trill of a flute drifted down the winding staircase.

Leah instructed them to each take a side handle on the first tureen. As soon as they lifted the heavy container full of sloshing hot cider a centimeter off the table, they switched to their combined levitation power. The fact that their robes had been too short to begin with was now a blessing as they navigated the endless flight of steep stairs.

At the top was an enclosed landing with two long tables—one empty, one covered with stacks of gold and silver serving pieces. On the other side of the landing, more stone steps went down in the opposite direction from the cookery. They set their burden down and went back for more while the other slaves began ladling the opium-laced drink into ornate gold and silver chalices studded with gemstones. After they brought up the last tureen, an older woman pointed out the row of peepholes in the wall that the slaves used to watch the meal's progress and note any hand signals from the nobles. She quietly demonstrated the different signals, then suggested Shara and Gabriel watch until it was time to get the next course.

Shara and Gabriel stationed themselves at two adjacent peepholes, but had to bend down to see through. Shara's gasp of wonder wasn't nearly as loud as Gabriel's expletive, but they were both instantly warned to remain silent.

They had a perfect bird's-eye view of the central court of the temple. The landing and peepholes were placed just above the heads of the crowd of nobles.

The entire central court seemed to be on fire, it glowed so brightly. The floor, walls, and enormous pillars were all covered with gleaming orichalcum. The ceiling and wall borders depicted elaborate scenes carved in ivory, and alcoves around the chamber housed statues of gold.

But the masterpiece of metalwork was on a raised platform at the far end of the chamber. An immense statue of a bare-chested, bearded Poseidon stood in a chariot. In one hand he held his trident and the other controlled the reins to six prancing winged horses. At the base of the platform were a multitude of sea nymphs borne by dolphins. The entire display appeared to be molded from the purest gold.

In front of the raised platform was a block of white marble the size of a large bed.

The sacrificial altar, Gabriel told her. *And that rectangular opening in the center of the court is undoubtedly the fire pit Ester referred to.*

Shara shivered with repulsion and turned her attention to the people. The men were all garbed in long, richly colored robes trimmed with gold, and a golden braid encircled their heads as well. The woman who had shown them the peepholes had also explained that the nine princes wore deep blue, the lesser noblemen wore other colors that depicted their ranks, and King Jupiter alone wore red. Based on that information, she was able to locate him. *Holy stars! He's the image of Hades.*

But from Jarad's account, he's even more demented than his arsonist ancestor was.

Four soldiers dressed in white girdles and carrying spears stood around the king, looking as if they were prepared to fend off an attack due at any moment.

The women in the gathering wore lightweight gowns of shimmering pastel materials in a variety of styles. Their trimming and head braids were of silver.

The nobles were all scattered haphazardly throughout the court, standing, sitting on benches and steps, or sprawled on the floor, making service extremely difficult. Yet every noble soon received a chalice of cider and was slowly sipping the drugged beverage.

The entire meal took several hours to serve, with each course lasting longer than the previous one as more cider was consumed. The long day and manual labor in the poppy field began to extract their toll on Shara. She was tired and sunburned and had yet to come up with a way to obtain hair samples from the crowd below. Even if she were assigned to serving them tomorrow, as Leah had said she would be, any slave who touched a noble without permission had his or her throat cut the next instant. At least Gabriel had been able to give Beauty an eyeful for posterity.

When the last of the serving pieces were cleared, King Jupiter called for the entertainment to begin. Shara and Gabriel were watching a troupe of musicians and scantily clad girls enter the court when they were tapped on their shoulders by the older slave woman. She motioned for them to return to the cookery. Thinking their tasks were over for the night, Shara began to relax on the way down the stairs. But what awaited them brought the tension back in a rush.

The soldier who had been at the entrance door was speaking to a green-robed nobleman. "They are the ones I told you of," he declared the moment he caught sight of them.

The nobleman walked up to Gabriel and ordered, "Stand erect. Head up. Hood back." As Gabriel obeyed, the much shorter man circled him, measured the circumference of his upper arm, then pounded on his back with his fist. "He doesn't seem diseased to me. But he is exceptionally large and strong. He should have been assigned to the monument, not women's work. Take him away and see that he is more properly used." He waved a hand at the soldier, who in turn used his spear to prod Gabriel toward the exit.

Gabriel! Shara thought to him in a panic.

It's all right. I wanted to get a look at the monument anyway. Keep the channel open, and don't do anything to call attention to yourself. I'll be back as soon as I'm able. Use your powers if you have to. Their gazes locked for a heartbeat, then Gabriel was given a shove out of the room.

"Now you," the nobleman said to Shara. "Remove

your hood and look at me." He walked slowly around her, but did not touch. "The soldier said you are a witch with very strong powers."

She breathed an inward sigh of relief that Ester's lie to Leah about the soldier ordering them to work there had not been uncovered. Meeting his gaze, she allowed him to see her pupils change shades.

"You may speak. Do you know the magic, as he said?"

From everything she had learned so far, she knew these people both respected and feared witchcraft. Her intuition told her to use that to her benefit. "Yes. I know some."

The nobleman squinted at her as if trying to discern whether he should believe her. "Come with me."

Shara followed him into a torch-lit corridor that led in a different direction than Gabriel had been taken, then watched the nobleman glance nervously around before telling her what was on his mind.

"Do you have a spell for . . . to improve a man's, uh . . . not that I have a problem, but some of the nobles have had difficulties . . ." He lowered his voice a bit more. "Their tools do not work as they once did."

As Shara realized he was speaking of maintaining an erection, she had to stop herself from saying her thoughts aloud. Considering the amount of narcotics consumed during dinner, it was no surprise to her that the men's sexual performance might be suffering. "I believe there is a spell that might help. I will need to think on it a moment." She paced up and down the corridor looking very thoughtful, while she racked her brain to come up with an impromptu plan that could bring her closer to her goal.

Shara. It's too great a risk. Don't do it.

She ignored Gabriel's warning, confident that he was incapable of physically stopping her. *If you don't like what I'm about to do, don't pay attention.*

"I remember now," she told the nobleman. "But it will only work if the man who has the problem is a descendant of one of those who came to Atlantis with Poseidon. If that is so, I would need a hair from that man, and the name of the ancestor."

"You will try this spell on me first, before I speak of it to anyone else. My sacred ancestor's name was Penelope." He plucked a hair from his head and handed it to her.

Holding his hair against her forehead, she made up what she imagined would look and sound like a spell. Closing her eyes, she spun around until she was dizzy; then, swaying in place, she called out the first nonsensical incantation that came to mind.

"Mumbo, jumbo, gumbo. Rim, tim, kim. The power of the stallion's tool should go to him." She then stared at his loins, sent him a suggestion that he was highly aroused, then used her kinetic ability to make his "tool" rise beneath his robe.

The nobleman's eyes widened in shock, and he lifted his garment to see for himself the magic she had wrought. But his expression swiftly turned to lust as he grabbed Shara and twisted her away from him. "Bend forward, witch. We will see just how well your spell works."

Shara's fears stabbed Gabriel just as he was being prodded onto a wide chariot drawn by four large black horses. The next instant he understood the cause. Heedless of any danger to himself, he whirled away from the soldier and took off at a run back toward the temple.

He felt the blow on the back of his head a moment before darkness descended.

21

A searing pain shot through the back of Shara's head, then went away, but she had no time to worry over it. The nobleman was now fully aroused and forcing Shara into an accommodating position as he bunched up the back of her robe.

"My lord, wait!" she exclaimed. Afraid that he might discover the tempometer belt and certain that physically resisting him could get her throat slit, she hurriedly said, "Please, you have not heard it all. This is only a temporary reaction to the spell. In order for it to be lasting, you must heed my instructions." She sent him a suggestion that his desire was ebbing, and he released her. She stood up and shook her robe straight. "If you do as I say, you will be the most potent male in all of Atlantis."

He narrowed his eyes at her. "Go on."

"Beginning now and for seven more suns, you must not drink any cider and you must not engage in any sexual activities whatsoever." If nothing else, perhaps she could give a few slaves a week's reprieve from this nobleman's attentions.

"And when the seventh sun sets, will I be able to perform as I did in my younger days?"

Shara smiled. "It will be better than your favorite memory." As he fantasized over the possibilities, she sent him another suggestion that would cause him to forget her and the spell upon awakening the seventh morning.

Satisfied that the sacrifice was worth the end result, he nodded and said, "There are others who require your assistance. Remain here."

Shara could not believe how nicely fate had smiled on her. With a little luck, the ones she was looking for would come to her without any risk on her part. As soon as the nobleman disappeared around a corner, she lifted her robe and opened the pouch tied to her belt. It was too dangerous to allow anyone to see something as sophisticated as her micropluter, so she got out some static paper and a pencil and reluctantly put off testing any samples she might obtain until she was certain of privacy.

Minutes later, another nobleman in a green robe came down the corridor. This time she was careful to only give his male anatomy a little twitch instead of a full erection and she issued all the warnings before she began her "spell." One after another men came to her, wearing every color robe save two—dark blue and red. Either Jupiter and his princes did not need help, or the lesser nobles decided to keep her spell a secret among themselves.

When a very long time passed without any more visitors, Shara returned to the cookery. The excitement of having been handed a way to get her samples had given her a much-needed charge of energy, but it was rapidly fading again. To her relief, Leah was still on duty, so she didn't need to come up with any explanations.

"You may have a plate of food, then take your rest."

Shara wasn't that hungry, but she had no idea

when she might get the offer of nourishment again, so she ate. When she finished, Leah assigned another slave to show her to their quarters below the cookery.

"My name is Shara," she told the young girl. "I'm new to the temple."

"I am Odette. The work here is hard, but we eat well and we are rarely beaten . . . unlike those assigned to the monument or the quarries."

Shara cringed at the thought that Gabriel might have to suffer abuse where he was being taken. *Gabriel?* When she received no answer, she first assumed he had blocked her out rather than find out what she had been up to; then she realized his mind was at rest. She consoled herself with the logic that if he had been beaten, he wouldn't be peacefully sleeping.

It was cooler on the lower level, but much darker, with only an occasional torchlight on the stone walls, and the stale, musty odor was suffocating.

Shara asked, "Do you know Rebekah—the girl who is to be sacrificed at the final ceremony?"

Odette frowned. "I know who you speak of. I tried to talk to her after they locked her in, but she only cries all the time."

"Is she down here somewhere?"

The girl nodded.

"I was with her parents all day," Shara continued. "Perhaps if I told her how they are and give her their love, she would feel a little better."

Odette thought that was a good idea, but she had to return to the cookery, so she could not dally. Before returning, she showed Shara the bathing room. "All temple slaves must rinse their bodies before reporting to work, lest they offend the nobility with a foul odor." She pulled down a lever on the wall and water flowed from an open pipe in the ceiling. As she pushed it back up, the shower stopped. The stone floor slanted sufficiently for the water to drain into a hole in the center. "You may relieve yourself in that hole as well."

The girl then took Shara to the sleeping area, where hundreds of women were laying on woven grass mats on the hard floor. After directing Shara to a vacant mat, she turned to go.

"Wait," Shara whispered. "Where's Rebekah being held?"

Odette pointed to a wooden door in the corner.

"Thank you," Shara mouthed, and touched the girl's cheek. Looking confused by the gentle contact, she hurried away.

As much as Shara wanted to speak to Rebekah, she needed to use the bathing area first. She was grateful for the sanitary measures, even if they were only for the benefit of the nobility's aristocratic noses. The warmth of the water coming out of the pipe was a welcome surprise to her tired muscles. She recalled Gabriel's comment about being sore tomorrow after crawling on his knees in the field, and she mentally reached out to him again. It was unusual for him to sleep so soundly that he didn't sense her thinking about him and instantly awaken. As she went back to the sleeping area, she kept part of her mind focused on Gabriel.

The wooden door Odette had pointed to had a large lock on the outside. There was no key in sight, but the door did have a much smaller door in its center which was probably used to pass food through. Shara opened it and bent down to look inside.

A torch within the enclosed cubicle allowed Shara to see a little girl curled up on a mat on the floor. She had long black hair and a white gown was tangled around her brown legs. Shara seethed with anger. The child couldn't have been more than ten years old! It didn't matter what she had to do, she was not going to stand by and let Ester's baby be murdered.

"Rebekah," she whispered. "Wake up, little one. I have a message from your mother and father." The girl stirred, and Shara sent her a mental message to bring her fully awake. The look of raw fear on her face wrenched Shara's heart in half. "I'm a friend of your mother's, Rebekah. She told me where to find you."

Rubbing her eyes, Rebekah sat up and tucked her feet beneath her. "Why hasn't Mama come to see me?" Her voice sounded as though she would start crying any second.

"Sh-sh. Let's keep our voices very quiet so that we don't wake any of the others. The soldiers won't allow your mama or your father to come, but they want to very badly. They love you, sweetie, and even Elo misses you."

"Elo?" Rebekah's eyes opened wide, and for a moment it looked as though she were about to smile, then sadness clouded her expression again. "I miss them, too. But the man who took me away said that this was a greater honor to my family than if I remained with them."

"Rebekah, I want to help you, if I can. Do you understand why you have been brought here?"

"Oh, yes. I have been tutored on many things since I have been here so that I will not displease the gods or King Jupiter during the ceremony. I must do everything that I am told and I must not cry or make noise of any kind, even if something hurts."

She sniffled. "Being a virgin sacrifice is a very great honor. You see, I am a woman now, and only little girls cry." Her voice cracked, and she sniffled again. "The first part of the ceremony does not seem so bad, but I have very bad dreams about the second. I am most afraid that I will cry out and shame my family."

Shara desperately wanted to reach through the little door and pull Rebekah out so she could give her the hug she obviously needed, then run off with her. "Your parents would never be ashamed of you, no matter what you did, and they do not consider losing you an honor. I promised them I would try to save you, but I need your help. Do they allow you out of here at all?"

Rebekah shook her head. "I will only be taken from here on the seventh eve."

"Have you been told anything about the ceremony? You mentioned two parts."

"Do you really think you might save me?" Rebekah asked, hope brightening her features.

"If I have to fight the king himself, little one."

That made her smile. "I was told that when the seventh sun of the gathering sets, I will be taken to the court and placed on the altar before the statue of Poseidon. I am to make my body ready for King Jupiter while the nine princes castrate the bulls they have brought to sacrifice to Poseidon. Then each one drinks a cup of their animal's blood that pours from the wound so that the bull's power flows into its master. Then the king will take my virginity."

Shara tried not to react, but Rebekah saw her concern.

"It will not be too bad," she reassured Shara. "A man and woman have given me many lessons in how to prepare myself and how to please the king. I am not afraid of that." Her little mouth twisted back and forth. "Well, not *too* afraid. But I do not believe that what he will do to me will end my life. That is left to his bull."

Shara felt the meal she had eaten churning in her stomach and fought down the nausea. "I'm sorry to ask you to speak about it, Rebekah, but I need to know as much as possible if I'm to be of any help."

"I understand. When the king is finished with me, each of the nine princes will take pleasure from my body. Then I will be put into the pit with the last bull—the one that belongs to the king. It will already be upset by its confinement in the pit. My virgin blood should excite it even more. I must not make it too easy for the bull to take my life. If God is pleased by how I behave with the nobility and the bull, He will make sure I pass on the first time I am gored by the beast's horn. I pray that is the way it will be because after the sand passes from the top to the bottom of the timing vase, the pit is set on fire and the bull and I will go to Poseidon together. The other nine bulls follow behind us. I know it is very childish, but I am most afraid of the fire."

The horror of the child's words was magnified by the fact that she had been told the gruesome details, so that she could dwell on it for days before her execution. The way she spoke of it, however, told Shara that she was repeating the words, but not fully connecting them with herself.

No plan came to mind immediately, but she hadn't had a plan to get the hair samples, either. Now she understood why none of the higher nobility came for her spell. They couldn't promise to abstain from sex for a week when they had to perform in two nights before an audience. Perhaps circumstances would simply work themselves out again. In the meantime, she would stay as near to the girl as possible and take advantage of the first opportunity that came along to free her.

"All right, Rebekah. I will do whatever I can. I have a friend named Gabriel who might be able to help, also. He's a very tall, handsome man with light hair. You can trust him. Go on back to sleep now. I'll try to talk to you again tomorrow."

She closed the pass-through door and went to the mat Odette had pointed out. The urge to lay down and close her eyes was difficult to resist, but the lure of testing the hair samples helped give her the impetus she needed to stay awake a little longer. She got out her microputer and the samples and went to work.

Right after beginning her work, she felt another sharp pain in her head that slowly settled into a throbbing ache. Once the pain lessened, she realized it wasn't her head that was hurting, but Gabriel's.

Gabriel? What's wrong? She felt his mind clearing and opening to hers, and she helped him block the pain.

I made a mistake.

I don't understand.

Gabriel abruptly remembered why he had erred. *Sweetling, are you all right? Did that cretin hurt you?*

She smiled as his sincere concern flooded through her. *I'm fine. I talked him into a week of celibacy instead. He was so pleased with my sorcery, he recommended me to his friends.*

I don't like you taking such risks! With effort, he stopped himself from lecturing her. *Any matches?*

No, but I haven't tested them all yet. Why does your head hurt so bad?

When I thought you were in trouble, I tried to get back to you. As near as I can figure, that soldier was an expert with a rock and slingshot. Got me in the base of the skull with one try. I've been out for hours.

Where are you now?

He sat up and looked around, careful not to move his head too quickly. *Holy stars! Can you see what I see?*

Shara closed her eyes and concentrated on seeing through his. He was in a large field, cleared of all trees, and at least a thousand other men were laying on the ground around him. The moon appeared to be a giant spotlight placed in the universe for the sole purpose of illuminating Jupiter's nearly completed monument—a pyramid of gigantic proportions.

That one's larger than the House of Spiritual Renewal in Innerworld, Shara thought.

And all the pyramids in Outerworld's Egypt put together, Gabriel added.

Shara recalled what both Jarad and Odette had said about the monument. *Gabriel, the slaves working there are beaten and killed. You've seen the monument; now get back here.*

He asked Beauty to give him directions and distance to Poseidon's temple. *I'm only about a kilometer away, just outside the royal city walls. But that's not the problem. My ankles are chained to the men's ankles next to me and they're chained to the men beside them, and so on. It looks like I'm here for the night.*

Dear heavens! What are you going to do?

I'll let you know as soon as I figure it out. Just stand by in case I need to borrow your power of suggestion. For now, though, why don't you finish your tests so we can both get out of here as soon as I'm free? Beauty is picking up severe ground disturbances all over the continent.

He stayed with her mentally while she checked the rest of the hair samples and felt her disappointment grow with each failure. When she was finished, she had checked off all but seven names on the list Misha had given them, the most notable of those being Poseidon. She had no idea how many other names he had not told them, or how many of the ones left had remained among the nobility. There was also the possibility that the two descendants she was looking for were among the women, since she hadn't gotten samples from any of them yet.

One more day, Shara. That's it. Gabriel sensed her pulling way. *What is it? You may as well tell me.*

I saw Rebekah.

He knew he wasn't going to like this. *And?*

She's just a little girl! She's acting very brave, but she's terrified. She let him know what Rebekah had told her.

He was sickened by the account, but it didn't change his attitude. *You know how I feel about this.*

Yes, I do, and you know how I feel. I'll help her escape if I can, without your assistance. She lay down on the mat and mentally turned away from him.

Gabriel started to do the same, but the movement caused a wave of dizziness to wash over him.

Are you going to be all right? Shara asked instantly.

Gabriel figured out how to position his head on

the ground for the least discomfort. *I'll live. I'm just not up to an argument with you tonight.*

She sighed. *Neither am I.*

I could really use that massage you promised me. He could feel her smiling and it made him feel somewhat better.

You'll have to come back to me to get it.

May I at least have a kiss good night, then?

Shara needed no further encouragement to set aside their difference of opinion for another night. In her mind she pictured them as they had been the last morning on the ship from Norona and invited him to remember with her.

She imagined bringing his face closer to hers and pressing their lips together. Mentally, her hands roamed over the body she now knew as well as her own. She felt his body hardening as his mouth moved to her breast, and her desire for him swiftly ignited.

Take me inside of you, sweetling. That's it. Hold me tight.

Yes! I can feel you.

Sensations of dreamy pleasure floated back and forth between their minds, carrying them out of their physical bodies to a shimmering place they had never been before. They hovered there together and discovered the unique sense of oneness that could only come from a spiritual and mental joining. Their release came not in a burst of physical energy, but in gentle waves of peace and contentment.

Shara drifted off to sleep, feeling his arms wrapped protectively around her.

Gabriel gazed up at the stars. He couldn't sleep after such an incredible experience. Having sought solitude for so long, it was extremely difficult to believe how sweet it was not to be alone anymore. He didn't understand how it had happened, but Shara was now as much a vital part of him as his own heart. As far as he was concerned, it no longer mattered that they had not willingly joined. He needed her in his life and he wanted to remain a part of hers.

But he knew she was still holding certain thoughts back from him. Was it simply that he sensed her continued intention to alter history regardless of everything he'd said, or was it more? Did she still harbor an underlying resentment for having her romantic dreams destroyed?

He couldn't change the fact that they were joined in such an unusual manner, and he would never allow her to interfere with history, so there didn't seem to be any way to convince her to open herself to him as fully as he wanted her to.

Until she did that, he couldn't shed the gnawing fear that she would one day leave him, and he would be forced to return to his silent, lonely world again.

The rising sun was accompanied by the rattle of chains as the slaves were roused. Gabriel was very relieved to discover that the chains were unlocked so they could move about somewhat freely. He discarded the serving robe and rewrapped the material of his tunic around his hips in the same manner as the other slaves. His paralyzer rod and Beauty were neatly concealed, yet accessible.

Breakfast was a bowlful of gray, tasteless mush and a cup of water, but his empty stomach and parched throat were grateful nonetheless.

The ache in his head was impossible to ignore, but the painful stiffness in his muscles distracted him a bit. He hoped Shara stayed asleep until he got control of the pain on his own.

A loud crack sounded behind him, and Gabriel turned to see a soldier holding a long whip. All the men around him instantly hurried toward the monument. The second it took Gabriel to comprehend cost him. Before he could start after the others, the soldier cracked the whip again, only this time it landed across Gabriel's back.

Shara awoke with a jerk. The burning pain across her shoulders brought tears to her eyes. *Gabriel?*

Gabriel blocked his pain from her and assured her he was fine as the soldier ordered him to stop.

"You are new here, are you not?" he asked Gabriel.

"Yes. I was just reassigned," he replied, humbly bowing his head.

"The first crack of the whip orders you to get to work. Quickly. If it is necessary to strike you again, I will not be so gentle. You appear to be strong. Go over there and help place the blocks."

Gabriel followed his direction and was put to work with a crew of men. Their task began by tying four long ropes around a large block of marble. With twenty men pulling each rope, they hauled the block up the side of the pyramid on a ramp, the center of which was constructed of logs that rolled in place. The trick was for the men to balance themselves on the stationary sides of the ramp. Gabriel was given a pair of sandals with metal studs on the soles and shown how to use them to secure a foothold on the steep slant.

Once they started up the ramp, no one man could afford to relax, let alone slip, without endangering everyone else, and the higher they climbed, the more precarious the trip became. Gabriel was afraid to use his levitation power with so many people involved, so he pulled his weight along with all the others. By the time they reached the top and pushed the block into place, Gabriel's muscles were vibrating from overexertion. They were given a short spell to catch their breath before going back down again.

From that higher vantage point, he could see the royal citadel in the distance, and he discreetly withdrew Beauty to get a recording to the entire area. It may only have been a kilometer away, but it was all open space from the monument to the royal city, with a small army of soldiers in between.

Escape was not going to be easy.

The crew was cautiously descending the ramp when a rumbling sound warned of approaching danger. The ground quaked and the entire monument trembled. The men on the ramp crouched down and hung on to the sides as the tremor ran its course.

Suddenly one man lost his grip and tumbled off the edge. His screams pierced the rolling thunder as his body plummeted to the ground. When all vibration ceased, a soldier ordered that the slave's broken body be dumped into the new crevice that had opened in the ground not far from the base of the monument.

Shara had seen enough. Gabriel had to get away from there this second! She was about to order him to do so when Odette knelt down beside her and captured her attention. At the same time, she felt Gabriel preventing her from seeing any more of what was going on at the monument.

"You are to come with me," the girl said. "Hurry."

Be careful, Gabriel thought, reassuring her that he was not blocking her out of his mind completely.

You just get yourself back here, she retorted. *I'll be fine.*

Odette led Shara up endless flights of stone stairs and down a corridor to a richly appointed room. Seated on colorful pillows on the floor and lying on plush divans were a dozen noblewomen. Odette bowed and left the room, closing the door behind her.

A petite, gray-haired woman sitting in the only chair in the room snapped her fingers at Shara. "Has no one trained you? Bow to your betters!"

Shara imitated the low bow she had seen Ester and Jarad perform.

"You may lift your head, but do not rise. You are much too tall for a woman, and I never look up at a slave."

"Are you really a witch?" an adolescent girl with heavy kohl around her eyes asked.

"Hush, Mirabel," scolded the elder. "I will determine the truth." To Shara she said, "Our menfolk could not pleasure their spouses last night because of a witch's spell. Was that your doing?"

Shara tried to choose the answer that would get her in the least trouble. "My spell will increase their desire for their spouses a hundredfold, but in order for it to work, the men must avoid all sexual activity for a time."

The spokeswoman pursed her lips and narrowed her eyes. She was clearly unconvinced.

"Perhaps there is something I could do for you," Shara offered.

The woman glanced at the others in her group, then said, "We are bored this morning. Tell us our fortunes."

Shara had the distinct feeling that this one

woman could do her more harm than all the men she'd met last night, but it also seemed as though another key had just been handed to her. "I will need a hair from your head and the name of any ancestor of yours that arrived on Atlantis with Poseidon."

Most of the women appeared excited by the prospect of having their fortunes told, but the eldest continued to look skeptical, even as she handed Shara a hair and said, "Penelope."

Shara had already checked off that name, but she knew she had to be convincing to this woman to get samples from the others.

"I must communicate with the spirits in private for a moment," Shara said. "May I go behind that screen?" Given permission, she slipped behind the divider in the corner of the room and quickly ran a test on the hair as a double-check. No matches.

Since Gabriel was first to construct a partial wall between them, she didn't feel all that guilty when she did the same thing to keep him from seeing exactly what she was doing. He had enough problems where he was without fearing for her safety as well.

She came out and knelt at the older woman's feet. "The spirits told me of your great wisdom. They know you have not always been treated with the respect you deserve, but they asked me to tell you to be patient awhile longer. What you deserve will be given to you before the next royal gathering."

The woman was delighted and encouraged the rest of the noble ladies to cooperate. Shara stepped behind the screen each time she got another hair, tested it, then made up a vague fortune for each, based on their appearance and demeanor. One was told of a secret admirer, while another was warned of an accident to one of her limbs that could be avoided by taking care when she climbed stairs.

In the end, they were all satisfied but Shara. She had eliminated three more names from her list, yet still had no match for Khameira or herself. The worst of it was that there were only four names of exiles left on Misha's list, but thirteen rebels' names remained on the original list recorded in the history texts. Added to that was the fact that most of the people on Atlantis did not survive to continue their line.

She had no choice but to face the strong probability that she had missed some Friends at Zeus's commune. With the way her luck had gone on this mission thus far, if she had an ancestor among the rebels, it was undoubtedly one of the people she'd failed to test. On the other hand, considering the evil strain that ran through Poseidon's descendants on Atlantis, it seemed quite likely that Khameira was located somewhere further down on his family tree.

When the women dismissed her, she returned to the slave quarters to let Rebekah know she was still around. From there she headed for the cookery in hopes of being assigned to meal service.

In spite of the law against touching the nobility, she was determined to get a hair from as many of them as possible before she and Gabriel left Atlantis behind.

22

Gabriel could sense that Shara was doing something she shouldn't, but it was taking all his concentration and energy to perform the task assigned him. The ache in his head and the welt on his back were now minor irritations compared to the rest of his body. The palms of his hands had gone from blistering to bleeding and his muscles and joints had been strained to the point where the pain was nauseating.

And it was only midday.

He needed to save himself. He had to get back to the temple and find out what Shara was up to. So far, however, no opportunity for escape had presented itself.

The eighty-man crew had another block of marble almost to the top of the ramp when something went wrong. It happened too fast to place blame, but suddenly the huge stone toppled over the edge, taking four men down with it. One was crushed beneath the block; the other three lay bent and broken around it.

Several soldiers marched over to the ramp and shouted for the rest of the men to descend. Other slaves were ordered to dispose of the bodies while the soldiers used their spears to prod the crew into one long line.

They were to be whipped for their clumsiness.

Gabriel tried to think of a way to prevent the beating without calling attention to himself, but neither his paralyzer rod nor his new powers were adequate against such a large force of soldiers. All he could do was try to block the pain as the whip cracked over his back five times, then moved on to the next man.

The salt of his perspiration mingled with his blood to set his torn flesh on fire. He almost reached out to Shara, but he knew there was nothing she could do but worry for him, so he held back his need of her.

By the time every slave had received his five lashes, at least twenty of them had collapsed. Gabriel was tempted to give in to the pain and exhaustion as well, until he saw that the fallen slaves were being dragged over to the bottomless crevice in the ground. If they could not stand on their own, they were tossed in with the dead.

The soldiers were demanding that the crew begin again with the fallen block. It would have to be in place before they would be given any nourishment, water, or rest.

A momentary reprieve was granted them as a horse-drawn chariot raced up to the monument. A soldier held the reins, but next to him stood a man in a purple robe. The noble scanned the swarm of laborers as his driver spoke to another soldier. That soldier nodded and pointed at Gabriel.

Gabriel didn't care why he was wanted. Whatever the nobleman had planned couldn't be much worse than another trip up the side of the pyramid, and one soldier was a far easier obstacle to eliminate than an entire army. He kept his head bowed as he let himself be pushed on to the chariot.

Having been at the top of the pyramid, Gabriel knew the departing chariot and its passengers could be seen the entire way back to the city. Thus, any aggressive action on his part could bring the army down on him. At any rate, he desperately needed time to regain a little strength before attempting an escape.

The chariot sped away as quickly as it had arrived, stirring up a dust storm that briefly shielded it from any onlookers.

"Here, *Friend*, drink this," the noble said in a loud voice, and extracted a covered crock from inside his robe.

Gabriel was gripping the side of the conveyance with both hands to keep from falling, but the offer of a drink was incentive enough to risk letting go. As soon as he removed the lid, he recognized the smell and color of the cider he had helped carry the evening before. Drugged or not, the fluid would help his body recover. It took great effort not to gulp the entire contents in one swallow.

He was halfway through the contents when he realized that the nobleman had called him *Friend*, but since he had no idea what the situation was, he held his questions. There was something familiar about the man's features, though Gabriel couldn't pinpoint what it was.

As the soldier drove them through the series of gates into the royal city, Gabriel finished the cider. The screaming pain in his body had been reduced to a whimper, which told him that the drink had indeed been laced with opium, but his mind seemed perfectly clear.

Other than the offer of the drink, neither the nobleman nor the soldier said another word to Gabriel during their trip. Even when they stopped in the rear of one of the smaller mansions near the citadel, the nobleman merely motioned for him to follow.

The moment they were behind the closed doors of the residence, however, both the nobleman's and the soldier's demeanors changed from indifference to solicitousness.

"Eva! Borok!" the nobleman called out, and immediately a young native couple hurried into the foyer. "Fetch our friend a large cup of cider and prepare a cool bath for him. He will need your ointments, Eva. They whipped him before I could get there."

Eva reached for Gabriel's hand, but when she saw the condition it was in, she grimaced and grasped his elbow to lead him away.

Gabriel welcomed the kindness being proffered, but he wanted a few answers before he took another step. "I don't mean to sound ungrateful," he said to the nobleman, "but why are you doing this?"

The man looked somewhat embarrassed. "Forgive me. In my excitement, I have overlooked good manners. My name is Daniel. I am one of a very secret group who have been waiting for your arrival for almost two centuries. I regret that you were forced to undergo mistreatment, but I only learned of your presence this morning."

Gabriel thought perhaps his mind had been dulled by the opium-laced cider after all. "Exactly who do you think I am?"

Daniel nodded. "You are right to be cautious. Jarad and Ester passed the word among our group that two Friends had finally arrived from the Other-world to save us. There are only two nobles besides myself who have held to the beliefs of Poseidon and the Friends. We know the truth of our origins, though we have kept it from the natives."

Eve handed Gabriel a cup of cider and he auto-matically took a large swallow of it as Daniel contin-ued to explain.

"The Ruling Tribunal of Norona sent three representatives to Terra to analyze the progress of the exiled rebels about two hundred years ago. They promised that help would be sent. We have been waiting a very long time and are most anxious to learn of your plans to deal with Jupiter."

Gabriel rubbed his chin as he correlated Daniel's tale with the various theories he'd been considering. "Are you certain no one else from Norona is on At-lantis at this time?"

"Absolutely. Any stranger to our land would be brought to my attention immediately."

"Jarad mentioned that *God* was talking to Noe—warning him that the end was coming. I assume Po-seidon is not really sending messages from the other side, and if we are truly the first Noronians visiting Atlantis in two centuries, then who is giving Noe in-structions?"

Daniel furrowed his brow. "I suppose it could be the Supreme Being, just as Noe has insisted for many moons. However, whether the warnings are real or imaginary, the ground quakings have wors-ened and the grumblings coming from inside the mountains grow louder with each rising sun. We had begun to fear that you would not arrive in time to put a stop to this upheaval of nature."

Gabriel swayed in place and blinked at Daniel.

He wanted to correct him about who he really was, but his mind and voice no longer seemed connected. He could see Daniel giving instructions to his servants and he knew Eva was taking him somewhere, but everything had taken on a dreamlike quality.

Though there was something important he had to tell them and someone he needed to find, he couldn't seem to remember the specific details. His body was being cooled and soothed. For a time he was aware of the gentle ministrations without being fully awake, then sleep stole even that awareness.

The cups and bowls rattled as the serving table shook so violently, it threatened to tip over. Shara helped the other slaves in their efforts to prevent everything from crashing to the floor. The quaking went on for several minutes and everyone agreed it was the worst they had ever felt inside the temple.

Gabriel? Shara reached out to him for the hundredth time in the last hour. As long as he had been blocking her, she knew he was all right, but this blank wall she was touching was exactly like what she had felt earlier when he had been knocked unconscious. She was furious with herself and him for separating their minds even for a short time. Something had happened to him and she had no idea how to help.

If that wasn't enough, it was beginning to look as though the end of Atlantis was coming closer by the hour. Time was definitely *not* on her side.

She had been working in the cookery all day without any chance of sneaking away or getting close to the nobility. When she was finally ordered to go upstairs and help with the afternoon service, the quaking began. It would be just her luck to spill a tray of food on a nobleman and get her throat cut for not being able to keep her balance during an earthquake.

Gabriel? Nothing. She told herself that he might be hurt, but at least he was alive. Somehow she would know if his life had been ended. He was a part of her now, and if he was gone, she would no longer be whole.

She was handed a tray of sweets and directed down the stairs toward the central court, where Jupiter and his princes were meeting. In spite of so much going wrong, she still had a mission to do. Concealing the tiny scissors in the palm of her hand, she headed for her targets.

Careful to stay behind the princes, she carried the tray from one to another as inconspicuously as possible, but the treats had been anticipated, so her presence was noted by all present. As she had been instructed, after each man had taken a sweet, she stood behind a column and waited to see if any of them wanted seconds. When the signal came, she went to that man first, then proceeded around the court with her tray.

The fourth prince she approached was sitting on a bench, engrossed in etching something on a golden table. Quickly she glanced around to make sure no one was observing her too closely. Pretending to be rearranging the few items left on her tray, she brought the scissors to the man's hair and took a snip.

"What are you doing there?" the prince exclaimed, jumping up and whirling around to her so fast he knocked the tray and the scissors out of her hand. "Clumsy oaf! Why were you breathing down my neck?"

With her heart pounding against her rib cage, Shara dropped to her knees and scrambled to pick up everything that had fallen. Just as her fingers reached out for the scissors, the prince's sandaled foot came down on them.

Slowly he moved his foot and picked up the implement. His fingertip tested the sharp tip and his eyes took on a wild look. With a powerful swipe, he backhanded Shara, sending her sprawling on the floor. "The slave tried to harm me!" he shouted toward Jupiter, and held up the weapon for everyone to see.

Shara saw Jupiter nod to one of his personal guards. She tried to get up and run, but her head was swimming from the blow and the serving robe got caught beneath her feet. As the soldier strode toward her, he poised his spear over his shoulder and aimed.

She hesitated long enough to see the spear leave his hand, then she rolled away. Her defensive action was so unexpected that no one moved for several heartbeats—long enough for her to get to her feet and head for the narrow flight of stairs up to the serving area. Midway up she stopped and waited for the first soldier to come into view. Forcing herself to concentrate in spite of her panic, she hurled a suggestion at the man the moment he appeared. Instantly he froze in place and blocked the others from getting past him.

Shara flew up the remaining stairs, pulling off the bulky serving robe as she went. Just as she crossed the landing and began her descent toward the cookery, a tremendous explosion sounded outside of the temple, followed by the strongest earthquake yet. Too frightened to stop and brace herself, she stumbled down the steps, falling against one wall and then the other. Another explosion sounded, and in her mind's eye Shara saw the top of a mountain spewing fire.

This was it! Their time was up. *Gabriel! We have to get out of here!* Shara staggered into the cookery to find total chaos. Tables were overturned. Pots and crockery were all over the floor. Slaves tripped over each other in an effort to find a safe haven.

Suddenly Shara pictured little Rebekah, trapped in her cell below the temple. Her gaze darted around the cookery and found a large cleaver that could be heavy enough to break the lock on the cell door. Grabbing it, she took off for the slaves' quarters.

Shara?

Gabriel's mental voice was weak, but she heard it. *Thank the heavens! The volcano has erupted and the ground hasn't stopped shaking. Are you still at the monument? Can you get away?* She felt his mind straining to understand, but there was something wrong with him. *Gabriel, please, wake up!* She turned down the corridor she thought should have taken her to Rebekah, but found herself in an unfamiliar area. Reversing her steps, she tried to figure out where she went wrong.

I'm in a nobleman's house inside the royal city. I'll explain later. Where are you? Gabriel asked a little more clearly.

In the temple. Beneath it, actually. She breathed a sigh of relief as she found herself back on the right path.

Get out of there right now. Keep your mind open so that I can see where you are.

As Shara complied, she felt him turn his attention

away from her to speak to someone else. With her thoughts focused on releasing Rebekah, she couldn't manage to listen to his conversation as well. Just as she neared the slaves' quarters, another horrendous quake shook the temple. Crashing sounds overhead alerted Shara to the possibility that parts of the structure were collapsing.

Picking up speed, she rounded the last corner, only to collide into someone else.

"Rebekah!" she exclaimed, holding the girl still. "I was coming to free you."

Rebekah was crying and trembling uncontrollably. "When all the noise started, I kept pounding on the door, but nobody came. Then all of a sudden there was one terrible shake and the door fell down."

Holding the cleaver in one hand, Shara clasped Rebekah's hand with the other. "Come. Let's get you to your parents!" Before they could take off, though, a menacing figure in a red robe stepped around the corner in front of them.

"You will not take the virgin anywhere but my chamber."

Shara yanked Rebekah behind her and raised the cleaver over her head. "Get out of our way or I'll split you in two!"

Jupiter blinked and the cleaver flew out of Shara's hand and down the corridor. She threw a suggestion at him to go to sleep, but he caught it and tossed it back at her. His hand raised to strike, and she instantly paralyzed his arm. Their minds met on a battlefield of wills, pulling and pushing, each straining to overpower the other, but they were too evenly matched for either to be victorious.

"The virgin must be sacrificed," he demanded. "It

is the only way to appease the gods and put a stop to the destruction."

Shara stared into eyes of pure madness. His black pupils were dilated to their fullest as he struggled harder to force her to bend to him. She felt her mind weakening and saw his deranged smile of satisfaction.

Hold on, sweetling. I'm coming. Suddenly Gabriel's mind melded with hers and her defensive position changed to an unexpected attack on the king's consciousness. The next instant, Jupiter's eyes rolled back in his head and he fell to the ground.

Gabriel appeared a moment later. "Let's go!" he ordered, grabbing Shara's hand and pulling her over Jupiter's body.

"Wait," she said as she reached down and plucked a hair from Jupiter's head. She took another second to slip it into her pouch. Then taking Rebekah's hand, the three of them ran for the stairs.

Shara noted the cloths wrapped around Gabriel's hands and upper body like bandages.

I'll explain everything later, he promised.

The closer they got to the surface, the louder the sounds of destruction were. But nothing prepared them for the sight of it.

As they exited through the side door where they had first entered, they heard the screams and shouts of a panicked population. Throughout the courtyard, statues and columns had smashed to the ground. A portion of Poseidon's temple had already collapsed and all around the citadel, buildings were crumbling. The earthquake alone was capable of leveling the entire city, but a more lethal destroyer was on its way.

Bright orange fire was bursting from the tops of

three mountains that could be seen from the citadel mound—one only a few kilometers away. The burning lava appeared to be creeping down the mountainsides, but there was no doubt in anyone's mind that it would not be long before it was flowing into the city.

Shara, Gabriel, and Rebekah were swept along with the hysterical crowd, all heading for the beaches in hopes of finding a way to escape the inevitable.

"Mama and Papa have a boat hidden," Rebekah shouted to Shara as they ran toward the first bridge. "If they have not left already, I am sure they will take the two of you with us."

"Thank you," Shara replied sincerely. "But we have a boat also. And don't worry, they won't leave without you."

The gates were already opened before the flood of terrified people arrived, but the narrowed bridge created a bottleneck. Some people climbed the walls and dove into the canal to swim across while others pushed and shoved their way onto the bridge, not caring who they trampled to get ahead.

Gabriel picked up Rebekah to keep her from getting squashed in the stampede. Shara's fear mounted with each minute that passed. The throng kept moving forward, but the fiery lava appeared to be coming faster. She had no idea how they would ever make it all the way back to where the raft was hidden before they were overrun by either the lava or the people.

Remember the vision we shared about the volcano, Gabriel reminded her. *We'll make it. Just have faith.*

Shara's efforts to think positively received a tremendous boost as they crossed the second bridge. Salvation, in the form of one enormous elephant, was trudging toward them against the massive flow of refugees.

"Elo!" Rebekah cried, waving her arm in the air. "Mama! Papa! Here I am."

Elo trumpeted a warning and fanned his ears, and a path was cleared for him. His sheer size and tusks were enough to keep most people away, but a few dared to hitch a ride. The elephant knocked them out of the way with his trunk and continued on to his little friend. In a flash, Gabriel handed Rebekah to Jarad, climbing up Elo's side himself, and pulled Shara up in front of him.

"Turn, Elo!" Jarad commanded. "Home. Fast."

Men and women grasped at the riders' feet and begged to be taken along, but Elo moved too quickly for them. In no time he was carrying his passengers through the last gate of the royal city ahead of most of the fleeing population. He never slowed his pace until he reached Jarad and Ester's shelter.

They dismounted quickly and Jarad gave Elo one last order. "Go to Noe, Elo. He has a mate for you and will take you both to safety." Jarad then turned to Gabriel and Shara and bowed to them. "Thank you for saving Rebekah."

Shara gave all three of them a hug. "And thank you for everything you did for us."

The ground rumbled beneath them, warning that time was up. They wished one another safe journeys, then went their separate ways.

As Gabriel and Shara approached the beach, they were shocked to see huge waves crashing onto the sand only a short distance from where their raft was hidden. They wasted no time getting into position and preparing for the hop forward in time.

"We *are* going home this time, aren't we?" Gabriel

asked as Shara worked the front crystal of the tempometer belt.

She tilted her head back, gave him a sweet smile, and sent them on their way.

23

At least the water was calm this time. Calmer than Gabriel. "What was that smile supposed to mean?" he demanded.

She laughed. "I was only teasing. I swear, the adventure is over. I agree with what you said about the risk of running into ourselves if we tried to backtrack. According to my calculations, we should have arrived here on the same day as it would be if we'd never left. In other words, the same three weeks we've spent hopping have passed in our own time. Based on Lantana's notes, I figured that was the safest way to avoid a paradox of any kind." She opened her bag and pulled out her special ring. "In a few more minutes I'll have us in Innerworld, and we'll get your body repaired."

He put his hand over hers to stop her from programming the ring for transmigration. "Not yet. We have a few things to discuss first."

She turned to face him. "Oh?"

"I want to know exactly what you did to help Rebekah escape."

"Almost nothing," she replied with a shake of her head. "I had every intention of breaking her out of that cell, but she got out on her own. Considering the fact that Ester and Jarad were on their way to get her, I think it would be safe to assume she would have been rescued without my assistance. So you can rest easy. I did *not* alter history."

"Fine. Then I have something for you." He reached inside the cloth wrapped around his chest and handed her a dark brown hair. "This is from a nobleman named Daniel." Gabriel told her about what happened to him on the slave crew, his rescue by Daniel, and their subsequent conversations.

"It doesn't sound like the Ruling Tribunal had a hand in Atlantis's destruction after all."

"No, but I can't prove that they didn't orchestrate it, either. Fortunately, Daniel and his group had made arrangements to escape in case the end came without the promised saviors showing up. I hated to disappoint him, but I had to tell him the truth about who we really were. I hope he made it."

Shara looked at the hair in her hand. "What made you get this?"

He shrugged. "Something about his eyes reminded me of you, and I thought maybe it was his ancestor you were looking for. That exile's name was Willem."

Shara knew that was one of the names left on the list. As she pulled out the micropouter, her hands began to tremble. "Whether this is the one or not, I thank you. It means a lot that you would do this for me." She leaned forward and touched her lips to his. Holding her breath, she fed the hair into the micropouter and ran the analysis.

She exhaled when no match with Khameira showed up.

She pressed the next button and stared at the miniature screen, willing it to come up with a match for herself.

Gabriel felt her anticipation. Then her dejection. There was no match. "I'm sorry, sweetling. I was hoping that was your answer."

She sighed. "I guess I wasn't meant to know."

"Go ahead and test the other one. I'd rather you do it in front of me than behind my back."

She forced a smile for him. "Can I do yours first?"

"Mine?"

"You and Apollo looked an awful lot alike. Aren't you curious?" Although he made a face at her, he pulled out one of his hairs.

She ran the test, then punched a few more keys. "Well, well. It seems you, Apollo, and Artemis do share an ancestor, but it wasn't Zeus or anyone else I've tested. Undoubtedly their mother remained on Norona and mated with another man."

"Very interesting," he said. "Now run the other test."

She had such a strong feeling that Jupiter and Khameira would match up that she hadn't wanted Gabriel to see the results, but he was right. He'd find out eventually. They may as well have their final argument now as later. She found Jupiter's hair in her pouch and threaded it into the micropyuter.

Seconds later, all doubts were removed. Khameira's memory molecule contained matches with Jupiter, his father Saturn, and his grandfather Poseidon. If Poseidon had not been exiled to Terra, he would not have mated with the native women and would never have begun the line through which Khameira descended.

Before Gabriel could begin a lecture on not altering history, she defended her position once more. "You personally experienced the horrors perpetrated by Jupiter, and his father was almost as bad. One day in the future, Khameira will cause the destruction of this planet, and who knows what wretched dictators came from the same line in between? How could eliminating such evil be a bad thing?"

Gabriel took a deep breath. "Before I answer that, press the other button—the one for yourself."

"It's not—"

"You're a scientist, Shara. Run the analysis."

Just to prove it was a waste of time, she pressed the button . . . and gasped. It had never occurred to her to test herself against Khameira, but the ugly truth was staring her in the face. Though she descended through a different line, Poseidon was her relative as well.

Gabriel quickly pointed out the only conclusion possible. "If you stop Poseidon from being exiled to Terra, not only do you prevent Khameira's birth, but your own."

Shara weighed the alternatives, then lifted her chin in a brave manner and said, "Millions of people die because of Poseidon's earthborn descendants. What is my life worth against all of theirs?"

Gabriel grasped her shoulders. "What is your life worth?" He was so upset by her words, it took him a moment to form a coherent argument. "Think harder! What about all the other decent people you'd be eliminating? What about your own mother? Are her contributions so worthless that you would erase her life with a wave of your hand?" He felt her horrified reaction to the idea of eliminating her mother.

"You're confusing me," she said softly.

"Good! Because I'm so confused right now, I don't

know if the rest of what I have to say is going to make any sense, but here it is anyway. If you still believe that you should go back and stop Poseidon from being sent to Earth, then you'd better find that ancestor Apollo and I share and prevent her from starting the line I descend from, too."

Shara frowned at him. "I don't understand."

"If you're not going to be born, I don't want to be, either." She gaped at him in such surprise, he released her shoulders and stroked her cheek. "You're my *shalla*, destined to be my soulmate. I truly believe that now, and I've been hoping that one day you would come to believe it also. The last thing I want to hear you say is that your life has no worth, when it means everything to me."

"I . . . I'm not sure what to say."

"Then don't say anything. Just do me one favor. Open your mind. Completely. Let me see what you've been hiding from me."

She closed her eyes and knew the truth of his declaration. With joy filling her soul, she lowered the last wall between them.

As her love poured over him and into his mind, he pressed his mouth to hers. *I love you, sweetling. There's only one way I ever want to be alone again, and that's alone with you.*

His thought sent a thrill of pleasure racing through her and she returned his kiss with a loving thought of her own. *Our coming together wasn't the way I dreamed it would be, but loving you and having that love returned is better than any dream I ever had.*

A strong wave lifted the raft, reminding them that they couldn't afford to get too demonstrative.

Gabriel held her away from him and looked into

her eyes. "Can I assume this means I finally found a way to convince you that the past should not be tampered with?"

She nodded. "Yes. You were right, and I was wrong. However, I am *not* convinced that nothing can be done about Khameira. I intend to come up with something better than the Tribunal's solution of leaving warnings for future generations."

He gave her a hug. "Fine. Just give me a chance to prepare before you set your next plan into action. And speaking of plans, I picked up that ridiculous notion in your head that I would consider journeying without you." He pulled her to him and kissed her with a hunger reminiscent of the fever. "If that's not enough of a reason for traveling together, you've ruined me for journeying alone ever again. Besides the way you fit into my sleeping pouch, I've grown accustomed to having you to talk to, have meals with, work beside. I'd even miss our arguments."

His compliments made her blush. "We do make a pretty good team."

"We make a *perfect* team," he corrected, stroking her cheek. "My work has to be done in the field, but it seems to me that you could do your work anywhere, as long as you had your equipment. It would only necessitate a bit of customizing of my ship. I can't promise you'll always have the most luxurious surroundings, but I'll do my best to keep you comfortable."

She gave him a deep kiss equal to the one he had given her. "I can't think of anything more comfortable than sharing a sleeping pouch with you in it." She sat back and wrinkled her brow in thought.

"There's just one problem. I hope you weren't planning on us embarking on a journey anytime soon."

"Why not?"

"There is no way I'm going to be able to tell my parents about everything I've done, then take off immediately afterward. I can't begin to imagine their reaction to my being joined with someone they've never even met."

Gabriel grinned. "After what we've been through in the past few weeks, explanations to your parents should be a breeze."

"Hah!" Shara said with a laugh. "You don't know my father."

"Under the circumstances, then, I suggest we both dress more appropriately for my introduction."

As they donned jumpers, Gabriel insisted he could postpone medical treatment until after they reported in with her parents.

A raft appearing in the middle of their living area was the last thing Romulus and Aster expected that evening, but definitely the most welcome sight they'd had in a long time.

"Shara!" Aster cried, and rushed over to her. "We've been worried sick about you!"

"You must be the historian," Romulus unsmilingly stated to Gabriel.

Gabriel extricated himself from Shara and their baggage, then rose and held out a bandaged hand. "Gabriel Drumayne, Professor of History and Chief Procurer of Antiquities for Norona."

Romulus extended his hand, but the shake was anything but friendly.

Shara quickly stood up and gave each parent a hug. "We'll explain everything, but first, what's the date?" Her mother told her and she smiled at Gabriel. "You see? I told you I could hit it right on the nose if lightning didn't interfere."

"Did I hear that right?" Cattar exclaimed as she hustled into the living room. "You figured out how to pinpoint the destination date?" At Shara's bewildered nod, Cattar said, "Quickly, give me the belt and show me what you've done. We don't have a moment to spare."

Shara handed the strange woman the tempometer, but looked to her father for an explanation.

Without giving every detail, Rom and Aster filled her in on the catastrophic situation the tempometer had caused. With each word, Shara's knees grew weaker until she gave in to the need to sit down. Nothing, not even the news that a portion of Innerworld's people had already been evacuated, was as devastating as learning that her selfish actions had eradicated Mack's existence. *How could she ever live with that knowledge?*

Gabriel sat down and put his arm around her. "We'll fix it. There has to be a way."

"That's right," added Cattar. "And your returning with the tempometer was the first step. If you truly figured out how to arrive at a specific time, that's the second. Now tell me everything you've done with the device since you left, while we head for the science laboratory. Governor, please notify the research team to meet us there immediately!"

On the way to the lab, Shara and Gabriel gave the others an overview of where they'd been, but the excitement of their adventures was quashed by the problems they'd caused. Under the circumstances, Shara decided to withhold the fact that she and Gabriel had been stricken by the mating fever and joined. It was hardly a time for celebration.

When Shara revealed that she had not only found Khameira's ancestor but her own as well, and how she had been unable to go through with her original plans, Cattar rolled her eyes skyward and said, "Thank you, Supreme Being!"

Looking back at Shara and her parents, Cattar prepared to give them the one explanation she had been keeping to herself. "Forgive me for not speaking all of the truth before, but I didn't see the need to add to your heartache. I told you that Lantana's mind was fogged. Unfortunately, it was more than senility. He was fanatical enough to use his dying hour to feed you all very convincing lies that would ultimately destroy you and your contributions.

"Khameira Chang Sung exists on Outerworld in my time, but he is merely a religious zealot with a few psychic abilities and a claim to Noronian ancestry. Most of his original followers lost interest in his magic tricks within a few years. And there was never a third world war whatsoever. All but a few small countries live in peace and conduct business with Norona. Or rather, they did before the time disruption began."

"I don't understand," Shara said with a frown. "Why would Lantana go to so much trouble to convince me to go back and eliminate the ancestor of someone whose importance is negligible?"

"Aah, but it wasn't Khameira he wanted to eliminate," Cattar said. "It was your mother he was after."

Now it was Aster's turn to claim confusion.

"You see," Cattar said, "Lantana was a member of a small group of Noronians who never approved of open communication or fraternizing with the Terrans. The older he got, the more rigid he became in his beliefs. In his twisted mind, he blamed Aster Mackenzie for everything that he believed was wrong with our society. She was the first Terran woman to join with a Noronian man and bear children, thus permanently ending the purity of the race. She was the one who encouraged the first trade agreements.

"He was convinced that if he could eliminate Aster Mackenzie, the Cooperative Age never would have come about. Because of Shara's work in genetics, he was able to learn that both Aster and Khameira shared an ancestor from some early time, but he didn't know exactly when or who it was.

"Fortunately, you didn't act on your discovery. The strange part is that in Lantana's early research on time travel he theorized that events in time cannot truly be altered. If one person is eliminated, the contributions he or she would have made to history would simply be made by another. If a particular tyrant was prevented from overpowering a culture, another tyrant would do it instead. Apparently he forgot his own theories in his quest to return to a time already past."

Shara shook her head in dismay. "It was all a giant hoax? I can hardly believe what we went through because of that man. When I think of all the risks we took, how many times we came close to being killed, how—"

She cut herself off when she saw the horrified expressions on her parents' faces. "I'm exaggerating," she assured them. "Hardly anything happened to be concerned about. But from what you've related, this planet is deteriorating and my brother's life was eliminated, all because of one man's prejudice!" She felt Gabriel giving her a mental hug and calmed down. With him by her side and the confirmation of her Noronian ancestry, she would never again allow another's bigotry to eat away at her.

Eight hours later, Cattar and the research team were absolutely certain the tempometer's flaws were corrected. They worked out the most probable way to reverse everything that had happened, and Romulus and Aster gave their authorization to implement the plan as soon as possible.

A complete report of the events leading up to that moment would be planted in the central communication system. It would contain a trigger for it to be transmitted to Cattar's residence two hundred fifty years in the future, prior to when Lantana timehopped back to meet Aster and Shara. Cattar included certain information that would convince herself that she had indeed sent the message during a trip into the past.

It was concluded that, to prevent a paradox or disruption of any kind, Cattar had to return to her time as close as possible to when she departed. Based on the assumption that someone traveling through time actually exists in a separate dimension, it was uncertain what would happen to the time-hopping Cattar if the message was planted before she returned to her own time. Would she simply vanish from present time, or would there then be two of her? Therefore, it was decided that the message to her had to be planted at the same moment she completed the time-hop.

If everything worked the way it should, Cattar would have stopped Lantana from ever using the tempometer in the first place, which would prevent all the other events that followed from happening. The tear in the time-space continuum would not simply be repaired, it never would have occurred. And since it never happened, no one would have any memory of it. The weeks that had gone by since Lantana's appearance in the Locke residence would be replayed the way they should have without his interference.

It all sounded very logical, and if it was successful, the results would be perfect.

For everyone except Shara and Gabriel. Their meeting, the journey through time, his historical recordings, and even their joining—all of it would be erased the moment the plan was set in motion. They requested a five-minute delay while they left the lab to speak in private.

The moment they were alone, they were in each other's arms.

"I don't want to erase everything that happened between us," Shara said, tears filling her eyes.

"Nor do I, sweetling," Gabriel assured her. "But there seems to be no other way. Even if we tried to go ahead in time with Cattar, according to what they're saying, we'd have no memory of each other because we only came together after the disruption began. We have to believe our love for one another is strong enough to overcome anything . . . even time. Somehow, some way, we'll find each other again."

Shara sniffed and looked up at him. "With you journeying in another galaxy and me working in my lab in Innerworld, it doesn't sound like that's likely to happen. But I know you're right. There is no other way." She wiped her eyes and straightened her shoulders. "We'd better get back and let them do what they must."

"One more minute won't matter," he whispered, then lowered his head to give her a kiss so sweet and tender, she began to cry again. Tipping her chin up, he stared into her eyes. "Remember me, Shara. Look into my eyes and *remember*."

Shara slid her tall frame a little lower in the chair and pretended to concentrate on the food in front of her. This was one time Mack would not get her support. She was going to stay out of this family discussion if it killed her.

"*Drek*! But that's unfair."

"Mackenzie Locke!" Aster glared at her son, whose sullen face had taken on a tinge of pink when he realized his slip. "I will not have that language in our home. In fact, I don't care for your attitude at all this evening, young man."

Beneath the table, Shara gently tapped her brother's shin with the toe of her shoe to warn him to give it up. He was spoiling their weekly family dinner . . . again. She wasn't surprised when he continued his argument.

"Shara has her own residence. All I want—"

"Shara," Romulus interrupted, "is a grown woman with an established career. You aren't even out of school yet."

That was the one argument Mack had no answer

to and, though he was clearly unhappy about having his request for more independence denied, he let it drop for the time being.

After dinner, a competitive card game got everyone back into a light mood, but Shara couldn't keep her mind on the game. The oddest feeling had come over her, as if something was about to happen.

A month later she was still being bothered by the same feeling, and it was beginning to wear on her nerves. Though she had never had premonitions before, the fact that she had other well-developed mental abilities prevented her from completely dismissing the feeling. But nothing of importance had yet occurred.

She was working on a difficult calculation in her lab one day when she heard the door open and close. Someone was speaking, but she blocked out the voice and kept her gaze locked on the monitor so as not to lose her train of thought before completing the calculation. The pressure of a strong hand on her shoulder accomplished what the voice had not. The most peculiar tingling sensation danced down her arm to her fingertips.

"*Ahem!*"

Annoyed at the interruption, Shara slanted a glance at the fingers spread over her shoulder. The closely pared, unpolished nails and the smattering of fine blond hair on the large hand identified her visitor as a man. Her gaze continued up a bare forearm to an aqua jersey loosely covering a pair of muscular shoulders. Intending to deliver a glare that would have most men pleading for forgiveness, she swiveled her chair toward him and raised her eyes.

Her intended glare lost its hostility as she caught sight of his attractive, almost boyish features. His crown of blond curls, sky-blue eyes, and long eyelashes would have seemed more fitting on a Terran angel. But the warm body standing much too close to hers was definitely not that of a spirit. A plain gold earcuff on his left lobe was the only adornment that was not given him by nature. He epitomized the type of man she avoided at all costs.

And yet she couldn't pull her eyes away from his. She was certain she had never seen the man before, though he seemed as familiar to her as her own brother. She literally had to restrain herself from moving closer.

"I'm Gabriel Drumayne," he murmured as his gaze moved over her face. He completely forgot his reason for coming into the lab, but he was inexplicably pleased that he had. "Have we met before?" he asked, staring into her chocolate-brown eyes with an expression of curious fascination.

"I don't believe so," she replied in a tone that revealed a similar sense of bewilderment.

"Perhaps if we discussed it over lunch, we'd discover why you seem so familiar to me."

Without giving it a second thought, she switched off her computer in midcalculation. "I'd like that very much."

He held out his hand to help her rise and the charge that passed between their fingers could only be described as electrical.

Suddenly Shara understood the nervous anticipation she'd been experiencing all month, the instant feeling of recognition, the tingling sensation when he touched her. The look in his eyes told her he was also aware of what it meant.

Her romantic dream of finding the perfect soulmate was coming true ... exactly the way her mother had promised it would happen.

Dear Reader:

I have always been as intrigued by the Greek gods and the lost continent of Atlantis as I am fascinated with the future. *Stolen Dreams* gave me the opportunity to blend all three with my love of romance.

I hope you will join me again next December, when Topaz Dreamspun and I embark on a journey to a new world in *Gateway to Glory*

I love to hear from readers (s.a.s.e for reply please): P.O. Box 840002, Pembroke Pines, FL 33084.

DREAM ON!

Marilyn
Campbell

DANGEROUS DESIRE